"...a fitting tribute couples of the ages! W of a bard, Douglas b.... engaging story of Luther's marriage to Katharina von Bora."

**ERIC LANDRY**, Executive Editor, *Modern Reformation*

"An engaging and personal look at a figure of towering importance to Western civilization. This is a must-read for anyone who would see these events through the eyes of one who was there."

**DR. DAVID L. BODDE**, Professor Emeritus, Clemson University

"Douglas Bond has a gift for capturing the living and authentic nature of historical figures and their times. In *Luther in Love* he has seamlessly woven together historical fact into an engaging and enduring love story of mutual comfort and support between a declared heretic and an apostate nun. An excellent read!"

**MYRA BAUGHMAN**, Professor Emeritus, Pacific Lutheran University

"Combining a historian's eye for details with a novelist's sense for a good story, Douglas Bond brings Luther down from the pedestal so we can walk beside him and get to know him as the man he really was. I recommend *Luther in Love* heartily."

**GREG BAILEY**, editor

"*Luther in Love* is a lovely book, a pleasure to read, a creative and astute project, a page-turner, faithful to Luther's voice as a Reformer, a preacher, a theologian, a son, a friend, a father, and a husband."

**AIMEE BYRD**, author of *Housewife Theologian, Theological Fitness*, and *No Little Women*

"...Luther through the exhilarating mind of one of America's most impressive Christian storytellers. *Luther in Love* is Christian historical fiction at its mesmerizing best!"
**DARREN J. N. MIDDLETON**, Professor of Literature and Theology, Texas Christian University

"I loved reading *Luther in Love!* I laughed, I wept—so much wisdom about biblical marriage! ...a tender and insightful look into how the Father of the Reformation, and his beloved Katie, applied the theology of the Reformation to their marriage."
**SUSAN HUNT**, author, *Spiritual Mothering;* former Coordinator, Women's Ministry (PCA)

"Master historical novelist Douglas Bond has done it again. The fruit of extensive research, this book brings to life the story of Martin Luther's legacy and his marriage to Katharina von Bora. Bond blends theological and biblical insight from Luther in a compelling book for all readers."
**MARVIN PADGETT**, Executive Director/CEO, Great Commission Publications

"...beautifully written, incredibly moving account of Martin Luther and his bride Katharina von Bora. Bond seamlessly takes readers back 500 years. ...richly told, deserves to be read and reread."
**ALISA WEIS**, journalist and author of *Swiftwater*

# LUTHER IN LOVE

Also by Douglas Bond

*Mr. Pipes and the British Hymn Makers*
*Mr. Pipes and Psalms and Hymns of the Reformation*
*Mr. Pipes Comes to America*
*The Accidental Voyage*

*Duncan's War*
*King's Arrow*
*Rebel's Keep*

*Guns of Thunder*
*Guns of the Lion*
*Guns of Providence*

*Hostage Lands*
*Hand of Vengeance*
*Hammer of the Huguenots*
*War in the Wasteland*
*The Battle of Seattle*

*STAND FAST In the Way of Truth*
*HOLD FAST In a Broken World*

*The Betrayal: A Novel on John Calvin*
*The Thunder: A Novel on John Knox*
*The Revolt: A Novel in Wycliffe's England*

*The Mighty Weakness of John Knox*
*The Poetic Wonder of Isaac Watts*

*Augustus Toplady: Debtor to Mercy Alone*
*Girolamo Savonarola: Heart Aflame*

*Grace Works! (And Ways We Think It Doesn't)*

*God's Servant Job*

# LUTHER

*in*

# LOVE

DOUGLAS BOND

IBP

INKBLOTS
PRESS

ISBN-13: 978-1-945062-02-5 (pbk)
ISBN-13: 978-1-945062-03-2 (ePub)
ISBN-13: 978-1-945062-04-9 (mobi)

Cover: from bronze relief in Eisleben, Germany; designed by Robert Treskillard

Printed in the United States of America

**Library of Congress Cataloging-in-Publication Data**

Bond, Douglas, 1958-

Luther in Love / Douglas Bond.

pages cm

Summary: Katharina von Bora, fearful of discovery, secretly pens a memoir of her apostasy, her forbidden marriage to Reformer Martin Luther, his life and legacy, their life and love together, their children, their trials and tragedies, and their joys and triumphs.

ISBN-13: 978-1-945062-02-5 (pbk)

1.  Martin Luther, - 1564—Fiction. 2. Reformation—Fiction. Germany—History—16th century—Fiction. Christian fiction. Historical fiction. Historical theology.

PZ7.B63665History 2017

[Fic]--dc23

2015001268

For
Gillian, Giles; Desmond and Shauna;
Cedric and Ashley;
Rhodric, Tori, Gwenna, Amelia, and Nova;
Brittany, Jesse, and Margot


With gratitude to my mother

"The first love is drunken. When the intoxication wears off, then comes the real marriage love."
Martin Luther

"My Katie is in all things so obliging and pleasing to me that I would not exchange my poverty for the riches of Croesus."
Martin Luther

"God knows that when I think of having lost him, I can neither talk nor write in all my suffering."
Katharina von Bora, of Luther's death

# CONTENTS

# 1

# THE PEN OF THE DEVIL

(November, 1545)

I was grateful for the battering of rain against the drafty leaded windows of the cloister, the sluicing sound of water running off the eaves into the rain barrel, and the spitting and hissing of the pine logs in the fireplace. These sounds, and my occasional humming, helped conceal the scritch-scratching of my all-unable pen—or so I hoped.

At a lull in the downpour, worried that the irritable strokes of my goosequill might give my scheme away, I hummed more loudly, *Ein' feste Burg*, I hummed. Though my quill, as my tongue, was no match for the exuberant vocabulary of my dear husband, yet did I persist, feeling an urgency about the task I had set myself upon.

"Katharina, whatever are you doing?"

My husband looked up from his book, his eyes narrowed into fleshy slits, and he tilted his head toward me in that manner of his, as if to say, "What subterfuge are you up to this time?" His lips were thrust toward me—more in wary suspicion, at the moment, than in affection.

Fanning myself with the goose quill, the flame of my candle trembling, I looked up innocently from the parchment before me. I gave him my most disarming smile and shrugged carelessly for answer, hopeful this would satisfy and halt further enquiry. Though after more than twenty years of marriage to the man—the shrewdest of men, whose eyes could scan the deepest motives of most men, and women—I should have known better.

"It is just a little family business; that is all." It was truthful enough, as far as it went. But tell him the whole? I felt certain I could not tell him what it was I was really doing, laboring desperately at now for two months. I felt equally certain that he would not approve if he knew.

Startled at a clattering noise, I turned. The leaded window opened itself—again, letting in the frigid November wind, moaning like a specter. I was relieved at the distraction. The fire in the grate shuddered at the blast of cold air rushing eagerly into the chamber.

"I shall get it, this time," said Martin, his voice raspy. With a grunt, he attempted to shift his bulky frame in his chair, as if to rise.

"Rest yourself, Herr Doctor," I said. "Allow me." The wind outside struck me in the face with tiny pinpricks of sleet as I pulled the window to and reset the latch, a worn and tired old latch, disjointed and decrepit, and with a mind of its own. Hiking my shawl up more tightly around my shoulders, I shivered. Winters were always like this in Wittenberg, vicious cold and unrelenting wet that worked its clammy fingers into the very marrow of the bones, especially so into old bones.

"Ah, there you are again, my rib," said Martin, wincing and heaving back onto his chair. With the assistance of his own hands, he lifted his left leg and set it on the stool near the fire. "My rib, I would not trade you for France or Venice." A breathy chuckle followed, but then caught in his throat. I knew it was coming. Why must he laugh at his own jests? Wheezing, his face grew blotchy red, and his frame wracked with a fit of coughing.

Each heaving expulsion of air felt like a blow to my stomach. I gnawed on the inside of my left cheek, a nasty habit of mine.

"Stop, Herr Doctor, you must stop coughing now." Saying the words as I used to chide Magdalena for not drinking her bowl of milk, I tucked the wool blanket around his gouty leg. As if that would help the coughing. Yet, I had to do something,

Coughing like this had become more frequent of late. And, though I tried to pretend it was not there, sometimes there was blood in the spittle hacked up with those coughs. I did what I could—I had great confidence in herbs, and poultices of my own invention, and my beer, brewed especially for the inflamed proclivities of his bowels—but, for all my efforts, blood in the spittle boded ill. I tried my best not to think of what it might mean.

Then to my great relief, he grew calm, the fit passing sooner than some. There, I told myself, he is better.

Pressing a thick hand into the center of his chest, he continued, cautiously, "I would not trade my poverty for all the gold of Croesus—if I could not have you, my Kette."

"Nonsense," I murmured but without conviction. There was no ignoring the warm flush of pleasure his words gave to me. Once when I had fallen ill, and he had feared I would not recover, with tears he had chided me, "Oh, Katie, do not die and leave me." I shall always cherish his words to me then, and the tremulous imploring of his tone. Perhaps it is why I recovered.

But now the table was turned. I knew it would come, must come. Though irrepressibly robust in character and manners, he had never been so in health and constitution. Now it had grown far worse: the coughing, the pain in his chest, the blood.

Twirling my quill pensively, I set it to my parchment and recommenced writing. I knew he was watching me, so I attempted feigning that I was making a list of items to sell at market, counting on my fingers from time to time for good effect. Family business. Or I would appear to be tallying the weeks before spring and Bertha would be delivered of her calf, God willing. I was merely the chronicler of ordinary family business.

"My dearest apostate nun." He cleared his throat cautiously. "There is more of sense in my words than you know." He gazed at the fire, brooding, his watery eyes unblinking, the firelight glittering on them. "I am a weary old man, exhausted from many labors. Kette, I have lived one and sixty years."

"*Nein*, you have done better than that, Herr Doctor. November is nearly passed. You have lived two and sixty years." The words no sooner left my lips and I wished I had not said them. What difference did a year make?

"You think yourself wise, woman," he retorted, "because you are mistress of the pig market." But there was no heat in the words, as once there would have been. He used to chide me when first he took me to wife. "A woman ought to recite the Lord's Prayer before opening her mouth," he would say. But that was then, when our love was new, untested, halting about as if on the legs of a drunken man. Perhaps he was right. Who, man or woman, would not do well to recite the Lord's Prayer more often? How many harsh words would be, thus, unsaid and damage, thereby, never done?

"Two and sixty, one and sixty. It matters not. In those years, I feel that I have worked myself to death." His voice was low, and gravelly like wooden shoes on a cinder path. "I have done enough."

"*Ja*, you have worked too hard," I said, not truly meaning it. God knows, he had labored night and day, waging warfare against the empire; against princes, dukes, popes and cardinals. I had come to know, however, that agreeing with him would rarely console him. Agreement made him suspicious. He wanted no superficial alignment from anyone. No, for my husband, Martin Luther, agreement in total was the safest way, the only way. But if he thought someone was calculating, conniving in their nodding acquiescence, it put the fight in him, and he became like a bull. My false words had awakened him to the fallacy of his own. He turned suddenly upon me.

"I have done nothing," he said soberly. "I simply taught, preached, and wrote God's Word." His eyes strayed back to the pulsing coals on the grate. "*Nein*, I did nothing," he repeated, his voice stronger, more guttural in its resolve, for an instant, like the old Martin, the younger, vigorous, and explosive one. "The Word did everything."

"*Jawohl*, it is so," I said, placing my hand on his shoulder.

"Indeed, *soli Deo gloria*," he said, punctuating each word with a nod of his head.

"Now, drink your beer, Herr Doctor. The night is cold and dark, and we should away to bed."

"My beloved Katie," he murmured, his voice barely audible above the sleet shying against the window panes and the hissing of the fire.

Dipping my quill in the inkpot, I pressed on. Just a few more sentences tonight. There was one more episode I wanted to complete before retiring to our bed. Others had penned the story of my husband, nay, he had penned the story himself; but I feared he had left out the human parts of the story, the ones that perhaps only a woman could observe and record.

Though I had encountered some of what others had written, I feared that none of them got it all correct, as it truly

15

was. Either they hated him overmuch—there had been many of these—and called him "the spawn of Satan," or "the disciple of the Devil." Or they had loved him out of all boundaries of sense and reason, "a living angel," the latter termed him.

I confess, though there were moments when my sympathies firmly aligned with the former, I was more often the latter, loving him in excess, frequently being forced to confess in my prayers that I looked to my dearest husband beyond measure, beyond what he could provide, expecting of him what came only from God above.

Albeit, I took some comfort in my excesses, for he had confided as much to me one time, with hand-wringing remorse in his tone, "I give more credit to you, my rib, than to Christ, who has done so much more for me."

The recollection warmed me deep within. I had absolved him of his crime, but only after prescribing his penance: No writing for a week, no visiting the sick and elderly, and he was permitted to preach but twice on the Sunday. If truly contrite, therein only could he make satisfaction for his crime.

Bellowing like a bull with a cow in heat across the fence, my husband declared it an impossible bargain and attempted to haggle over the terms of his penance. I remained harshly resolute—a posture I had learned from the undisputed master of it, my own husband. My way, or it was eternal perdition for him, so I had assured him.

"There you are, dear Katie," his words breaking in on my recollections, "smiling and blushing at your own cleverness."

He had been watching me.

"Beware the enchantment of the pen," he continued. "It may be the very devil himself. Do as I have done. Hurl your inkpot at the fiend." After another pull on his beer, he narrowed his eyes at me. "Whatever are you up to, *meine Frau?*"

16

# 2
# CAPTIVE DEMONS

My feeble efforts as chronicler began with the blood. When first his coughing produced blood two months ago, it struck me. As the first rains of autumn fell, the warmth of summer scurrying away from the chill air closing in on Saxony, and darkness glowering down on Wittenberg far too early—it was then, like lightning, that it struck me. I knew what I must do and scrambled for pen and parchment.

"Where I was born," he had said that same evening, frowning at the dark clouds and the falling rain, "on top of a high mountain—Pubelsberg, it was called—there was a lake into which if a stone was thrown a tempest would arise over the whole region."

I laughed, thinking he was jesting. "Surely you don't believe it, an old wives' tale, nothing more."

He turned slowly from the window. "The dark waters of that lake," he said, his voice low and ominous, "are the abode of captive demons."

"That is the speech of the unlettered peasant," I retorted, nable to quell another burst of laughter. "Surely, Herr Doctor, brilliant man of books and scholarship, you don't believe such nonsense?"

He nodded slowly and turned back to the window, rain pelting furiously against it. "I do believe in demons. Do not you, Katie?"

"*Ja*, of course," I retorted. "And the power of God to cast them into the pigs and drown them, one and all."

He grunted and nodded approvingly.

What followed was one of the first evenings of quiet I recall in our twenty years of married life together. There had been few quiet moments of any kind in our home, the cavernous Augustinian cloister gifted to my husband by Elector Frederick himself. Raising our own six children and four adopted dears, three of our deceased relations' orphans—God rest their souls—and myriad of students, fawning on my exalted husband, mouths agape at his words, yearning for knowledge, and for endless platters of my sausage and mugs of my best beer—the appetites of students these days!

But most of our children were grown, or with God, and I had driven away many of the students, not selfishly, of course, but for the sake of my husband's health. Until now, he'd had little time for lengthy conversation with his wife, what with teaching theology at the university, disputing with detractors and critics, translating Scripture into the common tongue, counting meter out for another hymn, reading the weighty tomes of the early church fathers, and writing yet another of his own books.

No, it mattered little how much I longed for intimate conversation with my beloved husband in those years. He was simply too much in demand. He holding court, as it were, in our one-time cloister—it was anything but a cloister now. It was as if the entire world hammered at our door, an endless mob of black-robed courtiers, eager to attend on him. There was absolutely no retirement or sequestration from the world to be had here. Until now.

So I had remained longsuffering, uncomplaining, and had carried on with my duties: milking the cow, slaughtering another pig, or gutting fat trout to load the board for supper—and to fill the gaping mouths of the countless young men that attended on my husband those years. Of course, I was never bitter.

But here my husband was, depleted, a hollow shell, worn out like an old shoe, sapped of his lifeblood as if by leeches. Yet, though he was sick, brooding, and melancholy, the room was quiet; we were alone, and he was voluble.

My pulse raced with excitement. I knew not how long the fit of it would endure, so it was I dipped my quill in the pot and began taking down his every word, determined in my account to set it down in total—Martin's story as it truly happened, unvarnished, without embellishment, free of fallacious statements of either excess or defect.

"Demons I had aplenty," he said with a shudder. "I recall in my earliest days in Mansfield seeing a devil depart the body of a possessed man. At the convent, just at the ringing of the bell at vespers, it was. That was my early life: bells, relics, priests and monks, steeples and spires, masses for the dead, last rites for the dying, and terrors on every side. Fear drove everything. My earliest recollections are of shivering.

"Eventually the bowels of the earth yielded a measure of wealth for my father, his boots besmeared with grime, and his hands coarse from labor. There were demons there, too. Sometimes he brought them home with him, so it seemed. And my mother caught them up, or was caught up by them. In a fury one evening, she took the switch to me—for what, I have no recollection—and beat me till the blood flowed." He paused, flexing the fingers of his right hand. "In her discipline of me," he continued, "she meant well, and God knows I often deserved it, no doubt, but I believed it was a demon brought up from the copper mines inadvertently by my father that made her do it so that night."

Fearful of breaking the enchantment, yet I could not help myself, and broke in on him. "What terrible deed had you done, surely you must know?"

After musing at the beamed ceiling for a moment, he snapped his fingers. "A nut," he said. "A hazelnut. That was it. I was hungry." He shrugged. "And stole a hazelnut from a bowl on the table."

"It sounds like for doing it," I said, "she cracked you like a nut."

Flexing his fingers again, he looked levelly at me. "She believed in demons, did my mother, and in witches. She claimed that her infant son, my little brother, died because our neighbor was a witch and put a curse on the baby."

"Was it so?"

"I believe he died," he trailed off, eyes dull and staring into the fire; I knew he was thinking of our sweet Magdalenchen. "I believe he died because Eve ate of the forbidden fruit in the garden."

"And Adam ate of it too," I broke in.

"But, my rib, there's no denying it, it was Eve who got things started down that pathway, and death ensued."

"Curious, though, isn't it, Herr Doctor, that Holy Scripture never refers to it as the sin of Eve, but always as the sin of Adam."

He frowned at me in feigned severity then broke into a smile. I feared he would laugh and another coughing fit might ensue. Why must I always wrangle with him so?

"My lord Katie wins again," he said tenderly.

"But in school you were poor." I wanted to get him back on the story. "I recollect you telling the children about your singing, door to door, for money, or food."

"My lute, Kette, would you pass me my lute?"

"*Die wittenbergisch Nachtigall*," I said, taking down his lute and handing it to him.

He gave a short, cautious laugh. "'The Nightingale of Wittenberg,' so some have called me. An exaggeration, to be sure. Perhaps I was at that time a sweeter singer than today, my voice now all gravel and chicken scratch. My singing, in any event, was a good thing. Like a poor mendicant, I sang my way from door to door in Eisenach. Had God not given me so sweet a voice in my youth, I fear I may have starved."

"Go on, then, Herr Doctor," I urged, my pen poised over my parchment. "I love the sound of your voice."

# 3

# BEATINGS

Mansfield Purgatory, we called it," continued Martin at my urgings. "Not only did I excel at singing—how I loved the *Magnificat* and the *Sanctus*!—but somehow I managed to excel in learning. I do not know how or why. But had I not done so, I would have died, either from beatings or starvation. In our recitations, all was to be in Latin, but being boys, German boys, who would not have slipped from time to time into German speaking? It was the donkey mask for the hapless lad who did so.

"Fifteen times, Katie, in one week alone, fifteen times I wore the donkey mask."

"Oh, my dear Herr Doctor," I broke in, "I would love to have seen you wearing the head of a donkey."

"As did my schoolmaster," he continued. "My mind had been otherwise disposed, and I had lapsed into German. I have no other excuse. The donkey mask, however, was but a momentary and light affliction. For failing to have my Latin verb conjugations memorized properly, I was caned fifteen strokes, till my flesh was raw."

"That is horrible," I interjected, wishing I hadn't. I feared breaking the spell of his volubility.

"Boys are more resilient, *meine Frau*, than you know. Sometimes such treatment can serve to toughen them for greater trials ahead."

"*Ja*, if they survive," I murmured.

"There was another and deeper consideration for me, then, my rib. And for that, I took a sort of pleasure in those strokes."

"Pleasure? What pleasure is there to be found in beatings?"

"I feared for my soul. *Nein*, the word fear is not strong enough. Mine was an irrepressible, grinding horror. I hoped beyond hope that perhaps by those strokes I could avoid the torments of hell, that by those beatings I might purge myself from my sins, satisfy Divine wrath, and find peace with God. Then again, perhaps not. My father, who prayed often with me, sometimes on his knees at my bedside, told me otherwise."

"'Martin,' he would tell me. 'You cannot do it alone. You must pray to the ever-Virgin Mary and the saints. They have extra goodness stored up as a farmer fills his barn with surplus grain to sell. So the Church has the keys to the barn and will sell goodness to you from the saints' treasury of merits. You must pray to them.'

"But I was in torment at these things. *Ja, ja*, to be sure, there were times when I felt carefree and happy. How I did love playing pranks on my fellows! But these were not my most thoughtful moments. I only felt free and jovial when I was not thinking of these things. I felt it in my bosom that I was better off thinking of them, thinking of them *now*, than weeping and wailing and gnashing my teeth that I had not

23

done so while burning in hell for all eternity. Do not you agree, dearest Katie?

"Kette? Are you paying attention, or am I merely speaking to that fat vermin crouching there in the shadows?"

"I am attending with great interest, Herr Doctor," I replied.

"Scribbling away on one of your market lists?" he retorted. "Your mind brimful with the price of beer, chicken eggs, and pork sausages—how can you attend?"

I felt the heat rising on my cheeks. "You seemed to enjoy your sausages at supper, sausages which come of my lists."

"*Ja, ja*, my lord Katie," he said indulgently. "But you cannot attend to my words and write your lists, Kette. It is not possible to do two things at one time."

I laughed. "It is what you have done these twenty years and longer, two things at one time. *Nein*, you have not done two things—you have done *ten* things at one time! Why cannot I do just two things, listen and write, merely two things at once?"

At my own words, I bit hard into the flesh of my cheek. One would think I wanted him to give up talking. Perhaps I ought to bite my tongue. How was I to continue my chronicle if he gave up talking to me?

I rose and poured more beer into his stein. "Please, do not stop speaking," I said. "You cannot know how much I love hearing your words, Herr Doctor. Be assured, I am most earnestly attending. I want to know every detail, with accuracy, honesty, and without contrivance of any kind. I *must* know. I desire that our children and their families know, that all the world know what is true, without ornament or embellishment. And if I appear to be inattentive, Herr Doctor, it is only the appearance, thereof. I assure you from the bottom of my devoted heart."

"It is so?" he said, taking the stein from my hand, his hand pausing tenderly on my own.

"*Jawohl*, it is so."

Straining to see my parchment, he frowned, making as if to rise. "What are you writing, *meine Frau?*"

"It is just family business, *mein Herr*," I said softly. "You were speaking of your fears, terrors of hell. However did you allay them, *mein Herr?*"

# 4

# UNJUST JURIST

(January 7, 1505)

B eware, lest you spoil the boy," said Margaretta Luther. "You are always spoiling the boy."

Hans Luther scowled at his wife but said nothing.

"Doting on him," she continued, clamping her lower lip in her teeth and thrusting her chin forward, "telling the rest of us how smart the boy is, how he'll be the staff of our old age, marry well, become a rich jurist, and dine with the *Bürgermeister*, so you are always telling us. It's not good for children to be told such things and doted on by their parent— *parent*, I say, not parents. Nothing good will come of it, you mark my words."

"Quiet, woman," murmured Hans. "Here he comes. Let us greet our son with joy, *meine Frau*. He has completed university sooner than anyone. I am told that with but one and twenty years he is the youngest ever in Erfurt to earn the Master of Arts. Our son, the youngest ever. Can you not find it in yourself to rejoice at that?"

"I'll find it in myself to rejoice," retorted Margaretta, "when he gets a situation working for a rich lord, and arranges good jobs for his brothers. *Ja, ja*, then I will rejoice."

"In time, in time, *meine Frau*. He will commence his doctorial study of law in a few weeks, but at his rate, in no time, he will become a doctor of jurisprudence—imagine it, our son a doctor. And then he will have his pick of the finest situations."

"He'll work for a bishop or a cardinal," said Margaretta, eyeing her husband.

"*Nein*, not the clergy for a Luther," said her husband with a scowl. "Advocate for a duke or a prince, that is the path for Martin." He gripped his wife's arm. "Here he is," he hissed.

"Martin, my son. I present this to you, Sir."

Martin studied the beautiful leather volume his father extended to him. *Corpus Juris*, the body of Roman law, a book he knew would have been enormously expensive for his father to purchase.

"Thank you, *mein Vater*, said the young scholar reaching for the book. Calloused and muscular, Hans Luther's hands held the book reverently toward his son. Martin looked at his own hands, pale, scholars' hands, fit for turning the pages of such a book, and fit for writing with the goosequill, but for little else. His hands, so different from his father's. Suddenly the whole exchange seemed profoundly significant to Martin.

His father began working with those same hands when he was old enough to walk, working the soil, ditching, hoeing, milking the cows, picking rocks, cutting hay. And when it was time for his elder brother to inherit the small farm, Hans Luther, the younger son, had turned to the copper mines. Of course his father's hands would be muscular hands; from ditching in the fields, those hands turned to the pick and shovel of the miner, and grew yet stronger, breaking rocks beneath the earth; more calloused, sorting through great subterranean mounds of slag and ore.

And here was Hans Luther passing on to his son a book he could not himself read, would never read. Yet through backbreaking labor in the bowels of the earth, he had prospered. Certainly *Corpus Juris* had been expensive—all books were expensive—but Hans Luther had taken a measure of pride in his ability to purchase such a book for his son. Martin could see this on his father's face. By diligent labor, and the help of St. Anne, patron saint of all miners, his father had come to own the copper mine and an interest in several foundries. He would never wear the ermine gown, or climb into a higher layer in the stratum of society, but he was a wealthy man—for a peasant.

In his father's hands, and in the terse line of his lips, and the perpetual scowl of his broad forehead, Martin felt he could read his father's thoughts. Here was a man enormously proud of his son, a bright and intellectually able son now squarely situated on the cusp of discovering a new vein of ore, a purer vein, a golden stratum of society.

All this was eloquently etched on his father's features. The arrow was nocked, the bowstring drawn taut, the trajectory calibrated; his son was about to be launched upward into an altogether higher class, into an exalted new world. There to make a name for himself, to prosper, to gain wealth, to become a man of importance and rank. And from those dizzying heights—his father was ever a practical man— Martin would be far more able to care for his mother and father in their old age, should they live to see much of the elusive thing called old age. Martin felt he was reading these things as surely in his father's hands and features as from the pages of a book.

Releasing the book, the thick hands fell to the big man's sides, then he folded them together at his middle, steepling his broad thumbs.

"*Danke schön, mein Vater,*" said Martin again. "Thank you, very much, indeed, Father."

There he stood, sturdy working man, gazing on his son, his features swelling with pride at his son's scholastic accomplishment. Martin did his best to smile in return. All about him in the cobbled courtyard of the university, his school fellows celebrated with their families and friends, joyful words and laughter abounding. Martin cradled the book in one arm and ran the sleeve of his other over his brow. How could he tell his father?

Martin had at the first found great pleasure in the rigor of his studies at the university in Erfurt, preparatory to his legal studies. He had accepted the study of law, the path his father had marked out for him. And at the first, submitting himself to the legal pathway had made him feel, if not righteous, at least he had felt less unrighteous. Perhaps it is what drove him to excel in so short a time at such a rigorous course of study. By becoming expert in the law, perhaps thereby he could appease the wrath of the Lawgiver. Perhaps as a jurist, he could become just, and at long last find peace with the Judge of all.

And then one day in 1503 he had an accident. Like so many accidents, it began with an embarrassingly silly blunder, which in a second escalated into an event that nearly marked the ending of his life. Trudging along the muddy roadway from Erfurt to his home in Eisenach, Martin suddenly felt his feet slipping from under him. The precise details of how it happened would remain a mystery to him. His sword lashed to his belt—no one dared travel that road without a weapon—became not a means of protection against a thief, but the implement of his own destruction. His breath caught in his throat as he felt himself falling, powerless to halt the plummeting. Landing with a splat in the filth on the road, he readied himself for the laughter of his school companions.

"Martin, you clumsy oaf!" laughed one of his fellows.

"Hush, he is merely falling to his prayers—again," said his friend Hieronymus Buntz to uproarious merriment.

29

But something was not right. Martin's leg felt as if on fire. Crying in agony, he sprawled on the road, excruciating pain throbbing through his foot and leg. And moisture filling his boot. But not cold road slime. This was hot and sticky. His heart sank. It was his own blood pulsing from a deep gash in his foot. Martin had fallen on his own sword.

"St. Mary, help me!" he cried. Vaguely he saw the merriment in Hieronymus's eyes freeze and turn to incredulous horror, his friend's face now slack and pale.

Like never before in his short life, Martin feared dying. What if this was the end? There was no priest ready to hand, no last rites. Dying was bad enough, but dying without confession, without penance—there was no time or strength for penance, lying in a pool of his own blood, what could he do? And dying without absolution, without satisfaction, his sins on his own head? Then what? Torment, incalculable ages of torment in purgatory? It was as if the flames were engulfing him then and there. Never had he felt such terror.

Yet, thanks to the level-headed thinking and the swiftness of foot of his friend Hieronymus, Martin did not die, not that day. He had been spared. But for what? His wound, though deep and arterial, had healed, and he had regained strength and continued his studies. But for what? To face it once again, real dying, without Hieronymus to rescue him, no coming back from the brink, no escaping the lapping flames, the taunts and torments of hell? For what, then, had he been spared?

No sooner had he regained his strength and returned to his studies, the bloody accident beginning to fade, than another horror descended. Plague swept through "Little Rome," as Erfurt was called. And the "nest of priests" became a place of horror, frantic clerics abandoning the nest and fleeing for their own lives, leaving behind a hell on earth, a torturous place where the Black Death reigned arbitrarily supreme, sparing one and taking off another.

To Martin's inconsolable grief, his friend Hieronymus was marked out as the latter, taken off in that wave of death. Yet was his grief shuffled aside by his paralysing fear: would he be next? His insides heaving with nauseous dread, Martin daily inspected his armpits and groin for buboes, the fatal tumors, harbingers of contagion. But nothing. More died around him, hundreds more, yet was he spared. Again. But for how long? When would his turn come? Was God merely toying with him?

Torments and sleepless nights followed. Martin gave himself to his studies, in part, to find in books some measure of relief from his fears. But it was no good.

Since his childhood, Martin had seen the woodcuts of the dance of death. "Depart from me you accursed ones into everlasting fire," they had read, the condemned dragged by the hair from their tombs and hurled into the flaming abyss. Rocking from side-to-side, Martin had clamped his hands over his ears to block out their howls of anguish. Writhing in his sweaty bed, throughout his childhood, he had felt an affinity with the damned in those images. He was one of them.

Surely these were mere childhood fancies, the dragons and demons of an overworked imagination, superstitions of an undereducated peasant boy. But it was not so. In university, in books, in the new learning, in the study of Aristotle, he had found no peace. Nothing could assuage Martin's fears. If anything, as knowledge increased, anxiety and unrest came on harder at the heels, and grew exponentially. No, the scholar's life had not mitigated his fears; it had augmented them.

But what of the Christ there on the crucifix above the door? Martin had read in the Gospels, from the pages of the Latin Bible, chained to the reading table in the university library, the first Bible he had ever laid eyes on, "Be perfect, as my Heavenly Father is perfect."

The sacred words sent a shudder throughout his being. He was not perfect. Of that much, Martin was certain. Hence, God in the Bible brought him no comfort, no hope. Martin was in terror of God, this perfect God. Perfection came easily enough for God, but what right did he have to require the same from his creatures? In the secret places of his innermost being, Martin even entertained thoughts of revulsion at so holy a God; he found at times, that, rather than loving such a God, he hated him. Yet all was lost if he hated God. He knew that much. It was unpardonable to hate God.

Inhaling, as it were, the sulphurous vapors of his own fears, with sinking heart, Martin became convinced that the study of law could not give him peace with the Lawgiver. Worse yet, he felt certain that the prosperous life of a lawyer, the sumptuous comforts of a life of ease, would only serve to heap up greater condemnation before the Judge of all.

How to allay his torments? The Church offered but one sure path.

Yet, here standing before Martin was his father, beaming at the advancement of the son of his hopes and dreams. Running his pale, trembling fingers over the leather boards of *Corpus Juris*, Martin felt barely able to breathe. How could he tell his father such things?

# 5

# THE WINK

A ll those fasts and vigils, Martin," said his fellow student Joachim, "they'll make you old before your time. Come along with us. We'll drink Torgau beer and celebrate."

"What is it we are celebrating?" asked Martin.

"The burying of your copy of *Corpus Juris*," said Joachim, closing the boards of the book with a clunk and a poof of vellum-scented air.

"Burying the body of law—*Jawohl*, that is a good one," said another, thumping Joachim's back with hilarity.

"Indeed, we are celebrating that The Philosopher," said Kaspar, drawing out the nickname and bowing to Martin with a flourish, "is not spending another Friday night staring into the stagnant blackness of his ink pot."

"Or frowning at the pages of the Vulgate in the library," said Joachim. "How you do scowl and fume at it, Martin!"

"There! That alone is cause enough for celebration."

"Come along with us, Martin," urged Joachim, "just this once."

As his friends bantered about the prospects of the evening of revelry, Martin reflected on his first months of law school.

In May of 1505 he had commenced his study of jurisprudence at the University of Erfurt. Within weeks, Martin was singled out by Jodocus Trutvetter for a debate over a passage from Plato's *Republic*. But it was the Augustinian lecturer Gerard Hecker who fascinated the budding jurist more than any other. While other professors were enamoured with the works of Cicero or Seneca, Hecker was fascinated with the Bible. From him Martin learned that the Bible was wholly unlike other ancient texts.

Cradling the Vulgate in his arms, Hecker would scan the hundreds of tomes that lined the walls of the university library. Inhaling the intoxicating smells of parchment, ink, leather, polished wood, and candle wax, the lecturer would then trace with his fingers the decorated leatherwork on the boards; nodding slowly, Hecker would say, *"Die Bibel ist vor allem Bücher."*

Martin was nothing short of astonished at Hecker's passion about the uniqueness of the Bible, to be esteemed above all other books. Martin had never heard anything like it before. What is more, Hecker believed that the Bible ought to interpret itself.

"But Master Hecker," said Martin, "does not the Church teach papal supremacy over the interpretation of the Bible's words? Does not the pope tell us what the Bible means? So we are told?"

"And the Church councils," added Hecker, nodding dutifully. "You must not forget them. And the magisterium, the collected teachings of the Church, and canon law. *Ja, ja,* you must not forget these."

But even as the man said the words Martin knew he was saying them out of obligation, not because he believed them himself. Perhaps it was his confidential wink when he said them. But Hecker had the unique ability to affirm with his words what Rome required of him, knowing full well what Rome would do to him if he did not, but then turn from his feigned acquiescence back to the sacred text of Scripture, "the fount," he affectionately called it. Looking over his shoulder, he would take a fistful of Martin's scholar's gown and draw him close, then whisper earnestly in his ear, "*Die Bibel wird Ihnen sagen, was die Bibel meint.*"

Hecker could not have fully understood the impression his words had on the young jurist: "The Bible itself tells us what the Bible means." There was no shaking free from the hold Hecker's words had on Martin.

Meanwhile, in the moment, there was to be no shaking free from the urgings of Martin's friends. Joachim and the others had collared him, and, arm-in-arm, led him off down the narrow cobbled streets of Erfurt to celebrate at the *Bierhalle*. It would be a night to remember—in ways Martin could not have anticipated.

# 6
# IN LOVE WITH DYING

"Another stein for our exalted friend, The Shiloph-osher," slurred Kaspar.

"You mean, Martin, The Philosh-opher," said Joachim.

"*Jawohl*, that'sh the one, The Philosh-opher," said Kaspar, slamming his empty stein on the table. "Now, while thish lovely *Fräulein*, refills our steins, let ush sing her a lovely song, together, for the lady." Inhibition long drowned in Torgau beer, Kaspar belched into the back of his hand and launched in:

> Every pretty girl I meet
> Sets my heart a-sighing;
> Hands off! Ah, but in conceit
> In her arms I'm lying.

The barmaid cuffed Kaspar in the back of his head. "'Hands off!' *Jawohl*. The best line in the song." Laughing, the skirts of her dirndl swishing, she spun on her heel back to the bar to refill their steins.

Following her with his eyes, Martin found himself musing on the intriguing differences between the sexes.

"You'll need to drop in for a good long sit down at the confessional after this night, Kaspar," said Joachim. "As will we all."

But, staggering to his feet, Kaspar waved off the suggestion.

"Careful, friend," said one of his comrades.

Kaspar, his face set in bewildered concentration, stepped onto the ale bench and stood there teetering. "Hear my confess-shun," he slurred. "Like a good monk, I will sing it to you, at you—that is, for at you."

Hear me prelate, most discreet,
For indulgence crying;
Deadly sins I find so sweet,
I'm in love with dying.

Laughing raucously, the others hoisted their steins. But Martin wondered how Kaspar, at so advanced a stage of inebriation, could even recall the words of the drinking song. But such words! Kaspar's was a confession of defiance, or was it merely a confession of honesty?

Martin scowled at the foam dribbling from the head of beer in his stein. Though he was repelled, even terrified, at the consequences of his sins, did he not also find sin so sweet?

As he mused on these things, the human tapestry of sound whirled into an indistinct clamoring: clunking steins, catcalls, drunken bellowing, laughter, belching, flatulence, scraping of benches on the rough floor—all faded as Martin's mind returned to his tortured fears. Though he was too frightened to make so bold a sung confession as Kaspar's, yet was sin so sweet to his taste, and, thereby, was he not equally in love with dying?

As Martin, surrounded by the seeming happiness of revelry, mused in his singular melancholy, a more distinct sound began to pierce through the others.

Perhaps what followed had been played out on the stage of reckless parties for millenniums: Young men too long at the ale bench laughing and jesting together. Then a jest that became an insult, a mocking accusation, ridiculing another student's mother, a heated rejoinder, augmented shouting, shoving, fingers pointed and jabbing, clenched fists, a broken chair, a fractured beer stein, teeth-gnashing obscenities. Raging for order, the proprietor of the *Bierhalle* used a trestle bench to herd them, shoving them like cattle through a gate, out onto the street.

Where the brawl continued with more heated words and cursing. Something flashing menacingly in the moonlight, a knife drawn from the folds of a scholar's gown. Cursing. Thrusting blows, screams of pain, frantic crying for help.

It was the crying out that broke through the fog of beer-addled brains. Martin found himself on his knees at the side of a fellow student. Blood was everywhere. In the moonlight he could see enough. It was Kaspar's blood pulsing from under the folds of his gown.

"Is it mortal?" cried Kaspar, his teeth clenched in anguish. He clutched at Martin's sleeve. "Is it?"

Though he knew nothing about doctoring, Martin pressed his hands over the gaping wound, hoping thereby to push the blood back into his friend's body. What else could he do?

"Is it?" asked Joachim, his voice hoarse.

"Get a priest!" hissed Martin.

"A priest?" Joachim's tone was slack with incredulity.

"They're everywhere. Get one!"

Joachim turned unsteadily, and lumbered down the street.

"Am I dying?" Kaspar's voice was barely a whisper now, and his face shone deathly pale in the eerie light of the waning moon.

There was too much of it. Blood, pulsing hotly out of his body. Nothing Martin could do would stop it, nothing. He had no words. Reaching with his hand, he stroked the boy's brow. Martin meant it for comfort, but it left a ghastly smear of blood on Kaspar's face.

Martin leaned low over the body, his ear close to the young man's pale lips.

With his final breath, Kaspar whispered, "Save me."

# 7

# THUNDERBOLT

(July 2, 1505)

S ave me." Martin had tried to save him, did what he could, but there had been no saving Kaspar. Not only did the dying student's final words haunt Martin, so did his frantic groping, his horrified eyes, and his life blood gushing onto the cobblestones and staining Martin's gown and hands. His life, it was over so quickly. One moment the young man had been singing love songs to a pretty *Fräulein*— then he was dead.

Though word of Kaspar's death spread overnight throughout the university and the city, his killer had vanished.

It was dark. Most everyone had been drinking. It could have been anyone. The man wielding the knife might not have meant to plunge its blade into Kaspar's body, might not even have known whose body it was. It may have just happened in the reckless mayhem of a drunken brawl.

Though the magistrate questioned everyone who had been at the *Bierhalle* that night, what they saw, what they heard, the story was the same. No one had any idea who had plunged the knife into Kaspar's body.

Bewildered and in shock, Martin and his friends could not concentrate on their books. In frustration, the rector of the university suspended lectures and tutorials for the week. Desperate to put distance between himself and Kaspar's death—his blood, his final words—to leave the horrible incident behind him, Luther trudged to Eisenach and his home.

Knifings at universities were not that uncommon. His parents had heard nothing. He told them as little as possible. Brooding and melancholy, Luther felt restless to be back at his books. Taking leave of his family, he set off to retrace his steps back to Erfurt, a long day and a half of walking.

"Infernal Saxony," he mused aloud. "Die of cold in winter on this road, or of this raging heat in midsummer."

Loosening his gown at the throat, Martin scowled at the muggy heavens. The orange ball of the sun winked bright and dim, bright and dim, then disappeared altogether, a column of gray clouds in its place.

"There's relief in that," he said aloud. "At least I'll not fry like an egg."

In a rolling pasture, across a ditch from the roadway, Martin heard the guttural lowing of bovine, a bull emitting deep bawling growls like a bear. Ears twitching, the herd of cattle huddled together, their tails swishing the sultry air.

Rolling up his sleeves against the heat, Martin's mouth felt dry. He tried to swallow.

Trilling in alarm, a flock of starlings darted for cover overhead. As he looked up, the breeze set a lock of his hair thrashing across his face. Flicking his head, he cleared the hair from his eyes.

It was no longer a breeze. Martin felt his heart beating hard in his temples. It was a gale of wind, accelerating and furious. Oddly, the movement of air did not give relief from the heat,

41

rather it seemed to infuriate the air as a bellows to the flames in a furnace.

The wide-bladed grass along the roadside ditch chattered in a frenzy. Martin's unease mounted with every gust. He sniffed the sultry air. It was pungent with a menagerie of scents, spicy with the sap of weed grass, stalks of wheat and barley, and fir needles pummelled and bruised in the wind.

Wide eyes darting at the heavens, Martin watched a young goshawk driven madly before the gale, its frantic wings clutching the air for control against the blast. Driven sideways, it disappeared behind the flailing branches of a pine tree. There was no repelling this inexorable force, not for bird or beast, or for man.

It was useless to resist. Try as he might, Martin felt his unease giving way to terror. Impending doom pressed down on him so palpably that he tasted it in his mouth. Had it come? Were those rowling black clouds the judgment of God?

"The one who doubts," the words from the pages of the Bible in the university library lashed defiantly at Martin's imagination. "The one who doubts is like the waves of the sea driven and tossed by the wind."

Martin began running, where he did not know, but doom and trepidation demanded it. He had to get out of this storm. His breath came in hot blasts, and he felt that his lungs would burst within him. Frantic, Martin scanned the countryside for some protection, some haven. It was dark at midday. His teeth felt like he had clamped down on a chunk of copper ore, and a tingling current radiated up his spine.

And then a low grumbling began along the tree line on a nearby ridge, as if the very bowels of the Thuringian hills were agitated. Martin's hair felt like it was lifting itself out of its follicles. If only he could find refuge under that giant fir tree just ahead. He threw off his burden and ran as if a demon were hot upon his heels. As he ran, the grumbling behind him grew louder. The bitter ache in his teeth increased, and it was harder to breathe. But he was there.

Collapsing under the fir tree, Martin tore at his gown, pulling it open so he could take in air. His heart sank. His eyes followed the great rugged trunk upward. Swaying in the gale, its branches moaning, the tree glowered down at Martin.

Then popping sounds erupted from the branches above him. The grumbling from the ridge grew louder, nearer. Like kettle drums being pounded before a battle, it rumbled, gaining momentum, wind mounting, the branches flaying back and forth above him, lurching violently in the maelstrom.

Martin clamped his hands over his ears. Was this the end of the world? He tried to pray. Had he so enraged the Almighty that it had come, judgment and condemnation? Was this hell?

*Crack!*

At the sound, Martin bolted from under the tree. Tripping on a root, he felt himself falling, then sharp pain in his chin and jaw, and grit in his teeth. Looking back, he saw a branch as thick as his thigh plummet to the ground. Inches from where he had just stood.

He had to get farther from the tree. What if it was smitten, incinerated, the massive thing raining fire down upon him? Clamoring to his feet, his hair now stiff and crackling, he lunged toward the ditch and the huddle of cattle. Maybe there was protection with them.

Suddenly, out of the blackness above, erupted a crash so deafening, so skeletal that Martin felt it in his bones more than heard it with his ears. Simultaneously there was light—blazing white, all-consuming. For an instant he could see nothing— nothing but flesh-searing whiteness.

"St. Anne! Help me!" he cried. "I will become a monk! Help me!"

# 8

# KEEPING VOWS

*J**a, ja*, you have had a frightening experience, Martin," said Joachim. "But surely you do not intend to do it?"

Walking up the hard cobblestones of Domstufen, Martin looked soberly at his friends, and turned away. He pressed his thumb and forefinger against his temples. Yesterday, when at last the storm had passed, somehow Martin had managed to get himself back to Erfurt and his room at the university. Collapsing onto his bed, he had lain awake trembling most of the night.

He pressed again at his temples. Ahead, where the street crested the high point of the city, was the east end of the Erfurt Cathedral. Its soaring arches were framed by two rows of half-timbered houses leaning over the street. Martin squinted at the sunlight reflecting off the stained-glass windows, the Gothic arches of its east end pointing heavenward. He halted. Was it another sign? Clasping his hands behind his back, he resumed walking, trudging as a condemned man led to the scaffold.

"It is not as if God himself called you to become a monk," continued Joachim. He spun on his heel, walking backward in front of his friend; looking Martin in the eye, he gesticulated earnestly as he spoke. "Come, Martin, be reasonable. You are The Philosopher, brilliant scholar, ahead of all the rest of us. The world lies at your feet, Martin. And you would throw all that away to become a mere monk?"

"My pig!" cried a girl's voice. "Hurt my pig and I'll—!" *Oink-Squeal!*

It was too late. Screaming in alarm, Joachim tumbled backward over the pig, his feet in the air, his backside in the street muck.

"That comes of walking front-to-back in the street," howled a companion. Staggering with hilarity, his friends did their best to hold their noses as they hoisted Joachim to his feet.

"My best gown, covered with it!" spluttered Joachim, "and all my companions can think to do is mock me." Wiping street filth off his gown, he grimaced, "Ugh!"

"H'm, now then," said Martin, "What was it you were saying? I believe you broke off in the midst of a disparaging rant against the monastic life. Before God and these witnesses, do carry on."

Scowling heavenward, Joachim blinked rapidly and crossed himself.

Continuing up the street, Martin shielded his eyes from the hot July sun radiating off the cathedral windows. "With clouds he covers the lightning." Words from the Vulgate in the library bore in on his imagination. "And causes it to strike the mark."

"Let me guess, Seneca?" said Joachim.

"*Nein*, it is Cicero, is it not?" chimed in one.

"Plato?" guessed another.

Martin eyed his friends incredulously. They were so different from what he was. For his fellows in law school,

45

religion was a matter of calculation, weighing the risks against the advantages, taking their chances, hoping for the best. But he had noticed they always chose to do what they wanted to do in the moment. Regard for future consequences, well, that mattered little.

"Surely you won't do it?" repeated Joachim, flicking a clod of muck from his sleeve. "Thunder and lightning, it is just what it is. The new learning, Martin, it is time to move beyond the puerile superstitions of the Dark Ages." He snorted. "It's not like thunder and lightning are caused by witches or demons."

Martin halted, turning on his friend. "Or by God?"

"Well, *ja*, there is that," said Joachim stiffly.

"I was called by heavenly terrors," said Martin. "God causes the lightning to strike the mark, my friends. And he did, and it did. And I was its mark."

"Martin, it is only the weather."

"And who makes the weather?" Martin almost shouted the question. "Joachim, I vowed to St. Anne."

"You were frightened, Martin. You didn't know what you were doing. Vows aren't binding when you don't know what you are doing, are they? And why St. Anne?" He slapped his hand on his forehead. "That's it! She is just a saint, a Fräulein one, at that. She is not God. There it is, you have a way out."

With an astonished shake of his head, Martin eyed his friend. "A Fräulein one, at that, you say? St. Anne is the ever-Virgin Mary's mother, grandmother of the Christ—"

"H'm, St. Anne, St. Anne," mused Joachim. "I have got it! Miners, they prefer to pray to her."

"*Jawohl*," said Martin. "Patron saint of miners, her name often invoked in my youth."

"Ah, so then," said Joachim, stretching out each word, "you—cried—to—St. Anne." He tapped his forehead with his index finger; unaware of the muck-green smudge left by the tapping, he put on what he must have considered to be

46

his most philosophical expression. "Tell me about this girl saint of your father's. Does she tend to be fickle—?"

Slapping his fist in his palm, Martin cut him off. "I vowed a constrained and necessary vow, Joachim. Do you think I vowed to become a monk freely or willingly, or to gratify my belly? I was walled around with the terror and agony of sudden death—I tremble to think of it—so constrained, I took my vow." He halted in the street facing his companions. Resignedly, he stretched his arms wide, the cruciform of the cathedral forming a backdrop. "As God is my judge, I intend to keep my vow."

Frowning, Joachim nodded. Then, brightening, he turned to his companions. "That is good. *Meine Freunde!* It will serve us well to have had a priest for a companion, do not you think so, my friends?"

"*Jawohl.* We are in need of all the help we can get!" Laughing jovially, Martin's friends clouted him on the back.

# 9

# MONKERY

D oubt makes the monk,' so goes the saying, my lord Katie." Setting aside his book, Martin took up his lute, plucking absently on the strings. "I certainly had more of that commodity than most."

Several days had passed since last we spoke of these things. The drenching cold of November had given way to the frigid snow of December, a lacy fleece shrouding the bare branches of the pear tree in the garden below our cloister home. Winter weather upon us, I had found more time to devote to my chronicle. And here was Martin, inclined to continue.

My quill suspended above my parchment, I mused on the vast difference between my experience of entering upon the monastic life and my husband's.

"You entered willingly, Herr Doctor," I said.

"Willingly? Only in a manner of speaking, Katie. I was constrained by the violence of heaven, marked out by the God of thunder and lightning, or so I then believed myself to be." He paused, adjusting his leg on the ottoman. "But it was not so with you, dear Katie?"

"I was not consulted in the matter," I said. "I too was constrained, but it was by my father's constraint. So I am told."

"You, my rib, were but a child," he said, "a child with, what was it, but nine or ten years?"

"Five," I said, shaking my head in wonder. "Continue to give yourself to theology, Herr Doctor. You have never had a head for numbers."

"*Nein*, it is so," he agreed. "And so, my Kette, there is yet another reason why God chained me to you. But five, it is very young for taking vows for life."

"I suppose it is. I have little memory of life before the cloister in Brehna. I have little memory of my father and none of my mother. She died when I was too young to remember her."

"Or was it a memory too painful for a little girl to bear?"

"Perhaps. I do not know."

"A mercy," he said. "But your father, surely he provided a dowry to the nunnery, to support you?"

"I do not know. I have neither seen nor heard from my father since he deposited me at the cloister."

"Why did he do it, my dear?"

"I only know what I was told by my aunt one of the sisters. I never learned why my father gave me up. But I have decided to believe that it was for the best, that perhaps he did not have money to care for me, that he did it for the best, that he believed the Benedictine cloister was the best place for me."

"An honorable little girl. My dear Katie, it is good for you to forgive him his debt, but I cannot imagine a father giving up his little girl. *Ja, ja*, it must have been some mammoth constraint acting upon him to give up one such as you, dearest Katie."

Cold as it was outside our walls, in our cloister sitting room there was warmth beyond that which radiated from the hissing flames and the glowing coals on the grate. I rose and tucked his blanket more closely around his legs.

"You must drink my beer, Herr Doctor," I said. "It is good for your bowels and for sleep."

"Bless you, my rib," he murmured, his hand resting on mine as I passed the stein to him. "And what next of your early days?"

I warmed my fingers over the candle. I preferred to hear of his early days. Mine were of little consequence. But he seemed to disagree.

"I found myself in the Cistercian monastery near Grimma," I replied. "You know the one."

Drawing in a long pull on his beer, he set it on the table. "Ah, indeed, I do."

"For fifteen years I lived there."

Counting slowly on his fingers, Martin frowned. "You had but nine years when they moved you to a new cloister." Strumming a gigue chord on his lute, he added triumphantly, "*Jawohl*, that is the reason why I said nine years. Why did they move you?"

"I do not know."

"Grimma is near Wittenberg." He smiled and reached toward me. "Who would have seen this in the stars, us together like this, a union of which the pope and all his crew are not worthy—nor am I. Ah, my runaway nun, yet God was in it, was he not?"

"It is entirely your fault, Herr Doctor. You wrote that treatise on marriage."

"*Ja, ja!* My fault, was it? What were nuns doing reading my treatise on Christian marriage in the first place? Apostate nuns! Clearly in violation of your vows."

"Our vows?" I stifled my impulse to laugh. I knew he would join me, and I could not bear to see his body racked with another fit of coughing. "There was little else to read. Pamphlets, printed sermons, treatises, whole books—all by a rebel Saxon monk called Martin Luther. What else were we to read? The Dance of Death?" I broke off. "*Nein, nein.* You must not laugh aloud. Be merry inside you, with your eyes, is good."

He wafted my words with his hand. "Rebel, how I despise being called rebel." His face clouded over. I knew what he was thinking: the mayhem caused by the peasants and another treatise he penned decrying their rebellion, much to his later regret.

I must divert him from this path. He would become sullen and melancholy, and it could endure for days. "It is the cloister that did this to you, is it not?" I said. "Ruined your health. No sleep, bad food, beatings, night vigils, all the rest. Herr Doctor, tell me more of those days, when first you arrived at the monastery."

"July 17, 1505, it was," he continued, his lute cradled in his arms as he had cradled our six children when they were young. "My friends threw a party for me, and then next morning I took my leave of my room at the university, walked across town, my copy of Virgil under my arm. I had sold the rest of my books, including *Corpus Juris*, gift of my father, but couldn't bear to part with Virgil. My stomach churning, I rapped upon the great arched door of the Augustinian cloister. 'What seekest thou?' so I was greeted.

"'God's grace and thy mercy,' I replied. I had read the manual. I knew the script. When they asked if I was prepared to deny myself all worldly endeavors, I gave reply, 'Yes, with God's help and insofar as human frailty allows.'"

He fell silent, scowling into the fire.

"I knew nothing but the cloistered life," I said, hoping to pull him from his silent brooding. "But, Herr Doctor, it must have been a big change for you?"

51

He grunted, took a drink of his beer, and continued. "I nearly collapsed of exhaustion that first night—I had no idea what vigils and deprivations awaited. The cloister bell clanging at one in the morning; indeed, being wrenched from sleep in the dark of night was challenging at the first. Making the sign of the cross, covering ourselves in the white robe, over that the scapular—one was never to leave his cell without the scapular. Robed and fit for heaven, we were sprinkled with holy water, and fell to our knees at the high altar for prayer. But it was the choir, and singing, dear Katie, it was the music that thrilled me, the art of the prophets. Next only to theology, it is music that can calm the agitations of the soul and put the devil to flight."

As he spoke, he caressed the strings of his lute with his fingers. "But only after theology. Without true theology, I learned that music was not enough. In the cloister, my agitations of soul increased. Far from finding comfort and solace, my terrors were augmented by it.

"Was the monastic life, taking up the cowl, was it the surest way to salvation? So the Church taught. One dark night while singing the *Salve Regina* my first doubts began to rear their heads and dance before my imagination.

"*'Save, O Queen, thou Mother of mercy, our life, our delight, and our hope... Thou our advocate, sweet Virgin Mary, pray for us, thou Holy Mother of God.'*

"My heart soared as we chanted, the polyphonic strains of our voices swelling, overlaying one another with perfect accord, rising higher, more majestic, reechoing from the vaulted splendors of the chapter house high above.

"Then I was struck, as if by lightning. Were we expecting too much from her? The more I read in the Bible—the monastery had several of them, and, O, how I longed to have such a treasure of my own—the more I read, the more I doubted her advocacy. 'Doubt makes the monk,' but it would be precisely my doubt that would defrock this monk."

Again, he broke off, brooding, pressing on his temples.

"So, my dear Herr Doctor, what did you do?"

"Do? Doing was my great problem. If ever a monk got to heaven by his monkery it was I. All my brothers in the monastery who knew me will bear me out. So strictly did I keep the rule of my order, that if I had kept on any longer with vigils, prayers, readings, and other work—I should have killed myself."

"There are times, Herr Doctor, when I fear you have killed yourself."

He waved his hand dismissively. "And then the time came. I knew it was coming, dread and torment pressed down on me like an upper millstone as the day approached. It was my death sentence."

"What so terrified you, Herr Doctor?"

"My first mass, saying my first mass nearly slew me."

My pulse quickening, I dipped my quill in ink, and readied a clean parchment to render the account.

# 10
# MISERABLE PIGMY

The air in the vestry of Erfurt Cathedral was a menagerie of holy smells: fine linen, golden thread, spicy incense, the fatty scent of candle wax, and the musty rigid smells of ancient cut stone. All of these entwined themselves with the not-so-holy smells of fear-induced sweat, the moldering remains of long-dead patrons entombed beneath the flagstones, mildew and dust, and vermin droppings.

Drawing in his breath, Martin Luther coughed. The blood pounding in his temples, only with great effort did he managed to suppress the urge to wrench himself free and run from the robing chamber. Feeling crushed with each new layer, he chafed under the load of vestments pressing down on his body.

"Stop fidgeting, Brother Martin," muttered Karl a fellow monk. He lowered the white surplice over Martin's head. Stepping back, he scowled. "Well, that is... better, anyway."

"They must be precise, my son," said the prior.

"Better is not good enough, then?" murmured Martin, doing his best to hide the tremor in his voice.

"Uh-uh." Karl shook his head vigorously.

"No, it is not," said the prior.

"Forget the seven deadly sins, Martin," whispered Karl, eyes wide, splaying his fingers as if he were casting a spell. He nodded confidently. "Compared to proper vestments, the seven deadliest are as a poof of smoke in the wind."

"You over speak yourself, Brother Karl," said the prior. "Nevertheless, it is so; there must be no mistake in robing you."

"And what of my—" Martin cleared his throat. "M-my voice?"

"No stammering. The words must be as precise as the vestments."

"And my soul? What of it?" There was no hiding it. The entire question came out as a stammer.

Tilting his head in scrutiny, the prior took Martin by the shoulders; he narrowed his eyes as if peering into his soul. "There must be no sin unconfessed, no sin."

"No sin," chanted Karl, aping the prior's words, his eyes half closed. He brushed an imaginary fleck from Martin's shoulder. "No sin."

"It is a holy thing you are about to do, Martin," continued the prior. "There must be no sin even in the corners of your heart."

"No sin, not even in the corners," chanted Karl, his eyes arched heavenward, his jowls waggling as his head convulsed with feeling.

Martin tried to swallow. He felt a tremor in his knees and feared he might collapse before entering the sanctuary. If he felt this way before entering the holy nave, what awaited him when he mounted the precipitous altar?

"But judging from your time spent in the confessional this last week," continued the prior, "—you were there for over four hours at one time—I think you need not fear for your sins. God will be merciful." The prior stepped back, frowning at Martin. "Remember, it is the sacrament which is holy, not the officiant."

"Is it futile, then," said Martin, "to confess and be absolved from my sin?"

As the prior opened his mouth to reply, the bells of the cathedral spire high above began ponderously ringing out the call to the mass. *Clang-clang! Gong-gong!*

Martin clamped his hands over his ears, swaying from side-to-side, desperate for the ringing to stop.

"Proceed! Proceed!" hissed Karl, poking Martin in the ribs. "The time has come."

"O sing unto the Lord a new song." Accompanied by the hammering rhythm of Martin's heart, the monks chanted in procession down the aisle ahead of him. He watched the rising and falling orbs of their tonsured heads, flaring into reflective globes as they passed through shafts of sunlight angling across the nave. Blue wisps of incense lurked above the aisle, circling, intertwining the monks, lurching forward in the wake of disturbed air, then drifting into hovering expectancy.

Martin's breath came in short, wheezing gasps. There was no avoiding the blue tentacles of incense, and he must draw breath, or die. Searching for air to draw into his lungs, air unpolluted by holy incense, it was no good. Suppressing a sneeze, Martin's eyes watered as he passed through a blue serpentine cloud. But he could not wipe them, not upon the sleeve of so holy a vestment.

"O sing unto the Lord a new song."

Martin wondered at the joyous words. Would not another psalm be more appropriate, he mused, his feet heavier with each tread, the high altar looming before him.

*"I am afflicted and ready to die from my youth up."* Should not his brother monks be singing this psalm on the occasion of

him saying his first mass? *"While I suffer thy terrors I am distracted. Thy fierce wrath goeth over me; thy terrors have cut me off."* Yes, this is what they should be chanting, their voices echoing Martin's inner turmoil off the stone vaulting, reverberating his terrors throughout the ambulatory and clerestory of the ancient structure.

As the monks divided and processed to left and right, Martin knew that he was to proceed forward, upward, onto the high altar, alone, before God, where his holiness dwelt. His feet were leaden as he climbed the ancient steps. *This must be the terror the condemned man feels as he climbs the scaffold.* Turning, Martin steadied himself at the table. Quavering before his eyes was the grand nave of Erfurt Cathedral, the monks in their black habits on either side, the nave filled with guests and family come to celebrate the grand event. His family, there to his left. He could not look at them, not now. He had not laid eyes on his father or his mother for nearly two years.

*"In nómine Patris, et Fílii, et Spíritus Sancti."* Shocked by the words, Martin realized they were coming from his own voice. He knew the recitation. All was going well. Or so he thought.

"We offer unto thee—" At the words, Martin lifted his arms heavenward. The wafer, in his hands, suspended above his head, Martin felt his arms trembling, the cascading sleeves of his vestments flagging as if with an approaching tempest. "We offer unto thee, the living, the true, the eternal G—" Martin's mouth was dry, and his voice clutched. Clearing his throat, he tried again. "The eternal God."

And then he stopped. There was much more Latin to recite, but, stupefied and terror-stricken, he stopped, his mind awhirl with doubts. *With what tongue shall such as I address such Majesty? Who am I that I should lift up my eyes or raise my hands to the divine Majesty?*

He swallowed and tried to recommence the recitation of the mass. But it was no good. Powerful fingers closed around his neck. His throat constricting, his conscience was plagued with unsupportable torment. *The angels surround him. At his nod the earth trembles. And shall I, a miserable little pygmy, dust and ashes and full of sin, shall such as I speak to the living, the eternal, the true God?*

Rivulets of sweat streaked down Martin's face, smarting in his eyes. Dozens of onlookers, including his father and mother, sat in awkward silence, the nave electrified with tension. His father had been livid with rage when he received news from the Augustinian cloister that Martin had presented himself to become a monk. What was his father thinking of him now?

Martin dared not look at the stern old miner seated in the front row. He did not need to look. He knew his father's postures, and the interpretation thereof. Spluttering with disgust, his father would have a thick arm stretched across his torso, his face buried in the hand of his other arm, his head shaking slowly in dismay.

"*Hoc est corpus meum.*" There it was, Martin's voice had resumed. "This is my body," it said. The miracle of transubstantiation was done. He had done it. The bread was no longer bread, the wine no longer wine. He held in his mortal hands, the very body and blood of the Son of God. With the awful realization, in his distress, there was a precarious instant when Martin nearly overturned the chalice, staining his holy vestments with its sacred contents.

Somehow, in spite of his terror-induced bungling, Martin managed to come to the final words of the rite. "*Ite Missa est.*" When the mass was ended, as the monks sang and withdrew from the cathedral, a new fear gripped Martin's mind. At the banquet that followed in the cloister hall, for the first time in two years, he would have to face the disapproving scorn of his father and take to the dance floor with his scowling mother.

*Dust and ashes, I am but a miserable little pigmy, indeed!*

# 11
# APPARITION OF THE DEVIL

Greta Luther bit her lower lip and thrust out her chin. "It is as I expected."

Martin could not help overhearing his mother. She had never been convincing as a whisperer. The heat rising on his cheeks, Martin saw from the downturned looks, the sideways grimaces, and the raised eyebrows of his brother monks at the table that he was not the only one who heard his mother's words.

"However clever you think he is, no good comes of doting on a child, so I've always said."

"Humph." Hans became engrossed in a minute inspection of the ham hock in his fist. Taking aim, he viciously sank his teeth into another bite.

His father said little during the banquet. He ate, drank his beer, and ate some more, sending occasional dark looks Martin's way across the table. Picking at his food, Martin glanced up, hoping to find a softening of his father's mood, so he could speak to him, reconcile with him. At last, when the novices had placed a steaming apple strudel before them, Martin saw his chance. Apple strudel was his father's favorite dish.

As his father, grunting approvingly, heaped his spoon with a second bite, Martin took his chance. "Dear father," he began.

His cheeks bulging with strudel, his father stopped chewing. As if seeing his son for the first time, he stared at him across the table.

Not at all sure how to proceed, Martin said, "Why were you so contrary to me taking up the robe of a monk? Is it not a becoming robe, Father? And the life here, it is so quiet and godly."

Setting down his wooden spoon with restraint, his father swallowed. Washing down his strudel with a great gulp of beer, he wiped the back of his hand across his mouth, and leaned over the table.

"You learned scholar," he began, placing more wait on the word learned than Martin thought necessary. "You *learned* scholar, have you never read in the Bible that you should honor your father and your mother? And here you have left me and your dear mother to look after ourselves in our old age."

The clattering of plates and cutlery fell silent at his words. Hans Luther had long ago learned the art of projecting his voice; workers could hear his voice deep down into the vast labyrinth of the copper mines; they feared cave-ins if he roared at them in anger. But throughout a life of hard labor, he had seldom managed to find any other volume for his voice. At the thunder of his words, all eyes had turned, wide and staring, on Martin and his father.

"Father, I can do more for you now as a... as a monk with my prayers than if I had stayed in the world and gained worldly riches as a jurist." Running a hand over his tonsured head, Martin felt keenly that inadequacy of his words.

Hans had resumed his work with the spoon, laying into the strudel as if it were a mound of ore that needed shoveling. At Martin's words he paused, eyeing his son over a generous heap of pastry.

"Besides, Father, as you know, I was called by God; the God of thunder and lightning called me to be a monk."

His father dropped his spoon and slammed his fist on the table, goblets and platters clattering. "Or by an apparition of the Devil!"

Like the whooshing of a furnace, there was a great indrawing of breath by the monks at Hans Luther's words. After an uncomfortable silence, whispered conversation gradually resumed, followed by the clattering and clunking sounds of eating.

Martin looked numbly at the untouched food on his plate. His mother, in a moment of tenderness, placed a hand on her husband's sleeve.

"Yet, it must have been of God," she said, with a tremor of emotion seldom heard in her tone. "For not accepting your new vocation, God has sorely punished us." Martin's estrangement melted as he saw the quaver in his mother's lower lip, and the tears whelming in her eyes.

"Your brothers," she continued, scraping her chair closer to the table and sitting up, rigid as a tombstone. She cleared her throat and, strained with effort, continued as if she were recounting the loss of the neighbor's dog. "Your brothers, they were, the two of them in one week, taken off with plague. Dead and buried."

Martin had heard the unhappy news, but this was the first he had heard of it from his parents. Seizing on it as an opportunity to press his point, he said, "As their brother, and as a monk, I can now pray for their souls and alleviate their suffering in purgatory."

"You becoming a monk," said his father, "is what done it in the first place!"

"It's our lot to make the most of our sufferings," said his mother, scowling darkly at her son. "Make the most of them, that is, with three fewer sons to help us do so."

Hans rose to his feet, his stein held high. "Come, let us drink."

Later that night, after taking leave of his parents, Martin knelt at the foot of his cot in his cell, sweat pouring from his body, his hands clasped more in agitated wringing than in prayer. "The devil comes as an angel of light." He had read so in the Vulgate. Had the lightning and thunder only appeared to be a divine calling by God? What if his father was right? And it was an apparition of the arched-fiend himself?

# 12

# NO SATISFACTION

O my sin, my sin, my sin!" Rocking back and forth, Martin knelt alone at the foot of his cot on the cold, stone floor of his cell. The pain in his knees had long ago subsided into numb oblivion. Shivering with the night chill, he clasped his hands so tightly they grew cold with lack of circulation. His confessor had urged him to seek God's mercy, that God delighted to extend his mercy to penitent sinners.

Martin had often heard it said that doubt makes the monk. But he had come to fear that his doubts were of a different order; they would kill the monk. Slouching back on his heels in exhaustion, he heaved a sigh. What if his father was right, and he was summoned, not by God, but by the devil?

At times, he felt that the cloister was his hell on earth. Purgatory would be better than the agonizing uncertainty of his days and hours. His confessor had urged Martin when in distress to pray the psalter. So he prayed the psalter. "My

God, my God, why hast thou forsaken me?" Over and over, he prayed.

That night in his cell, Martin was never certain what happened; it was a dream, more properly, a nightmare. As if in a dark tunnel, he vaguely remembered hearing a rooster crowing. *Cock-a-doodle-doo! Cock-a-doodle-doo!* Twice he heard it crowing. And then he felt as if his heart had stopped its beating. Doctor Staupitz his confessor had only that day told him to form a better judgment of God, that his bitterness at God's justice would bring down wrath from God more than mercy. But the rooster had crowed. In his thoughts, in the deepest recesses of his heart, had he, like Peter, betrayed the Christ three times? Here on his knees in his monkish cell, had he denied the Lord?

He had no answer. He despaired that there was any answer. Yet he prayed on. "My God, my God, why hast thou forsaken me?" How long he prayed, Martin never knew. Then it struck him. Perhaps God had forsaken him because he had forsaken God. That was how it worked. Forsaking God was blasphemy, and blasphemy was a mortal sin, too damning for expiation.

Suddenly, crying into his anguish, he heard voices. "Fra Martin, Fra Martin!" they called. Was it another summons? Had the demons come for him? There it was again. "Fra Martin, Fra Martin!" accompanied by pounding, earnest knocking, not to be ignored.

Suddenly, the plank door to his cell burst open. Towering above him like quavering apparitions were monks in black robes.

"Is he dead?" cried one, crossing himself and cowering beneath his hood.

Dropping to his knees, another brother bent over him and laid his ear on Martin's chest. After a moment of listening, he cried, "He lives!"

"Then what ails him?" asked another, cramming his hands into his sleeves and stepping backward.

"Fetch my Blockflöte," cried Brother Dieter. "Music will drive away the Devil. Make haste!"

The next thing Martin remembered was the sweet piping of Brother Dieter's Blockflöte, melodious, meandering, swelling and soaring, flitting playfully here and there, calming his spirit, reviving his soul.

"We thought we had lost you, Martin," said Dieter later that morning at breakfast. "Whatever happened to you? Was it ecstasy, like St. Theresa? Was it that?"

Expelling a sighing burst, Martin shrugged. He did not know.

"You were blue with cold," continued Dieter. "When did you last sleep, Martin?"

"I do not know."

"You look awful."

"*Danke*. Then my face does not lie," he said. "I feel as I look." Rubbing both his hands across his face, Martin pressed his thumbs in his temples.

"If any one of us gets to heaven for our monkery," said Dieter, shaking his head in wonder, "it will be you. And at this rate, it will be far sooner than later."

"*If* any of us gets to heaven," murmured Martin. "That is just it. I fear none of us will. Not in this way."

"Precisely! And that is why you must stop tormenting yourself. I fear you are taking the 'fastings, vigils, and mortifications' part of our vows too seriously."

"How can one take any matter of the soul," said Martin, "too seriously?"

"*Ja, ja*." Dieter waved his hand dismissively. "But you take these to greater extremities than is healthy for body or soul. Look at you. You look like a cadaver. Now, eat some cheese. And these sausages, they're heavenly. They will revive you." Dieter carved three thick rounds of sausage, placed them on a trencher, and stabbed his knife in the table. "Look at you. You need fattening, Martin. That is your problem. Now, eat, man!"

During vespers that evening, beside himself with exhaustion, Martin felt himself going down, the slackening of muscular tone, the skeletal disjointing, the slipping. His head spun. His brother monks drifted into sinister shadows encircling him, candlelight spluttering in between the shadows.

Once again it was the music that saved him, a soaring crescendo of polyphonic brilliance transporting him upon its ecstatic wings. Without the music Martin would have collapsed into a mound of monkish habit in his choir stall.

Barely able to walk, after vespers Martin approached his confessor. "Doctor Staupitz, I am afraid."

Staupitz gazed down at the young monk trembling on his knees. "Perfect love will cast out your fears, my son."

"That is why I fear, Doctor," said Martin, clutching a sleeve of his confessor. "Perfect love, you say. I have none. Not perfect, far from perfect. I am in torment! I must confess my sins."

Raising the young monk to his feet, Doctor Staupitz led him across the nave to the south transept and the confessional booth.

Once inside the confines of the confessional, Martin fell to his knees, facing the thin wall dividing him from Staupitz. "O, my sin, my sin, my sin!" he moaned. "I see specters, terrible figures, and, Father, I am terrified thereby.

"What have you to confess, my son?" said Staupitz, levelly.

"Father, forgive me for I have sinned."

"What sin, my son? Have you been tempted to sins of the flesh, lust for gold, lust for fame." He hesitated. "Martin, have you lusted after a woman?"

Martin did not immediately reply.

Interpreting his silence as admission of guilt, Staupitz pressed on. "Martin, have you seduced a *Fräulein?*"

Still no reply from Martin.

"Have you, Martin, fornicated with a woman? The sacrament of confession does you no good unless you confess with your mouth."

At last Martin found his voice. "I am not a stone, Father, but lust is most often scattered by terror, so that sins of the flesh are beyond me, out of my reach. I am crushed by sins that torment me, not so much in body, but inside of me. And I fear they sink me lower than the grave."

"What sins?" said Staupitz, shortly. "Martin, you did not sleep last night, and perhaps neither did you do so the night previous. It is late. What sins?"

"I do not know," stammered Martin. "Not of a certainty. But I fear I may have committed a mortal sin."

"What sin?"

"Pride, within my heart."

"And in what form does that pride appear?"

"I am ashamed to say it, but there are days when I feel that perhaps I am better."

The sound of drumming fingers came from across the confessional barrier. "This day, one may safely presume, is not one of those days."

"*Nein*, it is not. To myself alone, I say, 'I have done nothing wrong today.' But the words are scarcely uttered, uttered, that is, within the dark shadows of my own mind, and the chilling winds of exposure tear across my raw flesh. Pride was a sin. And if there was pride, what other sins might lurk as yet unawakened in my bosom? 'Have you fasted enough?' my conscience assails me. 'Are you poor enough? Have you deprived yourself sufficiently to win the favor of a holy God?' And worse."

After a pause, accompanied by more drumming of fingers, Staupitz said, "Within these sacred confines, Brother Martin,

I have heard the foul deeds of hundreds of monks in this confessional. I have heard of lying, thieving, lusting, fornicating, hating, and, yes, even murdering, mortal sins, all."

"And now pride, my pride," interjected Martin.

"Brother Martin, I do not understand you. Pride, as you have described it to me, is a venial sin not a mortal sin, slight, not vicious."

"But, Father, I willfully entered into the state of pride. Does that not make it mortal?" He hesitated. "And there is more."

"I was certain there was."

"I fear, Father, I may have committed—" He broke off, breathing heavily. "The unpardonable sin."

"Unpardonable? In what form?"

"Blasphemy," said Martin. "Is there any other? I have forsaken the Lord."

"You have not done so, Martin."

"How can you be sure?"

"Because you would not be here, caring so earnestly about your sins, if you had railed against God, had taken up your stand with the enemy of God and your soul, or had sworn your allegiance to the Devil. You have done none of these."

"O, but what if, within the dark recesses of my heart, what if I may have done so?"

"Martin, Martin. If the ultimate proof that one is a sinner," said Doctor Staupitz, "is that he does not know his own sin, then, Martin, you are no sinner, not that kind of sinner, not a mortal sinner, not a blasphemer. You know your sin, more so than any monk from whom I have ever heard confession."

"What must I do? Father, prescribe my penance."

"Your penance? Here is your penance, Martin. Instead of torturing yourself on account of your sins, throw yourself into the Redeemer's arms. Trust in him, in the righteousness of his life, in the atonement of his death. Listen to the Son of God. He became man to give you the assurance of divine favor."

"Assurance?" Martin's tone was bitter. "Is assurance possible? I have none. I am daily terrified."

"For such as you are, Martin, Christ does not terrify. He consoles the penitent. Now, go in peace. Love him who first loved you."

# 13

# DEVOUT DELIGHTS

(November, 1510)

H oly Rome," cried Martin in ecstasy, "I salute thee!"

"*Ja, ja.* Not bad," said Dieter, glancing at the skyline of the ancient city, its seven hills, its columns and domes. "Uh, Martin, do get up. Why are you prostrating yourself? It's not the burning bush. You're overdoing, again, making a spectacle. Others are watching. Rise to your feet."

Martin, who lay face down in the road, at Dieter's urging, rose to his knees, pausing there to take in the wonder of the Eternal City.

"All the way up, on your feet. Speaking of feet, mine are killing me," said Dieter, brushing dirt off of Martin's black habit. "You're disgusting. You cannot enter Rome looking like a Saxon peasant who's been groveling in the dung."

"I am a Saxon peasant," said Martin, still gazing at the city, his voice a husky whisper.

"Which I try not to hold against you," said Dieter. "But we must think aright about pilgrimage. It's not just about stuffing our account with more grace, not to diminish the value of the sacrament, mind you. But we must think of ourselves as diplomats, not merely pilgrims."

"Diplomats? What are you talking about?"

"We Saxons on pilgrimage must allay some of the misconceptions that abound toward us German barbarians. But, ugh, my feet; I do wish Doctor Staupitz had chosen us for a more local outing. As near as I can reckon, it's over 700 miles from Erfurt to Rome, and we've walked every yard of it on these feet."

"I wonder why Doctor Staupitz picked us?" mused Martin.

Ignoring him, Dieter continued, "Do you think they still have those Roman baths here? Ugh, it's not just my blistered feet; my whole body could use a good soak."

"The monastic vow of silence," said Martin, "it must have come at a great price for you."

"Don't know what you're talking about. But I do know why he picked us, at least why he picked you."

"Tell me," said Martin.

"So you could find peace. I believe Staupitz is afraid you will do yourself a harm if you do not find peace. And if peace can be had by the collected merits of the saints, Rome was the place to send you." He brightened. "—to send us!"

"'If peace can be had,' you say. Do you doubt it? Do you not believe that Rome is the greatest repository of the treasury of merit, the storehouse of everything I am lacking?"

"Available for a price, to the highest bidder," said Dieter, nodding philosophically. "Forty popes buried beneath these stones, the very ones we're treading on—my feet are killing me—the catacomb of St. Callistus alone contains the bones of 76,000 martyrs."

"You have done your research," said Martin.

"Staupitz gave me the pamphlet. It gets better. Rome has the chains that confined St. Paul, one of the thirty pieces of silver paid to Judas—imagine 1,400 years off purgatory for venerating a single coin; I call that devotional efficiency. And Rome has the remains of both St. Peter and St. Paul, a fragment from the burning bush, and the Scala Sancta, Pilate's steps on which our Lord trod at his final trial."

"His trial? It was in Jerusalem. This is Rome. How could they be genuine?"

"There's a skeptic born every hour," retorted Dieter. "Maybe they were brought to the Eternal City by Empress Helena, the benefactress of Rome. If the Church says they are genuine, who are you to doubt? Did you know, Martin, there's more merit to be purchased here in Rome than in Jerusalem? So says the pamphlet." He paused, frowning. "Imagine what our feet would feel like if we had to walk all the way to Jerusalem!"

"And here we are," said Martin, "the surplus merits of the saints waiting to enfold us with their grace. Dieter, do you ever wonder how the pope does it?"

"Does what?"

"Stores up merits," mused Martin, his brow furrowed. "And then dispenses them to pilgrims? How does he do it?"

"*Ich verstehen nicht.*" Dieter extended his hands, palms up, and shrugged. "But I do know one thing. We are in Rome, my friend. And I for one plan to enjoy it, talk as much as I can, take in the most valuable sites, feast on Italian delicacies, and come home enriched with a vast surplus of indulgences, having the time of our life in the process. Here, let's make a list of the bones we're going to venerate, and then we can check off the relics and adjust our tally as we go."

They arrived that evening at Santa Maria del Popolo, as the Italians called the church of the Augustinian order in Rome. Completed in 1477, it was a modern church for the people of Rome, built more along sturdy Augustinian lines,

Martin observed, than according to the reborn magnificence of the Italian Renaissance on display at most churches.

"Here are your cells, Herr Germanic Doctors." Brother Leonardo, assigned to orient them to the cloister as well as the city, was a rotund fellow, with a taunting manner, who seemed to enjoy hearing himself speak. "You will be expected to attend all the ecclesiastical hours of the monastic life of your Italian Augustinian brothers. But, have no fear, there is more than one kind of devotion of which to partake in Rome."

Winking and lowering his voice, Brother Leonardo drew Martin and Dieter in closer. "And when you step out of the cloister to take in the charms of the city, which you will no doubt do, be sure that you make your way carefully."

As he spoke, he clasped hands with Martin, pressing a folded piece of paper into his palm. Opening it, Martin saw a name and street address written on it.

"We do have our standards here in Rome," continued Brother Leonardo, in a pedantic tone that reminded Martin of his schoolmaster at the Mansfield Purgatory. "You must keep yourself pure from solicitations from the common herd on the common street corner. Beneath the dignity of your clerical office are these."

"I do not understand," stammered Martin. "Trastevere? Is that a district in Rome?" Dieter jabbed him in the ribs with an elbow.

"Oh, my good Saxon monk, you will understand. Now, tuck that away. I am confident you will not be disappointed." With another wink, he backed out of the room and closed the door.

"Give me that," said Dieter, snatching the paper from Martin.

"What is it?"

"Oh, nothing, nothing at all," said Dieter, wadding it up and thrusting it into the folds of his habit. Now, I think we should get a good night's sleep, lots of rest, especially for these feet. Rome is a vast city, with more moldering bones waiting to be venerated than anywhere. Brother Martin, you just follow my lead. Delights abound for the devout."

# 14

# MOLDERING BONES

I won't deny it," whispered Dieter, "this place makes my flesh to crawl." Clutching Martin's sleeve, his voice was pitched higher than usual.

An ominous *drip-dripping* echoed from the barrel vaulted ceiling of the subterranean passageway.

"*Jawohl*," agreed Martin. He did not trust himself to say more. Though it was cool in the catacomb of St. Callistus, sweat oozed from Martin's brow and smarted in his eyes; he tried to wipe them with his sleeve. At the sudden movement, his candle spluttered. Martin's heart skipped a beat. If its flame expired they would be in the dark, deep beneath the earth, surrounded by the moldering remains of tens of thousands, in absolute darkness.

A prolonged trickle of sweat crawled its way down Martin's spine. He felt an involuntary twitching under his left eye. Reaching out to steady himself against the rough stone passageway, he pulled back. Shuddering with revulsion, he frantically wiped the slimy substance on his habit.

"It feels like a labyrinth," whispered Dieter, cowering behind.

"It is a labyrinth," said Martin, flatly.

"But a labyrinth in hell. That's what this one feels like." Sniffing, he added, "and it smells horrible, like moldering bones."

Martin halted in front of a niche piled with bones. Doing his best to keep his hand from trembling, he reached out and closed his fingers around a skull. There was a hollow rattling as the bones settled. Holding the skull at eye level, the tremulous candle flame illuminating the teeth and cavity where once a nose had been, Martin stared unblinking into the gaping eye sockets.

"These are holy bones," he said, but with more confidence than he felt. "Bones of the martyrs, bones of popes, skulls and scapula of the saints."

"D-do you think this fellow was one?" asked Dieter.

Martin shrugged. Who could know? "The man who once inhabited this orb might have been a martyr whose treasury of merit alone could free my grandfather from purgatory. No, we must not think of this as hell; it is better that we think of it as the gateway to heaven. By praying in this place, we have the ear of this saint—and thousands more."

Stroking the lobe of his own ear, Dieter bent closer, tilting his head and narrowing his eyes at the skull. "A vast treasury of merit," he murmured. "Brother Leonardo told me this morning at breakfast that there was sufficient merit in the catacombs alone to empty purgatory. He may have exaggerated. But then, who would know?"

Martin reached out to return the skull to its resting place.

"Careful!" said Dieter. "The rattling of the bones—I cannot abide hearing them knocking together like that."

"Do you ever wonder," said Martin, "why he doesn't do it?"

"Do what?"

"The pope, why he doesn't just empty it. If he has the keys, and he is good, why would he not simply unlock the gates and free the tormented?"

Dieter laughed. "Imagine Julius II, the warrior pope, sword drawn, doing that! Martin, you are strange. We wouldn't have to work for it then. If we didn't have to work for it, if we didn't have to pay something for salvation, it would loosen the reins of our lusts."

Martin held the candle so he could see Dieter's face. "Loosen the reins of lusts? Have you not seen what lies all around us here in Rome? At the monasteries on our journey, the brothers living in lechery and luxury. You think me naïve, a blind novice in matters of the flesh. Unlike that skull there, I yet have flesh and blood, and eyes in my sockets. Everyone in Rome is here paying for their own or someone else's soul to be freed from torment. But in this meat market of the soul, one thing is clear to anyone with eyes to see: there is prodigious loosening of the reins of lust."

"Must you always be so earnest?" said Dieter. "Let's get out of here."

Martin turned. Dieter's eyes, illuminated by the candle flame, were wide and darting side-to-side.

"We've come this far, I for one intend to kneel down and petition this entire repository of dry bones. The only thing worse than being in this place of death is gaining nothing for our souls after having done so."

"I know you, Martin. You'll be at it for an hour. I do not believe I can endure another hour in this place. Besides, there are so many easier shrines at which to pray and gain expiation; Pope Julius II has just decreed a sweeping indulgence at the Scala Sancta; a quick *Pater noster* on each step—there's not really that many steps either—and purgatory disgorges our dearly departed." He snapped his fingers, the sound echoing through the passage.

"The warrior pope's indulgence?" said Martin doubtfully.

"Some call him that. I am sure he means well. Merit gained down here, in this moldering labyrinth, comes too dear, if you ask me. Let us be gone. *Blah-ha!* I feel skeletal fingers clutching at us from these mounds as we pass."

Listening to the ponderous *drip-dripping*, Martin felt much the same, perhaps worse. "I shall be brief." Determined to make the most of Rome, he fell to his knees. "*Sancta Maria, Mater Dei, ora pro nobis peccatoribus…*"

A half an hour later, Dieter flopped down beneath an olive tree. "I can breathe again," he gasped. "I say we get as far away from this labyrinth as we can. I've had about enough of groveling for grace at the bones of the ancient dead. I say we leave the bowels of the city beneath us and explore the living, breathing, pulsing Rome above ground."

"You mean her relics, of course?" said Martin.

"Of course."

# 15

# PRELATES AND PROSTITUTES

The catacombs of the long departed beneath them, Martin and Dieter resurfaced. On every side they were surrounded by ancient ruins—the coliseum, the Roman Forum, Constantine's arch of triumph, the Palatine Hill, the Circus Maximus. And they were surrounded by an emerging new world of reborn marble splendors—churches, palaces, fountains with muscular statuary—rising as if from the spirit of ancient Rome.

"This is not Eisenach," said Martin, his voice monotone but loud, to be heard above the bustling street sounds.

Eyes wide, Dieter grinned in reply.

"Sicilian spaghetti pasta," cried a vendor, extending a sample to Martin, "the finest in Roma!"

"Cheese, the finest Pecorino Romano! Get your cheese here!" announced another.

Inhaling the savory culinary aromas, the pilgrims from austere northern Germany, strolled in wonder through the boulevards and piazzas of the Eternal City. Encircled by a cacophony of human noises, they sampled the tomatoes, the peppers, the olives, the pasta, the cheeses, and an assortment of plump Italian sausages, baptized in paprika, fennel, oregano and other spices.

Bizarrely intermingled with the array of gastronomic wonders crouched beggars crying for morsels of food on one corner; a fulsome mendicant friar peddling indulgences on another, and a scantily clad woman peddling hers on still another.

"Where are we?" shouted Martin above the din.

"Trastevere," said Dieter. Halting in the street, he began patting himself down, searching for something inside his robe.

"What are you doing?" asked Martin.

"Ah, here it is," said Dieter, spreading out the note that Brother Leonardo had given them the night before. "It's got to be right around here."

"What holy relic could possibly be enshrined here?" asked Martin.

Dieter slowly turned completely around in the street. "Uh, perhaps a relic of Mary Magdalene, one from her old life."

"I do not like this," said Martin. "Why would an Augustinian brother send us here?" He voiced the question warily, afraid he already knew the answer.

Dieter shrugged. "It must be permitted if our order sanctions it."

Halting, Martin cut him off. "What is that man doing?"

Fascinated by the array human life, Dieter careened into Martin from behind. "What is who doing?"

"That priest just there," said Martin.

"There are priests everywhere in Rome," said Dieter. "Be more specific."

"The one speaking to that young woman."

"There are lots of young women hereabouts."

As they stared, the priest stepped closer to the girl, appeared to speak into her ear, and then caressed her cheek with the back of his fingers.

"His long-lost sister, perhaps?" said Dieter meekly.

Martin stood as if turned to stone, the press of people jostling him. Through clenched teeth he said, "You know better than that, my brother."

"But this is not the common variety," said Dieter, "the baser kind. Leonardo explained it. It is sanctioned. Harlotry regulated by and for the clergy. He told me all about it at breakfast. It's built into the monastic system, so he said. Whatever demerit one accrues here, not to worry, there's plenty of accumulated merit in the bottomless reliquaries of Rome to balance the scale." He paused, bobbing his head as if weighing out the merits of the argument. "He may just have a point, Martin."

"We must leave this place."

"No, wait. It makes sense when you think about it. Rome is the treasury of merit itself. If we stumble upon a bit of demerit, as I suspect is going on inside those walls, it can easily be put to rights. There is a relic to venerate and merit to be recovered just around the corner. That means there's really no better place to indulge in a bit of demerit than Rome."

Martin grabbed Dieter by the sleeve and spun him around, staring at him in disbelief.

"—so says Brother Leonardo," said Dieter, gesturing with his thumb over his shoulder back at the Augustinian cloister. "They're his words, of course, not mine."

Two friars arm-in-arm, each with a bottle of wine in hand, came toward them in the middle of the street, their faces puffy and red, singing at the top of their lungs. Martin and Dieter stepped aside to let them pass. Suddenly, Martin remembered Kaspar's drinking song, the words slurred out only moments before his knifing:

"Hear me prelate, most discreet,
For indulgence crying;
Deadly sins I find so sweet,
I'm in love with dying."

"Did you make that one up?" asked Dieter. "This evening at the cloister we must amuse the brothers, you on your lute, and I with my *Blockflöte*. We will render a Saxon consort."

"Did you not heed the words? Deadly sins, however sweet, are just that, deadly." Martin looked back at the drunk friars and the clerical brothel. "'Prelates, most discreet'? *Doch*, there is nothing discreet here; shameless, brazen, parading of transgression. Can there be an indulgence sufficient?"

"Brother Leonardo says there is, just around the corner. They have the pelvic bone of the mistress of Pope Alex—"

Martin cut him off. "I do not want to hear another word from Brother Leonardo. This place is an abyss. We must get away, before it is too late."

Dieter, looking at his fellow monk, grew sober. "You look ill. Are you not well, Martin?"

"Sick of this den of iniquity," he said, passing a sleeve over his brow. "Still more, I am sick of my own iniquity. If I survive this abyss, I will one day write a book on temptation."

"We must go," said Dieter, taking Martin by the sleeve. "I know just the place."

It was afternoon before Martin and Dieter knelt at the high altar of the Basilica di San Giovanni in Laterano, Rome's cathedral and the official seat of the pope.

"And that's where they have their heads," whispered Dieter, nodding with his toward an elaborately decorated shrine.

"Whose?"

"St. Peter's and St. Paul's. Did you not read the pamphlet?"

"Where is the rest of them?" whispered Martin.

"What?"

"Their bodies, arms and legs, the rest of their skeletal remains?"

"Various shrines in Rome have them. One must be willing to share."

"Why is it so fast?" said Martin. "The priest says the mass as if it were a chariot race."

"In a manner of speaking, it is." Clasping his hands in reverence, Dieter nodded. "Priest who say more masses bring in more revenue."

"Bread thou art," intoned the officiant, his voice diminishing in elongated piety, "and bread thou wilt remain."

Dieter turned suddenly. "Did you hear that?"

Martin nodded numbly.

"Latin, it has to be the same in Italy. You're a better scholar than I. Isn't it the same in Italy?"

"Of course it is the same."

"Perhaps it was merely a lapse in concentration."

Moments later the priest chanted, "Wine thou art and wine thou wilt remain," with the same quavering intonation.

"It is all a jest to them," whispered Martin. "They do not mean a word of it."

"Come, Martin. We should go. Across the street. I know just the place."

Five minutes later, they stood before a table, white-robed friars sizing them up. "Germans, are you?" one of them said. "That will be three gulden. See, I know of your coinage."

"Three gulden?" said Martin. "You charged half that to the monk before us."

"This, my barbaric brothers from the far north, is the Scala Sancta, the very steps on which our Lord descended from Pilate's court after his condemnation. The Holy Father has endowed these stones, the finest Tyrian marble, with special grace." Coins clattering, he shook his collection box irritably. "Take the indulgence or perish. Exercise your free will as you choose. Live or die eternally." He sniffed. "It is nothing to me either way. But do get out of the way. You're blocking others from the stairway to heaven."

Halfway up the stairs, Dieter groaned. "My knees are killing me."

"*Pater noster, qui es in cælis…*" prayed Martin.

"How many more steps?" hissed Dieter.

"*Sanctificetur nomen tuum…*" continued Martin, ignoring him.

"Will it never end?" groaned Dieter. "We still have to walk back to Germany."

"*Pater noster, qui es in cælis…*" prayed Martin.

When finally they had crawled on hands and knees to the top of the holy stairway, they were met by three friars. Thrusting a roll of paper into Martin's hand, the middle friar said, "Now move along, you German oaf. You're blocking the way to paradise." His companions laughed.

Repelled and bewildered, Martin stared at the indulgence, the warrior pope's seal certifying its authenticity. The paper trembled in his hand.

"Who knows whether it is so?" he murmured.

# 16

# BUILT OVER HELL

B eloved Katie," said Martin. "I would not have missed seeing Rome for 100,000 florins."

I looked up from my parchment. "We could use the florins," I reminded him.

"There you go, ever the mistress of the pig market. Balancing our accounts again."

"*Attempting* to balance them," I corrected.

"I never think of money," he said with a dismissive wave of his hand.

"I am well aware of that fact, Herr Doctor. Frequently your liberality forces me painfully to reckon with it. If only the master of the theological maxim would heed one of mine."

"One of yours?"

"Indeed, it is an economic maxim: One cannot give away that which he has already given away."

"And where in Holy Writ, my dearest, did you discover this maxim?"

"It is a variation, Herr Doctor, on 'Owe no man anything.'"

"Yet God has been amply faithful to us, has he not? Here sits a husband with his beloved wife, both erstwhile monastics, in our own cloister home, a rather large home for a peasant, don't you agree?"

"Large house or small, its roof leaks," I added.

Ignoring me, he continued, "And my rich lady of Zulsdorf, we own a farm: cows, pigs, and chickens. We have many temporal blessings, but none to compare with the eternal riches we have in the grace of our Lord Jesus, who though he was rich yet for our sakes became poor, so that we through his poverty might become rich." He looked triumphantly at me. "Lady Doctor Luther, I believe mine is an infinitely better economic maxim."

Shaking my head in resignation, I cuffed him gently on the shoulder. I had learned long ago that he was a formidable sparring partner. So I returned to our original topic. "But I thought you hated Rome." He had often told me how sickened he was by his pilgrimage.

"There was much to hate. It is impossible to imagine," said Martin, "what sins and infamous actions are committed in Rome; they must be seen and heard to be believed. Thus they are in the habit of saying, 'If there is a hell, Rome is built over it: it is an abyss whence issues every kind of sin.' No, I did the papacy no offense in my denunciations."

"And by them, Herr beloved Doctor, you did the common people much good."

"God in Christ did them much good, my dear Katie. I was merely an instrument. But had I not gone to Rome, seen it for myself, I would have always doubted whether I was not, after all, doing injustice to the pope."

"You did unleash some rather potent remarks about the pope."

He raised his eyebrows, as if in astonishment. "Did I?"

"Calling him a 'poisonous loudmouth.' Was that not a potent remark?"

"Not potent enough," he retorted.

"'A dragon from hell'?"

"That comes nearer the mark."

"But you went still further, Herr Doctor. How did you put it? As I recall, much to the glee of all Germany, as if to the pope's face, you said, "You were born from the behind of the devil, are full of devils, lies, blasphemy, and idolatry; are the instigator of these things, God's enemy, Antichrist, desolater of Christendom, and steward of Sodom."

Smiling broadly, he applauded my recitation. "Which he is. You would have said much the same, my lord Katie, had you seen Rome, once the holiest of all cities, now the most licentious den of thieves, the most shameless of all brothels, the kingdom of sin, death, and hell. It is so bad that even Antichrist himself, if he should come, could think of nothing to add to its wickedness."

"Calm yourself, Herr Doctor." I could see that his own words had aroused his ire, and I feared such rage would do his health no kindness.

Nodding, he continued, "I am quite satisfied on the point. Popes boast of possessing the Spirit, more of the Spirit than the apostles, and yet for centuries they have secretly prowled about and flung around their dung. The pope is a treacherous, secret devil who sneaks around in corners until he has done his damage and spread his poison." He warmed his fingers over the candle. "No, I am quite satisfied, now more than ever. I did the papacy no injustice."

"Your pilgrimage now ended, what did you do next?"

"Walk home," said Martin. "Stagger home, more like. You cannot imagine the havoc a 700 mile trek wreaks on ones feet.

While I had been away, good Doctor Staupitz had not been idle. I am convinced now that he had set in motion a carefully devised plan for me." He paused, a faraway look in his eyes. "I can see it now; if it had not been for Doctor Staupitz I should have sunk in hell.

"No sooner had I returned from Rome and Staupitz immediately accosted me. He had arranged for me to commence doctoral studies in theology, here at Elector Frederick's fledgling university. It was not Heidelberg, but I was young and inexperienced in academia. Staupitz, vicar general of the Augustinian order in Saxony, was not to be put off. Only later would I discover his real design. I was to make haste, gather my things—precious few of these—and be underway to Wittenberg, without delay."

"With no rest for your poor feet?"

"None. So it was that I arrived April 15, 1511 here in Wittenberg, at this very place, a peasant miner's son, an inexperienced Augustinian monk, troubled in mind about many things, as yet far from peace with God—and with no wife."

Our eyes met and held each other in their gaze. "No beloved wife." He smiled, his eyes moist with feeling. "Did you know, dearest Katie, that before we married the bed was not made for a whole year—perhaps longer—and became foul with my sweat. I worked so hard and was so weary that I tumbled into it without noticing. Did you know this?"

I could not help laughing at him. "Know it? I was the first one to change those filthy bed sheets. I would not have bedded down my pigs in them."

"They were that bad?"

"Indeed, worse."

"So many changes," he said, gazing into the coals and shaking his head with wonder. "We were two of the most unlikely candidates for wedlock under the heavens."

"Well, one of us was," I said, jabbing him playfully in the ribs.

"That is not unjust. I am guilty," he said, nodding his head. "I shall never forget that first morning," he continued, grinning at me like a schoolboy. "Awakening to find on the pillow next to me—a pair of pigtails that had not been there before!"

"On the *clean* pillow next to you," I added, placing my hand on his.

"First love is drunken," he continued tenderly. "But when the inebriation wears off, true marriage love begins."

"And never ends." I mouthed the words more than said them.

We sat in a glowing aura of silence for several moments, he cradling my hand in his and caressing the back of it with his stout fingers.

"When first I arrived in this place," he continued with a sigh, "I was yet in torment. Here I was, preparing to be a doctor of theology, an expert in the study of God, and I was the one assailed with doubts. Disillusioned with holy Rome, doubtful of the efficacy of the merits of the saints, utterly despairing in the sufficiency and goodness of my own works, I battered the doors of the confessional. Six hours one time."

"Confessing for six hours!" I said in astonishment. "What a prodigal transgressor I have got for a husband. What great penance was required of you for so much sinning?"

# 17

# SNARLING BARKER

After six grueling hours of confession, in which Martin had probed and ransacked every moral fiber of his being, Staupitz broke in. "Enough! God is not angry with you, Martin. You are angry with God, with the God who commands you to hope, yet in defiance of him you persist in hopelessness."

"Hopelessness," murmured Martin with a groan, shrouding his eyes with a hand. "It is yet another sin, Father. I must confess it."

"Look here," cut in Staupitz, "if you expect Christ to forgive you, come back with something that needs forgiveness! Parricide, blasphemy, adultery—real sinning that needs forgiving, not these peccadilloes!"

That evening after vespers, Doctor Staupitz took Martin by the arm. "Come, Brother Martin, take a stroll with me."

It had rained earlier in the day, but the clouds had past, and it was a warm spring evening in Wittenberg. Fresh blossoms were opening on the rose bush entwining its gnarly canes over the archway into the garden of the abbey. Martin, inhaling the sweet scents of springtime, marveled at all the changes that had occurred in his life, in so few months' time: his pilgrimage to the pretended grandeur and magnificence of Rome and now his new residence in the backwater insignificance of a sandbank village in Saxony.

"Wittenberg is not Rome, is it?" said Staupitz.

"No." Martin watched a black hen strutting and pecking the moist soil for worms, a brood of new-hatched chicks scurrying and cheeping about her feet. "It is a backwater, rows of small hovels covered with mud and straw. A miserable hole, some call it. Yet do I prefer it to Rome." He shook his head and looked at his confessor. "Licentious den of thieves, why did you send me there?"

Staupitz, clasping his hands behind his back as he walked, looked sideways at Martin. "I knew you must see it for yourself."

"But doing so gave me no peace," said Martin. "Far from it, Rome increased my doubts."

"As I knew it would, Martin."

Halting, Martin stared at his confessor. "It was an exceedingly long journey. Why did you send me, Doctor? To plunge me into everlasting despair, unrelenting hopelessness?" Martin resumed walking. "If this was your purpose, it has done your bidding."

Staupitz placed a hand on Martin's shoulder. "Martin, what is it you most desire?"

Martin expected his confessor, the vicar of his order, to chide him for his doubts and point him back to the Church, to the seven sacraments, the merits of the saints, to the pope, to Rome.

"Peace with God," said Martin.

"Where will you find this?"

Taking aim, Martin kicked a pebble out of the pathway. It clattered against the stone wall, echoing down the corridor of the cloister. "Not in Rome," he said.

"Then where?" persisted Staupitz.

Martin was silent. For six years he had tried the Church's way. The monastic life had given him no peace—it had nearly killed him. The merits of the saints? Rome itself smashed all that, only increasing his doubts in the efficacy of pilgrimage and indulgences.

Staupitz persisted. "Where will you find it?"

Martin recalled the first time he had ever laid eyes on a Bible, at the university library in Erfurt. "Perhaps in the Word of God?"

Smiling, Staupitz nodded.

"Priests and monks, they know Aquinas much better than Paul," said Martin. "Why is it that the Bible is rarely found in the hands of the monks, much less in the hands of university students?"

"It has long been that way," said Staupitz. "The patron of our order, St. Augustine himself, confessed his childish scorn for the Bible, 'The Scriptures appeared to me to be unworthy, for my inflated pride shunned their style, nor could the sharpness of my mind pierce their inner meaning. They were so simple and direct as to be understood by little ones—mere children—but I scorned to be a little one. Swollen with pride, I looked upon myself as a great one.'"

"What changed him?" asked Martin.

Staupitz smiled. "Pears."

Martin frowned. "Pears?"

"More precisely, the stealing of them."

At a gust of wind, Martin watched pedals swirling down from the pear tree in the center of the garden, its fresh green leaves shying in the breeze. He looked from the tree back to his confessor.

"Yes, we Augustinians are fond of our pear trees," said Staupitz. "The seeds of true repentance began when Augustine realized that he had stolen pears from a neighbor's tree, not because he was hungry, but because he loved doing wrong. From this he began to realize that specific sins were not his problem; his root problem was his sinful nature."

"He was in love with dying," murmured Martin.

Staupitz raised his eyebrows. "*Was ist das?*"

"It is just a song," said Martin, with a shrug. "A drinking song."

"Fitting lyric, nevertheless. Augustine realized he too was in love with dying. Until one day in a garden, not unlike this one, he heard children's voices chanting, *Tolle lege. Tolle lege.*"

"What did it mean?"

"Just what it said, 'Take and read.' Augustine did take up the Bible and read it. Martin, you asked me what changed him. It was the Word of God that changed him. 'Though once I myself had been a blind and snarling barker against the Scriptures,' he wrote, 'when I read the Bible I was all on fire.'"

Staupitz crossed his arms inside the wide sleeves of his habit and looked levelly at Martin. "I believe it will have the same effect on you, Martin Luther," he said. "Which is why I petitioned the elector for your appointment."

"What appointment?" asked Martin. "To read the Bible?"

"Yes, and to study the Bible," said Staupitz, "for your doctorate in theology. Your reputation proceeds you, and the chancellor of the university, Andreas Carlstadt, enthusiastically supports your appointment."

Martin smiled. "When first I saw a Bible, I longed to understand it."

Staupitz looked sideways at him. "Did I mention that you have simultaneously been appointed to *teach* the Bible?"

"To teach it? I who am full of doubt and sin? I am to teach others? No, you did not mention it. Surely it is a jest."

Staupitz shook his head emphatically. "I am rarely given to jesting. 'Physician, heal thyself.'"

Martin knew the maxim. "'—by healing others.' Or more likely killing them off with my own plague."

"There is no better path for you, Martin Luther," continued Staupitz. "Master the Word of God, my son. I, for one, am convinced that there is no better path to mastering it than teaching it."

"But surely there are many others more qualified than I?" Feeling trapped, Martin gestured toward the other black-robed monks strolling in the garden. "Any one of my brothers. What if I fail, become an embarrassment to the entire Augustinian order?"

"Oh, my son, I make you a solemn promise: on your own, you will indeed fail."

"I am to take comfort from such a promise?"

"The greatest comfort," said Staupitz. "You, Martin, are the man for this moment. You feel yourself to be nothing. And you are correct. But the Word of God is everything. It never fails. It never returns empty."

Clutching a fistful of Martin's gown, Staupitz's eyes flashed with excitement. "I have never been more certain in my life. Teaching the Word of God, this, my son, is your calling. And next to faith, this is the highest art, to be content with the calling in which God has placed you."

Staupitz, vicar general of the order, was not to be put off. Martin drew in a long breath, letting it out slowly. "If teach I must, I will not teach as those who have gone before," he said. "You won't find me spouting Aristotle from my tutorial lectern."

"Whom will you spout?" asked Staupitz.

It was futile to resist. Deep down, Martin felt part of himself no longer wanting to. "The Word of God," he said with decision.

"And what of the doubtful passages?" pressed Staupitz. "There are difficult passages, hard to understand. Will you simply give your private interpretation?"

"I do not know."

"Here again we Augustinians find wisdom in the words of our patron," said Staupitz. "'Let us not be too proud to learn what has to be learned with the help of other people, and let those of us by whom others are taught pass on what we have received without pride and without jealousy.' Let this be your pedagogic principle."

Martin felt he ought to make one last valiant effort. "But St. Augustine had something I sorely lack," he said.

Staupitz raised his eyebrows inquiringly.

"Eloquence. He was amply supplied with it and I am not."

"An argument sorely lacking in originality, Martin." Staupitz feigned a disapproving tone. "It works as poorly for you as it did for Moses."

Passing a hand over his tonsure, Luther tried again. "But surely, Doctor, you know how I am more given to fulmination than explanation."

"Abounding in eloquence himself, St. Augustine knew its dangers. 'We must beware of the man who abounds in eloquence, and not think that because the speaker is eloquent what he says must be true.' Martin, eloquence alone is never enough. Far more powerful than the eloquence of the rhetorician is the plain speaking of a broken heart. You have the latter."

Staupitz resumed walking. Clasping his hands behind his back, Martin followed.

"O, and I have failed to mention it," added Staupitz, touching his forehead with the heel of his hand. "The Stadtkirche, it is without a preacher at the moment."

Martin looked warily at his confessor. In his distraction, his toe collided with the stone border of a patch of tulips. Pain shot through his foot.

"The duke asked me for a man to fill the position," continued Staupitz, his voice casual, as if he were merely commenting on the pear blossoms.

Martin groaned. "Surely you are not thinking of nominating me for the position?"

"As a future consideration? No, of course not," said Staupitz. With a twinkle in his eye, he added, "I have already done so."

Halting abruptly, Martin felt the heat rising on his cheeks. "You nominated me, Doctor, I who am not qualified to pastor my own heart."

"There is no better qualification," said Staupitz, "than a broken spirit. Who can better feel the frailties of his flock than an under shepherd who so keenly feels his own?"

"You want to kill me, Doctor," said Martin, pressing his thumbs against his temples. "I shall not be able to carry on the thing for three months."

"Well, my son, if you die it will be in the service of the Lord. How noble a sacrifice!"

"But teaching *and* preaching? It will grind me down to the grave."

"Oh, I agree," said Staupitz. "Quite all right. God has plenty of work for clever men to do in heaven."

Martin felt like he was speaking to the hangman. "When?"

"Teaching begins first thing tomorrow morning," said Staupitz.

Martin groaned. "And preaching?"

"Calm yourself, Martin. You have fully two days before you deliver your first sermon."

"Two days!"

"Plenty of time," said Staupitz. "Elector Frederick is most anxious to hear you."

"The duke!" said Martin.

"Yes, Sunday, you are to preach before the elector at his Castle Church."

# 18
# MUTINOUSLY FALSE

Teaching in a lecture hall before boys of but sixteen or seventeen years, Luther soon found out, was of a different order than standing in the high pulpit of the Castle Church and delivering a sermon before Duke Frederick, Elector of Saxony, and his entourage.

"Preach out of the depths of your own heart, with honesty and sincerity," Doctor Staupitz had urged him.

Eyes darting over the faces gathered in the ducal church, Luther's heart rumbled like thunder. Flashing before his memory was that first mass, wherein, under the scowl of his parents, he had presumed to transubstantiate the very Son of God in the rite. Compared with delivering a sermon, entirely of his own words, regurgitating the words of the mass was nothing. Here there was no hiding

The candle flame illuminating the pulpit lectern hissed and quavered mockingly. Delivering a sermon required using ones voice; Luther was now to speak. He tried to swallow. His mouth was parched, as if filled with dry oats and no beer to wash them down. Before him sat the elector, self-assured and stout, regaled in the latest silk fashion, gold chain about his neck, the medallion of his office dangling over his broad chest, glinting at him like a cyclops. Tugging at the collar of his vestments chafing about his neck, Luther felt the man's scrutiny, the ducal eyes narrowed and penetrating, his bulbous lips thrust out and rimmed by a wide beard and moustache.

*Abandon hope!* screamed his conscience. Just when Luther was about to bolt forever from the pulpit, he saw in the congregation the face of Doctor Staupitz, his confessor: confident, resolute, calm—everything Luther was not. *"Preach out of the depths of your own heart, with honesty and sincerity."*

With trembling hands, Luther unfolded the parchment on which he had penned his sermon. Clearing his throat, he commenced reading the manuscript. He was never sure when it happened, but, looking up from his scripted sermon, he found himself speaking without the benefit of his notes.

"Is it not against all natural reason," he heard himself say, "that God out of his mere whim deserts men, hardens them, damns them, as if he delighted in sins and in such torments of the wretched for eternity, God who is said to be of such mercy and goodness?"

The duke frowned. The rustling of silk and satin, and the shuffling of boot leather on flagstones, sounded throughout the nave of the Castle Church. Signaling for a courtier to lean in close, Elector Frederick whispered in his ear. The courtier nodded appraisingly.

Luther continued. "And who would not be offended by this? I was myself more than once driven to the very abyss of despair so that I wished I had never been created. Love God?" said Luther, smacking an open hand on the pulpit. "I hated him!"

When his words ceased reverberating off the vaulted ceiling, stony silence descended over the sanctuary. Luther scratched his tonsured head. He fiddled with the parchment on the lectern. Clearing his throat, he scanned down the page and resumed reading. Somehow he managed to complete that first sermon.

After the service, his head hanging low, Luther followed his confessor from the Castle Church, through the cobbled streets of the village, back toward the cloister. "'Hate God'?" Staupitz broke the silence. "Martin, what were you thinking? You must speak more carefully." Breaking off, he called out, "Mind your step! The oxen have been here."

"You admonished me to be honest," said Luther. Propping himself against an archway, he scraped dung from his shoe with a stick. "Groping in the dark, there are times when I do feel that I hate him."

"As your confessor," said Staupitz, "I am well aware of this. But you must not offend the weak." He paused, eyeing Martin with suspicion. "Wait. Martin, are you attempting to get yourself removed from your obligation to preach?"

Tossing the stick in the gutter, Martin wiped his palms on his habit. "I do not think so."

"I assure you, it will not work. Next Sunday you begin your preaching duties at the Stadtkirche. But please, do not offend your flock by telling them you hate God. That will never do."

In spite of the rebuke, Martin sensed that Doctor Staupitz was not displeased with him.

They were now crossing the cobbled square in front of the town church where a begging friar stood on a pickle barrel, preaching to passersby. "Do you not love your dearly departed ones enough," cried the friar, "to secure them an easy passageway to heaven! I have here from Pope Leo X himself a certificate of—"

Scowling, Martin said, "Bad as it was, surely my preaching was not as vile as that charlatan's. Did my sermon offend the duke?"

Staupitz shook his head. "On the contrary."

"How can you be sure?"

"Because he spoke plainly to me about you. 'This Martin Luther,' said he, 'has profound insight, exceeding imagination—' (I agreed wholeheartedly with him about your imagination). 'He will trouble the doctors before he has done and excite no slight disturbance.'"

"The elector said that?"

"Indeed, those were his words," said Staupitz, patting Martin on the back. "So, my son, you need not fear; there will be no burning you at the stake—at least not today."

In the weeks and months ahead, Martin preached often at the Stadtkirche. Surrounded by the market square, in the heart of the village, the City Church of St. Mary's was not a ducal chapel. It was the people's church where the fishmonger attended with his wife and children, where the pig farmer gathered with his family, where the butcher, the tanner, the milkmaid, the boatman, and the brewer gathered for the mass. It was the Stadtkirche where the aged, the widow, the orphan, the infirm and the insane gathered to gaze in rapt wonder at the miracle of transubstantiation, to receive the bread of the sacrament. And now, more than ever, to hear Martin Luther preach sermons, much to their delight, no longer in Latin— but in German.

Jostling for the best places, the common people elbowed their way into the nave, eager to hear the young Augustinian who spoke like no priest they had ever heard before. When he offered them the bread in the mass, frowning and perplexed, he would sometimes chide them, "Do not run to the sacrament like a sow to the trough!"

Perhaps because their new pastor was peasant born, because he thought like a peasant and spoke as they spoke— and in their own language—his flock clamored to hear more. Week by week, with each sermon, Luther gained more energy, more freedom, more stamina, and more clarity.

"Not only did the world refuse to receive Christ," he declared one Sunday morning, "but persecuted him more cruelly than all others who had ever come forth from God. But it was not merely the world that railed against him. It was the religious leaders: the priests and friars, the monks and bishops, the popes and cardinals of his day. They condemned the holy gospel and replaced it with the teaching of the dragon from hell. It was pharisaic prelates, poisonous loudmouths, whose proclamations were un-Christian, antichristian, and spoken by the inspiration of the evil spirit!"

The nave of the town church, crammed with Luther's growing congregation, rumbled with approval at his words.

When not preaching or teaching, Luther pored over the Word of God. Scouring the sacred pages, he felt a dire urgency in his labors. How could he dispel the doubts and fears of his congregation, if he had yet greater doubts and fears himself? As if rattling the portcullis at a castle drawbridge, he labored late into the night, determined to get at the meaning of the sacred words.

"'My God, my God, why hast thou forsaken me?'" In his tower study at the cloister, by the flickering light of a candle, he read the psalm over and again. *I feel forsaken by God, and justly so for my great sins. But why did the sinless Son of God feel forsaken by God? I will give myself no rest until I know the answer.*

Next day in the lecture hall of the university, Luther gave out the text to his students, his own voice ringing with anguish as he read.

"Being forsaken of God," said Luther, pacing in front of the lectern, "there is no greater plight than being forsaken of God. To comprehend fully the weight of this tortured question uttered by the Son of God upon the cross, we must show first what God is. We can never appreciate fully the agony of being forsaken by one we do not know."

Spreading his hands wide, he looked up at the stone vaulting and continued. "God is life, light, wisdom, truth, righteousness, goodness, power, joy, glory, peace, blessedness, and all good! Therefore, to be forsaken of God is to be abandoned to all that he is not."

Clenching his arms across his chest and rocking from side-to-side, he continued. "Abandoned to all that God is not: death, darkness, ignorance, lies, sin, malice, weakness, sorrow, confusion, dismay, desperation, damnation, and all evil!"

As if he were alone, battering the door of the confessional, Luther's voice rose to a crescendo of agony. His students stared at him as if eyewitnesses to the Last Judgment; they sat in open-mouthed wonder, not only at his words, but at the tortured manner in which he uttered them.

"Christ, deserted by God," continued Luther, each word sharp and weighty. "Deserted by his own father. This is the greatest affliction—to feel the wrath of God and to be terrified before God, as if God had abandoned and condemned you."

Biting his lower lip, Luther looked out over the upturned faces, his students, so young, so full of life, so ignorant, so deceived, so bewildered.

"How is it that holy Jesus, who is without sin, has become the victim forsaken by God?"

And then a strange thing happened. Suddenly, the pages of Scripture Luther had assaulted and cajoled for months, raging for them to give up their meaning to him, did so. He felt on fire.

"He was forsaken not for sins that he had done. As the Apostle Paul says, 'Jesus was made a curse for *us*,' and Isaiah prophesied that Christ would bear *our* sufferings, and that he would be stricken by God for *our* sins. He counted his own soul an offering for the crimes of others, not for his own. Thus, Paul says, 'God made him to be sin for us who knew no sin.' Condemned as a sinner, the sinless Christ bore his father's judgment for the seditions of others, and, thereby, satisfied divine wrath once for all time."

Luther felt like an observer, listening in to his own voice. He paused. After a moment of breathless silence, a young man in the front row, raised his hand. "You may speak, Pieter."

His brow furrowed, Pieter spoke slowly, deliberately. "Did the Christ, Herr Doctor, bear all of his father's wrath against sin?"

Luther did not immediately reply. He was not at all certain how to reply. He felt as if he stood on a great precipice and to answer was to plunge into a terrifying abyss. The answer might be one from which there would be no turning back.

"Because if he did…," continued Pieter, his voice trailed off.

"If he did," said Walter, "then why must we do penance?"

"Or go on pilgrimage?"

"Or buy indulgences?" said another.

"Or why does the priest sacrifice Christ again and again on the altar in the mass?" asked Pieter.

"Would not these doctrines of the Church," said Walter, "if he is a God who is satisfied, would not Church doctrine be a reproach to God's satisfied justice?"

Pieter stood to his feet, his face pale. "And if so, would not Church doctrine, thereby, be mutinously false?"

Raising his hands at the barrage of their protest, Luther felt cornered. Staupitz was right. Teaching the Bible would force him to reckon with its manifest truths, he and his students. But to disparage the doctrines of the Church?

It was heresy.

# 19

# THE POPE'S PIG

The ark of Noah was enormous," said Luther. "If it were not in Scripture, I would not believe it. I would have died if I had been in the ark. It was dark, three times the size of Wittenberg's Augustinian cloister, and full of animals."

Luther looked out on the young men in the university hall. Some smiled broadly at his words, anticipating the next salvo of his satire. But all leaned forward, as if eager, yearning for knowledge. It didn't fool Luther.

It was the benches. He remembered from his student days. There was no other way to sit in them. Both feet firmly on the flagstones, and no drifting off; they were designed to disgorge the weary or inattentive in an ignominious heap. The furniture craftsman had been precisely instructed by the Church, no doubt with threats about his eternal salvation if he did not comply.

"Imagine the daily accumulation of dung!" continued Luther. "The stench! The baying, mooing, oinking, clucking, growling, snarling." He broke off, touching his forehead as if a thought had suddenly come to him "Though I would rather hear the clamoring of a thousand beasts than the vain prattling of a Dominican friar peddling his fraudulent indulgences. Which brings my discourse back to the subject at hand. Relics!"

Pieter and Walther grinned broadly in anticipation.

"Relics? *Nein*, Pig bones, all!" Luther stepped in front of his lectern, wandering down the aisle between the benches. "But I return to Noah. I venture to say that there are sufficient splinters from the cross of Calvary that, if brought altogether in one place, and somehow reconstituted into useful lumber—the pope should have no difficulty here: simply transubstantiate the splinters into whole boards. In the ranking of miracle performing, it would be the task of a schoolboy—Pieter, here, ought to be able to accomplish it before supper time."

Rowdy guffaws and laughter burst from his students.

"How difficult could it be in comparison with turning, say, common bread into the flesh of Christ, and wine into the very blood of the Savior, a miracle accomplished thousands of times a day by the pope and his devilish priests? Splinters into timbers for boat building? I would wager that in the reliquaries of Europe there is sufficient particles of wood from the cross to reconstruct all of Noah's ark, stem to stern!"

A bench toppled and clattered onto the flagstones. Holding their sides, the boys were beside themselves with laughter at his performance.

"*Nein*, there would be more than sufficient wood. Surplus, stacked and ready, for when it was time for Noah and his sons to replank the vessel."

More shouting and hooting.

"And there is, in the reliquaries of Christendom, sufficient hay from the manger of our Lord," continued Luther, "to feed all the animals confined on Noah's ark."

"For forty days?" asked Walther, grinning broadly.

"Till the waters receded—a year, at the very least," said Luther.

"A year of hay?" shouted Fritz. "Imagine all the manure!"

"Which brings me back to relics," said Luther. "What falsehoods there are about relics! One abbot claims to have a feather from the wing of the angel Gabriel, and the Bishop of Mainz has a flame from Moses' burning bush."

Luther broke off, shrugging in feigned bewilderment. "How does one have a flame from the burning bush? How does one keep a flame a-flicker for thousands of years and then present it for certification to the pope? I shall have to consult the church Fathers on the subject, perhaps write a book on it. What is more, how does it happen that, of Christ's twelve apostles, there are fully eighteen of them entombed in Germany?"

His students stomped their feet, thudding on their desks. Luther snatched up his lute, never far from hand, and delivered a flourishing fanfare on the strings, finishing with a drumming of his knuckles on the sounding board. The young scholars howled with delight.

Had the patron of the university stepped into the tutorial and heard what Luther was saying, and seen the raucous reception of his students to his words, he might have wondered at the growing popularity of his university—young men from all over Germany clamoring to enroll.

Word spread among scholars as well, some of the brightest young theologians seeking teaching posts alongside Luther at Wittenberg's university. But it was not just Germany. The provost of the university received letters from prospective students and professors from throughout the European world. Elector Frederick was, for the moment, elated.

Laying aside his lute, Luther raised a hand for silence.

"Indulgences are a scandal," he continued soberly. "A scandal that declares salvation to be had by contrition, confession—and contribution! The average Dominican fulminator placing considerably more weight on the contribution component; walk through the market square, linger on the steps of the town church, hear the slogans, the shameless hawking of forgiveness. What is all this? The funding of papal extravagance with the bodies and souls of Germany."

Luther, the heat rising on his brow, paced before his students. "What of Germany's working poor, of her orphans, her widows, those who cannot make a sufficient contribution to Rome? Is contrition and confession enough?"

Luther slammed a fist on the lectern. "No, it is not! What awaits the contrite poor of Saxony? Heed the words of a fraudulent friar and you will know: Hell and damnation! What of the dear mother whose child expires before baptism, or lives, but the widowed mother has no money to pay for the baptism? What becomes of the child? What is the dear woman told? Her child is consigned to a world apart, the absence of heaven, outside of the grace of the gospel of Jesus Christ. Ruined. And by such a lie, so is that loving German mother, her heart rent asunder. Beside herself with despair, anguish and hopelessness are her meat and drink; make no mistake, she has no other."

His cheeks hot with indignation, Luther broke off, the muscles of his jaw flexing as he ground his teeth.

"Herr Doctor," said Fritz timidly. "Is it possible these matters are too far above us? Is not our obedience to the pope sufficient? It is not ours to answer for abuses."

Pulling back, Pieter looked at Fritz as if his face was a mass of plague sores. "When it is the bodies and souls of Germany, we alone answer for them," he retorted, conking him over the head with a sheaf of parchment. "It is we alone who pay for his abuses."

"I just thought," said Fritz, rubbing his head, "that what with the pope being infallible, it wasn't our problem."

"Infallible? *Doch*!" said Pieter.

"Germany is the pope's pig," said Luther. He slapped a fist in an open palm, the slap echoing through the hall. "That is why we have to give him so much bacon and sausages."

# 20

# GATES OF PARADISE

Months passed during which Luther continued teaching through the Bible, the university gaining popularity with every lecture. And he was not alone. The chancellor of the university, Andreas Carlstadt, supported and encouraged Luther, and the young scholar from Tubingen, Philip Melanchthon, never far from Luther's side, became increasingly bold in confronting error.

Most doctors of universities chose their words so as never to offend those in power. They understood who their benefactors were: nobles who endowed universities, archbishops and cardinals who controlled the course of study, the Holy Roman Emperor who wielded civil authority over Germany and beyond, and the pope who exerted pontifical power over all. Run afoul of any of these and not only would a scholar's job be terminated—so would his life.

As chancellor, Carlstadt had to be more diplomatic, but along with Melanchthon, Luther seemed either not to understand these realities, or flagrantly to ignore them.

"The popes' hawkers of indulgences in Germany?" he told his students. "What bilgewater of heresies has ever been spoken so heretically as what they say at the very gates of Wittenberg? It is as if their brains have been transubstantiated into stinking mushrooms!"

But his lectures were far more than mere bluster and mockery at folly and error. Completing the psalms, Luther made his way carefully, as a scholar scouring an ancient text for wisdom, through Paul's Epistle to the Galatians.

"Paul makes it clear enough that it takes more than an Abrahamic pedigree to be a child of God," he told his students. "Or a Teutonic one! For Jew or German, to be a child of God requires faith in Christ. And Christ is no Moses, no law-giver, no tyrant, but the mediator for sins, the giver of grace and life."

From Galatians Luther moved on to Paul's Epistle to the Romans. It was here that Luther was inflamed, a man on fire, irrepressible, energized, inexorable. His students were rapt and speechless as they heard his words.

"I greatly longed to understand Paul's Epistle to the Romans," said Luther. He spoke with a common-man's honesty, earnest and without calculation. "Nothing stood in the way but that one expression, 'the justice of God,' because I took it to mean that justice whereby God is just and deals justly in punishing the unjust. My predicament was that, although an impeccable monk, I stood before God as a sinner troubled in conscience, and I had no confidence that my merit would assuage him. Therefore, I did not love a just and angry God, but rather hated and murmured against him. Yet I clung to dear Paul and had a great yearning to know what he meant.

"At last, meditating day and night on the justice of God and Paul's statement that 'the just shall live by his faith,' at last, by the mercy of God, I began to understand that the righteousness of God is that through which the righteous live by a gift of God, namely by faith."

110

So intent were Luther's students on his words, the hall was deathly silent. No wooden bench creaked, no leather sole shuffled on the flagstones, no quill scratched on the parchment. Every breath was indrawn, tense, suspended with anticipation.

"Here I felt as if I were entirely born again and had entered paradise itself through the gates that had been flung open."

Momentarily overcome with emotion, Luther paused. Nodding thoughtfully, a gradual expression of wonder spread across his features. His eyes brimming with joy, he looked into the faces of his students. Clearing his throat, he resumed.

"Whereupon, the whole of Scripture took on a new meaning. Whereas, before the 'justice of God' had filled me with hate, now it became to me inexpressibly sweet in greater love. This passage of Paul became to me a gate to heaven."

Luther's students looked on in wonder, their eyes, their faces, their posture riveted with expectancy, as if they were eye-witnesses to a miracle. But this was no pretended, hocus-pocus, cheap-trick charade played on the peasants in the mass. Their faces betrayed them. They believed they were seeing before their very eyes a true miracle.

Silent for the moment, Luther took up his lute and began plucking softly on the strings. Settling onto the edge of the table on which his lectern was positioned, he gazed up at the timbered rafters of the hall, his lips moving soundlessly. After several moments, his fingers stirring now more purposefully over the lute strings, he began singing—his words clear and sweet, not in Latin, but in German: *Ein' feste Burg*...

God is our fortress and salvation,
Our present help in tribulation.
We will not fear though earth may shake,
For God will keep us mid the quake.
Mountains may fall into the ocean,
But we will not fear such commotion.

With us the Lord of Hosts shall dwell,
The mighty God of Israel.

When the last chord trembled into silence, Luther set aside his lute. Standing before his students, his arms spread wide in appeal, he continued:

"He who sees God as angry—as I have for so long seen him—does not see him rightly but looks only on a curtain, as if a dark cloud had been drawn across God's face." Walking down the aisle, Luther placed his hands on the shoulders of several of his students.

"If you have a true faith that Christ is your Savior," he continued, "then at once you have a gracious God, for faith leads you in and opens up God's heart, that you should see pure grace and overflowing love. To behold God in faith is to look upon his fatherly, friendly heart, in which there is no anger, no ungraciousness."

When the last student left the hall, as Luther gathered his books, Melanchthon approached.

"I heard your lecture, Doctor Luther."

Luther looked bewildered.

"From behind a column, just there," said Melanchthon, pointing with a thumb at the back of the hall. "You are like Elijah, full of the Holy Spirit." He hesitated, a slight tremor on his lips. Passing a hand over his thin reddish beard, he looked intently at Luther and said, "Whatever lies ahead, I would rather die than be separated from you."

Luther set down his books and placed a hand on the young scholar's shoulder. "I am the rough pioneer," he said, "who must break the road, but you, Master Philip, God has richly endowed you with the gift of gentleness—a gift I know little of. You are his divine instrument for what lies ahead."

In the days that followed, Wittenberg was aflame. What those young men had heard and witnessed in the lecture hall settled over the region like dew on an October morning.

From the cabbage peddler in the marketplace to the gutters of the slaughterhouse, there was talk of little else. It was as if the gates of paradise were about to be flung open wide, not only for Martin Luther—but for all Wittenberg.

# 21

# LOVE NOT MERIT

There's talk of little else," said Carlstadt the next day. "You are like a petard, your words like explosions. What will you do now?"

Walking across the market square with Carlstadt and Melanchthon, Luther stepped carefully through the slurry oozing between the cobblestones, nudging a rotting cabbage aside with the toe of his shoe. There was no denying it. Studying and teaching—Staupitz had been right—so much had become so suddenly clear to him. What *would* he do?

"Onions! Best onions from Calbe!" A street vender broke in on his thoughts. It was early in the day and the vender's basket was still filled with sweet yellow onions.

The market square surrounding the Stadtkirche was alive with activity, with rows of canvas booths of farmers and tradesmen lining the square; it seemed that all Wittenberg had converged to buy and to sell.

Luther drew in a deep breathe. The pinching odors of street filth were being pressed down by the sweet scents of fresh produce harvested  that morning from the farms surrounding Wittenberg.

"*Spargel!* For your wedding soup! Mine's the finest," promised an asparagus vender.

"Well, Martin," said Carlstadt, biting into a piece of gingerbread. "—Hmm, delicious. You must try some. But I say, Martin, there's turmoil ahead for you. So just what will you do?"

Sprawling on a barrel, a vegetable vender narrowed his eyes, appraising them. "Beets, potatoes, leeks!" he chanted.

"Finest bratwurst in Saxony!" cried a sausage vender, extending his dagger toward them with a meaty slice on its point.

Chewing slowly, Luther's salivary glands burst with hungry pleasure at the rich sausage juices. What would he do? He swallowed.

"Torgau beer!" shouted the brewer, winking at them. "Nothing so good with his sausages," he said, with a toss of his head at the butcher, "as is my beer!"

"Martin, after this, you cannot expect business as usual at the university," continued Carlstadt. "Nor you Philip. None of us can. There is the matter of the duke."

"The duke?" said Luther. "His university has doubled in size. Doctor Staupitz assures me the elector likes me, likes all of us."

"*Liked* you," said Carlstadt, eyeing him sideways. "We shall see about the future tense of the verb."

"Rye bread, dark and heavy!" shouted the baker. Encircled by a powdery white apron the size of a bedsheet, the baker held a trencher with hunks of samples toward them.

"What will I do? Eat," said Luther, moaning with pleasure. "Right now, what I feel like doing is eating and then eating some more."

"Gingerbread, then?" called the baker after them.

"Alms! Alms for the needy!" cackled an old woman, her boney fingers curling, drawing them to come closer.

Luther halted, staring at the emaciated old woman. With all the market day bustle, he could have easily missed hearing and seeing her altogether. Seated on the ground beside her was a round-faced little girl, eyes set wide apart, her pink tongue bulging from one side of her mouth. She looked up at Luther; her dirty face spread into a grin.

"Then eat we shall," said Carlstadt.

"Dear woman," said Luther, ignoring his companions. Drawing up his gown, he squatted in front of the beggar and the child. "What is it you need? You and the little one?" The girl's grin was contagious, and Luther smiled back.

"Bread, Father," whispered the woman, her voice weak, her watery eyes searching his.

"You shall have it," said Luther. Then over his shoulder he called, "Carlstadt, buy the largest loaf."

"But, I thought—?" began his companion.

"Is that all?" said Luther to the woman. "When did you last eat a full meal?"

She ran her tongue over cracked lips. "Bread, just bread. Bread will help me feed her."

"Sausages!" called Luther over his shoulder. "Melanchthon, have him buy the best sausages." He turned back to the old woman. "Do you have means to cook for her, dear woman, and for yourself?"

The woman nodded slightly.

"And leeks," shouted Luther, "potatoes, some onions, and a cluster of the best asparagus, just there. Here is some gulden, Philip," he added, tossing a pouch. "Pay with this."

The little girl got up and stood in front of Luther, always grinning. "And, Philip," added Luther, "have Carlstadt buy the largest piece of gingerbread! Make it two pieces!"

Taking the little girl's hand in his, Luther asked, "Is she your child?"

116

"She is my grandchild, Father," said the old woman.

"And what is your name, little one?" asked Luther.

She scrunched her shoulders with delight. "Liesel," she said, intoning each word with care and effort. "My name is Liesel. What is yours?"

Her words were soft and slightly muffled, as if her tongue was too large for her mouth. Her grandmother made as if to rebuke her.

Luther smiled and placed a hand on the girl's matted hair. "Liesel is a beautiful name. My friends call me Martin. You may call me Martin."

"Martin," said Liesel, splaying her tongue around her lips as if tasting the name. "Martin is a beautiful name too."

Tears trickled down the old woman's cheeks as she gazed in wonder at the bounty Luther and his friends laid before her.

"Dear woman, feed your grandchild, but you too must eat."

Ten minutes later, as they neared the south gate of the village, Melanchthon said, "Some will be bewildered at your deeds, Doctor Luther."

"How will they be so?" asked Luther.

"Your display of good works," said Philip. "Why extend such benevolence, if merit cannot contribute to salvation? That's what you have been teaching. You're students might be confused, misinterpret your generosity."

"It is not for merit," said Luther, halting and looking at his colleagues. "That pernicious error is our entire problem."

"Others will wonder, if it is not to gain merit," said Carlstadt, "whatever is it for?"

"For love," said Luther. "We are justified by the instrument of faith alone in the grace and merits of Christ alone. Good works add nothing to justification, but they inevitably will flow from it. True faith results in true love, and will produce true good works, pleasing to God—but earning nothing from him."

"I doubt he would agree," said Carlstadt. He nodded toward a white-robed Dominican friar.

Mounted on a horse fit for a duke or an archbishop to ride, the friar had managed to adopt a facial structure, wan and sunken, like that of the stone effigy of a saint. On either side, the friar was escorted by two robed and mounted companions. Leading the procession, trumpeters blew a fanfare as if the harbingers of a papal visitation.

Luther felt the heat rise in his temples. "What mischief is this mountebank about to hurl at the benighted souls of Saxony?"

## 22

# PASSPORT TO PARADISE

T hat's him," said Carlstadt, nodding toward the mounted friar. "Johann Tetzel. Notorious scoundrel, here to do the pope's bidding."

"And Albert of Brandenburg's," added Luther, the muscles of his jaw flexing.

"Archbishop Albert, you mean," said his companion. "Or more accurately, Archbishop, Archbishop, Archbishop Albert. Archbishop three-times over is he. It is a bit of a mouthful to say."

"And more impossible to do." Luther snorted in disgust. "He already has Halberstadt and Magdeburg and now Mainz. Canon Law forbids three archbishoprics, especially for an under-age upstart like Albert."

"There's good money in archbishoprics."

"Indeed, but they come at a price," said Luther.

"But worth it, so some believe. The banking house of Fugger lent Albert the ducats. It's purely a business deal."

"Nothing pure about it, is there?" said Luther. "And the price is his eternal soul; who knows how many other souls along with him."

"Once a man has the revenue of an archbishopric," continued Carlstadt, "let alone three, he can live like a prince."

"Until he dies," said Luther.

"Dying and eternity seem entirely forgotten in Rome."

"Rome," said Melanchthon, a faraway look in his blue eyes. "I have never been. What is it like?"

"If there is a hell," said Luther, "Rome is built over it."

"Is it as bad as all that?"

"Worse," said Carlstadt and Luther in unison.

"If only the putrefaction would confine itself to Rome," said Carlstadt. "Word is Pope Leo X wanted Albert to pay 12,000 ducats for Mainz; to keep everything holy and biblical, the amount was meant to represent the twelve apostles."

"I have heard," said Luther. "And Albert countered with an offer of 7,000 ducats for the seven deadly sins."

"*Jawohl.* Word is, they settled on 10,000 ducats, a vast sum of money."

"Manifestly not for the Ten Commandments," said Luther, "of which neither of these charlatans has any inclination."

Carlstadt grabbed Luther's sleeve and looked both ways. "Martin, you must be more guarded. Someone might think you were referring to the Holy Father."

Shrugging, Luther continued, "Tetzel, Albert, Leo—what is the difference?"

"The difference? Martin, surely you are not that naïve. You can probably get by with criticizing a hireling friar, but an archbishop, still more, the pope himself? I can smell the faggots burning."

"Sniff away," said Luther. "Albert colluded with the pope for a commission from 'His Holiness' to sell a new and augmented indulgence. I for one do not take kindly to a

German prince colluding with a luxury-loving Italian to fleece my poor flock here in our Saxony." He frowned at the crowds pressing close to see the show.

"Just how augmented?" asked Melanchthon.

Nodding at the friar stepping up onto a makeshift platform, "I believe Tetzel is about to tell us," said Luther.

"My dearest people of Wittenberg," began Tetzel.

"Words dripping with fat," murmured Luther, "as a hog turning on the spit drips the same."

Smiling expansively at his audience, Tetzel continued, "I have come at the behest of His Holiness himself, Pope Leo X from Rome; the Holy Father has sent me from the Eternal City. And I come bearing rich gifts for all Saxony." At his signal, one of his attendants bowed before him, holding aloft a gold-gilded velvet cushion. With a flourish, Tetzel took a rolled parchment from the pillow. As if it were made of delicate lace, he unrolled it, and held if for them all to see.

"This, my good friends of Germany, is nothing short of your passport to the celestial joys of paradise. You priest, you noble," he gestured with the indulgence toward them as he spoke. "You merchant, you virgin, you matron, you youth, you old man, enter now into your church, which is the Church of St. Peter. Visit the most holy cross erected before you and ever imploring you." Here he paused, gesticulating dramatically at the cross held aloft by one of his courtiers. Draping from it was the scarlet banner and papal seal of Leo X, the banner fluttering in the breeze.

"Have you considered that you are lashed in a furious tempest," continued Tetzel, "amid the temptations and dangers of the world, and that you do not know whether you can reach the haven for your immortal soul? Consider that all who are contrite and have confessed—and made contribution—will receive complete remission of all their sins."

A murmur of wonder rose from the crowd.

"Complete remission?" came a voice from the crowd. Leering at the friar, the speaker pattered the tips of his fingers together expectantly. Ample flesh bulged around the edges of his greasy leather jerkin.

"Did I not promise you I was bearing rich gifts?" replied Tetzel, nodding knowingly at the fellow. "With one of these indulgences, each bearing the papal seal, as you see, you may indulge yourself in sins, that is to say, in the forgiveness of sins—past, present, or future ones—as you wish, and for whom you wish."

He broke off theatrically, cocking his head, cupping his hand to his ear. "Do you not hear them? God and St. Peter call you. Consider the salvation of your souls and those of your loved ones departed."

After placing the papal certification reverently back onto the velvet cushion, he continued, his voice quavering with apparent anguish. "Do you not hear the voices of your dead parents and other relatives crying out, 'Pity us! Have mercy upon us, for we suffer great punishment. With a few coins, you could release us from our misery. We have created you, fed you, cared for you and left you our temporal goods. Why do you treat us so cruelly and leave us to suffer in the flames, when it takes only a little to save us?'"

As if rehearsed, Tetzel's attendants brandished two torches, flames hissing, black tentacles of smoke hovering over the crowds.

Carlstadt leaned close to Martin's ear. "What a pious fraud, is this."

"As soon as the coin in the coffer rings," continued Tetzel, with obvious pleasure at his little jingle, "the soul from purgatory springs!"

At his words, his attendants yanked a drape from a bird cage. Wings beating the air, eight or ten white doves flew upward, cavorting over the wondering faces.

"Nothing pious about this fraud," said Luther through gritted teeth. "He is an infernal, diabolical, antichristian fraud."

"Lay a stone for St. Peter's in Rome," continued Tetzel, "and you lay the foundation for your own salvation and felicity in heaven!"

"The man is a mountebank," said Luther, "unworthy to call himself a Christian. This is foul, despicable!"

"So vastly generous is His Holiness in this indulgence," persisted the friar, "so kindly extended to the good people of Germany, that there is no sin beyond its reach. Go ahead. Let your imagination roam the transgress-atorial possibilities, the unrestrained, unbounded trespass-atorial opportunities. Go on."

Here, Tetzel proceeded to graphically describe the most horrific sinning that one could commit and yet Pope Leo's indulgence was sufficient. "So virulent an indulgence do I hold in my hand, that one could herein find remission for the most heinous of sins—" He paused dramatically, snatching up the parchment and letting it tremble over the upturned faces of the crowd. "—For the very sin of violating the ever-Virgin Mother herself!"

His congregation emitted a collective gasp at the thought. Nodding approvingly, Tetzel appeared satisfied with their response.

"Will you not then for a quarter of a florin receive these letters of indulgence through which you are able to lead an immortal soul into the fatherland of paradise?"

"Even Lucifer," said Melanchthon, shaking his head in wonder, "was not guilty of so great a sacrilege in heaven. God help us!"

"A false preacher, such as this cheat," said Luther, "is worse than the deflowerer of a virgin."

"Which according to common knowledge," said Carlstadt, his eyebrows raised, "Tetzel is a master practitioner of such deflowering." He shook his head in disgust. "Look at them. The working poor of Wittenberg leave the walls of their village to come out here and give their quarter florin to this despoiler of souls."

Luther's heart sank. "Wait! Is that not—? We must stop her. She has nothing."

Holding her grandmother's hand, little Liesel turned. Waving, she grinned at them.

"I believe a devoted woman such as she would gladly forfeit her own soul for her granddaughter," said Carlstadt. "Perhaps that is the currency with which she is buying the indulgence."

"A swine like Tetzel won't take souls," said Luther. "He cares nothing for that woman and the dear little one. He only wants her money—and she has none. I believe I am watching the old dragon from the abyss of hell, parading in all this trumpery before us."

"Wait for me," called Carlstadt as they marched back to the village. "You are angry, Martin. I cannot keep your pace."

"Who would not be angered?" said Luther, his jaw set, the folds of his black habit swishing at his ankles, Melanchthon jogging at his side.

"I fear for you." Carlstadt, breathing hard, called after him. "You must calm yourself, act with restraint."

"Rage suits me," said Luther over his shoulder. "I work better when I am angry, and I have work to do."

# 23

# HAMMER AND NAIL

(October 31, 1517)

Luther, his eyes bloodshot—he had been at his parchment and ink pot late into the night—a determined set to his jaw, marched down the main street of Wittenberg, a parchment roll under his arm and a hammer and nail in his clenched fist. Striding up to the door of the duke's Castle Church, he unrolled the parchment.

"*Guten tag*, Herr Doctor," greeted one of his students.

Luther turned.

"Good All Hallows' Eve to you, Herr Doctor," said Pieter.

"All Hallows' Eve? Yes," said Luther, "it is a good day."

"And what, Herr Doctor, have you written?" asked Pieter.

"Hold these for me," said Luther, handing the hammer and nail to Pieter. "I must make room. Why others post things without consideration of where the rest of us will post our messages is beyond me. Let me see, if I move this one from the Zulsdorf farmer selling a bull calf to the left a bit, and this wedding invitation to the right—there, now, that is better."

Luther placed his parchment between the two notifications. "Nail, please," he said, his palm opened. "And hammer."

His hammering sounded hollow against the distressed wood of the great door of the church, *Clonk, clonk, clonk!* and it echoed from the portico into the street. Luther stepped back, inspecting his work. He drew a deep breath.

Pieter, his nose close to the parchment, read aloud. "'Ninety-five Theses. Out of love for the truth and from desire to elucidate it,' and then your name, title, and Wittenberg, '...intends to defend the following statements and to dispute on them in that place. Therefore, he asks that those who cannot be present and dispute with him orally shall do so in their absence by letter.'"

Pieter broke off. "You will dispute with the Church?"

"If any will step forward," said Luther, scanning down his theses, frowning critically. "Yes, I will dispute them, happily."

Pieter nodded, then continued reading. "'In the name of our Lord Jesus Christ, Amen. When our Lord and Master Jesus Christ called men to repent,' and then you reference the biblical text—you're always doing that in tutorial, 'he willed the entire life of believers to be one of repentance. This word cannot be understood as referring to the sacrament of penance...'"

Pieter's voice trailed off but his lips continued moving as he read down the document, Luther watching him closely.

"*Was ist das?*" asked Fritz. He and Walter and several other students crowded around.

"What have we here?" asked Walter, leaning over Pieter's back.

Nodding at his parchment, Luther stepped back to make room. "See for yourselves."

"Stop shoving," said Pieter, bending over to read the final article. "I am almost finished." Moments later, he looked up and said, "I especially like the part about the tares of purgatory being 'sown while the bishops slept.'"

"And I the place here," said Fritz, tapping the theses, "where you wrote, 'The true treasure of the Church is the most holy gospel of the glory and grace of God.' Is this so?"

"Next to the gospel of grace," said Luther, "the pretended treasury of merit is but wood, hay, and stubble."

"But Herr Doctor," said Walter, "will not your theses run across the grain of the archbishop, the pope, and Rome itself?"

"And Elector Frederick himself?" added Fritz.

Luther nodded soberly. "I suspect there will be more who dislike them."

A cluster of people eagerly reading something on the Castle Church door, acted as a magnet. Dozens now jostled one another to read Luther's 95 Theses.

"Humph," grunted the brewer, scratching his head. "Infernal Latin." Searching the faces in the crowd, he hollered, "Wilhelm, you read a bit of Latin. Come, man, translate it. Give it to us in German."

Luther drew aside to make more room. His students followed.

"Herr Doctor," said Fritz, soberly. "You merely seek a polite scholarly disputation. What is the crime in that?"

"Polite or otherwise," said Luther, "I challenge anyone to dispute what I have written. Show me where I am wrong, just as we bare our cerebral knuckles and wrangle in tutorial. That is all I ask."

Walter nodded. "I fear the pope will think you are a wild boar."

"Word is, Pope Leo is fond of hunting wild boar," said Pieter. "If Elector Frederick withdraws his support," he continued, looking over his shoulder, his face pale, "it would be disastrous. Herr Doctor, your theses could end in more than a mere disputation."

"Our lives begin to end," replied Luther, "the day we become silent about the things that really matter."

127

"And this really matters?" said Fritz.

Luther nodded. "What is at stake," he said, "is heaven or hell."

# 24

# OFFENSE AND TUMULT

**M**artin, what have you done?" said Carlstadt, bursting into Luther's study. His face was red and, he wheezed with exertion from climbing the spiraling staircase into the high tower of the Augustinian cloister. "Everyone is talking about your theses."

"Everyone?" said Luther, fanning the wet ink on the parchment before him.

"Perhaps you could have sent them as a private letter," said Carlstadt, "servile, deferential, reconciliatory. But no, you had to nail them to the very door of the ducal church, as if firing a salvo from a cannon across the bow of the entire penitential system of the Church!"

"Everyone, you say?" Luther set down his quill and turned on his stool.

"Yes, everyone," retorted Carlstadt. "There is even a crude summation of them circulating by word of mouth in German, and the day is barely half over!"

"I do hope the common man gets it right."

"This is no time for jesting, Martin."

"I do want everyone, peasant to prince, dung man to duke, to get it right. Which is precisely why I nailed them to the duke's door."

"Have you gone mad? Tomorrow is All Saints' Day."

"I am well aware of the Church calendar," said Luther.

"When centuries of saints and martyrs are celebrated all over Christendom."

"Who have now become the objects of shameless idolatry," retorted Luther. "What better time to post my theses?"

"You are too angry, Martin. Yes, Tetzel is a scandal and needs to be silenced. But I have read your 95 Theses. Do you think that perhaps you have gone too far?"

"It is in my mind," said Luther, "that I have a considerable way yet to go."

"But surely you are aware of the duke's plans for the morrow? The elector who is, if I may remind you, our benefactor, our patron, our employer in his university."

"Unveiling his latest acquisitions? Yes, I am very much aware of it. Pilgrims already cramming the streets, eager to venerate the bone fragments of antiquity—for a price. Do you realize, Carlstadt, the duke's collection has swollen to such proportion as to be sufficient to grant a grand total of nearly two million years of penitential release from purgatory?"

"Who did the arithmetic?" asked Melanchthon, entering the study with a trencher loaded with bread, sausages and three steins of beer.

"I did," retorted Luther. "Using the elector's catalogue of 1509, the one illustrated so beautifully by our neighbor Lucas Cranach, which only included 5,000 particles in 1509, bone fragments, teeth, and the rest. But the duke has been voraciously diligent in his collecting in the intervening years. Including his latest acquisitions, his collection has swollen to nearly 17,000 bits and pieces of reliquary remains."

"Might not it be merely an old man's benign hobby?" suggested Carlstadt.

"A hobby that leads the weak to perdition," said Luther, "is never benign."

"Indeed," said Melanchthon, "the duke's is a collection to rival Rome."

"I've seen Rome's reliquary assemblage," murmured Carlstadt.

"Which is our noble benefactor's goal," said Luther. "His more cherished items include: an unconsumed twig from Moses' burning bush, a tooth of St. Jerome, four unidentifiable remains of St. Chrysostom, six fragments of St. Bernard, four bits and pieces of St. Augustine, four hairs of Our Lady, three threads from her cloak, four fragments from her girdle, and seven swathes from her veil on which fell drops of blood from Christ during his passion.

"Best of all, the elector's collection includes certifiably genuine relics from Christ himself: a thread from the swaddling bands, thirteen various fragments from the manger, including one bit of hay. Moreover, the duke has acquired from the wise men of the east a nugget of gold and three tiny portions of myrrh.

"But the nucleus of the elector's collection are the relics of Christ himself: a hair from Jesus' beard, an entire nail driven through one of his hands when crucified, a crumb of bread—one can only hope, an uneaten crumb—from the Last Supper, a chip from the stone on which Jesus stood moments before ascending to his Father, a barb from Jesus' crown of thorns, bearing papal certification that it did, indeed, pierce the brow of the Son of God."

Shaking his head in astonishment, Carlstadt looked at Luther. "You recited that like a lawyer who is a monastic."

Luther grinned. "I am a lawyer, that is, one without the status—or the wealth. And I am a monastic."

"But for how much longer?" said Carlstadt. "Keep this up and I fear you will be stripped of everything."

Luther, eyeing the sausages, shrugged.

"The duke is most pleased with you," said Melanchthon, "when you attack Rome for fawning on her relics."

"But the timing," said Carlstadt. "Your 95 Theses, Martin, launched the day before the unveiling of his latest treasures, is an affront to the elector himself. And we desperately need his continued support."

"Rome or Wittenberg, hoping for ones salvation in the buying of indulgences and the venerating of relics—it is all scandalous!"

"We all agree about that," said Melanchthon.

"Nevertheless, Martin," said Carlstadt, "we must be prudent with our prince."

"Complete remission of sins, past and future—for a contribution," said Luther bitterly. "Does it matter whether the contribution enriches Rome or an elector of Saxony?"

Carlstadt raised his palms as if weighing the two. "I believe, on a certain level, it does matter."

"Not to the soul deceived thereby," said Luther, pressing his thumbs into his temples. "Writhing in perdition, whatever degree of difference there is will matter not a whit to the poor souls of Saxony damned in hell."

"True, there is that," said Carlstadt. He chewed pensively on a hunk of rye bread.

"Have we no shame?" said Melanchthon. "All this done in the name of Christ's Church."

"I believe," said Luther, "that our Lord would long ago have uncoiled his whip and driven these money grubbers—Italian or German—from his Father's house."

Biting his lower lip, Carlstadt looked at Luther. "I fear it, if God has stirred you up to wield the lash."

"'As soon as the coin in the coffer rings, the soul from purgatory springs,'" recited Luther viciously. "Tetzel is full of poisonous refuse and insane foolishness. He is a man of flies.'"

"Speak thus of Tetzel," said Carlstadt. "But not so of the pope, not directly, not if you value your life."

"Of course not, of the pope," said Luther. "But fraudulent Tetzel spews brazen, sacrilege, a foul contagion that must be driven out."

"Yes, reserve your vitriol for Tetzel. The duke has banned the scoundrel from the streets of Wittenberg."

"You and I know why," said Luther, looking sideways at his friends. "So he can sell his own indulgences, and charge pilgrims for the veneration of his own relics. Not exactly the purest of motives for banning Tetzel from selling his."

"Of course it is not," agreed Carlstadt. "But you must be prudent, man. Say nothing offensive about the elector. Be the loyal subject, a true son of Saxony, show due deference to his patronage. Therein is your salvation."

"My salvation, the forgiveness of sins, comes through the Son of God alone."

"Yes, of course," said Carlstadt. "You understand my meaning."

"I do," said Luther. He held his stein up to his friend.

"Your premature death, Doctor Luther," said Melanchthon, "and ours with you, would restore the darkness, consign the poor to the fraudulent error of men like Tetzel, and hide the light of the gospel."

"But there does come a time," said Luther, "as there did for our Lord, when one must uncoil the whip and drive out the money changers. Many who say otherwise care more about gold than the souls of their neighbors."

"But I do fear," said Melanchthon, "that driving them out will bring about great trouble."

"I am certain of it," said Luther. "The gospel cannot be truly preached, my friends, without offense and tumult."

# 25

# INDIGNATION OF GOD

O n his way to the Stadtkirche on All Hallows' Eve, 1517, Luther watched the last leaf fall from the pear tree in the garden of the Augustinian cloister. Though there was a foreboding snap in the crisp autumn air that evening, the streets were crowded. Luther pulled his hood up more closely around his neck.

Bundled against the chill, the common people of Wittenberg jostled their way into the sturdy grandeur of the Stadtkirche. Amidst the murmuring of voices and shuffling of feet on the flagstones, breathing heavily, Luther climbed the steps into the pulpit of the city church.

There was no hiding in a pulpit. His heart pounded in his temples as it did that fateful day when he attempted to say his first mass. Writing his protest down was one thing. Here, in the pulpit, he was about to speak the words, words that would most certainly cause great tumult. Clutching the edges of the lectern, Luther scanned the faces of his congregation.

The nave was crammed with bodies, hard-working farmers, craftsmen, wives, and children. And the air in the musty church was perfumed with them and their varied occupations. Drawing in breath, Luther smiled. In spite of his fierce protest when Staupitz and the duke had dropped the weight of pastoral duties on his shoulders, he had come to love those duties, to love these his people.

Perhaps it was his own peasant roots, but Luther even loved the smell of his congregation: the fatty tallow smell of the candle maker, the potent acid stench of the tanner, the slimy aroma of the fishmonger, the pinching odor of the pig farmer, the barnyard hoppy whiffs of the brewer, the mysteriously delicious scent of fermenting cabbage, the earthy wafture of hay and manure mingling in, with, and under all the other smells.

"Many of you have heard it said," began Luther, "that 'As soon as the coin in the coffer rings, the soul from purgatory springs.'" At his words their chattering and rustling dwindled into silence. Leaning over the pulpit, he looked into their upturned faces.

"Some of you, wanting to believe it is true, have heard the clattering of your own coins in Johann Tetzel's coffer. 'Lay a stone for St. Peter's and you lay the foundation of your own salvation and happiness in heaven,' so he has told you. Moreover, you have heard the most outrageous claims for the indulgence he is peddling, that it is 'your passport to the celestial joys of Paradise,' full remission of your sins for a few coins."

Again Luther paused, looking about the sanctuary. And in the instant of that pause, the iron gray clouds of the autumn evening outside must have parted, and five or six brilliant shafts of sunlight radiated through the window panes. The faces of his congregation, now illuminated by the warm sunlight slanting across the nave, looked up at their pastor. Among those faces, Luther caught a glimpse of the old

135

woman and her granddaughter. Liesel, smiling broadly, raised a pudgy hand and waved at him. Winking at her, Luther continued.

"Full remission of your sins," he paused, spreading his arms wide, savoring the phrase. "That would be good news, indeed, would it not? But purchasing Tetzel's letters of indulgence will not secure this for you. He has lied to you. It is not true."

Murmuring rose from the congregation, bewildered looks, even angry scowls were on some of their faces.

"The revenues of all Christendom are being sucked into St. Peter's," continued Luther, "this unquenchable basilica. Instead of placing our coins in his coffer, we Germans ought to laugh at calling this Roman basilica the common treasure of Christendom. Before long all the churches, palaces, walls, and bridges of Rome will be built out of your money—yes, and yours, and yours.

"First of all we should build living temples, houses of worship for German Christians, and only last of all St. Peter's, which is not for us. Who among us from Wittenberg is going to get up on Sunday morning and go to Church at St. Peter's in faraway Rome?"

"Not I," said the onion farmer.

"Nor I," agreed the fishmonger, thumping his chest as he said it.

"I'll go," called a farmer. "Foot it down right after milking my cows. But I'll need to be home by supper time."

Smiling, Luther raised a hand to quiet their laughter.

Gesturing at the rough stones of the church, he continued, "Better that it should never be built than that parish churches like ours should be despoiled. The pope would do better to appoint one good pastor to a church than to rob us with his indulgences to build his. Why doesn't the pope build the basilica of St. Peter out of his own money? He is richer than Croesus."

Melanchthon, standing near the front below the pulpit, blinked rapidly; Luther tried to ignore Carlstadt next to him, who was burying his face in his hands, shaking his head side-to-side in consternation.

"He would do better to sell St. Peter's," continued Luther, "and give the money to the poor folk—to all of you—who are being fleeced by the hawkers of indulgences. If the pope knew the exactions of these vendors, he would rather that St. Peter's should lie in ashes than that it should be built out of the blood and hide of his sheep."

The murmuring accelerated to low rumbling.

"Moreover, good people, beware of those who say that indulgences reconcile you with God. Papal indulgences do not remove your guilt before God. He who is contrite, truly sorry for and repentant of his sins has remission—without the pope's keys and indulgences!"

The rumbling accelerated.

Holding up a hand for silence, Luther continued, "Tomorrow is All Saints' Day. I would deceive you if I did not declare to you the truth about this day. Saints, however holy, have no extra credits to confer on you. Every saint is bound to love God to the utmost, and no saint has performed more goodness than is required by a holy God. And even if he had, how could his surplus goodness be stored up for the use of someone else? Certainly not by dropping a coin in Tetzel's collection box!

"Christ alone has true merit, but, until I am better instructed, I deny that his merit can be got by purchasing a certificate of indulgence with a quarter florin or all the golden trinkets of Rome. Christ's merits, my beloved, are freely available to all who believe—without the keys of the pope. Therefore, I declare to you that the pope has no jurisdiction over purgatory."

"He don't?" blurted an old man. "But the pope, *he* says he do."

"I am willing to reverse this judgment," said Luther, "if I am convinced by Holy Scripture. If the pope does have the power to release anyone from purgatory, why in the name of love does he not abolish purgatory by letting everyone out? If for the sake of miserable money he released uncounted souls, why should he not for the sake of most holy love—empty the place? Free of charge!"

"*Jawhol! Jawhol!*" The nave of the Stadtkirche nearly erupted with stomping feet and shouts of agreement.

"To say that souls are liberated from purgatory as soon as the coin in the coffer rings is audacious—and positively harmful. I declare to you, dear people, indulgences make you complacent; they give you a false sense of security; they divert you from the love of Christ, and are ruinous to your salvation. 'With my certificate of full remission of sins in hand, my neighbor be damned; I can live as I please,' so says the one who has put his money in Tetzel's coin box.

"Christians should be taught that he who gives to the poor is better than he who buys a paper pardon. Did Christ say, 'Let him that has a cloak sell it and buy an indulgence'?"

"No!" shouted a peasant, thumping his staff on the flagstones with a clunk.

"He said no such thing!" cried a young man.

"Father Martin speaks sense," murmured others.

"Love," continued Luther, "covers a multitude of sins and is better than all the pardons of Jerusalem and Rome. He who spends his money for indulgences instead of relieving the needs of his poor neighbor receives not the indulgence of the pope—but the indignation of God!"

# 26
# COUNTER-BURNING

Luther awoke with a start. Blinking in the darkness, he sniffed the air in the room. His cell at the Augustinian cloister in Wittenberg had never smelled like a rose garden. Far from it. It reeked of sweat, his sweat, and of bedclothes long unchanged. Weary from study and teaching, he collapsed into bed without caring. But this was different. Again he sniffed the night air.

Smoke. Sitting bolt upright in bed, Luther felt the clutches of fear wrapping their fingers around his insides. Fire. It had long been one of his greatest fears. And his cell was high in the tower, far from the great doorway, the main egress from the cloister. He felt panic rising in his bosom. Being trapped in a tower during a conflagration—he would choose almost any other method of dying.

Tearing off his blanket, Luther bolted out of bed. Throwing on his cowl, he burst from his cell. His left hand sliding on the central column supporting the stair, his feet pounded on the worn treads of the circular stairway.

Other monks burst from their cells, converging in the great hall of the cloister.

"Is it fire?" cried one.

"Where is it?" cried another.

"There is shouting from the street," said Melanchthon.

Running through the courtyard of the priory and into the street, Luther halted. A bonfire crackled and hissed in front of the Stadtkirche, sparks disappearing into the blackness above the steep gables of the houses surrounding the square. Luther felt the wall of heat as he drew near. Shadowy cavorting figures were silhouetted by the fire.

Grabbing one of them by the sleeve, Luther accosted him. "What is going on? Pieter? What are you doing?"

"It's that scoundrel Tetzel!" shouted the young man, his cheeks flushed, firelight flickering in his wide eyes.

"He burned your 95 Theses in Frankfurt," said Fritz, wiping sweat from his forehead with a sleeve.

"And declared you a heretic," said Walter.

Pieter held up an armload of parchment. "And sent his counter-theses here to be posted in Wittenberg."

"Seeing as he burned your theses," shouted Fritz.

"It seemed fitting," cried Pieter, "that we consign his to the fires of purgatory!"

"Where they belong!" shouted another student, hurling a mound of parchment into the flames.

"Well done, *junge Männer*!" shouted Carlstadt above the din.

Luther was speechless. Watching a lone sheaf of paper, aflame and borne upward by the infernal air, he held a hand toward the flames. His fingers trembled.

"I do not like it," said Melanchthon. "We mustn't give the pope any ideas."

# 27

# SCUM OF THE EARTH

"Y ou did what?" cried Carlstadt.

"I sent a letter to Albert," said Luther.

"The archbishop?"

"Three times over," said Luther. "The very same."

It was the day after the burning in the square, and Luther and his colleagues had met after their tutorials for a walk along the River Elbe to discuss the latest turn of events.

"A letter to the archbishop?" said Carlstadt. "Martin, is not that a tad bit impertinent of you?"

"I gave him due deference," replied Luther.

"As you did the pope in your All Hallows' Eve sermon?" said Carlstadt, passing a hand across his brow. "All that about the pope being rich enough, and why doesn't he in the name of love empty purgatory?"

"It is a compelling question," said Melanchthon. "One that needs an answer."

"Indeed, I agree," said Carlstadt. "The pope, he is in faraway Rome, but Albert, he is here in Germany, and needs very careful handling."

They paused under an oak tree, its hefty branches angular and reaching out over a wide bend in the river. A flock of storks circled above the water, their black-tipped wings making powerful strokes, then easy gliding, red legs and feet stretching back in flight, head and bill thrust forward, mutely scouring the marshlands along the river for a dinner of fish and frogs.

"Hear for yourself," said Luther. "My letter began thusly, 'Father in Christ and Most Illustrious Prince,' wrote I, 'forgive me that I, the scum of the earth, should dare approach Your Sublimity… my insignificance, my unworthiness,' and so forth. No, I gave him due deference."

"H'm! Of course you did," snorted Carlstadt.

"Albert needed to know how his instructions regarding this indulgence are being distorted and exaggerated."

"Yet, Doctor Luther," said Melanchthon, "are not Tetzel and his ilk actually following the archbishop's instructions?"

"Yes, though with advantages," said Luther. "Yet charity leads me to offer him a way of escape from this scandal."

"Charity?" said Carlstadt. "I would say it is more shrewdness than charity."

"Why cannot they walk hand in hand? Might not shrewdness smooth the way for charity?"

The threesome walked back along the river to the village. Overhead, rapid tapping sounds came from large nests made of sticks, built in the high branches of trees along the sandy marshlands of the river. Beaks clattering and held aloft, the storks gave off their rhythmic percussion sounds with musical regularity.

A week later, Carlstadt burst into Luther's tower study, agitated and beside himself. "Martin, the pope received

Albert's letter—your letter, along with his own copy of your 95 Theses. Everyone is speaking of it."

"Everyone?"

"Everyone who matters in this dispute."

"Do we know how the pope responded?"

"Word is, he dismissed you out of hand. Being dressed for a boar hunt, he is reported to have said, as a page shoved on his riding boots, and I quote, 'This Luther is a drunken German. He will feel different when he is sober.'"

Martin threw his head back and laughed. "Well spoken by His Holiness Leo the Temperate himself."

"Another report I have heard," said Melanchthon, stroking his thin beard, "claims that the pope referred to you as a brilliant scholar, and that the whole row is stirred up by the other monks' envy at your brilliance."

"Brilliant son of a peasant!" Martin laughed still harder.

"Methinks you prefer the latter response," said Carlstadt.

"It is more amusing," said Luther.

"And far more accurate," interjected Melanchthon.

"I grant you that, Philip," said Carlstadt. "But, Martin, this is serious, deathly serious. Remember, Tetzel has declared you a heretic. And your enemies—there's a growing number of these—boast that they will see you burned within a month. Some say less."

Nodding soberly, Luther studied his hand, the one he had held toward the flames of the bonfire.

"Now that Johann Grünenberg has printed your 95 Theses in German," said Carlstadt, "I wonder if it makes you more likely for the stake, or less?"

"Hundreds of copies circulating throughout all Germany," said Melanchthon.

"I too wonder," said Luther soberly.

"The printing press," said Melanchthon, "a remarkable invention."

Luther nodded. "I am convinced that printing is God's latest and best work to spread true religion throughout the world."

"Carried on the Elbe," said Carlstadt, peering out the leaded panes of the window in Luther's study, "our little river, washing the banks of our little Wittenberg, the highway of reformation, transporting your 95 Theses in German throughout Europe. Imagine it!"

"I do wish, however," said Luther, "I had been consulted on the translation. Nevertheless, I am gratified. The poor of Germany, long held in the bondage of error and ignorance, deserve to know the true gospel, what the Word of God actually says."

"But what conniving is afoot," said Carlstadt, "when the pope appoints the author of the 95 Theses vicar of the Augustinian order? He is up to something."

"He knew a cardinal's hat would not suit you," said Melanchthon. "In any event, I doubt you would look good in red."

"Of course, Leo means to silence me by the back door, as it were. Quench me before I become a conflagration."

"And doing so, "said Carlstadt, "puts Tetzel and the Dominicans on the defensive."

Months passed, during which Luther was not idle. He seemed to have no capacity for idleness. He studied, taught daily in the lecture hall of the university, preached to his flock at the Stadtkirche, and wrote—always writing. Anything Luther wrote, the Grünenberg press printed, and reprinted, circulating sermons, pamphlets, treatises throughout Germany, his writing smuggled to faraway places like Scotland, even Spain. In the spring of 1518, Luther's writing was disrupted by a summons to an Augustinian disputation in Heidelberg.

"There are many miles of open road between Wittenberg and Heidelberg," said Carlstadt. "Rumors of plots to end your life on the journey are legion."

"Perhaps you should not go," said Melanchthon, his brow furrowed.

"On the contrary," said Luther. "I must go. Do you not see? I must."

"What if they send you on to Rome?"

Carlstadt shook his head. "Elector Frederick has promised. No son of Saxony will be sent for a trial in Rome."

"It is four long days of walking from here to Heidelberg," said Melanchthon. "And all the threats? Think what could happen around every bend in the road."

"Yet, it is God's call," said Luther, "and I will obey. I walked all the way to Rome. I am going to Heidelberg on foot."

Carlstadt held up his hands in defeat. "I feared you would say that. Hence, I came prepared. If go you must, then I must insist that you shall wear this."

Luther lunged to his feet, his stool clattering behind him. "I shall do no such thing!"

"You shall!"

Melanchthon covered his mouth with a hand.

"Consign me to the flames!" cried Luther. "It would be a mercy to wearing that!"

# 28

# BRAIN OF BRASS

Once in the precinct of the Count Palatine's grand castle overlooking the city of Heidelberg, Luther shed his costume and was greeted warmly by the brethren of the order, especially Doctor Staupitz.

"When was your last confession, my son?" asked Staupitz, a smile tugging at the corner of his mouth.

"Before a priest?" said Luther with a laugh, "it has been a considerable time. Before God? Just this morning on my knees, and graciously absolved of all my miserable offenses, from parricide to the seemingly picayune."

"And it did not take six hours?" said Staupitz, a twinkle in his eye.

"I had an immediate audience," said Luther. "Free access without gold or good works, my Advocate ushering me into the throne room on the instant."

The Count Palatine brought out the best food and the finest drink that first night. Savory aromas filling the air, the board of the great hall of the castle was loaded with roasted pork and venison, leeks and asparagus, onions and sauerkraut, wheat beer and hock, lavish and celebratory, as if for a royal visitation rather than a gathering of Augustinian monks. Luther felt like a guest of honor rather than a man being led to the stake.

"None dispute," began Luther next morning as the disputation commenced, "that our failings and shortcomings, our willful transgressions, are indeed sins before God. But the patron of our order understood and taught something long forgotten in our day. Even our good works are merely 'splendid sins,' as Augustine put it. Where did he learn this? In Holy Scripture itself wherein we are told, 'All our righteousness is as filthy rags before God.' How then, if our good works are of no avail, how then are we justified? Surely, by the merits of another, whose works alone are splendid obedience."

"If the peasants heard you say that," said Staupitz over luncheon, "they would stone you."

Though some of the elder members of the Augustinian order scowled and shook their heads at Luther's teaching, the young men were elated. While their rival order, the Dominicans, hurled invectives at Luther and called for his excommunication as a heretic, the majority of the Augustinians treated him as a celebrated hero. Especially a young man from Strasbourg, Martin Bucer.

"That which Erasmus has only insinuated," said Bucer, "you, Doctor Luther, speak openly and freely. In argument today at the chapel, you showed the acumen of the Apostle Paul."

Luther waved his hand dismissively. "I have great hope that as Christ when rejected by the Jews went over to the Gentiles, so this true theology, rejected by opinionated old men, will pass over to the younger generation." He lifted his stein. "To men like you, Martin Bucer, and you, John Brenz, and the rest of you!"

"*Zum Wohl!*" they cried, lifting their steins in reply. "To your health!"

The next day, after pageantry fit for a duke, Luther continued his argument, defending the patron of the order. "'To will is of nature,' wrote Augustine, 'but to will aright is of grace.' Therefore, 'God bids us do what we cannot, that we may know what we ought to seek from him.'"

"'What we cannot,' bah," retorted an elderly monk. Stooped and almost completely bald, he rose to his feet. "Your teaching, young man," he said, "will loosen the reins of lust—and destroy free will."

"With reverence, may I reply with the words of our patron. 'Grace does not destroy the will, but rather restores it,' so said Augustine himself. And furthermore, said he, 'Men do not obtain grace by freedom; they obtain freedom by grace.'"

Far from being defrocked and burned by his order, Luther was, on the whole, treated as a champion, and escorted home, not on foot, but comfortably ensconced in a wagon.

Once back in Wittenberg, while pouring over his copy of the Greek New Testament, Luther made a glowing discovery.

"Master Philip! It is here!" he cried with elation to Melanchthon. "The Latin has it wrong! For centuries Rome has built an entire theology of penance on a flawed translation. Whereas the Vulgate renders Matthew's gospel text, 'do penance,' the Greek actually reads, 'be penitent.' It is an entirely different sense, is it not?"

Lips moving as he read the two translations, Melanchthon nodded in agreement.

Furiously Luther studied the Scriptures, and just as furiously he wrote his findings in sermons, pamphlets, and more treatises, Johann Grünenberg snatching up what he had only just penned, setting it to type, printing and distributing it overnight.

Meanwhile, Pope Leo X was furious and placed Luther under the ban, forbidding him by papal authority to teach or write. Undaunted, Luther dipped his pen in ink and set it to parchment, attacking the very ban that forbade him to write.

"I will adore the sanctity of Christ and the truth," wrote Luther. "The merits of Christ take away sins and increase merits. Indulgences take away merits and leave sins. I resist those who in the name of the Roman Church wish to institute Babylon! I damn and denounce the papal decree!"

Careful to insure that he did not offend the pope, and equally careful not to forfeit up to Rome his prized professor, Elector Frederick dredged up an obscure imperial law that had long forbade a German from being tried anywhere but on German soil. As further protection for himself, the duke employed George Spalatin to act as go-between, his left hand never quite knowing exactly what his right hand was up to, or so the duke hoped it would appear to the pope and the emperor.

Frustrated, for the moment, by the shrewdness of Frederick and the intrepid boldness of Luther, the pope commissioned a Dominican theologian to craft a reply to Luther in defense of the inerrancy of the Roman pontiff. In a final salvo, the Dominican apologist referred to Luther as "a leper with a brain of brass and nose of iron."

"Insidious devil!" retorted Luther, not to be outdone. "You cite no Scripture." He went on to declare that popes can err as can Church councils. "Consider Boniface VIII, a pope who came in as a wolf, reigned as a lion, and died as a dog. If Boniface can err so can Leo. Scripture alone is the final authority."

This was too much. August 7, 1518, Pope Leo ordered Luther to appear before him in Rome where he would be tried for heresy and contumacy. He had sixty days to comply.

Behind imperial closed doors, wrangling commenced over whether the pope could compel Luther to be tried in Rome or whether it was the prerogative of the Holy Roman Emperor to try his case at an imperial diet—on German soil.

Meanwhile, the papal legate, Cardinal Cajetan, summoned Luther to appear before him in Augsburg. Fearing treachery, his friends begged him not to go. "I fear not their scabby tribe or the quacking of the cardinal." And so he went, not only to stand before the papal legate, but the Holy Roman Emperor himself held court in Augsburg.

When the cardinal demanded that he revoke his criticism of the pope, Luther replied, "His Holiness abuses Scripture. Show me from Scripture where I am wrong. I deny that the pope is above Scripture."

Thumping his staff on the tiled floor, the cardinal ordered Luther to be silent. "Speak when you can say but one word, '*Revoco!*'"

The emperor, all the while, was brooding and inattentive, too distracted by an impending war with the Turks to pay much attention to a renegade monk. For the moment.

When at last the audience with the cardinal was adjourned, Staupitz pulled Luther aside. "You must flee Augsburg with all speed." Glancing back at the palace, his grip on Luther's elbow tightened. "The cardinal is provoked."

"Cajetan was as suited to handle my case," said Luther, "as an ass to play on a harp."

"Indeed, he is not fit nor in the frame of mind for debate with you, Martin," said Staupitz. "Yet is he the pope's legate in Germany, with enormous powers. He was tasked by the pope to hear you revoke what you have taught—not to debate with you."

"I could revoke nothing," said Luther.

"I know, but now Cardinal Cajetan is provoked. This can only go one way. Which means there is but one thing for us to do."

Walking briskly from the cardinal's hall, Staupitz turned aside sharply, leading Luther into a dark corner of the cloister. "You must kneel," he said, pressing down on his shoulders.

"You are my father in the order," said Luther bewildered, "but also my friend."

"Kneel, Martin Luther. I release you from all of your vows. From this moment forward, you are no longer an Augustinian."

"But surely there is some other way!"

Staupitz signaled for Luther to rise. "You are free. My friend, use your freedom. And may God and his angels protect you. Now, there is not a moment to lose. A provoked cardinal is a dangerous one."

Staupitz led Luther to the stables where he had arranged for a horse. "Ride like the wind back to Wittenberg and the duke's protection. And pray God that Elector Frederick is not also provoked with you."

Under cover of darkness, Luther managed to clamor onto the back of the big animal. Staupitz slapped the horse on its rump, and Luther, clutching to the reins and the horse's mane, rode into the night, the folds of his monk's habit billowing behind.

# 29

# ONE-EYED FOOL

s Luther clung to the back of his horse throughout that long midnight ride back to Wittenberg, his mind was in torment. "Are you alone wise," he said to himself through gritted teeth, "and all the ages in error?"

Luther feared that Cajetan would have already dispatched a report of his insubordination to the pope. At the news, there could only be one ruling from Pope Leo.

He shuddered. Cold night that it was, the thought of the flames brought no comfort. "Now I must die. What a disgrace I shall be to my parents!"

Once back in Wittenberg, the net tightened and Luther found himself encircled by hostile forces in both the Church and the state. Counseled to be wary, to lie low for a time, to be silent, to observe the papal ban for his own life's sake, Luther would have none of it.

"These sons of Nimrod!" he shouted from his lectern at the university hall. "They grease palms. Shepherds in name only, they fleece the flock, and more German money flies over the Alps. Holy Pope Leo must stop these abuses!"

Leo, who had ears everywhere, had heard enough. In a letter to Elector Frederick, the pope called on the duke to stop Martin Luther, "son of iniquity, pernicious heretic!" Cardinal Cajetan ordered Frederick to send Luther bound to Rome or banish him from Saxony.

Luther countered by privately appealing to the elector for a general council to convene on German soil, to be presided over by civil authorities—not Rome. Mysteriously obtaining a copy of the appeal, Wittenberg's printer Johann Grünenberg set it to type. Almost overnight, Luther's private appeal circulated throughout Germany. The torch ignited and dukedoms throughout the realm rallied to support Luther and Germany against an Italian pope and a Spanish emperor.

So widely had printers distributed Luther's books and sermons, and so popular had he become, that there were public readings of his sermons in the marketplace in Nuremberg. Families read Luther at their supper tables in Speyer, and schoolchildren throughout Germany made transcripts, copying Luther's sermons into their lesson books and committing parts of them to memory. One papal prosecutor, gathering evidence for the case against Martin Luther, returned from Germany discouraged. "For every one supporter of the pope," he admitted, "there were three supporters of Luther."

While Pope Leo X prepared his canonical ruling on indulgences, readying himself for a final censure of Luther, he was abruptly distracted by a conspiracy of cardinals plotting his assassination. At the same time, an event occurred that suspended his plan to condemn Luther. January 12, 1519, the Holy Roman Emperor died. Since it fell to German dukes to elect the next emperor, and since Luther's patron Frederick was an imperial elector, the pope began currying favor with the duke. Luther was, for the moment, preserved by the wrangling, collusion, and intrigue of the pope, the dukes, and the cardinals.

In the lull, Duke George of Leipzig, intractable rival of Elector Frederick of Saxony, hosted a debate. Frederick's Martin Luther would face off with Duke George's champion Johann Eck at Leipzig.

Amidst great pageantry, the debate was to begin July 4, 1519, two hundred of Luther's Wittenberg students thundering at the gates for admittance. Aghast at the crowd amassing to hear the Saxon monk debate, Duke George was forced to move the proceedings to the great hall of Pleissenburg Castle; there the contest would last for nearly two weeks.

Though Carlstadt and Melanchthon were at his side, Luther keenly felt his inexperience at formal debating. He tried to ease the chafing of his cowl about his neck. Stand his ground against the eloquence and sophistry of Eck? He would need instantaneous recall of all his knowledge. But was it sufficient? Wiping his brow, Luther appraised his opponent.

Eck was a formidable giant. His face broad and fleshy, his voice trumpeting like an underfed steer, Eck was confident and pompous, a professional debater with an uncanny ability to recollect a phalanx of facts to support his contentions. And he was clever.

When the dust began to settle at the close of the heated opening volley of debating, Luther's knees trembled and he feared he might collapse. Though he took some comfort in a brief exchange he overheard.

"Doctor Luther," whispered Melanchthon to Carlstadt, "has the Scripture at his fingers' ends."

"A perfect forest of words," agreed Carlstadt. "Though Eck is pressing him hard. How Martin remains affable under attack is beyond me. I am ever slow in memory and quick in anger. Not so Martin. He is equal to anything."

"Let us hope so."

On the afternoon of the fifth day of debating, Eck droned on about clerical celibacy and why canon law forbade monastics to take a wife.

"Yet, according to Holy Scripture," interjected Luther, "Peter, from whom the popes are allegedly descended, had a mother-in-law, which means, of necessity, he had a wife."

"That is, according to Martin Luther's *private* interpretation," retorted Eck, "though not according to the popes, the councils, and canon law. With whom shall we agree? With centuries of Church tradition—or with this seditious son of a miner from Saxony?"

It was a warm July afternoon and Duke George's bearded chin had more than once settled onto his ample chest, heavy breathing coming from his open mouth.

At Eck's retort, he awakened with a snort. Smacking his lips, he set aside his ermine gown, and cleared his throat. "I propose an interlude," he said.

The duke then clapped his hands sharply, and a gangly courtier, party-clad in red and yellow, wearing a motley coxcomb hat with three donkey's ears and bells, burst into the hall. Bounding in a series of whirring cartwheels, bells jangling, the jester executed a final back flip and landed crouching on the table in front of Luther's lectern. Cocking his head, the fool eyed Luther.

"As you can see," continued the duke, "my fool, for all his other prodigious qualities, is missing an eye."

The fool, gasping in shock, began pawing at his empty eye socket, then checking his pockets. Back-flipping off the table, he began scrambling about on the floor, under benches, tables, even under the duke's vast chair.

"My eye! My eye! It must have popped out when I was popping into the room! Wherever could it have gone to?"

The crowd roared with delight.

Flopping onto a bear rug, the fool flinched and moaned, then began reciting a ditty.

"There once was a fool from Speyer
Who could never control his ire.
One blindingly blusterful night
He drank himself into a fight.
The butcher, he swore by his life,
He'd gouge out the fool's eye with his knife—"

Pausing, the jester flipped backwards, prostrating himself face-down in the shape of a cross before the duke. Lifting up his head pitifully, and goggling with his one good eye, he added a final line:

"O why won't you give me a wife?"

What followed was a seemingly ridiculous debate over whether a fool with but one eye was eligible to take a wife.

"Most certainly not!" snorted Eck. "On two counts: one, if he's missing an eye, who knows what else he might be missing, and secondly, he is a fool."

"Yet, everywhere in Holy Writ," rejoined Luther, "marriage is commended, and finding a good wife is wisdom. A fool, thus, could be made wise by a good woman."

As the two scholars wrangled, the jester, warming to Luther, came over and placed his head affectionately on his shoulder, nodding sagely at his arguments. When Eck countered, the jester ogled grotesquely behind the scholar's back. Offended, Eck tried to mimic the jester's appearance, but, no match for the fool, made one of himself.

On the final day of the debate, Eck went on full offensive. "Martin Luther, you call yourself an Augustinian monk, but you are a follower of the damnable and pestiferous errors of John Wycliffe. What is more, you are espousing the pestilent errors of John Hus—Hus, of *Bohemia*—justly condemned by a holy council of the Church—and burned!"

# 30

# HUSSITE!

At Eck's words, Luther felt a crawling along his spine. Sweat trickled from his brow, stinging in his eyes; he wiped a sleeve across his face.

Burning. He had read of Hus's end at the stake in front of the cathedral in Constance.

"What say you, man?" shouted Eck. "Condemned and burned, I say!"

"Condemned, yes," said Luther, finding his voice, "by a council made up of men, men capable of error."

"Doctor Luther, are you declaring that Church councils can err?"

"Err? Of course they can err," said Luther. "The Council of Constance that condemned Hus was called precisely *because* previous councils had erred."

"Do you deny the infallibility of the papacy, then?"

"Deny? I affirm that Scripture alone is infallible."

"There! Martin Luther, you are a Hussite!" Chin in air, Eck looked triumphantly at the audience.

The hall erupted in stomping of feet and rival shouting. "Hussite! Hussite!" chanted Duke George's supporters. "Martin Luther! Luther!" rejoined Elector Frederick's supporters.

"Order!" cried the moderator. "I say, Order!"

"I repulse the charge of Bohemianism!" cried Luther, pounding on his lectern for emphasis.

"I'm a loyal son of Saxony——" he cried, his words largely drowned out by the chanting.

The moderator shouted, "This debate is adjourned until after luncheon." He brought his gavel down hard on the table.

"Where are we going?" asked Carlstadt, breathing heavily. "We should eat. Martin, you don't eat sufficiently. And you walk too fast. Tell him, Philip. He looks gaunt, unwell. Martin, your bones are protruding from your flesh. And you walk too fast."

"*I* don't look well?" said Luther over his shoulder. "Your face looks like smoked herring."

"Bah!" said Carlstadt. "But I'll eat smoked herring, or any other meat you can set before me. Where are we going?"

"Ah, I thought as much," said Melanchthon, nodding knowingly. "The library."

"Imagine sly Eck implying that I am a Bohemian!" Luther yanked open the heavy double doors of the Leipzig university library. Inside the stone walls were lined with hand-written books, the air scented with leather, parchment, and polished wood.

Luther addressed the librarian, his voice hushed. "I would like to see your collection of writings from John Hus—the Latin, not the Bohemia translated version, if you please."

"So you will not eat?" hissed Carlstadt, eyeing the door.

"When I eat, my bowels revolt," said Luther, scowling.

"But without meat and drink," whispered Melanchthon, "you will expire."

"At times, I feel that if I eat I will expire," said Luther. "In any event, I cannot afford to have my bowels lurching and rumbling away whilst I give answer to Eck this afternoon. Aha, here it is. *De Ecclesia*, by John Hus."

"Eck is right about this much," said Melanchthon, "Our Bohemian neighbors, they are calling you the 'Saxon Hus.'"

"Eck simply wants to rekindle a century of old animosities," said Carlstadt, bringing his fist down on the table.

"Excuse me, sirs," said the librarian, scowling fiercely at them.

"Bad blood," continued Carlstadt, his voice lower, "between Saxon and Bohemian. It is clear what he is doing. Eck, with this ploy, attempts to turn loyal Saxons against you, against us."

"When first I read the books of this John Hus," said Luther, "I was overwhelmed with astonishment. Who would not be?"

"Why did Rome do it?" said Melanchthon. "I too have read Hus. Why would the Church burn a man who explained the Scriptures with so much gravity and skill?"

"They cooked that goose," said Carlstadt, "if ever a goose was cooked." He groaned, "Oh, but I mustn't speak of food. But why did they do it?"

"It was Hus who wrote," said Melanchthon, "'Seek the truth; listen to the truth; teach the truth; love the truth; abide by the truth; and defend the truth—unto death.'"

"Those who would destroy a man so in love with the truth," said Luther, "—they must *hate* the truth. Ah, here it is. Hus wrote, 'The one holy universal Church is the company of the predestined.'" He scanned down the page, his fingers sweeping ahead of his eyes. "And furthermore, 'The universal Holy Church is one, as the number of the elect is one.'" He slapped the page with the back of his hand. "That's Augustine."

"*Bitte! Bitte! Mein Herr!*" scolded the librarian, his voice echoing off the stone vaulting.

"Augustine, who got it from the Apostle Paul," added Melanchthon.

"And Peter," said Carlstadt. "Both of whom agreed about meat. 'Kill and eat.'" He moaned. "There is little time, and I am hot and hungry."

"Some compare Martin Luther," said Melanchthon to Carlstadt, "with the Apostle Paul."

Carlstadt narrowed his eyes appraisingly at Luther.

"I don't look anything like Paul," said Luther, absently, skimming the pages of Hus before him.

"How do you know that?" snorted Carlstadt. "What do you think Paul looked like?"

"He was short and scrawny," said Luther, with a toss of his head, "like Melanchthon, here."

"He needed to eat more sausages," murmured Carlstadt. "What I wouldn't do for a plate of sausages, boiled potatoes, dripping with butter, sauerkraut—and beer, cool from the cellar—oh, this infernal heat! It is too hot for debating."

*Gong-gong-gong!*

"It's the bells of the ducal chapel," groaned Carlstadt.

"There's no time to lose," said Melanchthon. "It will not do to be late."

Luther wiped a bead of sweat dangling from the tip of his nose. Scanning the page before him, he traced the words with his fingers, his lips moving silently as he committed key phrases to memory.

"It is nearly two o'clock," said Melanchthon. "The debate, Herr Doctor, it reconvenes."

Moments later, just as the moderator brought his gavel down with a sharp *thud*, Luther and his friends, breathing heavily, perspiration glistening on their faces, reentered the great hall of the castle. Scowling at them, the moderator resumed by letting Eck reaffirm his accusation.

"Among the articles of John Hus," replied Luther, wiping his brow with the sleeve of his habit, his voice clear and amiable, "I find many which are plainly Christian and evangelical, which the universal Church cannot condemn."

"The Hussite plague!" growled Duke George, jabbing an elbow into the ribs of a courtier at his side. "Ravaging my realm!"

Luther continued. "As for the article of Hus that 'it is not necessary for salvation to believe the Roman Church superior to all others,' I do not care whether this comes from Wycliffe or from Hus. No Roman pontiff is at liberty to construct new articles of faith. No believing Christian can be coerced beyond Holy Writ. By divine law we are forbidden to believe anything which is not established by divine Scripture. I cannot believe that the Council of Constance condemned the propositions of Hus!"

"Oh, but it did so," chortled Eck.

Carlstadt wiped a sleeve across his forehead and tugged on Luther's gown.

"Leave him be," whispered Melanchthon, gently. "I believe the doctor has a plan."

"All the articles of Hus?" said Luther, stepping from behind the lectern and clasping his hands behind his back. "It was nothing so simple as that. The council did not say that all the articles of Hus were heretical. It said, and I quote, that 'some were heretical, some erroneous, some blasphemous, some presumptuous, some seditious, and some offensive to pious ears respectively,' so concluded the council. Whereupon, since the words of councils are so endowed with authority, my esteemed opponent would do well to differentiate the precise meaning of its words. Tell us, which articles of Hus were which?"

"Whichever they were," retorted Eck, fuming, his face the color of beetroot, "none of them was called most Christian and evangelical; and if you defend them, then *you* are heretical, erroneous, blasphemous, presumptuous, seditious, and offensive to pious ears respectively!"

Eck smiled smugly as the Leipzig audience cheered. Flinging dark looks across the hall, Elector Frederick's entourage and Luther's two hundred students grumbled.

"Let me talk German," said Luther, signaling for his students to be silent. Thereupon, in German Luther spoke plainly and bluntly. "I assert that a council has sometimes erred and may sometimes err. Nor has a council authority to establish new articles of faith. A council cannot make divine right out of that which by nature is not divine right. Councils have contradicted each other, and have declared themselves to be above popes. Which is it? Who has the authority, popes or councils? And which ones, since they have so often disagreed?"

Here Luther turned from facing Eck, and looked imploringly at the general audience. "A simple layman armed with Scripture is above a pope or a council without it!"

At his words, there was one vast in-drawing of breath, and then a swelling reverberation of astonishment as everyone spoke at once to his neighbor.

Above the din, Luther continued, now almost shouting. "Neither the Church nor the pope can establish articles of faith. These must come from Scripture. Where they disagree with Scripture, we should reject popes and councils!"

Above the hollers of approval, Eck cried, "But this—this is the Bohemian virus! All heretics have appealed to Scripture. It is rancid, it is horrible to appeal to Scripture and say that popes and councils err. I tell you, Martin Luther, you are a publican, an infidel. I can no longer speak to you as a Christian!"

# 31
# SHEEP FOR THE SLAUGHTER

At last!" said Carlstadt. "Let us eat!"

Back in their chambers after the final afternoon of debating, the landlord of the inn placed a trencher of plump bratwurst, another heaped with sauerkraut, still another mounded with steaming potatoes, butter dribbling into a pool around them, a basket of fresh-baked rye bread, and three steins of local gose beer.

"It seems I must have liars and villains for opponents," said Luther after they had blessed the food. "I am not worthy in the sight of God that a godly and honorable person should discuss these matters with me in a Christian way?"

"The remarkable thing, Martin," said Carlstadt, between bites, "is that a man, accused of heresy as you have been, that such a man has been free to engage in public debate at all. It is truly remarkable."

"Eck was far more a man of method," said Melanchthon, "than of meaning."

"This is my greatest lament," said Luther. "If he were here, I would speak thusly to him: May the Lord Jesus protect us and all devout souls from your contagion and your company!"

"Well, he is not here," said Carlstadt, "or we would have to share our repast with him. What is more, it would do your digestion no service if he were."

"If it were only the Italians or the Spaniards," said Luther, taking a pull on his beer, "it would be far less bitter. Just when we thought we should have found favor among our own countrymen, preaching as we have to them the gospel of peace, life, and eternal salvation—but *nein*; instead of favor, we have found bitter and cruel hatred."

"Yes, but from few, Duke George and Eck, merely a few," said Carlstadt, sopping a hunk of bread in the melted butter, "and they of little account."

"Word is," said Melanchthon, cutting off a slab of sausage with his knife, "under the very nose of the Vatican, Herr Doctor, there are young men distributing copies of your evangelical writings. It is no longer merely Wittenberg's printer Johann Grünenberg getting rich by your books."

"No, indeed," said Carlstadt. "John Froben of Basel, has he written you more imploring letters? Word is he cannot keep your works in print, so rapidly is he selling them. There will soon be others."

Once back in Wittenberg, Luther found still more of his colleagues at the university rallying to his support. After Leipzig, renowned scholar, Nicolaus von Amsdorf, became one of Luther's most faithful cohorts.

Invigorated by the debate, Luther locked himself in his tower study and fell to writing, furiously writing, incessant writing, writing as if the world depended on it. One evening, he heard footfalls drawing nearer, scuffling on the flagstone stairs, winding upward, then pausing at the oaken door to his study.

*Tap, tap.*

"Come in! Ah, my friends, Philip, and you, good Amsdorf. You are most welcome, and just in time. I must have more parchment. And another pot of ink, and more goose quills. Slay them all. I must have goose quills!"

"I'll slay the goose," said Amsdorf, "and give you the quills, if you'll let us fat you up on a nice roasted goose."

"I'm sufficiently fat," said Luther absently.

"Here's another letter from the printer," said Melanchthon, holding out an envelope.

"Which one?" asked Luther.

"John Froben."

"Tell me what he says."

Melanchthon tore open the seal and scanned down the page. "It appears to be an urgent letter. Da, da, da. Froben says he has but ten copies of your last book. And he enquires as to your current project." He placed the letter on Luther's desk.

"I too am curious, Martin," said Amsdorf. "You've been holed up in this garret for weeks."

"What are you writing?" asked Melanchthon.

Setting his quill down, Luther stretched, flexing the fingers of his right hand. "See for yourself."

Amsdorf took up the parchment. "'The Address to the German Nobility,'" he read. "'The time for silence has gone, and the time to speak has come.'" Looking up, he said, "I very much prefer hearing it in the musical strains of your sweet voice, Martin. What is it you say herein?"

"It is simple, really," said Luther. "I don't know why I didn't see it before now. Are not temporal authorities, the German nobility, for example, are they not baptized with the same baptism as we?"

"Indeed, of course they are," said Melanchthon.

"Then why do we not treat the baptized with equity?" said Luther. "If a priest is killed, the offender and his land is laid under an interdict. But it is not so if a peasant is killed. Why not? Why so great a distinction between those who are called Christians?"

"Indeed, there are great inequities," said Amsdorf. "What is your solution?"

"It is not my solution," retorted Luther. "I simply declare what God says in his Word. It was Peter who declared of all Christian men in his first epistle that 'you are a chosen generation, a royal priesthood, a holy nation, a peculiar people; that you should show forth the praises of him who called you out of darkness into his marvelous light.' From this text I call believers in Jesus Christ among the German nobility to take up the mantle of their royal priesthood."

"Meaning?" said Melanchthon, raising an eyebrow.

"Meaning that if the Church refuses to reform itself, to correct its manifest abuses and doctrinal errors, it is the duty of believer priests to reform the Church."

"Nobles you call priests?" said Amsdorf, "and, thereby, you are calling civil authorities to reform the Church?"

"No, I am not," said Luther. He tapped an index finger on the open Bible before him. "God in his Word has called them to do so!"

Melanchthon unlatched and opened the single window. "Perhaps, Herr Doctor, you are in need of fresh air. A view of the garden will do you good. See there, the pear tree is laden with fruit, and the evening light stretches the shadow across the pathway."

Luther ignored him. "Moreover, I urge the nobility to commission a new translation of the Bible."

"Though you have found but few errors in the Vulgate," said Amsdorf. "Fewer still in the Greek New Testament."

Luther shook his head. "Latin, Greek—this translation will be in German, in our own tongue."

Joining Melanchthon at the window, he looked out at the scene below. "—in the language of that milkmaid shouldering her pails, just there!"

Amsdorf joined them at the window. "H'm, just as it should be."

"The Bible," continued Luther, "it is like a fair and spacious orchard, wherein all sorts of trees do grow, from which we may pluck many kinds of fruit: rich and precious comforts, learnings, admonitions, warnings, promises, and threatenings.

"My good friends, there is not a tree in this orchard on which I have not knocked, and have shaken at least a couple of apples or pears. I desire the same for every man and woman, boy and girl in Germany, do not you?"

They both agreed.

"The pope, however, will feel supplanted." Melanchthon looked sober. "Your pamphlet will make plain that you do not believe in papal supremacy, that you reject the pope as sole interpreter of the Bible. You are aware of what you are attacking?"

"I am," said Luther, soberly.

"And the cost of such an attack?" said Amsdorf.

Nodding, Luther murmured, "He who is baptized into Christ must be as a sheep for the slaughter."

"And we with you, Martin," said Amsdorf. Peering more closely at the parchments scattered on Luther's desk, he continued, "Till then, however, one must eat. Since Leipzig, you have barely stopped for food and drink."

"I have been rather preoccupied with another project," admitted Luther, returning to his desk. "Where is it now? Ah, here. 'The Babylonian Captivity of the Church,' I call it. Incomplete as yet."

"That allusion has been used before," said Melanchthon.

"It seemed the most appropriate," said Luther, "Rome having taken the true Church captive with her corruptions."

"Corruptions you herein elucidate?" said Melanchthon.

"I do. It is the foul contagion of the entire sacramental system," explained Luther. "By it Rome has fabricated another gospel, which, as Paul wrote in Galatians, is no gospel at all. Let Rome be accursed for making transubstantiation, indulgences, pilgrimage, baptism, marriage, monasticism, penance—all these wrenched into the means of earning salvation!"

Eyebrows raised, Melanchthon nodded. "You *have* been busy, Herr Doctor."

"I must be so, because Rome has been so busy mangling and distorting the sacraments until they now bear no resemblance to the institutions Jesus established. There are but two sacraments in Holy Writ: baptism and the Supper. Even these Rome has so garbled that they bear little resemblance to the ordinances given by Christ for his Church. What Rome has done with the sacraments I compare to a lie, which like to a snowball, the longer it is rolled the greater it becomes."

"What will you put in their place?" asked Amsdorf.

A smile spread across Luther face. "The Word of God. Grace, a justification that comes not of works, not of sacraments, but of Christ. Justification by grace alone, through faith alone, in Christ alone. That is what the Word of God restores to its rightful place."

Grasping his hands behind his back and studying the rough-hewn beams of the ceiling, Melanchthon asked, "And what of marriage? Is marriage no longer a sacrament, a means of grace?"

"You might as well ask me this about all the trumpery of the sacerdotal system Rome has invented. Monasticism, priestly celibacy, for example. Where does one find that in Scripture?"

"All this is contained in your pamphlet?" said Melanchthon, fingering the edges of the parchment. "This freeing of marriage, freeing from monastic vows, including ones of…" he broke off, looking out of the corner of his eye at Luther.

"Celibacy? Philip, don't look askance at me. We must speak frankly. Most certainly freeing us from false vows. Though taken in good faith, they remain false, and, thereby, no longer binding."

He paused, the heat rising in his temples. "It is scandalous that so many clerics habitually break their vows of chastity!" He slammed a fist on his desk.

Amsdorf caught the ink pot, steadying it.

"All the while," continued Luther, "there is no biblical warrant to make sacraments out of marriage and the office of the priesthood in the first place. The very ordinances which Rome has invented to extol marriage as a sacrament have turned it into a farce. Show me, Philip, or you good Amsdorf, where we read anywhere in Holy Writ that the man who marries a wife receives any grace of God thereby, for having done so."

"There is nothing to show," said Amsdorf.

"So you think little of marriage?" asked Melanchthon.

"On the contrary!" retorted Luther. "Marriage is the God-appointed and legitimate union of man and woman in the hope of having children or at least for the purpose of avoiding fornication and sin, and living to the glory of God. The ultimate purpose of marriage is to obey God, to find aid and counsel against sin; to call upon God; to seek, love, and educate children for the glory of God." He broke off, pacing back to the window, gazing down at the garden.

When he resumed, his voice was softer, less combative, almost tender. "To live with one's wife in the fear of God and to bear the cross; but if there are no children, nevertheless, to live with one's wife in contentment; and to avoid all lewdness with others."

"You set my mind spinning, Herr Doctor," said Melanchthon, a faraway look in his eye. "How is it you can speak so highly of something, yet not find it a means of grace?"

"There is only one true means of grace, Master Philip. And that is the merits of Christ alone, received by the gift of faith alone. Rome has turned marriage and celibacy into meritorious means of salvation, one of many ways to earn it by our works. God instituted marriage as a school of character, but not a means of grace, not in the sense in which Rome distorts the sacraments."

"You speak so tenderly of these things," said Melanchthon, smiling and narrowing his eyes at his mentor.

"I do," said Luther softly. "Because there is no more lovely, friendly and charming relationship, communion or company, than a good marriage." Diverting his eyes from his friends, Luther returned to his desk, shuffling distractedly at his papers. He glanced up.

"Stop looking that way, Philip!" Luther narrowed his eyes at the young scholar. "What it is? Speak your mind."

Melanchthon wadded the sleeve of his gown in his fist. "I, with your permission, Herr Doctor, well, that is to say, I mean to take a wife."

Luther was speechless.

"Herr Doctor, you stare as if I have contracted plague. Did you hear me?"

Luther nodded.

"Congratulations, my friend," said Amsdorf, warmly shaking his hand. "Who is the young woman?"

Melanchthon looked at Luther. "The daughter of the Bürgermeister is she."

"Katharina Krapp? How lovely!" said Amsdorf, shaking his hand again. "Martin, isn't it lovely?" Tilting his head, he looked sternly at Luther.

Luther cleared his throat and swallowed. "You are young, Philip," he began, "and, unlike me, gentle in manner. Gentleness has kept you from bringing down on your head the condemnation of the papacy, unlike me, and that gentleness will serve you well as a husband."

"Thank you, Herr Doctor," said Melanchthon. There was a moment of awkward silence. "You have written so warmly in defense of marriage." He hesitated, then blurted, "Will you not consider marrying?"

Luther laughed louder than he intended to. "And leave my wife a widow?" he retorted, shaking his head. "But you are young, and the Bible gives you freedom to marry." He paused, pawing through the parchment on his desk. "Which brings to mind another pamphlet I have labored on, 'The Freedom of the Christian Man.' It will, of course, seal my doom, though we are in God's hands not theirs. Though another reason I must never marry."

"And your premise?" asked Amsdorf.

"In short, I make the biblical case that the law exists for the sake of the conscience, not the conscience for the sake of the law."

"'Man was made for the Sabbath,'" quoted Melanchthon, "'not the Sabbath for man.'"

"Precisely. Hence, I argue, herein," said Luther, slapping the parchment with the back of his hand, "that if one cannot help both at the same time, then help the conscience—and oppose the law!"

# 32

# PAPAL BULL

Three months later, in a small chamber off the hall of the cloister, Luther sat brooding before dinner. His innards rumbled. His bowels constricted. Pressing a hand against his abdomen, he clenched his teeth. Wincing, he bent over with a moan.

In the intervening months, Luther's pamphlets had circulated to every *bauernhof* and hamlet in Germany. To many they were messengers of light and hope and freedom. "Never a man spoke thus," many cried. "It is the finger of God."

Meanwhile, others gnashed their teeth at his words; "The drunken Saxon monk is the spawn of Satan!" these cried. City officials in Cologne and Mainz ordered Luther's books to be publicly burned. Rumor had it that Duke George and Leipzig would do the same. To Rome Luther's most recent pamphlets had gone too far, final nails in his coffin, so the pontiff hoped they would be.

Luther had seen his parents but little in these years. So busy was he that there was rarely time to break away from his preaching, teaching, debating, and writing. His tireless vigor, though not by his intentional design, caused great discomfiture to the pope. "The pope, who rushes forward as an ass under the pelt of a lion!" cried Luther.

Meanwhile, Elector Frederick continued to play the German diplomat, appearing to acquiesce to Rome's demands, feigning to be the dithering old elector, yet behind the guise remaining determined that his prize professor—the source of enormous popularity for his university, for Wittenberg, for Saxony, and, increasingly, for all Germany—would never face trial, if trial there must be, in Rome.

The pope, frustrated by the stonewalling of the duke, and distraught at the ever-mounting popularity of Luther and his books, knew he must act. The die was cast.

July 15, 1520 Pope Leo X issued a bull of excommunication against Luther. The papal bull detailed forty-one propositions found in Luther's books and pamphlets deemed heretical by the pope. Given sixty days to recant or face excommunication, Luther knew that an appeal would be futile.

"For me the die is cast!" said Luther, his teeth clenched at the pain. "There are times when I want to start afresh and burn the whole canon law!"

"Do that," murmured Carlstadt, "and we'll all go up in flames with it."

"The pope's bull condemns Christ himself." Luther paced the floor of the narrow chamber, his fingers closing, the papal bull crumpling in his fists. "I am now certain," he said. "The pretended Vicar of Christ is the very opposite of Christ. *Nein*, the pope is the very wolf of Christendom, the true and final Antichrist!"

"As the Bohemian called him," said Carlstadt.

"Which he is," said Luther. "Little wonder a Jew would rather be a sow than a Christian. If I were a Jew I would suffer the rack ten times rather than go over to the pope, the croaking frog."

"Your mother and father," said Amsdorf. "They have come to see their son, to dine with you. They will not understand. Might I suggest you not call the pope a croaking frog in their hearing?"

"There. I hear them," said Carlstadt, nodding toward the door, "being shown into the hall."

Amsdorf grasped Luther's arm. "Be patient with them."

Jaw cocked to one side, Luther murmured, "Yes, their voices, my mother and father." He made to rise. Hesitating, he bit the edge of his lower lip. "I must go to them."

"Wait," said Carlstadt.

"I must go—" Luther's hand froze on the latch.

"Papal bull?" The door was ajar, and his mother voice was clearly audible. "Whatever that is, it cannot be good. I knew he would never amount to much."

There was an indistinct murmuring from his father.

"Exactly what is a papal bull?" his mother's voice continued.

"A citation, I believe." Hans's voice, though gruff, had a tone of resigned longsuffering about it.

"From the pope in Rome?" added his mother. "Just what do the words on the citation say?"

Hans did not immediately reply. Luther could see his father in his mind's eye, looking down at his hands, his fingers clasped together like intertwining sausages, so he had thought of them as a boy.

"Our Martin," he began, "he seems to have run afoul of the pope."

"Afoul? *Seems* to have?"

Luther closed his eyes, clasping his fingers on his forehead and rubbing his temples with his thumbs.

"*Ja*, and the pope in the papal bull," continued his father's voice, "commands him to retract what he has said and written."

"*Jawohl*, as I always say," said his mother. Luther could see her in his mind's eye standing before her husband, lower lip jutted, her hands planted on her hips. "As I always say, 'if folks don't like you or me, the fault with us is like to be.' That's what I always say. But it seems to me Martin was never listening when I said it. And now he's gone and got his self run afoul of the pope; by his own doing has he done it."

"There is something to be said, *meine Frau*, for getting correspondence from the Holy Father in Rome. Martin would be the first of us Luthers to get that kind of mail."

"There you go, always defending him," said his mother's voice. She stomped her wooden-shoed foot for emphasis; a *clonk* sounded on the flagstones. "So what happens next? Martin writes a humble letter to His Excellency the pope. And there begins an amiable letter exchange and eventual resolution?"

"His *Holiness* the pope," corrected Hans. Luther heard his father sigh heavily, then grunting and rustling sounds as he rose to his feet. "You must know, *meine Frau*. The papal bull condemns our son to excommunication."

"Has it come to all that?"

"*Jawohl*, and eternal ruin in the flames of hell."

"Fire," murmured his mother, "even as a boy, he's always feared the flames. Why would he do this and run straight into burning?"

"*Ich verstehen nicht*," murmured his father. "There must be a way of escape."

"Surely there is penance," said his mother, "an indulgence to purchase? If he had only become a jurist, it would never have come to this. And even if it did, a rich jurist would be able to purchase forgiveness and castrate the papal bull, would he not?"

"I have heard enough," hissed Luther, rising. "Far too much. I must go to them."

# 33

# HOUSEBREAKER

Amsdorf took Luther by the arm. "Perhaps this is a divine appointment, Martin. The papal bull has made a breach in the wall. Forgive them. They are your parents. Speak to them. Explain all to them."

"Nicolaus is right, Martin," said Carlstadt. "*Post tenebras lux*. Your parents have been lost in the dark. Bring them into the light. We shall pray as we dine."

Luther pulled the door open. "*Mein Vater, Meine Mutter*," he said.

At sight of their son so suddenly through the doorway, there was an instant of confusion, his mother's face darkening, his father's eyes flickering from adoring to rueful. Smiling warmly, Luther embraced them both, and invited them to sit beside him at the table.

Novices in black habits laid dinner out on the table— roasted beef loin, savory and moist, and falling from the bone; a whole boar, hocks and snout overflowing its platter; tureens of rich gravy, aromatic steam hovering over the board;

sauerkraut, asparagus, boiled potatoes, roasted beets, all in abundance—the hall filling with delicious smells, mouth-watering anticipation, and good cheer.

When prayers had been offered and the psalm had been sung, amidst the clattering of serving bowls, knives and forks, pewter steins and wooden bowls, they fell to.

After the first wave of hungry silence, punctuated by munching sounds and little grunts of pleasure, Hans turned to his son.

"This papal bull, Martin. What does it mean?"

"*Ja, ja,*" said his mother. "I'll tell you what it means. Martin wanted his way—again. Never could play nicely with the neighbor children, not our Martin."

Luther's knife clattered onto his plate. Just as he was about to speak, Amsdorf, seated across the table, prodded him none too gently in the shin with a foot. Snatching up his knife, Luther filled his mouth with boar flesh. He chewed slowly.

"Whatever did you do?" said Hans. "Your mother and I do not understand you. Why must you be so contrary?"

"*Ja, ja,*" agreed his mother, wagging her knife at him. "Are you alone wise?"

Swallowing, and wiping the grease from his lips with his sleeve, Luther nodded slowly and replied. "It vexes me greatly, my dear parents, that my actions, my calling, have been the cause of disappointment and grief to you. Yet am I most heartily willing to explain to you, so that you will truly understand, why I have been compelled to take my stand."

Conversation at the long table dwindled as Luther, his voice animated and passionate, attempted to help his parents understand.

"The Bible is alive," said Luther. He had turned his stool and looked earnestly at both his parents. "The Word of God, it speaks to me; it has feet, it runs after me; it has hands, it lays hold of me."

His mother, shaking her head slowly, cupped a hand and feigned to whisper in her husband's ear. "Have I not told you a thousand times if I've told you once, he is mad?"

Luther felt another kick under the table from Amsdorf's foot. Scowling at his friend, he continued.

"What I have come to know as the chief lesson in theology, dear Father and Mother, there is but one thing: well and rightly to learn to know Christ. It is in the Word of God where he is very friendly and familiarly pictured unto us. 'Grow up in the knowledge of Christ,' wrote Peter. Christ himself also teaches us that we should learn to know him only out of the Scriptures, wherein he says, 'Search the Scriptures, for they do testify of me.'"

Clearing his throat, his father interjected. "But what of the pope, the Church, canon law? Since my youth, I've been given to understand that these are the means by which we understand the Word of God."

For the next few moments, Luther launched into a near diatribe against the pope—"The very masterpiece of the devil's art!"—against indulgences and the sacraments, against justification by the works of the law. Wincing from a sharp blow to his shin, he halted. Looking fiercely at Amsdorf, he recommenced, but on a different path.

"In short, the Word of God has laid hold of me, has taught me the true way of salvation and peace with God. Mother, I daily interrogate myself with the same question, 'Are you alone wise?' And I answer it, '*Nein*! I am nothing. It is the Word of God alone that is wise.

"And the Word of God tells us that faith alone is the instrument whereby we are made righteous before God. But faith is not yet another work you must stir up by your own will. Faith is infinitely beyond all the power of our nature. It is an extraordinary and precious gift of God."

"What is faith?" Toying with a wooden spoon, his father murmured the words so softly they were audible to few else in the room. "I have long wanted to know."

Luther leaned closer. "Faith is a living, bold trust in God's grace, so certain of God's favor that it would risk death a thousand times trusting in it." He broke off. Eyeing the row of candles in the middle of the table, their flames quavering, tendrils of smoke coiling above each.

"That is faith," he continued, "and such confidence and knowledge of God's grace makes you happy, joyful and bold in your relationship to God and all creatures. All this the Holy Spirit makes happen through faith."

"Just faith? Without my good works, you say, then?" Hans narrowed his eyes at his son. "Just faith? I can be right with God without earning it by my good deeds?"

Taking hold of his father's calloused hands, Luther replied. "*Jawohl, mein Vater.* We are justified freely by God's grace; good works have nothing whatsoever to do with justification—nothing.

"Yet because of God's gift of grace, the true Christian freely, willingly and joyfully does good to everyone, serves everyone, suffers all kinds of things, loves and praises the God who has shown him such grace."

"Only grace, then, you say, my son?"

"Grace alone. There are not good deeds sufficient in ourselves for any of us, dear Father." Luther squeezed his father's hand. "I have not fulfilled my father's will. I know it and so deeply grieve that I have not pleased you, you and Mother. But it was only Jesus who could perfectly fulfill his Father's will."

Luther felt his father's fingers tightening on his own.

"Though works will never save anyone," continued Luther, "yet is it just as impossible to separate faith and works as it is to separate heat and light from that hot, crackling fire, just their warming us from the hearth!"

"But must you abandon Rome for your new ideas?" It was his mother's voice. She had pulled her stool close. Luther felt her pressing hard against him.

"They are not my ideas, *meine Mutter*, neither are they new. The Apostle Paul in all his epistles taught justification by grace alone, through faith alone, in Christ alone. And so it is in all the Word of God. Alas, the Church has departed from Holy Scripture, and so has led you and me and all Germany to look away from Christ's merits to our perceived good works, to the merits of the saints—by this we have been led into perdition."

Spreading his arms, his palms up, Luther continued. "I do not know why God called me. It is not because I am wiser than other men. I have learned he does not call the equipped; he equips the called. Therefore, it has fallen to me— unwanted, unsought by me—to sound the alarm. Like a violent physician, I must alert the world to watch out for false ideas and guard against good-for-nothing gossips, who think they're smart enough to define faith and works. It is the Church and all her crew who have become the greatest of fools."

Another blow to his shin. Luther bit the knuckle of his index finger.

"What are we to do, then?" whispered his father.

"Ask God to work faith in you," said Luther warmly. "It is the prayer he never refuses. Without his Holy Spirit's work you will remain forever without faith, no matter what you wish, say, or can do."

*"Ich verstehen nicht."* It was his mother's voice. "I-I do not understand." Her words were no longer harsh, but genuinely bewildered, with longing in her tone.

"And what of the law?" said his father. "Is not your Bible filled with law?"

*"Jawohl,"* so it is," said Luther, "to expose our guilt and condemn us, to demonstrate that 'By the deeds of the law shall no man be justified.' It is the gospel alone that can save

sinners—that can save you, *meine Mutter, mein Vater*." He broke off, rising to his feet, addressing the whole table.

"Failing to observe the distinction between the law and the gospel is what got us in this quagmire. Therefore, we must be most vigilant in observing the law and gospel distinction, for without it the law will always force me to abandon Christ and his gospel boon. In that emergency I must abandon the law and say:

"'Dear Law, if I have not done the works I should have done, do them yourself. I will not, for your sake, allow myself to be plagued to death, taken captive, and kept under your thralldom and thus forget the gospel. Whether I have sinned, done wrong, or failed in any duty, let that be your concern, O Law. Away with you. I have no room for you in my heart!

"But if you require me to lead a godly life here on earth," he continued, spreading his arms wide, "that I shall gladly do. But if, O Law, like a housebreaker, you want to climb in where you do not belong, I would rather not know you at all than abandon my gospel gift!'"

# 34
# BURNING THE BULL
(December 10, 1520)

"The die is cast!" cried Luther. Holding the papal bull before his students, he deliberately crumpled it into a wad, packing it as if he were making a snowball, readying it for launching at an opponent.

"I despise alike Roman fury," he continued, "and Roman favor." Tossing the bull upward and catching it in his palm three or four times, he at last hurled the bull onto the floor of the hall. His students looked on, wide-eyed, with mouths agape.

"I will not be reconciled nor communicate with them. They damn and burn my books. Unless I am unable to get hold of fire, I will publicly burn the whole canon law!"

A cheer rose from the hall.

"Might not we commence, Herr Doctor," said Pieter, rising to his feet, "with the bull?"

Luther reached down and picked up the wad of parchment. Unfolding the crumpled ball carefully, he laid it out on his lectern.

"Some call me too ferocious," he said. "But if a lion is met with a wolf, the lion must rage with fury if he is to prevail. I am a violent physician for violent times. I often wish God had called another. Pieter, here, he could do it for me." The students guffawed, slapping their classmate on the back. "But, alas, God has called me. I unsheathe my sword. We shall strike a blow at the wolf, this pestilent pontiff, who viciously preys on Christ's flock!"

Amsdorf was dispatched to carry an invitation for all students and faculty to gather at the Elster Gate of the city.

As if the pied piper in the legend, Luther stepped into the street, and the people of Wittenberg, as if by supernatural compulsion, left their homes and shops. It was a cold and wet December day; wet snow had fallen in the night and was turning the muck in the streets into a foul slurry. Nevertheless, in ones and twos, and whole families, they crowded at Luther's heels, shouting as they followed him to the eastern gate of the village where a column of smoke rose into the gray sky. The nearer they came, they could smell the burning and hear the crackling of the bonfire.

"All of Wittenberg is here," said Melanchthon, blinking as smoke blew into his eyes.

"Amsdorf, just there, and many of our good colleagues at the university," said Carlstadt. "And George Spalatin, the duke's functionary." Carlstadt nodded at a tall man dressed in the silken garments of the court. "I wonder, does he come to join us?"

"Or to bring an ill report of us back to his master," said Melanchthon. "I do hope it is the former."

Luther stepped onto an upturned barrel set in front of the fire. The heat was strong on his back as he looked out over the crowd. Though the wall of heat felt comforting on such a frigid winter day, it also made him tremble. Fire must be like the way of a man with a maiden, he mused; congenial and full of pleasure in its proper boundaries, but twisted and destructive outside of them.

He lifted a hand for silence. Over the crackling and fizzling of the conflagration, he began to speak.

"When on this same site the fire was ignited over Tetzel's absurdities and extravagances, the fate his counter theses merited, I was not aware, nor did I wholly approve, of such action. I then, three years ago, thought that the pope would see sense, acknowledge his manifest errors, and commence reformation within the Church." He paused, looking out over the flushed cheeks and eyes sparkling in the brightness of the bonfire.

"I was wrong!" he shouted. "The pope and his satellites call for the same to happen to me; chains, fire, and flames for Luther. I am called ignorant, stupid, and unlearned, a paltry imitator. They roar and rage in their vociferations against me. Against all of you. They declare Germans deplorables— heavy, drunken blockheads.

"What are we to say? How are we to respond to their juggling quips and craft? This odious despotism which blinds and keeps poor souls in chains must be stopped. Hence, I am compelled to answer geese in their own language.

"You see, when the dawn appears," he continued, "Satan becomes impatient of the light; he resorts in a thousand ways to subterfuge, evasion and indirection; but everything turns out wrong, as inevitably happens when anyone tries to maintain and defend an open lie against the manifest truth.

"The pope and his lies will not prevail. It is impossible. Glory, power, victory, salvation and honor are worthy of the Lamb that was slain and rose again. All these are ours, together with him, the sole possession of everyone who believes that Christ was slain and rose again for them. Christ, on our behalf, will prevail!

"Yet do we doubt. What is it about our own miserable works and doings that makes us think we could please God more than the sacrifice of his own Son on our behalf? About this there is no doubt."

Stepping off the barrel, Luther moved as close to the flames as he dared. "Since they have burned my books," he shouted above the noise of the crowd and of the fire, "I burn theirs!" Holding the papal bull above him, now crumpled and torn, he hurled it into the flames.

A great cheer rose from the crowd. The flames leapt higher. More parchments were thrown on the fire, some loose pages borne up on the heat, suspended, hovering, then bursting into flame and hurtling into the inferno below. More joyful shouting, children with rosy cheeks clapping with glee. Lucas Cranach the painter squatted in a doorway, sketching the scene with a lump of charcoal.

Meanwhile, Luther's students gathered more copies of canon law, and letters and pamphlets written against their teacher. Shouting in defiance, they pitched these onto the fire.

What happened next would have the profoundest impact on Luther. One of his students began singing. It was the *Te Deum*, and he sang the first stanza all alone and beautifully, his clear young voice echoing off the stone walls and close-packed houses forming a corridor along the street.

*Te deum laudamus te dominum...*

All in Latin. On the second stanza and throughout the remainder of the ancient Trinitarian hymn Luther's students and many of his colleagues joined in singing. In Latin.

Luther too joined in, heartily singing the ancient text, his voice deep and resonating, his heart swelling with wonder:

The holy Church throughout the world,
O Lord, confesses thee,
that thou Eternal Father art,
of boundless majesty.

Thine honored, true, and only Son;
and Holy Ghost, the Spring
of never-ceasing joy: O Christ,
of glory thou art King.

When the final strains of the hymn fell silent, thrilling as the moment had been, Luther realized that something was missing. Something was deeply wrong. He scanned the faces of the crowd. Only his students and colleagues had sung. The townsfolk had not been able to sing, "The holy Church throughout the world, O Lord, confesses thee."

They did not understand the Latin. They had fallen dumb. Silent and awkward, they stood detached, listening to beautiful music but not understanding its meaning, disenfranchised, cut off, not invited or able to join in.

That realization struck Luther like another bolt of lightning. And like that first lightning bolt, he felt he would never be the same thereafter.

As the villagers returned to their various callings, his students parading a copy of the papal bull impaled on a sword through the streets, Luther walked slowly back to the Augustinian cloister and his tower study.

"Doctor Luther," called a voice from behind him.

Luther turned. "Herr Spalatin, George, it is good to have friends in high places."

Spalatin lifted his caplet and nodded in an abbreviated bow. "You do not always make things easy for His Excellency the duke."

"No, I suppose I do not," replied Luther, "for which I am truly sorry. I wish I could fulfill my calling without so many bits and pieces of imperial debris falling about his head."

"There are times," said Spalatin, shaking his head in wonder, "perhaps today is one of these, when it feels more like you have been the cause of fire and brimstone raining down upon the great duke. Yet, without wholly declaring himself so, he remains your defender. I am instructed to convey His Excellency's own words to you, 'Luther ought not to be condemned unheard, nor ought his books to be burned.' So speaks the great duke."

"I am honored by His Excellency's continued patronage—and his patience. I realize I have been a trial to him at times."

Spalatin cleared his throat in his fist. "At times?" Eyebrows arched, he smiled. "Nevertheless, anticipating today's activity at the bonfire—word does travel so very fast in Wittenberg—he has written a letter to the emperor, to the effect, 'If now Martin Luther has given tit for tat by burning the papal bull, I hope that His Imperial Majesty will graciously overlook it.' So wrote the great duke, that is to say, so I penned on his behalf. His message is sealed and en route to the emperor as we speak."

"His words or yours, George? I sometimes wonder about the secretaries of great men."

Spalatin waved a hand in protest. "Entirely His Excellency's words, and my honor to deliver on his behalf."

"But why so?" said Luther. "I believe he has spoken fewer than twenty words to my face."

"Do not take it as an insult," said Spalatin. "Quite the contrary. He says you are 'the finger of God. That you teach not as the scribes and Pharisees, but as the direct mouth and organ of Almighty Power.' Yet, keeping his immediate distance from you is essential to the elector's scheme."

Grasping Luther's hand in his own, Spalatin grew sober. "There's a time coming when the duke can do no more. You have reckoned with this fact?"

Luther nodded slowly. Spalatin gripped his hand more tightly. For an instant he looked at Luther as if admiring a Cranach painting or a woodcut masterpiece of Albrecht Durer. "May God protect you." The elector's servant bowed and turned to go.

Luther watched the retreating figure of Spalatin; hunkered into his cloak against the cold, the ducal secretary, dodging a mud puddle, picked his way back to the castle.

Once back in his study, Melanchthon and Carlstadt following, Luther lowered himself into his chair and said, "I was wrong."

"Wrong?" said Carlstadt. "Wrong about not approving the burning of Tetzel's counter theses? You already confessed that."

Luther gave a short laugh. "I am only getting started, my friends. Recall, I once tried the patience of my confessor for six hours. Yet do I have more to confess. Herein, I do so: I once said that indulgences were the pious defrauding of the faithful."

"That was wrong?" said Melanchthon, raising an eyebrow.

"Yes, and I recant of it," said Luther, crossing his arms in the sleeves of his habit and eyeing his friends.

Carlstadt groaned. "He's up to something."

"Recanting the former," continued Luther, ignoring him, "I now declare that indulgences are the *most* impious fraud and imposters of the *most* rascally pontiffs, by which they deceive the souls and destroy the goods of the faithful."

Carlstadt frowned. "That is recanting of nothing."

"O, it is recanting of a sort," said Melanchthon. "You, Herr Doctor, did not state it as strongly or completely as you now know it to be. Am I right?"

Luther smiled. "Ah, my friends, there is more," he said, spreading his arms wide. "I was wrong about another matter, for which I now recant. I misspoke regarding the articles of John Hus. Not merely some but *all* of Hus's articles are most Christian and evangelical. And if Pope Leo X stood beside us at the conflagration on which we burned his bull today, I would say it to his face. And add for good measure that his articles come from the synagogue of Satan and are downright impious and diabolical!"

It was Carlstadt's turn to hold a hand near the flames. "You are determined to end up like the bull—consumed by the flames. Do bear in mind, it will be us with you."

Luther shook his head. "I have a great aversion to fire. Fire and lightning bolts—neither are my favorite things. But it is clear to me now. So far I have merely fooled with this business of the pope."

# 35

# WORLD GONE WRONG

U nless I am held back by force," said Luther, sharpening a goosequill with his penknife, "or Caesar revokes his invitation, I will enter Worms under the banner of Christ against the gates of hell."

"Held back by force?" said Carlstadt, weighing the words, his fingers steepled. "So if we were to chain you hand and foot and throw you in the duke's dungeon—?"

"It could be arranged," said Spalatin with a laugh. "The pope has wanted you in chains since Leipzig."

"But, my friends," said Luther, "you would deprive me of my recantation before the emperor."

"Which, of course, you will not make," said Melanchthon.

"Oh, but I will," said Luther. "This shall be my recantation at Worms." Rising, he slumped his shoulders, drew in his cheeks in a wan servile expression. "'Previously I referred to the pope as the Vicar of Christ. I recant.'" He thumped his knuckles on the desk. "'Now I say the pope is the adversary of Christ and the apostle of the Devil.'"

"Bravo," said Amsdorf, applauding.

Carlstadt buried his face in his hands. "Whereupon, the emperor will have you on a gibbet."

"But, Martin," said Spalatin, "you fail to take this summons seriously. It is an imperial diet. You will be standing before the emperor."

"Who has the power to stop you," said Carlstadt, snapping his fingers, "like that."

"Nonsense!" Luther took up his lute and sat on the edge of his desk. "This is not Spain."

"True, but Charles V, Holy Roman Emperor," said Spalatin, "is Spanish."

"I am ready to go on, to be sacrificed, if need be," said Luther. He thrummed idly on his lute. "I would rather die than retract any truth I have maintained."

"Perhaps the elector can avert violence," said Melanchthon. "You are his confidant, Herr Spalatin. You could make that happen, could you not?"

"Surely, you could, George, if anyone could," said Carlstadt.

"You over estimate my influence upon the duke. Heretofore, he has shown prodigious support for his favorite doctor of theology, apologies to present company. Reckless support, some call it."

"But when the elector is seated in judgment with his peers at the diet," said Carlstadt, with an in-drawing of breath, "it may be altogether another matter."

"He is a man of honor," said Spalatin, "yet is there only so much a good man can do against the empire."

"Against the world," added Amsdorf.

"Even if I am too sick to stand on my feet," said Luther, "I will go. If Caesar calls me, God calls me."

"Martin Bucer has sent word," said Melanchthon. "'Do not enter the city of Worms,' he warns."

"As has the imperial confessor," said Carlstadt. "Imagine it! Even the emperor's priest warns you not to go. They will burn you in Worms. Yet, do you listen? *Nein!*"

Luther waved a hand. "If violence is used, as well it may be, I commend my cause to God. He yet lives and reigns who saved the three youths from the fiery furnace of the king of Babylon, and if he will not save me, my head is worth nothing compared with Christ. *Herren*, this is no time to think of safety. The gospel must not be brought into contempt by my fear to confess and seal my teaching with my blood."

Two weeks later, on the afternoon of April 16, the wheels of Luther's Saxon cart clattered ominously on the paving stones of the main street of Worms. Imperial herald Caspar Sturm, commissioned to insure Luther's safe conduct, sat with rigid dignity on his black charger, the eagle on the imperial banner snapping in the spring breeze.

Haughty and condescending when he first arrived in Wittenberg, the imperial herald gradually began to change. As Sturm witnessed the masses of people cramming the streets of village after village, and city after city, hailing Luther as if he were the emperor himself, his hauteur dissolved into respectful silence; at times there was a trace of fear in his eyes. Luther had noticed. Sturm's features betrayed him, the longing in his eyes, and the furrow on his brow.

Though the emperor's promise of safe conduct had forbidden Luther to preach en route to the diet, pressed by the locals, he often exhorted villagers from the oxcart. At the roadside inns where they ate their meals and spent the night, Sturm appeared to have a growing appreciation for Luther's music, his jocularity, and the warmth and passion that emanated from the man.

Now, April 16, 1521, Luther, accompanied by Amsdorf, sat lurching in an oxcart down the cobbled streets of Worms. His stomach churning, Luther looked up at the imposing round tower of the cathedral rising high above the city. It had come. He had appealed to the emperor, and now it had come. Shouting brought his mind back to the immediate present.

"Luther! Luther!" as in Erfurt and Oppenheim, the streets were crammed with people, waving scarves, stomping their feet, shouting his name, laughing, and crying with joy. Others chanted, *"Buntschuh! Buntschuh!"*

Luther felt the heat rising on his brow. *Buntschuh*, the wooden working clog of the common farmer—the word had become the partisan cry of the peasantry on the eve of revolt. He gripped the edge of the cart; he wanted to rise, rebuke them, stop their chanting. Perhaps it was a scheme of his enemies, stir the rabble into a revolutionary frenzy and thereby discredit gospel teaching.

"Steady, my friend." Amsdorf clamped his fingers around Luther's arm.

Luther slept little that night. After breakfast on the morning of April 17, he spent the day in prayer and study, sometimes feeling confident and exhilarated, more often feeling crushed by the weight of the foreboding cloud pressing hard down on him. "I am fearful and trembling," he admitted to Amsdorf.

Accompanied by an imperial marshal, Caspar Sturm arrived in the afternoon to escort Luther before the emperor, Amsdorf attending. One plodding foot in front of the other, Luther felt like he was being led to the slaughter.

His stomach lurched as he heard the clanking of the latch, the creaking of the hinges as the great double doors were flung open before him. At the far end of the room, seated on a throne, was young Emperor Charles V; radiating around him was an assembly of six electors, Frederick the Wise near the middle, and two dozen apologists. Imperial marshal at one elbow and Caspar Sturm at the other, Luther felt himself prodded forward.

The imperial sovereign narrowed his eyes at Luther. Jutting his chin, the corners of his mouth downturned with scorn, Charles leaned over to the pope's ambassador, Girolamo Aleander. "That fellow will never make a heretic of me," he quipped in an audible whisper.

"Has the whole world gone wrong," replied Aleander, "and this Satan alone has eyes to see?"

Luther's mouth was parched, and his throat constricted. Who was he, the peasant son of a miner standing before the newly crowned heir of an illustrious line of Catholic rulers, sovereign of Germany, Austria, Burgundy, the Low Countries, Spain, and Naples—Holy Roman Emperor, governing more domains than any sovereign since the days of Charlemagne.

His pulse thundering in his temples, Luther felt numb. How had it come to this? Who was he, low-born, simple monk, to stand before such splendor? Either this trial would be the final gasp of endangered grandeurs giving way to a new world order, one of the common man—or it would prove to be more of the same, the hasty crushing of a gnat under the grinding heel of yet another tyrant. Which would it be?

# 36

# HERE I STAND

L uther passed a hand over his brow. Would he be the gnat crushed beneath the heel of yet another tyrant?

"Greater is he who is in you," murmured Amsdorf close in Luther's ear, "than he who is in the world."

The prosecutor, an official of the Archbishop of Trier, paced before a table on which had been arranged rows of Luther's books and pamphlets.

Robes swishing, the prosecutor lifted a stack of books, held them suspended for an instant, then let them drop onto the oak table with a *Thud!* As it echoed through the hall, the voices of the delegates dwindled into silence.

"These books," said the prosecutor, "are they yours?"

Attempting to clear his throat, Luther nodded, fearful that his voice would not sound when he opened his lips. "The books are all mine," he managed at last, "and I have written more."

The prosecutor spun on his slippered heel, parading before the emperor, his back to Luther. "Do you, Martin Luther, defend them all, or do you care to reject a part?"

Luther did not immediately reply. Stepping closer to the table, "If I may?" he said, taking up first one and then another of his books in hand. "This one touches on God and his Word. This book is about the salvation of souls." Setting the books down, Luther turned toward the emperor. "Christ said, 'He who denies me before men, him will I deny before my father.' To say too little or too much would be dangerous. I beg you, give me time to think it over."

Waggling his head, the prosecutor feigned amazement, his arms spread wide. Touching his forehead in mock bewilderment, he said, "Think it over? Give you time?" He flung an arm in a wide arc over the pile of books. "It takes a very long time to write a single book. Here lie dozens of your books, and you wish us to believe you require more time?"

While the diet fell into deliberation of the request, the hall was abuzz with speculation. "He is stalling," growled one delegate. "Look at him. He is terrified," said another. "Perhaps, at last he has come to his senses."

Luther stood unblinking, hearing all, wincing at the lurching and gurgling coming from his intestines. His mind raced back to Erfurt Cathedral, his first time to preside over the mass, the abject terror he felt standing before and in the place of God. His mind was in turmoil, haunted by that inner voice: "Are you alone wise?"

"It is over," said Amsdorf, taking Luther by the elbow and leading him from the hall, "at least for today. The emperor extends his clemency until tomorrow."

Wiping sweat from his brow with the back of his sleeve, jostled by the press of the crowd, Luther followed.

That evening Ulrich von Hutton, vassal knight, poet, and man of learning called at the Johanniterhof Inn, Luther's lodging.

"It is time to strike a blow," he said, pacing before Luther, candle light shimmering on the intricate etching on his breastplate. "We have an army, ready and awaiting the word."

"An army?" said Luther. Agitated he too rose and paced the room.

"Between knights loyal to Franz von Sickingen and my own," continued Hutton, "we have a sufficient army. When we advance, others will join us in the glorious cause. At present, much of the emperor's army is occupied, fighting the Turks. The time is ripe."

Luther halted, his hands raised in protest. "I commend you for your zeal, my friend. But taking up arms? Defending the innocent, perhaps. But advancing the gospel by the sword?"

"We are at our strength," said Hutton, slapping his gauntlet across his palm. "If we wait, we are doomed."

"My friend, it is our enemy who is doomed," said Luther. "It is not in our own strength that we face the foe. We have the right man on our side, our champion Jesus Christ. He must win the battle for us."

"True, indeed. But by means of our sword," said Hutton, laying his hand on the hilt of his own.

"'He who lives by the sword,'" said Luther wearily, "'perishes by the sword.'"

"Well said, my friend," said Amsdorf when the knight finally left them.

Throughout the long night, Luther's stomach felt like a lump of dough being pummeled and kneaded by the iron fingers of the baker. He slept little. The waiting was agonizing. His summons to appear did not come until late in the afternoon of the next day.

Unlike the previous day, the bishop's palatial hall was crammed with bodies: scarlet-clad cardinals, silken-robed princes, scowling archbishops, and Roman apologists. The chaos of noise—the undulating roar of voices, the scuffling of feet—was deafening. The emperor and electors were seated in gilded chairs. Everyone else stood, crammed shoulder to shoulder and back to front.

At a nod from Charles V, the hall fell silent. Without further ado, the prosecutor confronted Luther, restating his question of the previous day as if no time had elapsed.

Luther groaned. He felt it rising in his gorge, that all-too-familiar wave of nausea. Clenching his teeth, he took a deep breath. "Most serene emperor, most illustrious princes, most clement lords, if I have not given some of you your proper titles I beg you to forgive me. I am not a courtier but a monk. You asked me yesterday whether the books were mine and whether I would repudiate them. They are all mine, but as for the second question, they are not all of one sort."

The prosecutor frowned, drawing breath to speak. "This is not a debate. You are here to answer our questions not pose your own." At a wafture of the emperor's hand, the prosecutor fell silent. The emperor nodded for Luther to continue.

"They are not all of one sort," repeated Luther, reasonably. "Some deal with faith and life so simply and evangelically that my very enemies are compelled to regard them as worthy of Christian reading. Even the bull itself does not treat all my books as of one kind. If I should renounce these, I would be the only man on earth to damn the truth confessed alike by friends and foes. A second class of my works inveighs against the desolation of the Christian world by the evil lives and teaching of the papists. Who can deny this when universal complaints testify that by the laws of the popes the consciences of men are racked?"

"No!" cried the emperor, leaning forward in his throne.

A rumbling of angry protest rose from the cardinals and bishops. The prosecutor called for order. Scowling, the emperor sat back but signaled for Luther to go on.

"Our German nation has suffered under an incredible tyranny at the hands of greedy popes. Should I recant at this point, I would open the door to more tyranny and impiety, and it will be all the worse should it appear that I had done so under pressure of the Holy Roman Empire.

"A third class," he continued, "contains attacks on private individuals. I confess I have been more caustic than comports with my profession, but I am being judged, not on my life, but for the teaching of Christ, and I cannot renounce these works either, without increasing tyranny and impiety. When Christ stood before Annas, he said, 'Produce witnesses.'

"If our Lord, who could not err, made this demand, why may not a worm like me ask to be convicted of error from the prophets and the Gospels? If I am shown my error, I will be the first to throw my books into the fire. I have been reminded of the dissensions which my teaching engenders. I can answer only in the words of the Lord, 'I came not to bring peace but a sword.'

"If our God is so severe, let us beware lest we release a deluge of wars, lest the reign of this noble youth, Charles, be inauspicious. Take warning from the examples of Pharaoh, the king of Babylon, and the kings of Israel. God it is who confounds the wise. I must walk in the fear of the Lord. I say this not to chide but because I cannot escape my duty to my countrymen. I commend myself to Your Majesty. May you not suffer my adversaries to make you ill-disposed to me without cause. I have spoken."

"Martin Luther, you have not sufficiently distinguished your works," said the prosecutor. "The earlier were bad and the latter worse."

Laughter rose from the papal delegates and some of the electors.

The prosecutor brought his fist down on a pile of Luther's books. "Your plea to be heard from Scripture is the one always made by heretics! You do nothing but renew the errors

200

of Wycliffe and Hus. How can you assume that you are the only one to understand the sense of Scripture? Would you put your judgment above that of so many famous men and claim that you know more than they all? I ask you, Martin Luther, answer candidly and without horns, do you or do you not repudiate your books and the errors which they contain?"

The hall fell strangely silent. Everyone held their breath, not wanting to miss a single word. Sweat dribbled off Luther's nose and chin.

"Since then Your Majesty and your lordships desire a simple reply," he began, his voice growing stronger, "I will answer without horns and without teeth. Unless I am convicted by Scripture and plain reason; I do not accept the authority of popes and councils, for they have contradicted each other. My conscience is captive to the Word of God. I cannot and I will not recant anything, for to go against conscience is neither right nor safe. God help me. Here I stand, I cannot do otherwise."

"Not in your German, if you please," said the prosecutor, his arms crossed, drumming his fingers on his sleeve. "In holy Latin."

Luther swallowed, wiping his sleeve across his forehead.

Amsdorf called from the audience, "If you cannot do it, Martin, you have done enough."

Luther repeated the words in Latin. "My conscience is captive to the Word of God. I cannot and I will not recant anything. God help me. Amen!" Throwing up his arms in triumph, he shouted, "Here I stand, I cannot do otherwise!"

While the hall erupted with hissing and shouting from the papal inquisitors, Hutton and Amsdorf surrounded Luther and escorted him back to his lodging.

Spalatin joined them later that night. "The duke was elated. 'Doctor Martin spoke wonderfully before the emperor, the princes, and the estates, in Latin and in German, but he is too daring for me.' So spoke the elector."

"It was a marvelous stand," said Amsdorf, "words of great power hurled before the emperor."

"Balaam's ass," said Luther, waving his hand dismissively, "was wiser than the prophet himself. If God then spoke by an ass against a prophet, why should he not be able even now to speak by a humble man against the pope and emperor?"

"But will Frederick persuade the council?" asked Amsdorf.

"Certainly not." Spalatin shook his head. "At least four of the six electors will cast their vote against you, Martin." There was silence in the room. "You will be condemned."

Amsdorf stood up, his chair clattering onto the flagstone floor. "We must flee. There's no time to lose. We must get Doctor Luther to safety before it is too late."

"Safety? Where is such a place?" said Spalatin. "Martin, the emperor will declare you a notorious heretic."

"We can only hope and pray," said Amsdorf, "the promised safe conduct is honored."

Spalatin wrung his hands. "I am more concerned about papal thuggery. The emperor may officially honor the safe conduct, but behind closed doors turn a blind eye to the gnashing schemes of papal inquisitors."

"What are you implying," asked Luther, "treachery?"

Spalatin bit his lower lip. "There are many desolate miles of road between Worms and Wittenberg."

# 37

# ABDUCTION

Throughout the duration of the diet, Luther had slept poorly at the Johanniterhof lodging in Worms. The strain of the trial before the emperor, the constant grinding in his stomach, his own doubts, combined with the lack of sleep, had depressed him and made him restless.

The lurching rhythm of the oxcart clattering along the roadway put him into a disjointed trance, a delirious lethargy coming over him, wherein he was aware of things going on around him but only vaguely, as if observing them from the tops of the massive fir trees deep in the Thuringian Forest through which the roadway now traversed.

Yet even in such a restive state, his mind was active, muttering to him as if from the treetops flicking by overhead. "Do I believe?" he murmured. "Then I must speak boldly. Do I speak boldly? Then I must suffer. Do I suffer? Do I confess my faith? The cross must follow. And I shall be comforted."

The cart lurched in a pothole. Luther's head clonked against the side rail of the cart.

"What is it, Martin?" Armsdorf appeared to have been dozing himself.

"Was I speaking?" said Luther, grimacing and touching his temple with his fingers.

"Indeed, you were."

Luther rubbed his eyes. He looked forward, past the slumped figure of their taciturn driver and the broad shoulders of the oxen, and rubbed them again. Turning around, he frowned at the vacant road snaking into the gathering darkness behind them.

"Where is he?" He sat up, straining to see better. "Caspar, our imperial escort? Where did he go?"

"He left this for you," said Amsdorf, handing Luther a folded piece of paper.

Eyeing Amsdorf, Luther took it and read, "'God is your fortress. He will rescue you.'" He turned it over. "It is unsigned. Why would he not sign it?"

Amsdorf looked at Luther reproachfully. "Logic, Herr Doctor. He is herald to the emperor who just condemned you as a notorious heretic. If Sturm signed such a friendly message, he could be condemned for aiding and abetting you." He drew his index finger across his throat.

Luther nodded, rereading the note. "Is he attempting to warn us of treachery?" He glanced behind them as he spoke. "Do you hear it?"

"Hear what?" said Amsdorf. "Apart from the plodding hooves of the beasts pulling our conveyance, I hear nothing."

"Springtime deep in the forest," said Luther, "and you hear nothing. Where are the song birds? Where is the merry calling of the warbler?" He hesitated. "Or the grunting of the bear, or the howling of the wolf?"

"*Nein.* There is nothing." Amsdorf's voice was low and strained. He gripped the rail of the cart; his knuckles shone white.

Luther narrowed his eyes at his friend. "Do you know more than you are telling?"

Palms up, Amsdorf shrugged. "What is there to know?"

In a sudden gust of wind, fir branches reaching out over the roadway above them rustled and moaned. As if answering the trees, a lone wolf howl pierced the silence: mournful and menacing.

"Not entirely silent." Luther's voice was barely a whisper. To their cart driver, he said, "Is there an inn, a cloister, anything nearby where we might find refuge from this demon forest?"

"Schloss Altenstein lies hard by," said the driver.

At his words, dark clouds shrouded the pale sunlight that had occasionally flashed through the dense stand of trees that encircled them.

Heaving and blowing, the oxen came to a stand.

Eyes darting at the shadowy forest, Luther felt his heart beating in his gorge.

Suddenly, from all sides, erupted the sounds of pounding hooves, snorting horses, creaking harness leather, clanking armor and weapons, and shouts of men. Five mounted knights, their faces shrouded and indistinct, accosted them.

"Halt! Which of you is Luther, the heretic Martin Luther?"

"I am he." Luther raised his hand, and began rising to his feet. "Let these others go."

Without another word, they yanked Luther to his feet and dragged him from the cart. Cramming a coarse sack over his head, they tied it roughly around his neck.

From that blind, muffled world, Luther was forced to piece together the subsequent events without the benefit of sight. His sense of hearing and smell, however, were intensified by the hood and his lack of sight. Strong arms shoved him forward; amidst grunting and cursing, he was hoisted onto a horse. He felt a cord being tied around his wrists, then drawn tight against the horn of the saddle. As the horse lurched beneath him and began trotting, Luther hunkered forward, gripping the animal with his knees. By the sounds around him, his captors had hemmed him in on all sides. There was no escape.

During that dark and grueling ride, Luther's mind was awhirl. Who were they? Common thugs? Not infrequently there were robberies and knifings, stories of ruffians bludgeoning a traveler to death for the coins in his money pouch. Anything could happen on these roads. Then why did they not slit his throat and be done with it? And why prey on a penniless monk? Luther feared the worst. These were henchmen on a murderous undertaking commissioned by the emperor or the pope.

Every bone in his body ached, and the sack cinched so tightly at his throat restricted his breathing. Just when he feared he was about to faint, his horse suddenly halted.

Then new sounds: the bulky rattling of chain, winding of gears, clonking of heavy wooden planking against stone. His horse lurched forward again, hooves clopping on wood—a bridge, perhaps a drawbridge, surely it must be. And then again the sounds of chain and gears, and the portentous closing-to of heavy iron-studded gates.

"Enough of this!" said a voice.

# 38

# WARTBURG

E nough of this!"
Luther felt the grip of his captors lifting him from
the saddle. As his feet met the ground, pain shot
through his legs; he feared they would crumple beneath him.
There was fiddling at his throat, then a quick jerk.

Though it was full dark, he squinted; impulsively he raised
a hand to block the light. He smelt something burning, and
heard the hissing and popping of flames and tallow fuel. Heat
radiated near his face. Was it a nightmare? Had the devil
returned in new guise to torment him? Blinking, he peered at
the light. Casting eerie shadows, torchlight illuminated the
faces of his abductors. There were more than five men
surrounding him now.

"I am Burkhard von Hund," said one of them. He broke
into a smile and extended his hand in greeting.

"And I am John of Berlepsch," said another,
"commandant of Schloss Wartburg, your new home."

Luther had never been more bewildered. In the light of the torches, he looked around him at the massive square towers rising into the moonlight. Thick walls formed a crenellated fortress around the courtyard and the inner buildings of the castle. Across the courtyard, candlelight flickered from inside rows of round-arched stained glass windows.

"You are weary from your travels, no doubt," said Burkhard. "I will show you to your quarters and have refreshment brought to you."

Luther, so bone weary he remembered little else about that first night, awoke the next morning feeling more rested than he had for weeks.

Stepping to the window, he peered through the round leaded panes. His room must be in the highest tower of the castle, and judging from the panoramic view of the Thuringian forest and hills, morning mist clinging to the valleys, the castle sat atop the highest point for miles.

Unlatching and opening the window, Luther looked straight down the stone wall to the rocky foundations of the castle and the forest floor far below. His stomach lurched at the sight. Looking to his right, he could see the crenellated wall zig-zagging as it followed the irregular contour of the ridge line. He had little to fear from an attacker in this place. Likewise, would there be no escaping from such a fortification.

*Tap, tap*, sounded at his door. "*Guten Morgan*! It is Burkhard von Hund. May I enter?"

Luther opened the door. His host had brought a hot breakfast from the castle kitchen. While Luther ate, Burkhard explained everything.

"But who is my benefactor?" asked Luther.

"I have given my word," said Burkhard, with the toss of his head and a wink. "Now, then. Whilst you are in our protection, you are no longer Martin Luther. Your new name is *Junker Jörg.*"

"Ridiculous! Why am I to be called Knight George?"

"Your protector wishes it so," said Burkhard simply. "To complete your disguise, and for your greater protection, we must destroy your old garments," he continued. "You will now wear the garb of a vassal knight."

Burkhard had a servant boy lay out Luther's new clothes. He rose to go.

"My lute?" said Luther, his brow furrowed. "I had it with me in the cart."

Burkhart smiled. "I will have it sent up."

Luther looked confused.

"We were given very precise instructions," said Burkhart. He turned to go, but stopped himself. "One other small matter. You are not to shave." The warden touched his own head and pattered his fingers at his chin. "No shaving tonsure or chin. Knights are very fond of hair on head and chin."

Luther stared at the trousers and hose, the tunic and leather jerkin, the knee-high riding boots and spurs, the breastplate and buckler, the dagger, the sword. He rose and went back to the window.

His first robing at Erfurt Cathedral at his first mass, the recollection flooded him. Everything had to be perfect. The monk's habit was sacred, a sign of innocence and renunciation; it was everything to a monk. A monk who died without his cowl would be denied entry into heaven by St. Benedict, could only peep in at the glories but never partake—not without his monkish habit. Luther ran a hand over the shaved crown of his head. And now this.

"Farewell, you miserable cowl," he said, "insufficient to ransom from sin and from death! Farewell, proud robe, which they compare—nay, which they prefer—to the spotless robe and precious blood of Jesus Christ. Farewell!"

209

Relating it later, Luther felt this was a critical pass. Though he had been formally defrocked for his own freedom by Staupitz, deep down, he had continued to cling to his monastic vows. This was a final test. He was not being asked to sacrifice his only son—just his wardrobe, and the haircut he had so long worn. Laughing out loud, long and hard, he unlaced the Augustinian habit he had worn for over fifteen years and tore it off his body.

"If man is saved by grace through faith alone, this is what becomes of the monastic life. Monkery and salvation by grace are in flagrant opposition. Monkery must fall! Monks are the pillars of the popedom." He was shouting, almost singing the words.

Frantic, Luther sat down at the writing desk; dipping the quill in the ink pot, he wrote. "I will throw down these pillars. God has made nothing which Satan has not mocked in caricature; and because it was God's will to have a nation of priests, Satan has made a nation of monks. No! I am not a monk! I am a new creature, not of the pope, but of Jesus Christ. Christ alone, Christ without a mediator, is my bishop, my abbot, my prior, my Lord, my Father, my Master; and I will have no other!" He paused, dipping his pen. "The monks, the fleas on God Almighty's fur coat, must be gone!"

A flutter on the wide sill of the open window caught the corner of his eye. Luther rose to investigate. "Ah, my feathered friend. You have come to spy on me, see if I will give it up. Did the pope send you? Or was it the emperor?" With a flick of its wings, the lark took to flight. Luther watched as the bird plunged and cavorted, at last disappearing in the forest far below.

When Burkhart returned with Luther's lute, he had a servant in tow, the boy's arms loaded to his chin with more parchment. "We are instructed never to let you run out of paper and ink. Food and drink, perhaps, but never paper and ink. So we were instructed."

As Luther thanked them, he felt something nudging against his feet.

"Ah, forgive me; we have left the door ajar," said Burkhart. "Though there are few people, there are many cats at the Wartburg. This fat one believes he is lord of the castle."

Luther narrowed his eyes at the cat. Flicking its tail, it purred loudly, rubbing its long wheat-colored fur against his shins.

Burkhart signaled for the servant to pick up the cat. Luther held up his hand. "*Nein*. He will give me someone to talk to, perhaps throw things at, if necessary."

Later in the day, the warden showed Luther around the castle. Built nearly five hundred years before, the castle was like no other Luther had visited. Though there seemed to be hardly any occupants to enjoy it, he could not help but admire its splendid columns, rounded arches, soaring ceilings, the gilded vaulting adorned with intricate mosaic images.

"This is the Singers' Hall," explained Burkhart, "where people have gathered for centuries to engage in singing competitions, rather gladiatorial ones. Legend has it they escalated to serious life or death contests, with death to the loser."

"How barbaric!" said Luther, his words echoing throughout the stone hall. Charmed by the vibrant acoustics, Luther could not restrain himself; he broke into the *Te Deum*, his clear voice swelling and resonating throughout the chamber.

Burkhart grimaced. "I pity your singing competitor."

Luther's mind raced back to the burning of the papal bull and his students singing in Latin. He felt it coming over him, anger that bordered on rage. Energized by singing, and by his recollection, he returned to his chamber.

The instant he stepped into his room, he knew something was wrong. The window, open as he had left it, and there was the lark, perched on the sill. But crouching on Luther's writing desk, quivering with anticipation, was the wheat-colored cat, ready to pounce.

"It is so with the pope," said Luther with a laugh. The lark fluttered away to safety. "Leo watches me, ready to pounce upon me if I go out of these walls, if I try to escape this kingdom of the birds, my Patmos, my wilderness, my dungeon."

Luther reached down and stroked the cat, its spine arching at his touch, its tail twitching. "But I fear him not. I am more afraid of my own heart than of the pope and all his cardinals. I have within me the great pope, Self." The cat rumbled, purring contentedly at his touch.

"Perhaps, my feline friend, I have discovered a name for you. *Jawohl*, I shall call you 'Pope Leo.' You are so like the pontiff: luxury-loving, living to be served, caring for your comfort alone, bowing to none, and covering yourself in gold. 'Pope Leo' it is."

Luther took up his lute. With a wafture of his hand, he said, "I dismiss you, Pope Leo. I have work to do."

For several hours, as if nothing else mattered in all the world, Luther sat at his desk, lute on his knee, alternating plucking out a tune, snatching up his quill, muttering to himself, scribbling notes and lines of poetry, and then back to the lute.

"There now," he said at last. "I dedicate this to Pope Leo." And then he sang, not in Latin, but in German:

In devil's dungeon chained I lay,
The pangs of death swept o'er me.
My sin devoured me night and day
In which my mother bore me.
My anguish ever grew more rife;
I took no pleasure in my life,
And sin had made me crazy.

There were several more stanzas, all in German, comprising a poetic and musical confession of faith. Curled at Luther's feet, Pope Leo purred rhythmically along with the music.

"Music is the art of the prophets," murmured Luther, setting aside his lute and taking up his pen. Still purring, Pope Leo batted with a paw at the lute strings.

"Music is the only other art," continued Luther, writing as he spoke, "alongside theology, which can calm the agitations of my soul—and put the devil to flight."

# 39

# GOOSE QUILLS

Weeks plodded into months at the Wartburg. Luther learned snatches of the latest news from his protector. Or was it his captor? Sometimes he resented Burkhart and saw him more as a prison warden. But he did bring Luther news.

Apparently Luther's disappearance was on the lips of all Europe. While his enemies rejoiced, hoping it was the end of him, German peasants were on the verge of revolt; their champion had been destroyed, and they would have their revenge. While the emperor wrung his hands at the tumult in his realm, scholars, artists, and students grieved and speculated.

At word of the disappearance of Luther, it was rumored that the celebrated artist Albrecht Durer was in anguish. "I know not whether he lives or is murdered, but in any case he has suffered for the Christian truth. If we lose this man, who has written more clearly than any other in centuries, may God grant his spirit to another. His books should be held in great honor, and not burned as the emperor commands, rather burn the books of his enemies. O God, if Luther is dead, who will henceforth explain to us the gospel? What might he not have written for us in the next ten or twenty years?"

Beautifully situated though the Wartburg Castle was, Luther felt like a caged bear within its vacant walls, and fell into depression. Fresh food was scarce, and his stomach grew worse. Bent double, he groaned under the relentless agony. When he wanted food, he became anxious, even fearful. Food wanted him. Hungry though he was, when he ate, the meat and drink, like the pope, seemed to turn on him, gnawing away on his innards.

So he labored night and day with his pen, working until he collapsed onto his bed with exhaustion. There, perversely, he could not sleep, thrashing in his sweat through the long nights.

"They will take advantage of my absence," he moaned into the darkness, "and undo the work I have begun. Some fools will charge me with running away, being a deserter. I would rather be stretched on burning coals than stagnate here rotting, half dead."

Plagued by sleeplessness, tormented in the bowels, and oppressed by the enemy, Luther, at times, delirious with bitterness, raged aloud at the devil.

One night, as he slumped over his desk, numb with exhaustion, but attempting to write, the candle flickered; his pulse thundered in his temples, and his vision blurred. Wiping a hand across his sweaty face, he moaned.

Pope Leo, purring at his feet, suddenly leapt onto the desk and curled up opposite the writing things, watching Luther. As Luther stared back at the creature, the candle flickered again, and the animal's face began to change. He rubbed his eyes. From smug, whiskered contentment, the cat's features became fleshy; jowls emerged where fur had been; the luxurious wheat-colored coat on its back metamorphosed into a red cape, and the creature's dreamy eyes became black orbs of condescension and haughty ambition.

At the crimson apparition taking shape before him, Luther was terrified. He snatched up the nearest thing. His inkpot. Cocking his arm, about to hurl it at his oppressor, he hesitated, blinking rapidly. Ink could be difficult to come by. He turned the pot in his hands, eyeing its ebony depths. Better to drive away the devil with the ink in the pot than waste it. Shape the ink into defiance, and thereby drive the devil back to the pit where he belongs. "Satan, I defy thee!" he shouted, thudding the ink pot back onto the desk where it belonged.

Burkhart came to see him in the morning. He looked anxiously at Luther. "Herr Doctor, are you not well?"

Luther waved a hand and attempted to laugh. "It is well with my soul," he said, "though not so much with this decaying carcass." He paused. "There are times when I feel oppressed, as if the devil is here in my chamber taunting me, tormenting me, in body, mind, and spirit."

Burkhart, a master of the art of listening, nodded encouragingly. Luther continued, unburdening more of his troubles to the sympathetic warden.

When Luther fell silent, Burkhart, nodding kindly, said, "I have read many of your books with great encouragement." Gently, and without chiding, the good caretaker summarized Luther's own writing on learning from Holy Scripture, by the Holy Spirit, 'the only master and tutor to teach us therein,' especially when weighed down by the devil's trials and temptations.

"But best of all," continued Burkhart, "these words of yours have come to my aid: 'When I find myself in temptation, then I quickly lay hold and fasten on some text in the Bible which Christ Jesus lays before me, namely, that he died for me, from whence I have and receive comfort.'"

While the good man spoke, Luther had gone to the window. Smoke from charcoal burners rose in a dense cloud atop a ridgeline in the forest. As he watched, a breeze rustled across the treetops. The charcoal smoke thinned, then dissipated altogether, and sunlight flooded the scene.

"You have been a beacon, good Burkhart," said Luther, turning from the window and grasping the man's hand. "I see my way more clearly. God is in this exile. He wants me captive here in this dungeon. And so I will use my captivity. I will use it to translate the New Testament into German, into our mother tongue."

"All of it?" said his warden. "It is a great work."

Luther turned, pacing the floor of his chamber, agitated, enlivened. "Scripture without comment, it is the sun whence all teachers receive their light. Oh, if this book," he said, snatching up his Greek New Testament, "if this book could but be in the hands, still more, in the hearts, of all!" He laughed. "Then Luther must retire, and the Bible advance; this poor man must disappear, and God in Christ appear!"

Invigorated, Luther resumed his work. Though he felt out of the fray, a castaway, idle while others labored, that work was prodigious. In a few short months he translated the entire New Testament into German.

Meanwhile, stimulated by his careful study of the precise meaning of the words of the biblical text laid out before him, Luther would pause in his translation work, writing in one place a treatise on the Lord's Supper: "Blockhead pontiffs got it wrong. It is not a sacrifice but a celebration, a thanksgiving." And close on its heels, he wrote another treatise on giving both elements of the Supper, bread and wine, to all confessing Christians.

Whole books expounding passages from the Gospels and the Epistles followed. And he wrote letters, one to Albert of Mainz, urging him to be a shepherd not a wolf, and halt at once the renewed peddling of indulgences, "Or I shall write a tract against you!"

The devil, so it appeared, frantic at Luther's output, redoubled efforts to torment him. Luther felt and heard bats circling his head in the night, and wine casks tumbling down the staircase from his bower chamber.

"The best way to drive out the devil," he told Burkhart one morning, "if he will not yield to texts of Scripture, is to jeer and flout him, for he cannot bear scorn."

Opening the window to let the morning light in, the warden nodded encouragingly.

"Worst of all," said Luther, "the fiend hates goose quills!"

"Well, then," said Burkhart, "give him more to hate."

# 40

# APOSTATE MONK

As the months passed, Luther watched the seasons change on the forested hills surrounding the Wartburg Castle. Birch leaves turned golden, dry and raspy in the autumn breezes, then fell from their branches. Winter set in. Through the round leaded panes of his bowyer window, now rimed with frost, he watched snow dusting the trees as midwinter approached.

All the while, Luther wrote. "Give the devil more to hate," so his kind warden had urged him. Warming his fingers over the candle, cutting a fresh point on his quill, Luther gave himself up to the task.

While writing an exposition of the epistle to the Ephesians, Luther found himself arrested by Paul's words to husbands, "love your wives as Christ has loved his Church and has given himself for her." His mind immediately bolted back to what he had discovered about the subject in previous study.

"Marriage, the God-appointed and legitimate union of man and woman… to seek love… to live with one's wife in contentment and in the fear of God… There is no more lovely, friendly and charming relationship, communion or company than a good marriage."

Cold as midwinter in the Thuringian forest is, Luther's heart grew warm. He labored on a treatise that would become a grand apologetic for Christian marriage. One evening he asked Burkhart to read over it. "This is the book that will empty the cloisters," said his warden with feeling. "And make families, happy ones with many children in them."

When not occupied with translation and other writing, Luther gave himself to expounding the Psalms, trying his hand at versifying the ancient Hebrew poetry into German hymns. From there he labored at poetic expositions of other passages, hymns on themes found in the Epistles and the Gospels. He explained to Burkhart one evening what he was attempting to do.

"Music is a great gift of God," he said. Frowning, he continued. "But I shall never forget seeing most of my flock in Wittenberg fall silent when it was time to shout and sing; since they knew not the Latin, they fell mute, like a herd of cows staring at a new gate."

"So what will you do?" asked Burkhart.

Luther toyed with a parchment on his desk. "When God speaks to us in his Word, German Christians need to reply to him with hymns—sung in German." He twirled his pen between his fingers. "For which I need more poets— German poets! O, but how the devil hates these goose quills!"

"I have seen you at it," said Burkhart, "gnawing on your tongue, scribbling at your poetry."

Luther shrugged. "I am never sure if it is my gift. Writing poetry occupies not just the fist or the foot while the rest of the body can be otherwise disposed; it occupies the whole man. Perhaps I am not fit, and my energies should be expended elsewhere, leave hymn writing to the real poets."

Burkhart smiled. "Perhaps, Herr Doctor, you *are* a real poet." His features brightened, and he slapped his knee with a gauntlet. "I have it! Come with me to the Singers' Hall. There is no better place to hear music. We shall settle this, I as judicator."

Once inside the ancient chapel, Luther blew warmth into his fingers and began tuning his lute.

"As of old in this Singers' Hall," said Burkhart, "let the competition commence!"

Luther hesitated, eyeing his warden. "Not, I hope, a singing competition to the death?"

Burkhart laughed. "*Nein.* To the life—the life eternal!"

Cocking his ear toward the pear-shaped body of the instrument, Luther fine-tuned the strings. He felt the fighting sternness that so often roiled within him subside. He closed his eyes, breathing in the mysterious tranquility of the music. As it anointed him, settling over his spirit, he felt a softening of the rigid places, a sweetening of the bitter turmoil that had taken hold of him.

His fingers moving skillfully over the strings, Luther played through a hymn tune, one that had come to his imagination simultaneously while writing the lines of poetry. And then he sang, the expressive tonality of his lute conjoining with his voice. The Singers' Hall came alive, the barrel vaulted ceiling resonating with a new song, one about love, children, the incarnation, the birth of a baby, the Son of God.

All praise to thee, Eternal Lord,
Clothed in a garb of flesh and blood;
Choosing a manger for thy throne,
While worlds on worlds are thine alone.

Once did the skies before thee bow;
A virgin's arms contain thee now,
While angels, who in thee rejoice,
Now listen for thine infant voice.

A little child, thou art our guest,
That weary ones in thee may rest;
Forlorn and lowly is thy birth;
That we may rise to heaven from earth.

Thou comest in the darksome night
To make us children of the light;
To make us, in the realms divine,
Like thine own angels round thee shine.

All this for us thy love hath done;
By this to thee our love is won;
For this we tune our cheerful lays,
And sing our thanks in ceaseless praise.

Luther remained still as the final strains of the hymn reverberated throughout the medieval hall. In the hush that followed, he laid down his lute, studying his warden's face. "Well?"

Leaning forward, elbows on his knees, Burkhart stared intently at Luther, his face perplexed, as if doubting what had just transpired before his senses. When he spoke, his voice was hushed, reverent, halting as if groping for the right words.

"It is a marvel. I have never heard the like. 'Rise to heaven from earth,' it is what you have, herein, accomplished. The music, the voice, the lyric—it is the very finest." Burkhart rose to his feet, pacing the chancel. "Though, in truth, you must know, I am but a coarse man, unfit to be judicator of such high things."

Burkhart halted, regarding Luther closely. "Yet, I will make bold to say, this hymn sounds as if it were penned by the tender father of infants and children, the husband of a wife."

Rapping his knuckles on his instrument, Luther grunted. "While all the while it was written by a peasant son of a miner, a violent man, unfit for domesticity, a celibate monk."

Burkhart laughed. "Now an apostate monk!"

# 41

# LUSTY SINNERS

After eleven months of solitude, sometimes maddeningly tedious months they were at the Wartburg, Luther's heart swelled as he stepped into his pulpit at the Stadtkirche and looked out over his Wittenberg flock.

Something had changed. His time in exile made it more obvious to him. There was an atmosphere of jostling restlessness emanating from his congregation. Melanchthon and Amsdorf had warned him in letters that some in the town were worked into a frenzy. There had even been violence. Students had attacked some of the twenty-five priests still employed to say mass at the Castle Church. Luther scanned the walls of the Stadtkirche; not a statue remained. In his absence the stonework had been smashed.

As he began his sermon, his eyes passing over the familiar faces, he again marveled at how vociferously he had protested at becoming their pastor. There was little Liesel, merry eyes wide apart, smiling up at him; a bit older now, and her grandmother, more stooped, more wrinkled, more haggard, yet still alive. As he read out his text and commenced his exposition, he felt the balm of his own message washing over himself.

"The doctrine of justification by faith alone is a fragile doctrine. Not in itself, of course, but in us. I know how quickly you and I can forfeit the joy of the gospel.

"All your good works, your best efforts, without this justifying gift of faith—are idle and damnable sins! To the man who comes to God's house this day, proud of his good conduct, preening himself that he is not like that festering neighbor of his, I have a message for you. Sin for all you are worth. God can only forgive a lusty sinner!"

Murmuring rippled through the congregation.

"Christ did not come to call the self-righteous, dear people, but to call sinners to repentance. God works by contraries so that a man feels himself to be lost in the very moment when he is on the point of being saved. When God is about to justify a man, he damns him. Whom he would make alive he must first kill."

Luther's voice rose with energy, filling the city church, resonating into the darkest crypt, the loftiest vault, and, he hoped, into the deepest recesses of every heart.

"God's favor is so communicated in the form of wrath," he continued, "that it seems farthest when it is at hand. Man must first cry out that there is no health in him. It is then, when a man believes himself to be utterly lost, that light breaks. Peace comes in the word of Christ through faith. He who does not have this, however morally upright is his conduct, and though he be absolved a million times by the poisonous exhalations the pope vomits forth, that man is lost.

"Dear people of Wittenberg, week-by-week, you are so prone to forget that sinners are justified freely and solely by God's unmerited grace. Thus it is that, week-by-week, you and I must listen to the gospel. It tells me not what I must do, but what Jesus Christ the Son of God has done for me."

After the service, when Luther had been greeted warmly by his congregation at the door of the Stadtkirche, Amsdorf accompanied him back to the cloister and his study.

"'Sin for all you are worth,'" repeated Amsdorf. "'God can only forgive a lusty sinner!' Martin, are you certain you meant to say such a thing? Will it not open the floodgates?" Amsdorf tapped on Luther's Bible. "Does not Scripture everywhere commend upright living?"

Luther smiled at his friend. "Ah, so that is why Jesus reserved his most vociferous denouncements for the upright living Pharisees?"

"All right, he did; there's no denying it," said Amsdorf reasonably. "But you have made statements that could so easily be misconstrued, distorted, made into a license for sinning. After all, did not the Apostle James himself declare that we are not justified merely by faith but by our works as well?"

"Wrongly understood, James is an epistle of straw!" retorted Luther. "True faith is a living, restless thing. It cannot be inoperative. If there be no works there must be something amiss with faith. Mingle works with faith and there will be something amiss with both."

"But your critics, Martin, they will say that you denounce the law and all good works."

"And Paul's critics did not so accuse him?" said Luther. "They railed at him for preaching that one could continue in sin that grace might increase."

"Which he did not preach," said Amsdorf.

"Yet it was precisely his preaching of free grace that left him open to that criticism. No man would ever criticize Pharisees for such preaching."

"Well, that is different."

"Is it so?" said Luther. "I am certain that if the gospel we proclaim does not invite such criticism, such distortion, it is not the same gospel Paul preached."

Amsdorf nodded pensively. "H'm, there is that, and, I admit, Paul was so accused in more places than one."

"You know me, Nicolaus. I am a violent man. It is my method to awaken lethargy in my hearers with thunderclaps. Come now, my friend. I have for these long months been in chains."

"Chains?" said Amsdorf, laughing.

"In a manner of speaking," said Luther, rubbing his wrists and laughing with him. "I did feel so useless. But I must know, Nicolaus, what is the state of things. I felt like a caged animal in the Wartburg, knowing next to nothing. And now Wittenberg feels like a den of lions, and I about to be torn limb from limb by them."

"There have been some rather sweeping changes in your absence," said Amsdorf.

"Such as?"

"New rules for the Supper," he said, not meeting Luther's eye. "Dispensed without ceremony and in both elements to the common people."

"As it should be," said Luther. "Though we must choose our battles carefully. There must be no impediment to freedom in Christ. What else?"

"He removes all images from the Stadtkirche."

"As I observed today," said Luther, nodding. "'He,' you say? Of whom are we speaking?"

Amsdorf cleared his throat. "Uh, Nicolaus."

"Carlstadt?"

"*Ja, ja.*"

"Was it done in an orderly manner?" asked Luther, "or otherwise?"

"The young men," said Amsdorf, biting his lower lip, "you know how over wrought they can become?"

"With violence, then," said Luther, frowning and stroking his beard. "I want no idolatry, certainly. But we must make changes with care, more gradually, within the boundaries of law and order. The people have been long steeped in error. We must not imagine that we can undo centuries of error—" He snapped his fingers. "—just like that. I fear to ask. What other changes?"

Amsdorf did not immediately speak. "He follows young Melanchthon's example."

"Carlstadt?"

"*Ja.*"

Luther looked bewildered. "His example in doing what?"

Amsdorf cleared his throat in his fist. "Taking a wife."

"Carlstadt?" roared Luther, slapping his knee. "Who would have him?"

Amsdorf laughed. "Anna Mochau, has already done so."

"I know the girl," said Luther. "The Bürgermeister's other daughter. Is she of marriageable age?"

"Her family approved the match."

"Then so do I," said Luther. "And he is happy?"

Amsdorf smiled and nodded. "So contented is the man with his wife, he makes the case for replacing mandatory priestly celibacy with mandatory priestly marriage, an obligatory wife for every pastor."

Luther frowned. "But what of freedom in Christ?"

"He makes his case very potently," said Amsdorf.

"As will I," said Luther. "I say there is freedom to marry for every pastor who desires marriage and is so called to marriage—that is, assuming he can find a wife. But never required. Any new regulation that is not expressly found in Holy Writ, I shall always oppose. Always!"

A sharp knock immediately sounded at the door.

"*Komm herein,*" called Luther.

Carlstadt entered the study. "The door was ajar."

228

"For friends, my door is always ajar," said Luther, greeting him warmly.

"I could not help overhearing," Carlstadt said. "What is it you shall always oppose?"

"Surely you know, my friend," said Luther. "I oppose any regulation that restricts liberty in Christ."

"But the time for change is now," said Carlstadt. "There are many practices that are impediments to true Christian worship."

"Such as?"

"Many things," said Carlstadt. "For one, I say we relegate organs, trumpets, and flutes to the theater."

"And lutes?" Smiling, Luther took up his and plucked an impromptu flourish on its strings.

"In the worship of God, yes, excluding lutes," said Carlstadt.

"As you do away with musical instruments," said Luther, "will you also do away with the psalter? 'Praise him with trumpet sound; praise him with lute and harp!' So it reads in my copy."

They haggled for a quarter of an hour about musical instruments in old covenant worship. "We should no more use lutes in our worship," cried Carlstadt, "than we should slaughter bulls and goats in our worship!"

Carlstadt described a number of other regulations he had either enforced during Luther's exile at the Wartburg or was about to enforce.

"And begging in the streets," said Carlstadt, "it is shameful."

"Poverty is a great tragedy," said Luther.

"Indeed, 'He who will not work, must not eat,'" said Carlstadt. "Thus, saith the Lord."

"What of those who cannot work?" asked Amsdorf.

"There's always something useful they could be doing," said Carlstadt. "I say we must pass laws against begging, rid the streets of Wittenberg of all beggars."

Luther felt the heat rising, his pulse pounding in his temples. "So you will replace the canon law of Rome with a new canon law of Wittenberg? Is that it? Just how will you enforce these new laws?"

"By church discipline," retorted Carlstadt, "by civil penalties, and the like."

"Before we pass laws against begging," said Luther, slapping his palm on the desk, "we the Church of Christ must embrace the needy poor with the love of Christ. Laws against begging friars, charlatans who prey on the poor, well and good. But any law that takes one crumb of bread from the mouth of an orphaned child or an aged woman with no strength left to work, with all my being, I oppose such a law."

Carlstadt drew in breath for a retort, but Amsdorf dug his fingers into the man's sleeve. He remained silent.

"I know you mean well, my friend," continued Luther, "but in our zeal for change, we can so easily forget God's grace. Christ has come to set up his kingdom in our hearts, not with sword, nor with scepter, not with another legal code, nor with another canon law. Our Lord turned the other cheek when he was smitten. He was not a man of violence. He did not call his followers to take up the sword and hack their way through the rabble and place a crown of gold on his head.

"Antichrist, as the prophet Daniel wrote, is to be broken without the hand of man. Violence will only make him stronger. We preach, we pray, but we do not pick fights. We do not set up new laws. We do not stir up the mob to tear down images. Constraint will be needed, for surely there are abuses that must be corrected, but we must never be over hasty, and whatever corrections there must be, they must be exercised by the constituted authorities."

"But what law shall guide those authorities?" asked Carlstadt.

"The law of Christ alone," replied Luther, "heartfelt love for God and self-giving love for our neighbor—especially the hungry poor."

# 42

# EMPTYING CLOISTERS

B lockhead Duke George," muttered Luther, halting before a door, its knob area blotched with painted fingerprints. Rapping on the door, he continued, "Imagine him forbidding the sale of my German New Testament in Leipzig!"

"So beautifully illustrated by Lucas Cranach," said Amsdorf. "It matters little. The September edition has sold out, and Herr Lotther readies his type for another before Christmas."

"No thanks to Duke George," said Luther, knocking again.

The door opened. A short man stood blinking at them, his long hair hanging in matted strands, with streaks of red, blue, and yellow around his face where he must habitually push it aside with his hands. He wore an artist's smock so stiff with paint it looked like it could as easily be stood in the corner as hung from a nail.

"Greetings, Herr Cranach, my friend," said Luther.

Wiping more paint from his hands onto his smock, the artist greeted them. "*Komen herein*," he said, beckoning them to follow him into his studio.

Lucas Cranach's house studio smelled of egg whites, horse-hair-bristle brushes, glue, and drying paint. One wall of the studio was lined with finished paintings, and a fresh canvas stretched onto a wooden frame leaned on an easel near the window.

"Herr Cranach, you are a marvel," said Luther, gesturing toward the row of paintings. "The gifts and calling of God come in many shapes. Yours is a remarkable one."

Cranach smiled, nodding modestly. "Mine is a humble calling, but one from which I derive great pleasure, greater still when others do too."

"As does everyone who views your paintings," said Luther. "I am certain your exquisite illustrations account for the rapid sale of the German New Testament."

Cranach bowed and smiled. "Rome has been such an enthusiastic patron of art and artists," said Cranach, inviting them to sit. He narrowed his eyes at them. "Some have feared that your reformation will destroy art—and, thus, artists."

"It is not my reformation, Lucas," said Luther. "And may I remind you that Frederick the Wise is both your patron and mine. There need be no hostility between art and reformation."

Cranach nodded distractedly. Adjusting the position of his stool, he settled himself in front of the new canvas. Leaning from behind the canvas, he made a rectangle with his fingers, and peered critically at Luther.

"The misuse of art," said Luther, "is another matter."

"The misuse?" said Cranach, frowning, his brush poised in hand.

"While the Word of God celebrates the achievement of artists, it calls men to destroy the misuse of art."

"Idols?" said Cranach.

"*Jawohl.* Art becomes an idol when it is venerated by worshipers," said Luther. "Whereupon, idols must be removed."

Cranach dabbed a brush on his pallet. "I make no idols," he murmured under his breath.

Luther eyed a row of finished paintings lining the wall. "You are most prolific, Lucas." His eyes rested on a painting of Adam and Eve in the garden. Luther cleared his throat in his fist, and diverted his eyes.

Cranach peered from behind his canvas. "'Naked they were, and not ashamed,'" he recited, nodding confidently, his eyebrows raised. "Nor ought you to be."

"Indeed, they were naked," said Luther, "as you have so vividly portrayed them. But that was before the Fall, before men became bond slaves of temptation and sin."

"Eyes forward," said Cranach. "And do hold still."

"May I speak?"

Cranach muttered, "It will take more than my rebukes to stop Martin Luther's mouth."

"I've never succeeded either," said Amsdorf. "Neither has the pope."

"Or the emperor," added Cranach.

"Your painting of the old man, just there," said Luther, ignoring them, "laboring over his book, skull presiding over all."

"Jerome," said Cranach. "You approve?"

"Indeed, I do," said Luther. "Yet even holy Jerome confessed to being confronted with temptations of the flesh. Finding himself all too often, as he put it, 'in the midst of the vain delights and pleasures of the wild wilderness,' he admits that even in his cloistered life, 'I thought myself oftentimes to be dancing among young women, when I had no other company, but scorpions and wild beasts. My face was pale with fasting, but my mind was inflamed with desires in my cold body: and although my flesh was half-dead already, yet the flames of fleshly lust, boiled within me.'"

"Turn toward the window," said Cranach. "*Nein*, not that much. Back, just a bit. *Ja, ja*, that is it. Now try not to move."

"If such a one as sainted Jerome," continued Luther, chin toward the window, "could find himself inflamed with fleshly lusts, how much more you and I. I am no sexless stone myself, so allow me to be blunt. Some of your paintings, dear Lucas, they most assuredly will be a means of awakening the wilderness of passions that boil within all our hearts."

Remaining hidden behind his canvas as he worked, Cranach's voice was barely audible. "Humph, art simply mirrors nature," he murmured. "I can't be blamed for what is real."

Luther nodded. "But are all parts of nature equally worthy to be shown? After all, God did clothe Adam and Eve, a rather conspicuous omission in your portrayal of them."

Silence from behind the canvas.

"My artist friend, are you listening?"

A short grunt from behind the canvas.

"The man who creates art," continued Luther, "art that puts on display the barest realities, must the artist not reckon with the consequences our Lord prescribes for the man who causes another to stumble?"

More scratching of charcoal from behind the canvas, accompanied by indistinct muttering.

"The devil and temptation will come," continued Luther. "We cannot prevent the birds from flying over our heads, can we? Yet must we beware not to let them build nests in our hair. One must not, in the name of art, invite the devil and all his fellows to a feast."

Cranach worked in silence for several more minutes, no sign of him from behind the canvas.

"Do not mistake me, Herr Cranach," said Luther. "I am not of the opinion that all the arts shall be crushed to earth and perish through the gospel, as some bigoted persons pretend, but would willingly see them all, and especially music, servants of him who gave and created them."

Luther stood up, pacing before the window.

"Daylight, Herr Doctor," said Cranach, waving Luther aside. "You are blocking it."

"Of course, forgive me," said Luther, returning to his seat. "May I see your work?"

Cranach grunted but made no reply.

There was an awkward silence. Amsdorf cleared his throat. "We have come, Herr Cranach, bearing a proposal for you."

Luther nodded. "*Jawohl*, we have."

One stern eye peeked around the canvas. "Well?" said Cranach.

"Would you and your good wife," began Luther, "ever consider taking on another domestic?"

"Another servant?" said Cranach. "Our domestic needs are amply staffed by the duke."

"I am beset," continued Luther, "with something of a problem."

"So I have heard," said Cranach. "A wagon load of vestal virgins has been unloaded at your doorstep. It is the gossip of all Wittenberg. You do have your hands full, Herr Doctor."

Amsdorf laughed aloud.

Luther ignored them. "We may have need of a place for a young woman or two."

"A woman?" said Cranach. "Or two?"

"Nuns, former nuns," said Luther. "Fleeing the cloister, and until we are able to find them husbands, they will need proper housing, a vocation, only until such time as suitable marriages can be arranged."

"Doctor Luther's treatise on marriage," Amsdorf attempted to explain, "has begun to empty the cloisters. The monks fend for themselves, but the nuns, the women, they need assistance."

"We have done well finding husbands for most of them," said Luther, "have we not, Amsdorf?"

"Most definitely."

"It should not be long," continued Luther. "Barbara, your good wife, could she not use the help with your growing family, and all these new apprentices hovering about eager to learn your art?"

"Or steal it from me," muttered Cranach. Framing Luther with his thumbs and index fingers again, he continued drawing.

Luther rose to his feet. "I am beside myself with curiosity, Lucas." He peered at the canvas. "May I?"

Cranach shrugged. "It is a mere sketch, and, with all your talking, unfinished."

Luther scowled. "Why with a beard?" His fingers strayed to his chin.

"I chose to portray you as *Junker Jörg*, from your Wartburg exile."

"My beard as you have drawn it," said Luther, "looks very like Elector Frederick's."

"I am his court painter," said Cranach, drawing in breath and crossing his arms on his chest. "The stylistic imitation will please the duke."

"Will you do it, then?" asked Luther.

Cranach blinked rapidly, then touched his forehead. "Ah, that. *Ja, ja.* Only until you find a suitable husband for her. Does this *Fräulein* have a name?"

Luther nodded. "Katharina von Bora."

# 43

# BARRELS OF NUNS

## (April 4, 1523)

P ickled Herring! It would be weeks before I, Katharina von Bora, was to sniff the last of them. What made things worse, the next day was Easter. Herring is good in its place, like so very many things. But in one's hair, and lingering and fermenting upon one's clothing. But there was no other way, so Leonard Kopp the herring merchant had assured us on Martin Luther's behalf.

"Escaping a nunnery in Germany," he had reminded us, "is a capital offense! They execute women for such things." Kopp was a bit of a showman, and took great delight, eyes goggling, in running an imaginary knife across his throat at his own words. "We must take great pains for your concealment—or else." For good measure, he repeated the gesture.

But just then as I was jostling inside my barrel, wadded into a most undignified posture, along with eleven other of my sister nuns stuffed in theirs, all of us stowed on Kopp's wagon, lurching and bumping behind his oxen (I believe he managed to drive into every pothole on the journey)—I wondered about the whole mad scheme.

My barrel had a knot hole near the lid, and I found that if I crammed my head up sideways against the lid, I could just see out of. I did my best to follow our progress from the Cistercian monastery of Marienthron in Nimbschen, near Grimma, my home since I was a little girl, to what we hoped would be our new home, far from the cloister, in Wittenberg, there to meet the man who had inspired, unbeknownst to him, this mad escapade.

Lurching into view through my knothole came my first glimpse of Wittenberg. I suppose in my mind, what with reading the emancipating books of Martin Luther, I expected it to be more grand, domes and spires, splendors glittering from every rooftop, perhaps its streets paved with gold.

Looking back, it was the first of a number of amendments I would be required to make in my thinking. Put bluntly, Wittenberg was wholly unimpressive from a distance; I would find it all the more so moments later when I alighted from my barrel and my feet sank into the street muck.

The twin spires of Wittenberg's Stadtkirche and the bulky round tower of the Castle Church squatted along the drab sandbank of the River Elbe. Grubby peasant faces flicked past my line of sight, and, at the eye-ball-gouging edge of my knothole, a rickety looking wooden bridge came into view.

Gnawing on the inside of my left cheek, a nasty habit I began as I child, I worried about what would befall us there. Meeting Martin Luther—*the* Martin Luther—hearing his voice sound from the pulpit, but, perhaps, even hearing him speaking directly to us, to me, it was too much to be believed. His words I had only read on the pages of his books and treatises smuggled into the nunnery and devoured by most of us. Sometimes with giddiness and longing, even blushes and laughter. And now this. I confess, I pinched myself on the back of my hand until it hurt.

My barrel suddenly began jostling and chattering. It must be the cartwheels passing over the river on the timber bridge. Folded nearly double to fit in my barrel, I flexed my arms and knees hard against the inside of the barrel to steady myself against the bone-jarring motion. I heard one of my sister nuns cry out in alarm, and a shriek of fright from another.

"None of that, my Fräulein fishes," called Herr Kopp from where he drove the wagon. "Not until I've delivered you safely inside the walls of Wittenberg. You can make all the racket you want then."

Moments later, we arrived safely inside those walls. "Good heavens!" retorted Luther upon seeing us disgorging from our barrels. "They won't give me a wife."

These were the first words I heard from the lips of Martin Luther. With a pry bar, Herr Kopp had tediously released us one-by-one from imprisonment in our herring barrels, and we stretched and groaned as we were deposited onto the streets of Wittenberg. I pondered Luther's words. Were they spoken with envy, even longing? Or wariness and bachelor certainty? Or were they a mere jest? It was my primal lesson—there would be so many more tutorials—in the nuanced complexity of the man.

Word of our arrival had gotten out. Grinning faces eyed us from everywhere we looked. By the wide-eyed looks, the whispers behind the backs of hands, we must have been a frightful sight: two days hidden away in herring barrels, no food, grimy with filth, and smelling profusely of fish. From a clump of young men near Luther, all robed in black scholar's gowns, I overheard snatches of their comments.

"A wagon load of vestal virgins has just come to town," said one, laughing as if it was a great jest.

"More eager for marriage than for life, I shouldn't wonder," observed another. "After a good bath."

"God grant them husbands lest worse befall," quipped a third.

"*Ja*, and may he grant them a good wash first."

When later I caught a glimpse of myself in the glass, I did not blame them overmuch for their remarks.

In my first hours in Wittenberg, I learned that Martin Luther, whatever other failings he might have had, was a man who got things done. While his friend Kopp masterminded our escape, the great reformer had not been idle. The parents of four of the youngest nuns were there to collect their daughters, while he had already secured husbands for five of us. Betrothals followed hard on the heels of our arrival. Though I rejoiced for my sisters, I was not one of the five.

The eldest of my sister nuns, I had four and twenty years when first I arrived in Wittenberg and was apparently considered too elderly for marriage by some. Hence, I was put to service with the Cranach family; my yet-unwed sisters were placed in other households.

Frau Cranach treated me, if not as a daughter, as a large plaything, a doll to dress and fret over. "This lovely yellow cotte," she cooed, "my dear Fräulein, will enhance every contour." Robing me, my mistress fussed over every pleat of my new costume. She pulled the cotte over my head and, as it fell down over my body, I admired the split sleeves of the shift, how they burst with color and shimmered in their velvety texture. As she laced my bodice, I gazed in some astonishment at myself in the looking glass, the yellow cotte blousing alluringly over my kirtle.

Frau Cranach stepped back, inspecting every fold and crease of my costume. "Lovely. If I do say so, lovely, indeed!" she pronounced. "Turn and spin, now."

I felt a thrill at setting aside forever my blockish nun's habit. Heat rising on my cheeks, I gazed at the figure staring wide-eyed back at me in the looking glass, its lips parted in wonder and its cheeks flushing the color of ripe strawberries in summertime. It smoothed its hands over where the blousy shift fell around its curvaceous hips.

"And now for your hair," said Frau Cranach, "such a lovely shade, the color of beech leaves in October. Be a shame to stuff it all under a hood." She rummaged in the dressing cabinet. "A headband and lovely net snood, that's the thing, your autumn locks glistering through all."

As she fussed with my braids, I felt mildly troubled that Luther in his prudent zeal had already arranged things as he had. How had he foreseen that there might be unmarriageable nuns in his herring harem? He yet had three runaway nuns on his hands, though Frau Cranach seemed intent on doing her part to find one of them a husband, if clothing and adornment alone could do the deed.

As the months passed, I came to believe that Wittenberg was the most rampant rumor mill in all Germany. Spalatin the duke's secretary made a private jest to Luther that in a matter of hours spread throughout the town to great hilarity. "Martin, you could solve this in a trice. Marry all three." Spalatin was not the only one who thought it a humorous remark. Though it failed to spark amusement in me.

Though Herr Cranach was a trifle odd—I had heard rumors about something called the artist's temperament—his wife was, on the whole, delightfully normal, and doted on me, as I did on their children. As months turned into a year, and more months followed hard on the heels, I began to resign myself. Perhaps I, like Martin Luther, was not meant for marriage. "They won't give me a husband," I mused to baby Ursula as I changed her diaper. Grabbing at my nose and lips with her chubby fingers, she giggled at me.

Since any communication from Martin Luther to me came through an intermediary, it was not unusual when one day his friend and colleague Philip Melanchthon, a happily married man himself, brought news of my matrimonial status from Luther. But, as events would prove, I wish he had not.

242

Luther had managed, so he thought, to find a match for me in a Nuremberg nobleman's son, a student of his. I longed to hold my own babes in my arms, and my heart warmed at the domestic prospect. Until Melanchthon returned a week later, wringing his hands in his cap, profoundly apologetic.

Plans for betrothal were off. Apparently I was too beneath the station to wed into so exalted a family, especially with having broken my vows; suspicion abounded among some that an apostate nun might be a precarious match. The young Nuremberger was strongly urged not to vow himself to one who had already violated hers.

Weeks passed, and, disappointed though I was, I was the more determined to find contentment in my station.

Every week, I saw and heard the voice of Martin Luther. He was my pastor at the Stadtkirche. His sermons encouraged me, sometimes thrilled me, and I found the gospel of Jesus Christ becoming clearer in my thinking and in my heart with his every word.

"Just as workers with brawn are prone to despise workers with brain," he declared one Sunday morning from the high pulpit of the city church, "so are scholars and clerics, and poets and courtiers prone to despise men of what are considered baser vocations. I can just imagine the astonished people of Nazareth at the judgment day. 'Lord, were you not the carpenter who built my house? How did you come to this honor?'"

We all laughed at his words. We often did while he preached. His expressiveness, his inflections, his imagery—he had such a remarkable way of making plain what he was teaching from the Bible.

"The hosts of heaven," he continued, "visited humble shepherds with the glorious news of Christ's birth. What did those shepherds do after visiting the Christ child? We can read it in Holy Writ. Rejoicing and praising God, they went back to care for their sheep.

"But you will say to me. *Nein, nein*! Surely that must be wrong. We should correct the passage to read, 'They went and shaved their heads, fasted, prayed their rosaries, and put on monks' cowls.'"

Again, we could not help ourselves, some guffawing aloud at his parody.

"But what does the Bible say?" he asked us.

"They hastened back to their sheep!" shouted a man dressed in the coarse tunic and britches of a farmer.

"Precisely!" agreed Luther, slapping his palm on the lectern. "The shepherds returned to being shepherds. The sheep would have been in a sorry way if they had not."

Someone bleated like a sheep, and the congregation burst into laughter, Luther with them.

"Noah was a farmer and a shipwright," he continued. "Moses was a shepherd and so was David. The lowlier the calling the better! The milkmaid is above the cardinal, and the mucker of manure is above the pope! Away with all this strutting nonsense about exalted callings. We are all one in Christ Jesus our carpenter Lord!"

Next his sermon progressed to the family, the roles of fathers and mothers, babies and children, husbands and wives. Oddly, as he continued in this vein, I felt that he was avoiding looking in my direction, though I confess my eyes were riveted on his.

"Maternity is a glorious thing," he said, "since all mankind has been conceived, born, and nourished of women. All human laws should encourage the multiplication of families.

"As for mothers, they are the living breathing exhibit of the love of God. Just as God's love overcomes sin, so a mother's love overcomes soiled diapers."

"*Jawohl, Jawohl*!" called several women at the same time. Affirming laughter pattered throughout the congregation.

The sermon came to a close, the service ended, and, conversing warmly, we filed from the church through the wide arched doors, there to be greeted by our pastor.

"Thank you, Herr Doctor," I said. Taking hold of his extended hand, as was proper, I curtsied.

Blinking rapidly, he squeezed my hand, and seemed about to say something, but, oddly for him, no words came from his lips. Leaning forward, he narrowed his eyes, his jaw cocked to one side, as if studying me. To my chagrin, I feared that he was taking a tally of my flaws, an inventory of my deficiencies, attempting, thereby, to discern why no man would have me for wife. It did not then occur to me that this marked the very first time he had noticed me, clean and properly dressed, since my ignominious disgorging from the herring barrel.

I felt the color rising on my cheeks. Something must be said. "It was a fine sermon, Herr Doctor," I blurted, then hesitated, he still holding my hand in his. What was I to do, to say? Ought I to say what was on my mind? Was it proper? I took a deep breath. "Your words about families, children, husbands and wives, women and motherhood—Herr Doctor, your words went deeply into my heart."

# 44

# CONSENSUAL

**W**onderful news!" cried Herr Amsdorf later that same week. "At long last."

When he accosted me, I was being jostled at the market, basket in hand, haggling over the best clump of asparagus for the Cranach household. I confess, my heart leapt within me; I had lain awake for three nights, fearing I had over spoken, been indiscreet in my words to Doctor Luther after service. The inside of my poor cheek had undergone considerable gnawing.

"It's as good as settled," he continued. And then he began telling me about a man Luther had discovered, a potential husband for me called Doctor Glatz.

Amsdorf avoided eye contact as he continued, feigning a minute inspection of a large crock of pungent sauerkraut in the next stall. From there he diverted his attentions to a mound of plump sausages. My suspicions mounted.

"How old did you say?" I asked.

"Old enough, indeed," retorted Amsdorf, looking shocked that I would enquire. "Marriageable aged, have no doubt."

I thanked him for his kindness, paid for my asparagus, but made no commitments. I was determined to make my own enquiries and did so. The intelligence I gathered was shocking. I sent an urgent note to good Amsdorf, asking him to come to the Cranach house. I must discuss the matter with him immediately.

"What a burden I have been these two years to Doctor Luther and to you, Herr Amsdorf," I began. "But I feel ill-suited to wed a man old enough to be my grandfather. And the eccentricities I have learned about this man? I have no choice. I am compelled to refuse him."

Deflating, Amsdorf breathed a heavy sigh, slumped onto a settle in the Cranach parlor, and began plucking idly at the fringe on a cushion.

"I am a reasonable woman," I continued. "But I must say, before I would wed a man such as Doctor Glatz, I would take almost anyone. I would marry you—or Martin Luther himself before Grandfather Glatz!" We both laughed heartily at my levity.

What transpired next I later learned from Martin Luther himself. "While on a visit to Eisenach, sitting about the table with my mother and father, I shared what a troublesome young woman you were being," he told me after the fact.

"One can hardly blame the girl," said Mother Luther.

Hans Luther scowled as he listened to his son's dilemma. "Why not you?" he said.

"Me?" said Martin. "Father, surely you are not serious?"

Hans's glowered. "I am deeply serious about the Luther name. Marry the girl yourself, and with her make me more Luthers."

Martin Luther later told me that his father's words began their work on his mind; I wanted to believe that they equally began to do their work on his affections.

His friend Spalatin would give him no rest, tormenting him, accusing him of a preoccupation with women. Calling him so great a lover for having not one but three wives, the three of us for whom he had so miserably failed to find husbands. Meanwhile, Luther claimed he had no intention of marrying only to leave some poor woman a widow when he was led away to the stake there to burn for heresy.

Shortly thereafter, Luther did manage to secure husbands for my other two sister nuns. More than slightly humiliated, I alone of the original twelve apostate nuns remained steadfastly in a state of husbandlessness. Frowning at my figure in the looking glass one evening, I wondered if I had been a trifle unreasonable about Doctor Glatz.

The pear blossoms had already fallen to the ground when in May of 1525 matrimonial rumors fluttered about the city of Wittenberg. It seemed to me that Luther's moods and opinions carried so much sway that if he merely commented on the weather, his words would be rumored throughout the city, and would as likely appear in print before day's end.

"I believe in marriage," so Luther was rumored to say. "I am ready, though I am not infatuated. Since I can find no one else who will have her, I will marry Katharina von Bora before I die, even though it should be only a betrothal like Joseph's was with Mary."

Imagine it! Was it unjust of me to feel anger boiling over like a pot of broth too long on the coals? I think not. The man had said no such thing to my face. I was left to learn of it on the wings of the rumor, Frau Cranach returning breathless from the market, gushing and kissing on me at the joyous news. Bustling about the wardrobe, she began planning my marriage costume on the instant.

But there was more. "My motives for marriage?" so it was reported that Luther expostulated. "To give joy to my father, to give grief to the pope and to the devil, and to seal my witness before they burn me."

As the rumors spread, I was more than slightly miffed, I confess it. Heat intensifying on my cheeks, I was about to gather up my skirts and march down the street from my situation in the Cranach house to the doorstep of the Augustinian cloister and give him a piece of my mind. But I did not.

Martin Luther saved me the trouble. I had just finished braiding five-year-old Anna's locks, when a tentative rapping came on the Cranach door. I swung it open, and there he stood. To say that there was an awkward silence is wholly inadequate to describe the intensity of wordlessness that began that conversation. But at last we found our voices, mine, I confess, clanging more like a fishwife's, at the first.

"Is it proper that all Wittenberg learns before I do of your intention to wed me before you die? And a betrothal like Joseph's not a proper marriage? And 'since no one else will have her'? All this without consulting me?"

"Without consulting you?" cried Luther, his arms raised as if I were about to fall upon him and he was fending me off for his life. "It was Katherina von Bora who did the proposing." There was a twinkle in his eye, and he was smirking in that maddening fashion of his. "Amsdorf told me what you said—without consulting me—'I would marry Martin Luther,' so you said. It was I who was forced to learn of our betrothal from another."

I stared at him in astonishment. "Amsdorf nearly burst his bowels laughing with me. It was spoken entirely in jest."

"Entirely?"

Not meeting his eye, I spluttered for answer.

"Fräulein, Katharina—am I meant to call you that?"

I nodded.

"Katharina, away with all this blockhead nonsense about marriage as a sacrament. Biblically, God made them male and female—made us male and female. Hence, matrimony is based on the mutual consent of one and of the other, of a male and of a female, that is, a man and a woman."

He broke off, running his thick fingers through his hair, his eyes searching the flagstone floor as if in its cracks and undulations to find proper words. We sat in consensual silence for several moments, neither of us certain what was to be said next. Glancing at him out of the corner of my eye, and he at me, I was struck with the awkwardness of our lives. I a celibate nun with twenty-six years, who had rarely even seen a man since my fifth year of life, much less sat down to have intimate conversation with one.

When I didn't think he was observing, I studied his features. Shrouded in his scholar's gown, he looked bulky, like a black bear, and there was a sobriety to his brow, not quite severity, but a face lined with near ferocity, and pinched with discomfort; I had seen people in pain. Martin Luther was in pain. Whether it was physical, emotional, or otherwise, I would soon learn.

He was a celibate monk with forty-two years, the last twenty spent entirely around other men. He had only heard the confession of two women in all those years—I had learned these precise details from Amsdorf and Melanchthon, who, perhaps out of pity, had taken it upon themselves to prepare me.

"You see, Katharina," he said at last, "Scripture calls a betrothed bride a married woman. Do not be offended that I vowed a betrothal." He shuffled his feet awkwardly. "It is just as much a marriage after public consensual betrothal as after the wedding. The wedding is the celebration only; it is just the revelry."

I nodded. I felt ill-equipped to speak. What was I to say to so great a man? Would I have him? Would I consent? It was beyond my wildest dreams. Would I have him? With all my heart, but I knew not how to speak the words. We never rehearsed for such conversations in the cloister.

"Katharina, they want to make me a fixed star," he continued, shifting his bulk on his chair. "But I am an irregular planet, sometimes out of all orbit, wandering in the blackness. If you will consent, if you will have me, wild boar, coarse peasant that I am—" he broke off, wringing his hands.

Glancing up, our eyes met. He smiled, almost sheepishly. I liked what happened to his eyes when he smiled. The bearish ferocity melted away, and in its place came a boyish sparkle.

I nodded, and, judging from his expression, must have been smiling in return. I felt lightheaded, breathless. I wanted to sing, to dance. "Forgive me. There were no tutorials at the nunnery for this."

His smile broke into laughter. I found myself joining him. "My lord Katie, I believe we have a betrothal to prepare for! Correct me now if I am mistaken."

I made no correction. Whereupon, he became almost giddy, and I found myself feeling very much the same. It was a delightful sensation, one I had never had before. Little did I know the intoxicating pleasures that lay ahead.

"We must let Leonard Kopp know the happy news," he said, laughing. "Who would have read this in the stars?" He rose abruptly to his feet, frowning. "I have many letters to compose to our guests—always letters."

"May I assist you?"

Lips parted, glancing to left and right, he looked bewildered. "I cannot take you to the cloister, to my study, to my bed chamber, not yet." Not meeting my eye, he bit his lower lip. "It is a man's world. In all its life, its cavernous halls and vaulted passageways, they have never felt the tread of a woman, heard her voice, her laughter, been adorned by her graces, been bathed in her loveliness."

251

His voice changed as he said the words. The thundering bombast had departed; in its place was quiet tenderness, the expressiveness of a poet. I could scarcely breathe. Suddenly, I realized his dilemma and its solution.

"There are writing things here," I said. Hurrying from the parlor, I returned moments later with pen, ink, and parchment, laying them out on the table.

"*Ja, ja*, we have work to do. Letters to write—wedding letters!" He snatched up the pen.

I made my way behind him, looking over his shoulder. "May I?"

He nodded, his quill already dipped and scratching furiously on the parchment.

"While I was thinking of other things," he wrote, "God has suddenly brought me to marriage with Katherina. I am going to get married. God likes to work miracles and to make a fool of the world. You must come to the wedding." He paused, smiling up at me over his shoulder and twirling his pen.

"Just this morning," he said, "before coming to you, I received a letter enquiring about long engagements." He set aside the letter he had begun and reached for a clean parchment. "Here shall be my answer." He dipped his pen. "Don't put off till tomorrow! By delay Hannibal lost Rome. By delay Esau forfeited his birthright. Christ said, 'Ye shall seek me, and ye shall not find me.' Thus, Scripture, experience, and all creation testify that the gifts of God must be taken on the wing."

He sat back, grinning with satisfaction.

"'Don't put off till tomorrow,'" I said, biting my cheek. "What precisely does that mean?"

He laughed. "Today is Monday. What about Tuesday?" He gazed unblinking at me. "But that would be putting off till tomorrow though."

Heat rose on my cheeks, and I felt a constricting in my throat. It was all so sudden. "Thursday," I stammered. "What about Thursday?"

He snatched up another blank parchment.

"Dear Herr Kopp, I am to be married on Thursday. My lord Katie and I invite you to send a barrel of the best—"

"No, no, not herring?" I broke in on his writing.

Laughing, he gestured with a nod of his head at the letter and kept writing. "Send a barrel of the best Torgau beer, and if it is not good you will have to drink it all yourself."

I laughed aloud at his words. "Where are we to live, Herr Doctor?"

"I have already consulted with the duke on our plans to marry," he replied.

"The duke and everyone else in Wittenberg," I added, cuffing him lightly on the shoulder.

"And he has gifted us a home."

"A home, just for us?"

Martin looked away, blotting the ink he had been writing. "It is ours, and it has ample room."

"Where?"

"Wittenberg, of course. The Augustinian cloister. It is all ours, our new home. There we shall live, love, shout, and sing!" His voice became tender. "And there we shall, God willing, make more Luthers, as my father desires for us to do."

While he spoke the words, my hand impulsively had strayed to his shoulder. He reached up and placed his hand upon mine.

I had seen the cloister, though had never been inside; apparently no woman had ever been inside; that would be shockingly clear to me three days hence. I had observed it from the street. One entered an archway into a large garden courtyard. Rising above the garden was the cloister, wide as a church, several stories tall, bigger than five or six houses in Wittenberg.

"It is enormous," I ventured. I had spent endless hours as a girl on my knees until they were bloodied and raw scrubbing what had seemed like acres of floor in the Marienthron cloister. "So very enormous," I said again.

"And it is all ours," he repeated, squeezing my hand, seemingly oblivious to my fears. "Ours to live in—together, as male and female."

I eyed him, grinning up at me, and amended, "As husband and wife."

# 45

# PIGTAILS ON THE PILLOW

I shall never forget the experience of being the first woman ever to enter the confines of the Augustinian cloister in Wittenberg. Inhabited exclusively by men since its construction in 1504—inhabited exclusively by *German* men—I must confess, I did not find the experience a particularly pleasant one, at least, that is, on all levels.

It was called the Black Monastery for the dark complexion of the gowns of its inhabitants. Sniffing the stale air, however, and wiping a finger across the table, that first day upon entering its walls, I thought it a most appropriate name, but for entirely different reasons.

On the morning appointed, my betrothed husband had taken my arm at the door of the Cranach house and escorted me, as if I were a princess. The streets were lined with all Wittenberg, cheering as if Martin Luther were St. George and had just slain the dragon, and I was his lady love. Drums rumbling and pipers skirling, we were led in triumph to the portal of the Stadtkirche, its bells chiming till I feared its twin spires would collapse, crushing us all. In the shadow of the city church, with little pomp or ceremony, the entire city gawking at us on all sides, we solemnized our vows to one another.

Words fail me to fully describe the wonder of that day. I felt as Hannah must have felt and cherish the memory to this day, yet fresh and warm in my bosom these twenty years hence.

After that, the party began. A banquet in the cloister dining hall, then dancing at the town hall, and more feasting and drinking, the magistrate finally scurrying the last of the guests to their beds.

And we to ours.

I have already labored to describe the awkwardness of my life and Martin Luther's, how ill-prepared we were for matrimony, and all the intimacy that it entails. I have never felt such an exhilarating combination of longing as I did that first night as Martin Luther's wife, longing intertwined with more than a little fear.

Nor did I feel as much commingling of revulsion at his bed chamber, particularly the disgusting bed sheets, foul with his sweat, besmeared with a soiled imprint of his hulking body, and at the same time the delirious anticipation of being taken in the arms of my husband—I an apostate nun, formerly resigned to a life of celibacy and childlessness—now to be taken up in those strong arms and loved.

*Knock, knock, knock!*

"Who on earth would be pounding on the door at this time of night?" roared my husband.

"And on such a night," I murmured.

The knocking persisted, echoing through the halls. I followed Martin down the endless corridors of the cloister, candle light flickering on the walls and elongating his vast shadow before me, the persistent knocking growing more impatient. At last my husband threw open the front door.

"Carlstadt!" he exclaimed. "You're a mess. What are you doing here?"

For the next hour, Carlstadt told of violent peasant revolt, his flight from the city of Jena, and his narrow escape from the mayhem and burning. "I knew I could find refuge here with you." He looked from Martin to me as if seeing me for the first time. "And with you, Frau Luther, I presume."

I could see from my husband's features, the deep furrows in his brow, his agitated pacing before the fireplace; news of peasant revolt troubled him deeply.

"I abhor violence," he murmured, "bloodshed of any kind. But especially peasant blood, women and children." He looked at Carlstadt.

"Do not blame me." Carlstadt's face grew red with anger. "You're the one who started the violence!"

"I who abhor violence started it?"

"With your hammer and nail!" Carlstadt slammed his fist onto the table, bowls and platters rattling.

"While I preached *against* rebellion," retorted Luther, "you preached the opposite. Stirring the peasant hoards into a frenzy. I who abhor rebellion have never countenanced violence!"

Their quarrel I could do nothing about. It seemed a good time for me to retire, and I hastened back to our bed chamber. Hands on my hips, I assessed the unkempt situation. Rummaging on shelves in the hallway, closet doors banging, I at last discovered fresher sheets. Holding my nose, I wrenched the foul, oily cloth from the bed, then did my best to fluff up the mattress and tuck the clean sheets in their place. Scowling at the dirty ones, I wondered if I would ever be able to pronounce them clean again.

I was in the midst of doing what tidying up could be managed under the odd circumstances, the night nearly spent, when my husband returned to me. Though we were physically spent, and now emotionally troubled with Carlstadt's news and untimely visitation, and though the first cock would crow within an hour, it was our wedding night, and we were husband and wife, with clean sheets.

"First love is drunken," whispered my husband next morning at my side. "And there is ever so much to get used to, dear Katie, now that you are flesh of my flesh and bone of my bone." He paused, toying with my hair. "For one thing, one awakens to find pigtails on the pillow next to him that were not there previously."

I batted at his hand playfully, yawned, stretched, and got up. "There is no time to lose," I said, pulling on my clothes. "It was most generous of the late elector to gift this house to us, this enormous house to us, but it does sorely lack a woman's touch." I pointed at the mound of dirty laundry. "When did you last change the sheets?"

With feigned bewilderment, he shrugged. "One is meant to change them?"

I shook my head in wonder.

"A year, perhaps longer," he confessed. "I work so hard and am often so weary, I tumble in without noticing the sheets. That is, before now."

"I shall commence," I said. "There's a great deal to do to make this cavernous place livable."

I only had the vaguest inkling of the many accommodations that lay ahead. For the two of us, there would be far more to grow accustomed to than mere pigtails on the pillow.

# 46
# THE WAGER

I tied up my hair, girded up my skirts, bared my arms, and set to on that musty monastery. I was determined to conquer every dank and foul corner of its passageways.

After several hours thus occupied, I collapsed onto the settle in our cooking chamber, the heat rising on my cheeks. There sat my idle husband, book open on the table, lips moving, his fingers skimming the page.

"What is it you are reading, Herr Doctor?" I ventured.

"Sola Scriptura, my beloved Katie," he said, glancing up from the pages. "It is difficult to imagine it. My first twenty years of life I never so much as laid eyes on the Bible. Even in the monastery, it was seldom read. Now I cannot live a day without feasting on its sacred pages."

I moved to his side, looking over his shoulder at the book.

"I did not see a Bible," I said, "until coming to Wittenberg."

"Did you not read it at Marienthron?"

"*Nein,* I have never read it," I said, "not all through."

"You must make the journey, beloved Katie," he said. "It is like no other. The true Christian pilgrimage is not to Rome or Compostela, but to the prophets, the Psalms, and the Gospels."

"I do not know where to begin," I said, sitting at his side. "Is it not too difficult for me, a mere woman? You, the great Martin Luther, great man of books and of learning. But what of me?"

"This is the great fallacy of Rome," he retorted, his face clouding over. "The Word of God is for everyone, man or woman, husband or wife. It is why I have labored to translate it into our German, the language the mother chatters to her children; that is the language of Scripture. Katharina, the Word of God is for you, for all of us."

"Can I not receive the Word from sermons?" I asked, "your sermons, of course?"

"Preaching is good," he said. "But how will you know if you are being deceived? Johann Tetzel was a preacher and so was Leo X, quacking preachers, who preferred their words to God's. You must beware, be equipped to hear the error."

"How?"

"Christ ties us solely to the Word," he said, fingering a corner of the open page before him. "He will not have the Holy Spirit separated from the Word. Therefore, if you hear anyone boast that he has something by inspiration and suggestion of the Holy Spirit but it is without God's Word, whatever it may be, it is the work of the wretched devil."

Slapping his palm on the table, he laughed. "Would you like to read it, all of it?"

I told him I longed to read the Bible.

"Then you shall, and I shall make you a wager. Finish reading the whole of Scripture by Eastertide, and I shall pay you fifty gulden."

I studied his features grinning back at me. "We have not one gulden, Herr Doctor. How will you pay me fifty?"

Bewildered, he looked at me. "No gulden?"

"*Nein*, no gulden, no money," I said. "We have none for buying bread, meat, cheese, beer. How will you find fifty gulden to pay me for reading Holy Scripture?"

He shrugged and waved a hand at me.

I soon learned that, not only was my beloved husband challenged in matters of hygiene, he understood not the first principle of economics. I believed then, and yet more firmly now, that he truly never thought of meat and drink, or of the money to acquire such necessities. The full extent of his prodigality I would learn. It knew no limit, to the orphaned beggar in the marketplace, to the poor scholar in thread-bare gown, recklessly he gave away what he did not have.

"What have you done for food?" I asked, "before we wed?"

"I am given a stipend from the university," he began, holding out his thumb. "And the duke sends fish and game from time to time." He added his index finger to the tally, then as an afterthought, added another finger. Frowning, he stroked his chin and fell silent, apparently unable to discover another source of revenue.

I had read his books, attended diligently to his sermons, heard of his acumen in disputation with great men. But never had so brilliant a man in matters theological been so dull in matters of the home, the table, and the pocketbook. As with a burst of lightning, I saw clearly that morning the role God had for me with this mammoth and yet so helpless individual.

"Herr Doctor, is there land attached to the cloister?" I asked.

"I believe there is. Yes, of course there is. There is the garden, with a lovely pear tree in it." He pointed with a thumb over his shoulder toward the window.

"I cannot feed us merely from the garden," I said, looking out the window. "We will need more than a few pears. Besides, it is too small. Is there not other land, cultivated for raising food, pasture for keeping animals? The monks had to eat."

"That? *Ja, ja*, there is land," he said. "I suppose it is ours. Pasture for cows and pigs, and fields for growing vegetables, outside the Elster Gate, hard by the village."

He said this as if realizing for the first time where his food came from.

"I shall go inspect them," I said, rising to my feet and untying my kitchen smock.

"But your Bible?" he called after me. "When will you commence?"

"This evening," I called over my shoulder.

"Man shall not live by bread alone!" he called after me. "Or woman!"

"If we don't eat we die of hunger," I shouted back. "A corpse cannot read the Bible."

Thus I became a farmer. After inspecting my fields, I set my face toward the market and bought a cow. It would be the first of many.

"That will be twenty gulden," said the farmer.

Stroking the heifer under her russet chin, I blushed. I explained to him that I had no money, not so much as a florin, but asked him if he would like a copy of my husband's German Bible.

"And who be your husband?" he enquired, inspecting me doubtfully.

"Martin Luther," I said.

He gapped, his eyes growing wide. "Martin Luther's Bible for my very own? In exchange for my heifer?"

I assured him that if he wanted to add a bull calf to the bargain I would not complain, and I would make arrangements and the Bible would be sent to his doorstep.

All my husband's labor—and the printers never gave him a penny for his books. I would see to it that at the least they gave him copies of the books so I could barter with them.

Then we could eat. It would take shrewdness to keep my husband alive, that much was clear to me.

# 47

# TABLE TALK

Months passed, deliriously happy months they were. One bright autumn morning I returned from the edge of town and my labors as a farmer and overheard my husband speaking with students who had assembled to hear his words in our house. I confess, I longed to listen into his world, so different from mine.

Without entering the cooking chamber where I envisioned them all seated about the great square trestle table therein, I found myself a quiet window seat in the corridor and listened, they unaware of my presence. Perhaps it was wrong, but here is what I discovered of their talk about our table.

"What, Herr Doctor, was God doing," asked one student, "before he created the world?"

My husband emitted a roar of contempt. "He was busy creating hell for foolish students who pry into such questions!"

Raucous laughter and the thumping of backs sounded from the chamber. There followed a grammatical question from one of them, which discussion made little sense to me, at the first.

"Even grammarians and schoolboys on street corners know that nothing more is signified by verbs in the imperative mood than what *ought* to be done, and that what *is* done or *can* be done should be expressed by words in the indicative. How is it that Erasmus and so many theologians are twice as stupid as schoolboys? As soon as they get hold of a single imperative verb they infer an indicative meaning, as though the moment a thing is commanded it is done, or, more to the point, *can* be done?"

"Yet, Herr Doctor, we are commanded to hear, to come, to repent, to believe, to resist the devil, to obey, are we not?"

"We are," said Luther. "And might I add, we are commanded to be holy, to be perfect, as well. How has mankind done in those departments? But all these passages of Scripture you cite are imperative; and they prove and establish nothing about the *ability* of man, but only lay down what is and what is not to be done."

"I never thought of it in grammatical terms," said a young scholar.

"You must," said my husband. "Sound grammar leads to sound theology. For example, does it follow from the imperative 'turn you' that, therefore, you *can* turn? Does it follow from the command, 'Love the Lord your God with all your heart' that, from the very command, you can and are able to love with all your heart? What does Erasmus prove with this argument? He supplants the grace of God with the free will of man, by an abrogation of grammar!

"What is more, Scripture is imminently clear on this point. Paul speaking in the indicative tells us none are righteous, none seek after God, none come of their own free will, believe of their free will, repent or obey as an act of their free will. All the Bible's indicatives make clear that no sinner, dead in his trespasses, has any degree of ability to do any of those things commanded in the imperative.

"Why then the law?" asked a timid boy's voice.

"'By the law is the knowledge of sin,'" said my husband, "so the word of grace comes only to those who are distressed by a sense of sin and tempted to despair. When God is about to justify a man, he damns him. Whom he would make alive he must first kill."

"How then is it that one man believes and another rejects?"

"It is hidden in the decree of God," answered my husband, "God who, according to his own counsel, ordains such persons as he wills to receive and partake of the mercy preached and offered."

There followed heated discussion, even near shouting at times, my dear husband's voice rising above all with the last word. "All objections to predestination proceed from the wisdom of the flesh. Is it not wonderful news to believe that salvation lies entirely outside ourselves? And since salvation is totally of God's doing, the doctrine of election comforts those who believe. We can say, 'I belong to God! I have been chosen by God. I am one of his sheep!'"

I had been on the verge of rising and tiptoeing away, their discussion seeming at first to be theoretical, impractical, the wrangling of schoolmen. But something about my husband's words arrested me, as they so often did, and went deeply into my heart. I repeated his words softly to myself. "I belong to God! I have been chosen by God. I am one of his sheep!"

While I was thus ruminating, the table tutorial discussion deflected itself down a different pathway. I remained in my window seat.

"Though Paul commends marriage," said a young scholar, his tone dubious, "is it not better to remain unwed, thereby to devote one's self more fully to the work of reformation?"

I strained to hear. What might my husband reply when he is wholly unaware that his wife is hearing all? My breath quickened, and perspiration broke on my brow. Perhaps I did not truly want to hear. After all, we had only been wed for a few month's time. But I found myself unable to move, my ears straining to hear all.

"Christ sayeth not," said my husband, "Abstain from the flesh, from marrying, from housekeeping, and the rest, as the papists teach, for that were even to invite the devil and all his fellows to a feast."

His fist must have crashed onto the table; I feared for the crockery. "I say, be gone devil and all his fellows. I will feast with my beloved wife." He gave a laughing roar. "I got into the pope's hair and married an apostate nun. Who could have read that in the stars?"

"Yet are not your energies divided now, Herr Doctor?" pressed the young man.

"I saw just yesterday in the market place," said another, "a husband and wife going at each other hammer-and-tongs. I thought they might do each other harm."

"*Ja, ja,* there can be trouble in marriage," said my husband. "Adam has made a mess of our nature. Think of all the squabbles Adam and Eve must have had in the course of their nine hundred years together. Eve would say, 'You ate the apple,' and Adam would retort, 'You gave it to me.'"

More raucous laughter, and puerile hilarity emitted from the chamber. And this they called learning? I could not see what was so humorous in his words.

"And what of your squabbles, Herr Doctor?" said one of the young me, "yours and Frau Luther's?"

I felt the heat rising on my face. What business was that of theirs?

In the hubbub of voices I did not hear the first part of my husband's rejoinder. Then I heard this: "First love is drunken." His voice was low and earnest. "But when the intoxication wears off, then comes real marriage love." There were no comments, no laughter, no interruptions from his students as he continued.

"Perhaps it is in the home where our greatest need for reformation lies, in the family, in marriage. Katharina von Bora, my wife, she makes me glad to set aside my studies and return to her. And it is my daily goal to make her sorry to see me leave, glad to see me come home again. There is a learning to be found in marriage unavailable in any other school."

He was silent for a moment, then continued. "Katharina reads Holy Scripture daily now. She is hard at it and is at the end of the fifth book of Moses. Though I wonder if she did not read ahead. She lives every hour as if she skipped ahead to the last words of Proverbs and committed them entirely to heart. She is astonishing in her labors for my comfort and sustenance.

"She plants our fields, pastures and sells cows, slaughters pigs, chickens, even a bull with her own knife. Watching her wield that knife makes me behave better."

They laughed heartily. I knew their laughter encouraged him.

"And there is nothing like her sausages, her rounds of cheese, but best of all is her beer!"

"Herr Doctor, your wife brews your own beer?" asked one of the young men incredulously.

"The very finest," my husband retorted. "Better than the bilge water that passes for beer in Leipzig."

They roared again with laughter. "She does it for my bowels. Argh, my bowels," he moaned, to more laughter.

"Marriage ordained by God," he continued, "though it is a school of character and I very much in the lowest class, it is chief among God's good gifts to man. My Katie is in all things so obliging and pleasing to me that I would not exchange my poverty for the riches of Croesus."

As I listened to his words, and he all unaware, my passions rose. Tears formed in my eyes. It was only with great difficulty that I suppressed my desire to bolt into the room and fling my arms around my husband's thick neck, and smother him in kisses, careless of propriety. I did not. Yet was my heart all the more devoted to him.

# 48

# DIAPERS

It was not a week later that I woke up in the morning feeling my insides in turmoil, undulations of nausea rolling over me, as if I had eaten spoilt meat, cheese gone bad, or water slimed with the street filth. Martin was beside himself.

"Dearest Katie, do not die and leave me," he begged, kneeling at my side, grasping my hand in his. "It is I who must be sick always," he said, rocking back and forth, caressing my hand. "*Nein, nein*, do not die."

I confess that, so delightful were his entreaties, I considered not telling him the true cause of my discomfiture, basking for as long as I could in the warmth of his devotion. While considering just how long I might hold out, there came a final heaving, and I was suddenly and violently sick. There was no stopping it. There lay my breakfast all in a masticated rubble on the floor next to our bed.

"Oh, dear Katie!" he cried, caressing my brow, tears streaming down his face. "Do not die and leave me!" he begged.

Feeling somewhat relieved after disgorging my breakfast, I managed to smile at him.

"Ah, it is gone, and you are well?" he asked, his eyes imploring it to be so.

Sitting up, I could not help myself. I laughed aloud at him. "My dear, Herr Doctor," I said. "You do not know what this is?"

"I know illness, bowel disorder and rowling flatulence. But it is for me, not for you."

I laughed again, his face easing at my mirth. "This is your fault, Herr Doctor. It is entirely by your doing that this disease has taken hold of me."

His face grew slack with wonder. "Is it—? Are you—" he stammered, breathlessly.

"I believe I am with child," I said, squeezing his hand. "God enabling me, you are to be a father, my dear Herr Doctor."

Though it is something of an understatement, I will say it, my husband could be explosive. When angered by the pope or rejoicing in the grace of God—either way, he could erupt with irrepressible emotion. As he did that day. He was never a good dancer—more of a clumsy oaf, truth be told—but he footed it well at the news, dodging the remains of my breakfast strewn upon our bed chamber floor. Then he snatched up his lute, never far from hand, and sang:

A new song here shall be begun—
The Lord God help our singing!
Of what our God himself hath done,
Praise, honor to him bringing!

I believe, though I am not absolutely certain, that he composed it upon the joyful instant. And then furiously he fell to with pen and ink.

"What are you writing?" I asked. He had insisted I remain in bed, and he would care for me. Though well meant, they were astonishing words coming from a man so entirely incapable of caring for himself.

"My Katherina is fulfilling the words of Genesis, 'Be fruitful and multiply and fill the earth'!" he read aloud. "There is about to be born a child of a monk and a nun. Such a child must have a great lord for godfather. Therefore, I am inviting you. I cannot be precise as to the time."

I smiled at his words, his exuberance, his sheer delight at the prospect of a child. Though he somehow in the next months managed to continue his work, preaching, writing, teaching, arbitrating conflicts from within and without, he doted on me, often interrogating me. "How do you feel, dearest Katie? How does the baby feel? When will it be time? Whatever can I do?"

I urged him to pray. At times, I confess, I felt the cold fingers of anxiety clutching around my heart. So many women died bearing children. I feared dying less for myself. Far more I worried what would become of my poor husband left to fend for himself. He did pray, long and earnest praying, sometimes with boisterous wrestling as with Jacob on the banks of the Jabbok.

"My, how he does kick so!" my husband said, his hand upon my swollen middle, his face slack with awe, a tremor in his tone.

And then the longed for day arrived. June 8, 1526, I feeling intensely weary, yet glowing with gratitude. The infant coughed, spluttered, then thrust out his lower lip and bellowed out an affronted cry. Laughing for joy, Martin threw open the windows of our upper bed chamber, and, like a bull, announced to the entire village. "My dear Katie has just brought into the world, by God's grace, a fat little boy, Hans Luther!"

I heard a mighty cheering of delight, the clanging of pots and pans, the clonking of wooden shoes on the cobbles, a joyful cacophony rising from the streets of Wittenberg. "I-I need you, Herr Doctor," I called to him, less because I felt weak; more because I wanted him away from the window.

"Ah, I must stop. Sick Katie calls me," he said, resetting the window latch.

"Mary pondered these things in her heart," I chided softly, cradling little Hans in my arms. "And only the shepherds knew."

"My dearest rib, all the hosts of heaven knew and proclaimed the Savior's birth. I, but one man, just gave out the joyous news discreetly to a few neighbors."

I shook my head in wonder at the man. "He looks like you," I said.

"Like Knight George, strong, muscular?"

"H'm, I believe the similarity lies more with your fleshy face, your dimpled double chin." We laughed together.

As I wrapped little Hans tightly in a blanket, my husband said, "Kick, little fellow. That is what the pope did to me, but I got loose."

Months passed and Hans grew fatter. And louder. "Why is he screaming like that?" my husband called above the clamor.

"Feel here, in his mouth," I said, taking my husband's fingers and running them along the slobbery gums of our little boy.

"Cutting his teeth," said Martin, nodding, "and making a joyous nuisance of yourself, aren't you?"

"The pear not falling far from the tree," I said under my breath.

"Allow me." My husband took Hans up in his big arms, bouncing, cooing, and singing to his firstborn son. "These are the joys of marriage, dearest Katie, of which the pope is not worthy."

To any who might read this, I promised when commencing this memoir that it would be about my husband, Martin Luther, not about Katharina and our children. I intend to keep that promise, though I have come to realize that it is not possible to examine the whole man without intimate vignettes from our home life.

Looking back, I wonder if the most important legacy my dear husband left Germany, perhaps the whole world, is the reformation of marriage and the family. I believe so, and am, thereby, encouraged to divulge something more of his family in the months and years that then lay ahead.

"Child, what have you done that I should love you so?" cried Martin in exasperation. "You have disturbed the whole household with your bawling."

We sat down to table, now with three-year-old Hans, his little sister Elizabeth, born near Christmastide 1527, and Magdalena born also near Christmastide but in 1529, and surrounded by more of my husband's students.

It was as I had previously looked about that same table crammed with our growing family and a growing number of young scholars, when the idea had struck me. Eyeing those young men shrewdly, it occurred to me; there was another source of revenue I had, heretofore, overlooked.

My husband's students—eager, earnest, thronging about him as if he were a championship jouster, fawning upon him as if he were a master swordsman—had to live somewhere, had to eat, didn't they? As they seemed to prefer eating our food at our table anyway, we decided to open the doors of the cloister and our home as a boarding house for university students. We had as many as twenty-five of their kind at a time. I acquired more cows, pigs, chickens, even fish for the pond. Of course it was a bit like an asylum, and more work for me, but since they were eating up all the victuals at my

274

table anyway, it made sense to charge them money for the courtesy. Which meant I was able to take on some help.

One afternoon I was making cheeses, hanging the whey in nets, and at the same time attempting to get the yeast right on my beer, and equally at the same time, attempting to calm baby Martin, named for his illustrious father, born in 1531, and gnawing and drooling away on everything, cutting his first tooth. Baby Martin's father was at that very moment engaged in table tutorial, as I referred to it, with our borders, most of them my husband's students.

"This is the sort of thing that has caused some of the Church fathers to vilify marriage," said my husband, heaving a sigh. "But now God has brought back the majesty of marriage to its proper esteem."

It was at that moment that little Martin soiled his diaper, with red-faced straining and flatulence nearly equal to his father's.

"Dearest Herr Doctor," I interjected. "I must change poor Martin, and it is the last one."

His tutorial suspended, my husband drummed his fingers on the table top. "The last what, my lord Kette?"

"Diaper," I said. "The last unsoiled diaper. I have washed others, but they need drying. Would you, my dearest Doctor, put out the clean ones on the dry line? There's a breeze and a bit of sun. It won't take long."

My request was met at first with stony silence, and I feared I might have overstepped boundaries.

"The majesty of marriage, Herr Doctor?" said one of his students. "Are diapers also matters of which the pope is unworthy?"

There was a snorting, as if a young man had been holding something back, but could do so no longer. I heard the methodical scraping of chair legs on the flagstone floor of our dining room. I immediately felt guilty at what I had asked my husband to do. Others were snickering; some had given off all restraint and were now fairly bursting with hilarity at the picture, their exalted professor pinning diapers on the line in the back garden. The floodgates burst. There was hooting, slapping thighs and backs, boys bursting with amusement at the comical scene unfolding before them.

"Let them laugh, my lord Katie," said my husband, hefting the laundry basket brimming with wet diapers. He planted a kiss on my cheek. "God and the angels smile in heaven."

# 49

# PRECIOUS

One morning as I readied a chicken for the pot, scalding the bird to remove its feathers—it was a juicy, fat one, and would make a lovely soup—I glanced up. Through the window I caught sight of my husband returning from his labors.

As I gutted the bird, sorting through its internal organs, gizzard, heart, and the rest, I frowned through the window. His posture was eloquent, shoulders slumped, eyes on the ground, his gait mechanical.

Must he leave us for some disputation? Or was it the interminable letter writing? I wondered if he was not the most popular man in Germany for correspondence, from printers to popes, from dogmen to dukes, magistrates to milkmaids, he received hundreds of letters, and was determined to answer them one and all. I felt a twinge of guilt. I too had added to his mound of letters when in the cloister, seeking his counsel for our escape.

"I could use two secretaries," he told me one evening, moaning and flexing the fingers of his writing hand. "I do almost nothing during the day but write letters. I am a reader at meals, parochial preacher, director of studies, overseer of eleven monasteries, superintendent of the fish pond at Litzkau, referee of the squabble at Torgau, lecturer on Paul, collector of material for a commentary on the Psalms, and then—overwhelmed with all these letters! You see how lazy I am, dear Kette."

I had assured him I thought no such thing, nor did anyone else who knew him.

Increasingly, my husband resented obligations that took him away from Wittenberg, away from his family. I believe some of his boorishness in Marburg with his friend Martin Bucer and the Swiss Reformer Ulrich Zwingli (decidedly not his friend)—he recounted the dispute to me, blow-by-blow—his boorishness was a result of his bad temper from being away from the children, and, I wanted to believe, from me.

"You agreed on a dozen important points of doctrine," I had chided him upon his return, "yet became belligerent at but one, thereby alienating a man with whom you had so much in agreement?" I wish I had been there, caught his eye before he retorted again and again, "This is my body." He admitted it. But it was too late. The damage was done.

Then there was his Schloss Coburg exile. He had felt like a caged bear at Coburg Castle, surrounded by one hundred knights appointed for his own protection—he called them his prison guards—while the German princes debated the Augsburg Confession, the realm teetering on armed revolt.

He was away from us for months, during which time I received a letter. "My father has died," he wrote. I later learned from an attendant that at the sad news he took his psalter and wept in his chamber for two days. Though he assured me of his confidence that both his parents were hoping in Christ alone, how I longed to be at his side to comfort him, render my ministration to his gnarled back, the fused tendons of his neck, bring him some of my own beer. Who knows what pigswill they made him drink in the castle, and the havoc it would wreak on his digestion?

About the unceasing demands and obligations pressing down on him, when in better temper, he merely quipped, "There is, I suppose, one advantage to it all. As it stands, I have no time for temptations of the world, the flesh, and the devil."

Reflecting on his words, I plucked off a few stray feathers and hung my chicken over a basin to drip. When Martin came through the door, my heart sank. Distress was etched in every line of his face.

"Herr Doctor, what is wrong?" I said, rinsing blood and chicken trimmings from my hands. "Must you go away? Or is it those infernal letters again?"

"*Nein, nein,*" he said, collapsing onto the settle.

"I am preparing a plump chicken for your supper." I dried my hands "Here, drink some beer."

Taking the stein from my hand, he said, "You have seen her, little Liesel."

"*Ja, ja,* the sweet thing, favorite of yours, with her aged grandmother, in the marketplace. What is wrong?"

Staring at me, he shook his head, but did not reply.

"It is her grandmother. She has died, hasn't she?"

He nodded. "Liesel is not like other children. Anyone can see that. The dear old woman died in the night, Liesel at her side till morning, tears streaking her cheeks. What a stupid ass I am. I should have done more for her, long ago. Now she must mourn alone. And who will care for her?"

I wrenched off my smock, tossed it onto the table, and placed my hands on my hips. "We shall!"

He looked at me, shook his head in wonder. I confess, I do so feel a quickening of my pulse when he sets his eyes on me in that fashion.

279

"I need more help with the children," I explained, "and the cows, the student borders, the pigs, and the orchard."

He nodded his head slowly. "God is the God of the humble, the miserable, the afflicted the oppressed, the desperate, and those who have been brought to nothing."

"And such a God is Liesel's God," I whispered, consoling him.

"H'm, you know we must be prepared to do more for her," said my husband, "than she can do for us?"

"We may be surprised," I said. "Her face alights every time she catches sight of Martin Luther, you who have been so kind to her."

"Never kind enough," he retorted.

"But never too late," I added, taking his arm. "Though it will be if we don't stop sulking about it."

"You are an empress, dearest Katie," he said, kissing my lips. "Now, you make haste to the market and fetch her. There's not a moment to lose. I'll go to the Bürgermeister and make it legal."

Liesel would not be the last child adopted into our home. There would be three more. My husband reflected with a catch in his voice, "Just so it is in the gospel of Jesus Christ: we are all adopted children, grafted in."

Over the coming joyful years, in God's great kindness, Hans, Elizabeth, Magdalena, and Martin were blessed with another brother, Paul, and another sister, Margaretta, named for her grandmother. Ten children in all, not to mention my pied piper's brood of two-dozen, sometimes-cocky, student borders. Ours was a full house, a happy one, and often a noisy and chaotic one.

"Christ tells us we must become as little children," my husband called to me above the din of squealing voices one morning. "Surely God does not expect us to become such idiots!"

Martin sometimes referred to his children as a band of little heathens, and we their parents charged with the solemn duty of leading them to Jesus Christ. It was in this spirit that my husband penned a children's catechism, for his own, yes, but for the aid all German parents to teach their children the gospel. In my opinion, it was one of his crowning achievements. I delighted to hear him tutoring his own children in the gospel.

"I believe in Jesus Christ," recited Hans before bedtime. "Who when I was lost and damned saved me from all sin and death and the power of the devil, not with gold and silver but with his own—" He broke off, stammering for the next word.

"Precious," came a lisping voice near the hearth, Liesel's voice. My heart swelled within me. Blinking rapidly, my eyes met my husband's, his brimming with joyful tears. I dropped a stitch in my knitting.

"Thank you sister," said Hans, then resuming. "—but with his own precious, holy blood and his sinless suffering and death, that I might belong to him and live in his kingdom and serve him forever in goodness, sinlessness, and happiness, just as he is risen from the dead and lives and reigns forever. That is really so."

"Can I be next?" cried Magdalena and Elizabeth, jostling one another.

From this episode, my husband coined a nickname for our little Liesel. 'Precious,' he called her, and soon everyone called her that. There may never have been a more fitting name for a child of Luther, for a child of God.

For my husband there was no dispute about what labor of his was most important: The Word of God, and translating the whole of it into German, "the German the mother chortles to her infant," he would say. Along with writing new hymns, he spent his months at the Coburg translating the Bible. Never satisfied, for years after, he doggedly revised and recast the verbiage, both for accuracy—he explained to me that the Bible was given by the Holy Spirit in different languages, Hebrew and in Greek—but equally he revised for accessibility to the common man, woman, and child.

Though my husband was a doctor, a man of learning, a university professor himself, his love for God's Word made him anxious about Wittenberg's university, about all universities, all learning.

"I am much afraid," he told me after the ceremony conferring degrees on his students, "that the universities will prove to be the great gates of hell, unless they diligently labor in explaining the Holy Scriptures, and engraving them in the hearts of youth."

"As you do, Herr Doctor," I interjected, taking his arm, wanting to divert him from melancholy on the subject.

"And I shall soon die," he retorted. "Then what? I advise no one to place his child where the Scriptures do not reign paramount. If I were Carlstadt, I would impose a rigid law about it, but I am not. Thus, I am afraid. What will it take, dear Katie, a year, ten years, a century? And the Word of God silenced, even in these very halls."

Sunlight slanting through a gothic window glistered in his eyes. "Every institution in which men are not unceasingly occupied with the Word of God must become corrupt—the very gates of hell."

So much did my husband love the Word of God, and long to do its sacred words justice in German, I believe he may have been wrestling with his Hebrew and his Greek in the oxcart on his final journey away from us, resolute to the last, to get every word correct.

"Words are like children," he said one evening, after ours had finally settled down for the night, the last cries for milk or a slice of pear had drifted into heavy breathing. "The more attention you lavish on them the more they demand."

# 50

# CHRISTMASTIDE

A light dusting of wet snow fell in the night, and I admit it, I fretted about the cold and damp as I dressed the children for worship. It was the Sunday before Christmastide, a joyous time for all, save those sick with fever, or dying with plague—or mothers with diapers to change and too many children to dress for church.

"You'll not step foot out of this house," I chided Magdalena, "without your scarf snug about your neck. You'll catch your death of cold."

Squirming, Paul resisted Liesel as she attempted to tie his scarf about his neck.

"Paul, let sister tie it properly. Precious, if he continues to resist, you have my permission to cinch it a great deal tighter."

Hans gripped his own neck, feigning the sounds of strangulation at a hanging.

It was times like these when I was tempted to doubt my husband's laziness. While he prayed quietly in the vestry before service, calming his soul, communing with God, here

I was, noses and bottoms to wipe, hands full of all his unruly children.

"We must all bundle up," I said, darting a prayer of forgiveness heavenward. "In the dead of winter, the chill inside the church is little different from the cold outside."

"But all the people make it warmer," said Elizabeth.

"And smellier," added Hans, pinching his nose.

"Margaretta spilled her milk," said Paul, as if it were a crime akin to stealing a relic from the duke.

"Help her," I snapped. "The Reverend Doctor Martin Luther's family mustn't be late for service. Nor attend looking like ragamuffins with drool and milk stains on their tunics."

Breathless, we at last arrived at the Stadtkirche, pressed tightly on every side by our Wittenberg neighbors and friends, I smiling and nodding, and doing my best to appear unruffled, capable, the perfect mother.

After prayers and singing, my husband read out his text from Luke's gospel. And then he commenced.

"How unobtrusively and simply do those events take place on earth that are so heralded in heaven! On earth it happened in this wise: There was a poor young wife, Mary of Nazareth, among the meanest dwellers of the town, so little esteemed that none noticed the great wonder that she carried. She was silent, did not vaunt herself, but served her husband."

He, unaware of the high turmoil rowling in my bosom, smiled in my direction, and I believe gave me a wink.

"They simply left the house," he continued. "Perhaps they had a donkey for Mary to ride upon, though the gospels say nothing about it, and we may well believe that she went on foot. On foot, great with child! It would be like walking from Wittenberg to Leipzig—days it would have taken, all on foot, Mary about to be delivered of a baby! Joseph likely thought, 'When we get to Bethlehem, we shall be among relatives and can borrow everything.'

"A fine idea that was! Bad enough that a young bride married only a year could not have had her baby at Nazareth in her own house instead of making all that journey when heavy with child!

"It gets worse. When she arrived, there was no room for her! The inn was full. No one would release a room to this pregnant woman. She had to go to a cow stall and there bring forth the Maker of all creatures because nobody would give way.

"Shame on you, wretched Bethlehem! The inn ought to have been burned with brimstone, for even though Mary had been a beggar maid or unwed, anybody at such a time should have been glad to give her a hand.

"There are many of you in this congregation who think to yourselves: 'If only I had been there! How quick I would have helped the baby! I would have washed his diapers and hung them on the line to dry. How happy I would have been to go with the shepherds to see the baby Jesus lying in the manger!'

"Yes, you would! You say that because you know how great Christ is, but if you had been there at that time you would have done no better than the people of Bethlehem. Childish and silly thoughts are these!"

He paused, scanning our upturned faces.

"Why don't you do it now? You have Christ in your neighbor. You ought to serve him, for what you do to your neighbor in need you do to the Lord Christ himself."

There was a rustling and murmuring undulating through the congregation. I felt it. I contributed to it, his words cutting me to the quick, making me ashamed of my impatience, my feeling hard put upon in my labors, my indifference toward my needy neighbor.

"The birth was still more pitiable," he continued, returning to his narrative. "No one regarded this young wife bringing forth her first-born. No one took her condition to heart. No one noticed that in a strange place she had not the very least

285

thing needful in childbirth. I now know something about childbirth. There she was without preparation: no light, no fire, in the dead of night, in thick darkness. No one came to help, no tender ministrations from her mother, and no midwife.

"The guests swarming in the inn were carousing, and no one attended to this woman. Joseph and Mary, no doubt, wondered what they would use for swaddling clothes, some garment she could spare, perhaps her veil—certainly not Joseph's breeches. They didn't get ripped into swaddling bands. I've seen them. They're in a reliquary in Aachen, and at a bargain price: two-dozen indulgent years off purgatory for a few *Hail Marys* and florin!"

His congregation roared with laughter, men slapping each others' backs at the jest. He had taught them well to mock and flout papal indulgences, and they loved him for it, as a man being freed from prison loves the rattling of the key in the lock. I shook my head, smiling indulgently at his wit.

"Think, women," he continued, "there was no one there to bathe the baby. No warm water, nor even cold. No fire, no light. The mother was herself midwife and the maid. The cold manger was the bed and the bathtub. Who showed the poor girl what to do? She had never had a baby before. I am amazed that the little one did not freeze."

He hesitated, glancing my way. I felt my features grow pale, and my heart thundered in my bosom. I feared the worst. He would launch into one of his excurses, expostulating on my delivery of one of our children, sparing none of the more graphic details of childbirth, and my groaning therein. With a hasty shaking of his head, he continued. I let out my breath with relief.

"Do not make of Mary a stone. She was a young woman of feeling. For when God favors us with his presence, he makes us tender by his grace.

286

"Let us, then, join them in tender feeling and meditate upon the Nativity just as we see it happening in our own babies. Behold Christ lying in the lap of his young mother. What can be sweeter than the babe, what more lovely than the mother!"

Again, my husband glanced in the direction of his somewhat disheveled family, and smiled.

"What fairer than her youth! What more gracious than her virginity! Look at the child, knowing nothing. Yet worlds on worlds belong to him. Your conscience should not fear but take comfort in him. Doubt nothing.

"To me there is no greater consolation given to mankind than this, that Christ became man, a child, a babe, playing in the lap and at the breasts of his most gracious mother. Who is here this morning whom this sight would not comfort?"

He paused, letting his words sink into our hearts.

"Here is the only one to overcome the power of sin, death, hell, conscience, and guilt. Flee to this gurgling babe, and believe that he is come, not to judge you, but to save you."

After drawing his sermon at an end, Luther lined out a new Advent hymn he had prepared for his congregation. As our voices joined with his deep resonating one, the clouds outside seemed to thin, and as we continued our carol praises, a pale shaft of winter sunlight angled through the stained glass, illuminating and warming our upturned faces.

From heaven high I come to you,
I bring you tidings good and new;
Glad tidings of great joy…

Welcome to earth, thou noble Guest,
Through whom the sinful world is blest!
In my distress thou com'st to me;
What thanks shall I return to thee?

That afternoon, as I rubbed thyme between my hands, sprinkling it on the pork for our Sunday dinner, Elizabeth remarked, "The church was full this morning."

"And warmer than I feared," I said.

"But it did stink," said Hans.

"Yes," said their father, "they had manure on their boots."

"I shouldn't wonder," I said, "if we Luthers didn't have it on ours."

Drawing in a deep breath, my husband declared, "It is a perfume I heartily welcome. After all, manure would have been one of the first odors our Lord would have smelled at his birth, wafting into his sacred nostrils from the cows. It is an aroma more pleasing to the Lord than the rancid incense of Rome."

He frowned. "I do wish I had included this in my sermon."

# 51

# SOLA KATHARINA

One morning while little Paul was smacking and mulling at my breast, my husband smiled and said, "Child, your enemies are the pope, the bishops, Duke George, the emperor, and the devil. And there you are sucking unconcernedly."

Throwing his head back, Paul let out a howl. I cradled the baby over my arm and patted his back. Wiping the little fellow's mouth, I smiled at my husband. "He belches like his father," I said, and resumed nursing him.

My husband laughed. "Herein lies a lesson, dearest Katie. We no more earn heaven by good works than little Paul earns his food and drink by crying and howling."

Just then, our Magdalena bounced into the dining room singing a song, pinching the corner of her frock and twirling to her own music.

"What is it you are singing, dear one?" asked my husband. "Where is my lute? I must accompany your beautiful song."

She laughed, and sang again:

Luther teaches that we all
Are involved in Adam's fall.
If man beholds himself within,
He feels the bite and curse of sin.
When dread, despair, and terror seize,
Contrite he falls upon his knees.
Then breaks for him the light of day…

"Did you pen these words, Herr Doctor?" I asked, though I felt certain he had not.

"Only a clod would pen words using his own name!" he snorted.

"It is the shoemaker's song, papa," said Magdalena.

"Shall we invite our cows in to sing it with us?" asked their father, to raucous laughter.

"They are not people, papa!" said Elizabeth.

"Moo! Moo!" bellowed little Martin. "Imagine what it would sound like!"

"—and smell like!" said Hans.

"Pigs and chickens joining in," said Martin.

"Cows—pigs and chickens, too—have their own way of singing," said my husband, the children gathering around to listen. "But they are not made in God's image. His precious gift of music has been bestowed on men alone to remind us that we are created to praise and magnify the Lord."

He plucked softly on his lute strings as he continued, shaking his head in wonder. "But when our voices are sharpened and polished by art, then one begins to see with amazement the great and perfect wisdom of God in his wonderful work of music.

"Where one voice takes a simple part—" He played the same note, three times over, then dropping lower and swelling in undulations, a martial-sounding melody, to my ear. "And around that simple melody sing three, four, or five other

290

voices—Hans, Elizabeth, Magdalena, Martin—your sweet voices. And then add leaping, springing round about, marvelously gracing the simple part, like a folk dance in heaven with friendly bows, embracings, and hearty swinging of the partners."

My husband set aside his lute and snatched up my hand, spinning me around, the skirts of my frock swishing about the family room. Not to be outdone, the children joined it.

What followed was nothing short of a family frolic, spinning, looping arms, whirling in circles, singing, shouting, laughing as if this place, this once-sober black cloister had been transformed into the light and beauty of heaven itself.

At last we were forced to stop and catch our breaths. The warm glow in my bosom was reflected in the animated features of my children and my dear husband, their father, cheeks flushed and rosy with exertion and the exuberance of the moment.

"He who does not find this an inexpressible miracle of the Lord," said my husband, breathing heavily, "is truly a clod and is not worthy to be considered a man!"

"*Jawohl!*" the children agreed.

"This shoemaker's song," said my husband, "where did you learn it, my dear one?"

"All the children sing it in the market," said Magdalena. "It is like the catechism, but in a song. And there is more, all about angels, heaven, and the Lord Jesus."

"My dear child," he said, taking her up onto his knee, "if only we could hold fast to this faith."

"Why, papa," she laughed, holding his face in her hands, "don't you believe it?"

Twirling her curls in his fingers, he turned to me and said, "Christ has made the children our teachers. I am chagrined that although I am ever so much a doctor, I still have to go to the same school with our children, with you, sweet Magdalena."

He became sober.

"Who among men can understand the full meaning of this Word of God, 'Our Father who art in heaven'? Anyone who genuinely believes these words will often say, 'My Savior is Lord of heaven and earth and all that is therein. The Angel Gabriel is his servant, Raphael is his guardian, and the angels who meet my every need are ministering spirits. My Father, who is in heaven, will give them charge over me lest I dash my foot against a stone.'"

"*Jawohl*, I believe that," said Magdalena with a toss of her curls. Laughing, she squirmed and sprang from his lap, skipping out to play in the garden with her siblings.

"At times, dear Katie, just when I am affirming this faith," he continued, his voice low, "I fear that my Father will wrench all this joy from me—you, the children—and suffer me to be thrown into prison, drowned, or beheaded. Or, worst of all, burned. Then faith falters and in weakness I cry, 'Who knows whether it is true?'"

I dreaded his bouts of despondency, and by the vacant staring of his eyes, I feared he was plummeting into another one.

"I feel like a fugitive," he continued, his voice barely above a whisper, "fleeing for his life, staggering in the blackness up a staircase, winding ever higher—too high, too ancient, too dizzying a tower. My head spinning, my foot unsure, then slipping. Plunging to my ruin, I grope, my hands torn against the rough, barrel-round walls. Clutching for something, anything firm, I find and lay hold of a rope. On the brink of ruin, my fall arrested, I find the rope is affixed to something."

He paused, staring unblinking into the coals.

"Affixed to what?"

"A bell. It is too cruel—as I catch my fall on the rope, the bell begins ringing, clanging, interminable. I hear it yet today in my ears."

Not having words to bring him comfort, as was my habit, I massaged his shoulders, his neck, his arms, he emitting appreciative little grunts at my ministrations.

"Before we wed," he said, his voice monotone, trancelike, "when I went to bed alone the devil was always waiting for me. When he began to plague me, as he still attempts to do at times, I gave him this answer: 'Devil, I must sleep. That's God's command. He wants me to work by day. Sleep by night. So, devil, go away.'"

"Does he go away?"

"Not always. If that doesn't work and he brings out a catalog of sins, I say, 'Yes, old fellow, I know all about it. And I know some more sins of mine you've overlooked. Here are a few extra. Put them down.' If he still won't quit and presses me hard and accuses me as a sinner, I scorn and taunt him. 'St. Satan, pray for me. Of course you have never done anything wrong in your life. You alone are holy. Go to God and get grace for yourself. If you want to get me all straightened out, I say, come back when you've been absolved of the legion of all your transgressions.'"

"You speak thus to the devil?" I asked.

He nodded and looked at me as if to say, "Doesn't everyone?"

"And I sometimes dispute much with God with great impatience," he continued. "I hold him to his promises. As did the persistent Canaanite woman who besought Jesus for the crumbs that fell from the children's table.

"The Gospel account was written for our comfort so we can see how God does not slack his promises because of our sins or hasten them because of our righteousness and merits. He pays no attention to either.

"All Christ's answers in the Gospels sounded like no, but he did not mean no. He had not said that the Canaanite woman was not of the house of Israel. He had not said that she was a dog. He had not said no. Yet all his answers were more like no than yes.

"Katie, this shows how our heart feels in despondency. It sees nothing but a plain no. Therefore, it must turn to the deep hidden yes under the no and hold with a firm faith to God's Word."

"With the devil there is only no," I said. "Yet you contend with the devil, expose his hypocrisy in accusing you, and argue with him?"

He shook his head. "Don't argue with the devil. I don't recommend it. He has had five thousand years of experience. He has tried out all his tricks on Adam, Abraham, and David, and he knows exactly the weak spots.

"And he is persistent. If he does not get you down with the first assault, he will commence a siege of attrition until you give in from sheer exhaustion. Better banish the whole subject. Seek company and discuss some irrelevant matter as, for example, what is going on in Venice."

"Which brings to mind," I interjected, "a question that has puzzled me. Is the prime minister of Prussia the duke's brother?"

He blinked rapidly, as if unable to get his mind from one subject to another.

"I shall make enquiries," he murmured. "But as I was saying, shun solitude. But do not go it alone. Eve got into trouble when she walked in the garden alone. I have my worst temptations when I am by myself.

"Seek out some Christian brother or sister, some wise counselor. Undergird yourself with the fellowship of the church. Then, too, seek convivial company, feminine company, dine, dance, joke, and sing. Make yourself eat and drink even though food may be very distasteful—ugh!" he groaned. "Fasting is the very worst expedient for despondency. Though when my bowels are heaving and contorting themselves, I am tempted to a perpetual fasting."

He groaned, rising to his feet, breathing heavily, his face contorted with pain.

"Herr Doctor, you are not well," I said. "You must lie down here on the bed."

Moaning, Luther lay on his side. Sitting next to him, I persisted in my massage, working with my fingers into the knotted muscles of his neck and shoulders what healing I could manage.

"There are three things," he said, his voice low, "to alleviate pain, whether pain of the body or of the mind. Faith in Christ is the first. Second is anger; I find nothing that promotes work better than angry fervor. For when I wish to compose, write, pray and preach well, I must be angry. It refreshes my entire system, my mind is sharpened, and all unpleasant thoughts and depression fade away."

I shuddered. "That is almost frightening."

"You have nothing to fear," he said. "I reserve my rage for the pope and the devil. Never am I angry with you, my mistress of the pig market, my lord Katie."

"Never?"

"Impatient at times, more my fault than yours, but never angry."

I bent down and kissed him soundly on the cheek, still kneading away at his gnarled muscles. "You said three things," I reminded him.

"I did," he said. "Though faith in Christ remains the first. The third far and away exceeds the second. The third way to dispel despondency, pain, misery of every kind—is the love of a woman."

I scowled at him. "Any woman?"

He laughed. "*Nein, nein.* There is only one: *Sola Katharina.*"

# 52

# VILEST MISCREANT

**K**atharina alone," so he claimed, and I wholly
believed him—there were no other lovers. Seldom,
however, did we have our evenings to ourselves.
After the children were at last snuggled in their beds, the
scholar hoards descended. My husband's students and
colleagues somehow believed that Doctor Martin Luther was
theirs by right. At times like these, I was certain we did not
charge them enough gulden for their privileges.

One such evening, I knitting a new scarf for Magdalena—
poor dear, so prone at the first chill to catch a nasty cough
deep in her chest—as I say, there followed a somewhat heated
discussion with Philip Melanchthon. I include this exchange
as faithfully as I can, and do so because my husband so often
said, next to his children's catechism, his book *Bondage of the
Will* was his most important.

"Philip, my friend," cried my husband. "Your words
sound like Erasmus of Rotterdam. You make me weep. Are

there no greater differences with Rome than our use of German in the service?"

"Well, I hesitate to go that far," said Melanchthon, studying the creases on his palms minutely. "Why do you insist on being at odds with him?"

"Erasmus?" retorted Luther. "I do appreciate something about him."

"Indeed?" laughed Melanchthon, eyebrows arched in mock astonishment. "Erasmus, the greatest humanist scholar of the age, and you have stooped to find something you appreciate about him."

"I have. I am deeply indebted to him for the accuracy of his Greek in the New Testament. For this I applaud him. Moreover, in our disputation on free will, only Erasmus has taken it to the heart of the problem."

"Which is?"

"The nature of man," said Luther simply. "Is man irretrievably lost if left to himself? Or is his will free to believe and act according to God's will? Therein, lies the difference between Rome and the true gospel. Everything else is footnote."

"Surely man's will must have some degree of freedom," said Philip.

"Which is exactly what Erasmus argues: man in his free will is able to believe and come to God. Contrary to exalted Erasmus, however, the Apostle Paul does not agree. So neither do I. Free will is a divine term; only God has it. Man's will, dead in trespasses and sins, is in bondage and can only be made free by the grace of God in Christ."

"Who then will believe?" asked Melanchthon.

"No man *will* believe," replied my husband, "because no man *can* believe. Not without grace. It is only the elect who are reborn and graciously enabled to believe."

Shaking his head decisively, Melanchthon said, "Erasmus does not agree."

"Of course, Erasmus does not agree. He sneers at St. John. Why does he do so? Because John declares without equivocation that 'salvation comes not by the will of man but by the will of God who shows mercy.' Furthermore, your great humanist scholar sneers at St. Paul and ventures to say, that the Epistle to the Romans, whatever it might have been at a former period, is not applicable to the present state of things.

"What am I to say to a man who takes such a low view of God's Word? Shame upon you, accursed wretch! For this, Erasmus of Rotterdam is the vilest miscreant that ever disgraced the earth. He sits back and makes his mows and mocks at everything and everybody, at God and man, at papist and protestant, but all the while using such shuffling and double-meaning terms, that no one can lay hold of him to any effectual purpose. Whenever I pray, I pray for a curse upon Erasmus!"

I caught my breath at his words and dropped a stitch. Melanchthon was speechless, lips parted but no words.

"You think my words over harsh. But they are not. Why? Because it is erudite scholars, the lofty learned, men like Erasmus, who superciliously lead generations of others into error—and, thereby, into damnation."

Melanchthon made no reply.

"My great fear, Philip," continued my husband—I heard the anguish in his tone, "is that in your conciliatory zeal you will eviscerate doctrinal reform and betray the gospel, as Erasmus has done."

"But, Herr Doctor, what of love, unity?" asked Melanchthon. "Can we not find a middle way with the pope and with Rome?"

"I am not permitted," said my husband, "to let my love be so merciful as to tolerate and endure false doctrine. And what greater false doctrine is there than that which supplants Christ. Rome says the true treasure of the Church is the merits of the saints—and charges mounds of gold and silver to buy that merit. While the Church's true treasure is the merits of Christ in the gospel of grace, which comes freely of God's will. There is no middle way with error."

"But could not the papacy be reformed," said Philip. "The pope corrected, reconciliation and peace restored?"

My husband rose to his feet, agitated, pacing before the hearth. "Reconcile with a pope who declares King Hal of England, Defender of the Faith?" He scratched his head. "And why does the pope call a fornicating monarch thus? Because he penned a treatise against mine on justification by faith alone. That is why. Have you read it?"

Philip shook his head.

"The ignorance of this king is beyond all compass. He understands less about faith and works than a log of wood. I don't care a straw about this royal driveller of lies and poison. If a king of England spits his impudent lies in my face, I have a right and obligation in my turn to throw them back down his very throat."

"Is there, Herr Doctor, no moderating of your opinions?"

"Which is exactly what the pope and his pet monarch want me to do," roared my husband, "moderate my teaching."

"But your opinion, what you think—" began Melanchthon.

"What I think, Philip, matters nothing. What Erasmus thinks matters nothing! What matters is what God thinks. And what he thinks about free will he makes profusely plain to us in his Word, that is, if we shut our mouths and open our ears to hear what God thinks.

"Hal's problem, the pope's problem, everyone's problem is that we don't shut our mouths and open our ears; instead we open our mouths and stop our ears to God's Word. And what says the Word of God, Philip? It tells me not what I must will or do, but what Jesus Christ the Son of God has done for me."

"I agree," interjected Melanchthon. "Free will must have the assistance of Christ and his grace."

"But don't you see?" said my husband, his voice earnest. I could tell he genuinely wanted his colleague, his friend, to understand. "Free will without God's grace is not free at all, not while words continue to have precise meaning. Man and his will without the grace of God is the permanent prisoner and bond slave of evil, since no man by will alone can turn himself to good."

Melanchthon spread his arms and shook his head. "How can an obtuse doctrine such as this be the heart of the problem, the great difference between Rome and reformation?"

"Obtuse doctrine?" said my husband. "The most damnable and pernicious heresy that has ever plagued the mind of men was the idea that somehow he could make himself good enough by an act of his will to deserve to live with an all holy God."

Melanchthon, squirming in his chair, picked with his fingers at his thin beard before replying. "The pope and King Henry of England," he said, changing the subject, so it seemed to me, "they wield enormous powers. Their servants do their bidding."

Looking bewildered at his words, my husband halted in his pacing and shrugged his great shoulders. "Princes and popes are often great fools, great knaves, hangmen in high places. What care I if a thousand churchfuls of Henrys rise up against me? I have the Divine Majesty on my side. Go on, pope of Rome, declare this faithless king Defender of the Faith. He is a liar and a rascal. To Hal, to Erasmus, to the pope and all he defends, I say, come on, pigs that you are, burn me if you dare!"

I dropped another stitch. At this rate, my little girl will never get her new scarf, not before the cold and damp of winter sets in.

"Is this the doctrine," asked Melanchthon, "for which you want them to burn you?"

Sitting back down at my side, gazing unblinking into the flames of our fire, my husband reached over and placed his hand upon my arm. "For this or any other true doctrine," he said, his tone calm and resolved, "my body they may kill."

My knitting idle on my lap, I gripped his hand.

Melanchthon leaned forward, elbows on his knees. "Why is it so important?"

"Because by their false doctrine," said my husband, "this monarch and his defenders cast their filth at the throne of *my* monarch—*my Christ!*"

# 53

# IN DEATH WE LIVE

It was one of the moments a wife and mother cherishes, our children gathered around us, playing, singing (occasionally squabbling, I confess it), all of them, at the moment, in health; my husband, his temperament raucously joyful, his pain manageable (pain was his unremitting companion); good cheer, gingerbread, laughter, roasted apples, crackling fire, light flickering on the walls and beamed ceiling, autumn rain pattering against the leaded window panes. Presiding over all was my husband, improvising on his lute, teaching us a new hymn, telling stories, to his children's delight, and, I admit it, to my own boundless pleasure.

Over-awed as I had been at first laying eyes on Martin Luther, married now to him for these many years, I knew his weaknesses: his impatience, his proneness to despondency, his inclination to depression so deep I feared it would take him off, his proclivity for scurrilous, bombastic vitriol with his enemies—and sometimes with his friends—and there was always the matter of his bowels. Intimate with the whole man, his frailties not excluded; nevertheless, did I daily struggle with loving him overmuch, an ardent conflict that made itself more cruelly felt as the days, weeks, months, and years of our lives hastened by.

Setting aside his lute, my husband took up the family Bible, our daily custom. "Hans, it is your turn," he said passing it to our eldest, now almost sixteen years of age.

"Stop fidgeting, Paul," I admonished. "Margaretta, sit like a lady. Elizabeth, stop pouting. Liesel, dear, sit by your father and keep Paul from fidgeting. Magdalena, stop coughing, dear, and sit here, close to the hearth."

When all was settled, Hans read out the text from midway in the book of Genesis, his voice now so like his father's: deep, resonating, at times expressive and boisterous. A hush came over our sitting room. It was a sobering account he read out. Even the little ones seemed to feel it.

"Imagine it, children," my husband began, when Hans had finished reading. "Abraham was told by God that he must sacrifice the son of his old age by a miracle, the seed through whom he was to become the father of kings and of a great nation. Imagine how Abraham must have felt.

"I imagine he turned pale. Not only would he lose his son, but God appeared to be a hangman. He had said, 'In Isaac shall be thy seed,' but now that same God said, 'Kill Isaac.'

"Who would not hate a God so cruel and contradictory? How Abraham longed to talk it over with someone! Could he not tell Sarah? But he well knew that if he mentioned it to anyone he would be dissuaded and prevented from carrying out the deed. The spot designated for the sacrifice, Mount Moriah, was some distance away. Read that bit again, Hans."

"'And Abraham rose up early in the morning, and saddled his ass, and took two of his young men with him, and Isaac his son, and split the wood for the burnt offering.'"

"Abraham did not even leave the saddling of the ass to others," continued my husband. "He himself laid on the beast the wood for the burnt offering. He was thinking all the time that these logs would consume his son, his hope of seed. With these very sticks that he was picking up, the boy would be burned."

I glanced at the children, each in turn. What was he thinking? I wondered, was this an appropriate bedtime story?

"In such a terrible case," he continued, "should he not take time to think it over?"

"*Jawohl,* he should think it over." Little Martin nodded vigorously, eyes round and unblinking.

"Could Abraham not tell Sarah?" my husband continued. "I would so want to talk to your mother about such a matter. With what inner tears he suffered! He mounted the beast and was so absorbed he scarcely knew what he was doing. He took two servants and Isaac his son. In that moment everything died in him: Sarah, his family, his home, Isaac. Children, this is what it is to sit in sackcloth and ashes."

Magdalena raised her hand. "Why did God not tell him it was only a trial?"

"Only a trial?" said my husband. "My dear Lenchen, if he had known it was only a trial, he would not have been tried by it. Such is the nature of our trials that while they last we cannot see to the end. 'Then on the third day Abraham lifted up his eyes, and saw the place afar off.' What a battle he had endured in those three days!

"There Abraham left the servants and the ass, and he laid the wood upon Isaac; he took the torch and the sacrificial knife in his own hands. All the time he was thinking, 'Isaac, if you knew, if your mother knew that you are to be sacrificed.'"

I confess, I wanted to stop my ears, to halt the telling of the story. I scanned the attentive faces of our children; how could I bear to lose one of them? The tears were whelming up in my eyes. I sometimes knitted during our family prayers, but not this night. The wool grew damp, and I could not see to stitch.

"The sacred account proceeds," continued my husband. "'And they went both of them together.' The whole world does not know what here took place. They two walked together. Who? The father and the dearest son, one not knowing what was in store but ready to obey, the other certain that he must leave his son in ashes."

Nearly overcome with his own telling, my husband paused, reaching a hand over and laying it on Hans's shoulder, then stroking his hair. The little ones sat, eyes wide, mouths agape at the telling.

"Then said Isaac, 'My father.' And he said, 'Yes, my son.' And Isaac said, 'Father, here is the fire and here the wood, but where is the lamb?' He was worried his father had overlooked something. Abraham replied, 'God will himself provide a lamb, my son.'

"When they were come to the top of the mount, Abraham built the altar and laid on the wood, and then he was forced to tell Isaac. I can scarce imagine the moment. The boy was stupefied. What would you have thought, Hans, or you, Martin, or little Paul?"

"I would have been frightened," said Martin, swallowing.

"I would have questioned my father," said Hans.

"I would not have," said Paul, thrusting out his lower lip.

"I imagine Isaac would have protested," continued their father. "'Have you forgotten? I am the son of Sarah by a miracle in her old age. I was promised and through me, your only son, you, Father, are to be the father of a great nation? You've always said it was so.'

"Abraham must have answered that God would fulfill his promise even out of ashes. Then Abraham bound his son and laid him upon the wood. The father raised his knife. The boy bared his throat. If God had slept an instant, the lad would have been dead.

"I could not have watched." My husband's voice broke; he blinked rapidly, firelight glistened on the tears brimming in his eyes. "I am not able in my thoughts to follow. The lad was as a sheep for the slaughter. Never before in history was there such obedience. But God was there, watching with all the angels. The father raised his knife; the boy did not wince. The angel cried, 'Abraham, Abraham!' See how divine majesty is at hand in the hour of death. We say, 'In the midst of life we die.' God answers, 'Nein, in the midst of death we live.'"

Margaretta had clamored upon my lap; I was grateful and clutched her tightly to my breast. "I scarcely believe it," I said. "Surely God would not have treated his son like that."

"Ah, but, Katie, my love," he said. "He did. He did. God the Father gave his only begotten Son, the Lord Jesus for love. And still more so than Isaac, Jesus knew it, felt it, the horrible wrath of his Holy Father poured out on him.

"And there was no staying the hand of the Father at Calvary. No longed for, 'Abraham, Abraham! Do not slay your son!' That is why Jesus cried in agony, 'My God, my God, why hast thou forsaken me?'

"There was no other substitute. No ram caught in the thicket. No frantically happy untying of the cords freeing his son. No wrestling the substitute lamb to the altar. Christ was himself the lamb that God alone provided for the sacrifice. If only the hard-hearted sons of Abraham today knew and believed what our precious Lord Jesus came to do, 'give his life a ransom for many.'"

Liesel, thrusting her hand in her father's, whispered, "Precious." Squeezing her hand, he leaned close, smiling and pressing his forehead to hers.

# 54

# GRIEF AND LOSS

(Winter, 1543)

My dear husband, alongside his hymns, would entertain our children by crafting dramas for them to perform around our hearth of an evening. It warmed my heart seeing him so animated with them, coaching them on their inflections, gestures, and pronunciation.

He often played his lute, accompanying their performance, improvising interludes for scene changes, when something sinister occurred, or when something went awry and there was a need for distraction, as when a child fell from her chair, or dropped a vase accidentally, shards of crockery littering the floor, or when an actor was wildly gesticulating only to wack a sibling in the face. More than once there were bloodied noses, and on one occasion a broken tooth.

"Now, then," he announced. "Who would like to be the pope this evening?"

The boys' hands shot up accompanied by eager grunts and squeals.

"All right, it shall be Pope Paul this evening. And who would like to be our Lord?"

The girls' hands shot into the air, all of them sitting up straight, attempting to look very holy and good.

"Magdalena, you shall have the honor."

What followed was a drama the children knew by heart.

Pope Paul cleared his throat, leapt onto a chair, thrust out his chin, and declared, "Sicily is mine. Corsica is mine. Assisi is mine. Perugia is mine."

"I have not where to lay my head." Magdalena recited Christ's words, softly, reverently and with feeling.

Pope Paul leapt onto another chair. "He who contributes and receives indulgences will be absolved."

"I am the Way, I am the Truth, and I am the Life. No one comes to the Father but by me." Our Magdalenchen said the words as if she were confessing her own faith.

Stomping his foot, his chair nearly careening over, Pope Paul retorted. "*Nein, nein*! Rome is the way, the truth, and the life. No one comes to the Father but by Rome!"

"Feed my sheep," said Magdalena, spreading her hand wide.

"I shear my sheep!" cried Pope Paul, snip-snipping with his fingers. Hans bleated pitifully into his cupped hands.

"Put up your sword." As she spoke, Magdalena made a graceful motion as if doing so.

"Nonsense! Pope Julius killed sixteen hundred in one day with his sword." Flailing the air, Pope Paul gave a frightfully convincing imitation of a vicious warrior pope.

And so it went. I sometimes wondered if it wasn't a tad bit irreverent, but my husband was convinced that it was both a helpful and an enjoyable aid to our children. By such a participatory method—there were other family dramas—he was convinced that our children came to know the vast difference between the pretended Vicar of Christ, the pope, and of Christ himself, our only Savior.

The drama neared its climax, Christ always having the last word. Looking heavenward, Magdalena drew in breath to speak. There was a catch in her voice. I froze. Then coughing. Instantly, I was at her side, my arm around her shoulders, supporting her. "There, now, it is enough. Try to breathe slowly. No, don't gasp so."

"Thump her on the back," said Hans. "That sometimes helps."

Her face was red, tears whelming in her eyes. And still she coughed. "We must get her to bed," I said.

"Dear Magdalenchen," said my husband, caressing her cheek with the backs of his fingers. "I shall get the physician," he said, snatching up his cloak and hat.

I had known. But I had refused to think on it. She often coughed, but it grew worse when the rains of autumn fell, and worse still when the ice and snow of winter descended. The winter of 1543 was colder than usual, more snow, blocks of ice clogging the river.

She trembled as I tucked her into her bed, drawing in breath in lurching undulations. Reluctantly, I felt her forehead, knowing what I would find there. A fever, burning like hell fire.

"Elizabeth, fetch me a bowl of cool water and a wash rag. And the rest of you, ready yourselves for bed. Let us allow Magdalenchen to rest in hers."

I studied the furrows of the physician's face as he examined our daughter. He stroked her cheek, shaking his head slowly. Gesturing for us to follow him into the corridor, he rose from her side.

"Herr Luther, Frau Luther," he said, his voice low and grave; he bit his lower lip. "You must prepare yourselves. There is nothing I can do for her. God alone can save her."

"He has," murmured my husband.

We took turns throughout that long night vigil, my husband and I, neither of us sleeping while the other sat at Magdalenchen's bedside. Lying awake on our bed, I strained my ears, investigating every sound from the next room.

"O God, I love her so," I heard my husband praying, his voice trembling. He was silent for a moment. I heard him breathing, sighing heavily. Then, after a faint undulating moaning sound, he continued, "But thy will be done."

"Father?"

Her voice was faint, but I was on my feet in an instant, wrapping my nightgown tightly against the chill.

"Magdalenchen, my little girl," he said, taking her hand in his, his words strained, catching in his throat.

In the quavering darkness, a single candle cast a faint halo of light around the silhouette of my husband's bowed features. This man, this pastor, who had been at the side of many of his flock as they lay dying, now must summon up his own courage, find words to comfort his own daughter as she lay dying, words to comfort himself, to comfort me. I sat on the edge of her bed at his side, leaning heavily upon him.

"You, dear Lenchen," he continued, his voice a husky whisper, "you would like to stay here with your father and your dear mother?"

"Yes, dear father, but only as God wills."

Her words were breathless, transparent, but something in her tone made me firmly believe that she was speaking for his comfort, for our comfort, more than for her own.

"And, my dear little girl, I think you would be glad still more to go to your Father in heaven?"

Her face now blending in hue with her pillow, she drew in her breath—frail, weak, with a feeble rattling sound like the brook makes as it passes over the pebbles behind the cloister.

"Yes, dear father, as God wills." With her last strength, she reached a pale hand up and touched her father's cheek.

He laid over her, gently enfolding her, his shoulders hitching up and down, she breathing her last in his arms. Moments later, our rooster in the garden crowed out an anguished lament, rending the night, calling forth a grim, unwelcome morning.

Tenderly, my husband lay our lifeless Magdalenchen back on her pillow. Beside ourselves with grief, rocking and sobbing in each other's arms, we felt her body grow cold next to us.

Later that same day, my husband stared without blinking as they lowered our daughter's body into the dark hole. "I am blessed more than all the bishops of Rome," he whispered. He stooped, took up a clod of mud and rubbed it through his fingers, sprinkling it onto our daughter's casket. "Why then, cannot I give thanks to our Heavenly Father?" His voice broke off.

"You are so loved, Lenchen," he managed at last, "you will rise, you will shine like the stars and the sun." He turned to me, wiped a tear from my eye with his thumb, and took me in his arms. "How strange it is to know that she is at peace and all is well, and yet we here below—and so full of sorrow."

# 55

# A MIGHTY FORTRESS

Looming only days away after Magdalena's death was Sunday. My husband spent most of those days isolating himself in his tower study, high atop the cloister. I mounted the narrow stairway twice daily bearing food and drink, but he barely touched it. I listened at the door to his anguish, his prayers, and joined him in his not infrequent weeping, my forehead pressed hard against the oak planking of the door—the outside of the door.

I confess, I was angry at times. It was he who had taught me when despondency threatened, "Shun solitude." Those were his very words. I set my jaw, and I readied my fist to pound upon his study door, to fling his own words back in his face, to rail at him for being careless of my grief, of his children's sorrow. Then, the heat subsiding, I lowered and unclenched my fist. How could I add to his woe by troubling him further with my own?

Moreover, I knew he felt compelled to prepare his sermon, all the while wrestling with his grief. He was their pastor; he must ready himself to feed his flock. Yet what of feeding his family?

Finally the Sunday arrived. The congregation shuffled into the Stadtkirche soberly, as if on tiptoe, eyes diverted, glancing cautiously, pitifully, at their pastor as he moved toward the pulpit.

His face drawn and pale, his movements stilted, mechanical, like a wooden figure marking time in a horologe, Martin Luther climbed slowly up the steps into the high pulpit. Opening his Bible, he looked out on our faces, many of them as sad as his; this I knew for a fact.

"God is our fortress and strength," he read, "a very present help in trouble. Therefore, we will not fear though the earth gives way..." More than once throughout the reading his voice broke, trailed off, then with a tremor, recommenced. "The Lord of hosts is with us; the God of Jacob is our fortress."

At the conclusion of the psalm, he prayed.

"Lord, you alone give help and comfort. You have said that you would help me. I believe your Word. O my God and Lord, I have heard from you a joyful and comforting word. I hold to it. I let go of everything in which I have trusted. I know you would not lie to me. No matter how you may appear, you will keep what you have promised, that and nothing else."

It was far from his most eloquent prayer, further still from his most vitriolic. Halting, groping for words, there was a needy honesty in that prayer. Though he was perhaps wholly unaware of it, I believe more of his congregation were helped by this halting prayer of a man in distress, yet clinging, held fast by his God, than his most rousing and articulate prayers.

Nor would the sermon to follow be his most eloquent; his words meandered, and were interrupted by moments of awkward silence as he struggled to compose himself in his grief. Yet, as with his prayer, if a sermon is to be judged by its effect on the hearers more than by its structural perfections, then this may have been his finest hour in the pulpit. Not all will agree, but there were no critics sitting back with arms crossed, none looking askance, eyes narrowed; not that day.

"What is the greatest thing in the psalter but earnest speaking amid the storm-winds of every kind? A human heart is like a ship on a wild sea, driven by violent winds from the four quarters of the world. Here it is struck with fear, and worry about coming disaster; and then comes grief and sadness because of present evil and loss."

Breaking off, he stared dumbly at the open pages on the lectern, his jaw working. After an awkward silence, he regained composure, and continued.

"Here breathes a wind of hope and of expectation of happiness to come; there blows security and joy in present blessings. These storm-winds teach us to speak with earnestness, and open the heart, and pour out what lies at the bottom of it."

He paused again, this time pressing his hand hard against his chest. It was no affected orator's gesture. I knew and felt it, pain and hurt so real, so mortal, wrenching at my own heart.

"He who is caught in fear and loss," he persisted, "speaks of misfortune very differently from him who floats on joy; and he who floats on joy speaks and sings of joy quite differently from him who is numb with fear. It is seldom from the heart when a sad man laughs or a glad man weeps. At such times, the depths of his heart are not open, and what is in them does not come out.

"What is the greatest thing in the psalter but this earnest speaking amid these storm-winds of every kind? Where does one find such words of joy as in the psalms of praise and thanksgiving? There you look into the hearts of all the saints, as into fair and pleasant gardens, nay, as into heaven, and see what fine and pleasant flowers of the heart spring up from fair and happy thoughts of every kind toward God, because of his benefits in Christ."

He hesitated, eyes returning to the psalm laid open on the lectern before him.

"On the other hand," he continued. I heard the quaver in his voice and silently prayed that God would be his strength. "Where do you find deeper, more sorrowful, more pitiful words of sadness than in the psalms of lamentation? There again you look into the hearts of all the saints, as into death, nay, as into hell. How gloomy and dark it is there, with all kinds of troubled outlooks on the wrath of God!

"And when the psalmists speak of fear and hope, they use such words that no painter could so depict fear or hope, no orator so portray them.

"The best thing of all, they speak—nay, they sing—these words to God and with God. This gives the words double earnestness and life, for when men merely speak with men about these matters, what they say does not come so strongly from the heart, and burn and live and press so greatly."

Warming to his argument, he became more animated, his delivery more unencumbered with the weight of his grief. I blessed God for it.

"Though the preaching of the Word," he continued, "is the highest worship of God, for thereby are celebrated the name and the benefits of Christ, close on its heels is music, singing, poetry. In the poetry of the psalter we are safely guided how to think, come what may: in joy, fear, hope, and sorrow. Here we may learn to think and sing as all the saints have done before us.

"In this inspired poetry before us this morning we see the true Church painted in living color, its true form put in one little picture, a bright, pure mirror that shows us what the church is, who we are, who Christ is. Hence it is that we need more poets, poets hewn and fashioned by the psalter.

"And musicians alongside those poets. In this precious gift of God, this noble art of music, are all the emotions swayed. Nothing on earth is more mighty to make the sad happy and the happy sad, to hearten the downcast, mellow the overweening, temper the exuberant, or mollify the vengeful.

"Hence, the fathers desired that music should always abide in the Church. That is why there are so many songs created in imitation of the psalms. A psalm such as we have before us this morning. 'God is our fortress and strength, a very present help in trouble. Therefore, we will not fear though the earth gives way...'"

What followed was a sermon poem. I know not what else to call it, but I believe it represented the whole man, the anguished moment in which he struggled, the source of hope and conquest in that mortal struggle.

Based on the psalm text he had read to us, my husband now read out the words of the poem. I say read, in actual fact, looking out over our faces, he recited them, sometimes his words moving from speech to song, breaking into singing on whole lines. Pausing at times, he then commented, elucidated, and made application for himself and for us his flock and family.

> A mighty fortress is our God,
> A bulwark never failing;
> Our helper He, amid the flood
> Of mortal ills prevailing:
> For still our ancient foe
> Doth seek to work us woe;
> His craft and power are great,
> And, armed with cruel hate,
> On earth is not his equal.

His recitation of the last lines of this stanza were charged with boisterous indignation levelled at the ancient foe, his teeth barred almost shouting his defiance.

Calming himself, he continued, earnestly explaining to us how we are to read the psalms, how we are to read all of Scripture. "I see nothing in Scripture except Christ and him crucified. Whenever I see less, I am most unsatisfied. Christ is the central point of the circle; everything else in Holy Writ revolves in orbit around the Redeemer. Though it may look and sound differently on the outside—as in this psalm where there is no explicit mention of Jesus Christ—yet when you look into its inner meaning, the Word of God is concerned only with Christ, the Living Word of God made flesh for our salvation. *Solus Christus*! Away with all confidence in our own strength or striving!" And then he returned to the hymn.

> Did we in our own strength confide,
> Our striving would be losing;
> Were not the right Man on our side,
> The Man of God's own choosing:
> Dost ask who that may be?
> Christ Jesus, it is he;
> Lord Sabaoth, his name,
> From age to age the same,
> And he must win the battle.

"Be gone foul fiend," he continued. "The Man of God's own choosing has won the victory." Shaking his fist, fire in his eyes, his voice was strong and defiant. "Threaten away! Do your worst! You are a conquered foe."

> And though this world, with devils filled,
> Should threaten to undo us,
> We will not fear, for God hath willed
> His truth to triumph through us:

The Prince of Darkness grim,
We tremble not for him;
His rage we can endure,
For lo, his doom is sure,
One little word shall fell him.

"Put up your sword, devils!" He laughed, his arms wide enfolding his congregation. "We wrestle not with flesh and blood. But, dear people of God, know this: the Prince of Darkness? His doom is sure. Tremble not, beloved people. The Word of Christ alone has conquered."

That Word above all earthly powers,
No thanks to them, abideth;
The Spirit and the gifts are ours
Through him who with us sideth:
Let goods and kindred go—

His voice suddenly clutched, broke off. After a moment, composing himself, he continued.

Let goods and kindred go,
This mortal life also;
The body they may kill:
God's truth abideth still,
His kingdom is forever.

# 56
# GHOSTS AND BOOKS

*E*in' feste Burg, the hymn he taught his congregation after Magdalenchen's death three years ago, had rapidly become our children's favorite, my own favorite, his congregation's favorite, and time alone would tell how far beyond Wittenberg it would be sung by God's people. I often hummed its melody while at my duties, and while engaged in my secret endeavor, writing this account. When I was alone, I sang out the words. I must have been humming it that cold February evening in 1546.

My husband, suddenly looking up from his book, snapped it shut. "When I die I want to be a ghost," he announced.

I stared dumbly at him. Often immediately before unleashing a scathing denunciation of the pope or the emperor, or any number of other enemies he had developed, a boyish smirk animated his features—as it was doing at the moment.

"A ghost?" I wondered if he was slipping into a delirium. "Do we believe in ghosts?"

"Of course we do, and devils, and the Prince of Darkness grim."

"Why, pray tell, Herr Doctor," I said, twirling my quill, "would you want to be a ghost?"

"I want to be one so I can continue to pester the bishops, priests, and godless monks until they have more trouble with a dead Luther than they ever had before with a thousand living ones."

"You do not need to be a ghost, Herr Doctor. Your pen is your ghost. Your words in your books live after you. So many books. Surely they will continue to pester the godless who have enslaved the peasants and led them astray."

"They still burn my books." He nodded, staring into the fire.

"As you burned the papal bull," I reminded him. It was before I came to Wittenberg, but it made me shudder to think on it. Burning the papal bull! There had been nights when I had awakened, certain that I heard an advancing papal delegation, armed with swords and clubs, descending on Wittenberg, seizing my husband, dragging him away in chains to do to him as he had done to the papal bull. Though often in my dreams, somehow they had not yet come for him.

"It is in my mind," I continued, "that there is no better way to get the young to read books than when someone is burning them."

"Perhaps," he grunted. "Surely for every book they have burned Melchior Lotther and now his sons print another to take its place."

"*Hundreds* to take its place," I corrected. "Printers, yes, they see gulden when you write another book. Of course they print more books so they can sell more books."

I frowned at my own words. "Why do you not make any money from your books? Why do only the printers enrich themselves from your pen?"

He shrugged. "I did not write them for money."

"*Jawohl*, but the printers print them for money. Should not the man who labored to write them get more of the money?"

"And his family?"

"Of course, his family! Sometimes, Herr Doctor, your carelessness about money, it feels like carelessness about your family."

Sitting up straighter in his chair, he turned to me. "Imperfect clod that I am, there is nothing in all the world I care about more than my children. Except their mother, my beloved runaway nun. If that is true of a sack of maggots such as I am, how much more is it true of our perfect Heavenly Father, and his Son our beloved bridegroom whose mercies are new every morning, who will never leave you, dearest Katie, or forsake you?"

I smiled, comforted in measure by his assurances. He reopened his book. Watching him out of the corner of my eye, cautiously, I dipped my pen and recommenced writing. I now believe it was a trap.

"My lord Katie, whatever are you doing?"

# 55

# HIS KINGDOM IS FOREVER!

## (February 18, 1546)

M y lord Katie, whatever *are* you writing?" he asked again.

It was a trap. My husband was not reading his book. Eyes wary, he leaned toward me, attempting to see what I was writing.

Fanning myself with the goose quill, the flame of my candle trembling, I looked up innocently from the parchment before me. I shrugged carelessly for answer. I knew I was treading on thin ice, as when Hans and his brothers had attempted to skate on the fish pond before it has sufficiently frozen over. I feared a similar disaster awaited me.

"It is just a little family business." I had said the same before now, and it was truthful enough, as far as it went. Somehow I had managed, all these months, to keep my memoir from his gaze.

"Which reminds me," he replied, sighing heavily, "poor maggot-sack that I am, I must pull my bones together and attend to a little family business myself, in a manner of speaking."

I looked up in alarm. Hans and Elizabeth were both grown. Had some news arrived of them and their families? Our dear Magdalenchen was with God, and the three younger children, Margaretta with eleven years, Paul with thirteen, and Martin with sixteen years, were already in their beds. Liesel, our precious, however much older she grew in years, she would always be a child, always be with us, until such time as God saw fit to take her to himself.

"What family business, Herr Doctor?" I asked.

"The magistrate in Eisleben," he said, "claims that I am urgently needed to arbitrate some dispute with the local counts."

"But you have not lived in Eisleben for more than forty years. Why you?"

"*Ja, ja.* I do not know. But there is a dispute with the Mansfield authorities, urgent business; the magistrate is convinced I must act as mediator."

"You must not, Herr Doctor. Cannot it wait? Could you not write a letter, thereby reconcile the dispute? You are very good at letters. Surely, it does not require your actual presence?"

"I have inquired about sending another in my place," he replied.

"Melanchthon," I said. I cannot fully express the relief I felt. "He is young. You could deputize him and he could take your place. It is settled?"

"Philip is ill, unfit for the journey."

My heart sank. "*You* are ill, Herr Doctor. Unfit for the journey, especially in winter." I heard my tone, shrill, demanding. It was a failing of mine. I bit the inside of my cheek. "Besides, there is snow on the ground. And by the feel, more on the way."

"My bones tell the same tale."

323

"Could not it wait until spring?"

"The Mansfield Counts in Eisleben think not." He broke off coughing.

My heart sank. I rose to massage his shoulders. Sometimes that helped alleviate the coughing, so I believed. I leaned over, my lips touching his ear. "Please, Herr Doctor. Do not go," I whispered. "Your Kette, who loves you, who needs you, begs you not to go."

"My lord Katie, you have a husband that loves you," he whispered back. "But you must let someone else be empress."

I sat back, I confess it, pouting in my chair.

"The body they may kill, my Katie," he continued. "I have long feared the flames. But I do so no more. I have lived long enough."

Fearing a bout of despondency coming upon him, I tried another stratagem. I often prayed aloud. He had taught me the importance of prayer. "To be a Christian without prayer, my rib, is no more possible than to be alive without breathing." So he had taught me.

"O Lord," I began, intoning the words in a fashion that I hoped would move him. "You who guide the rolling spheres, I beg you, halt the snows of winter, moderate the cold and damp. Or if you will not, you who turn the hearts of princes, turn the heart of the magistrate of Eisleben, the petty squabbling of the Mansfield Counts. Or if you will not, turn the heart of my dear stubborn husband from the folly of—"

"Yes, why not, Lord?" he chimed in. "We have persecuted thy Word and killed thy saints. We have deserved well of thee."

I broke off, feeling hurt. Why must he jest when I am in earnest, when I am afraid? "I have premonitions," I blurted. I was desperate.

"Premonitions?" he said. "Of what?"

Exasperated with him, I smoothed my frock with my hands and sighed heavily.

"My dearest Katie, if it be God's will, we must accept it. You are mine and I am yours. But more importantly, we are God's. Rest assured of that. Should I die on this journey, he will care for you. It is his promise. Hold to God's Word."

"I am not thinking just of myself and the children," I said, swallowing hard at the tears whelming up in my eyes, threatening to catch in my throat, to choke me with foreboding. "There are so many people that need you." I broke off, unable to say more.

"I did want to write another book," he said, steepling his fingers under his chin, looking intently into the fire. "But God's will be done."

"My dear Doctor," I said, "if it is God's will I would rather have you with our Lord than here, though my heart breaks to say the words."

"Take heart, my dearest Katie," he said. "In this world you will have tribulation. But we must never forget, our Lord has overcome the world."

Smoothing my frock again, I folded my hands on my lap, nodding and staring at the flickering of the firelight on the walls of the sitting room. Save for the crackling of the flames, we sat in silence for several minutes.

"As he has always done," he continued, "God will provide for you and the children." And then his shoulders began hitching up and down in silent mirth.

"Think on it, dear Katie. God has made us rich. He rains down upon us corn, wheat, barley, wine, cabbage, onions, grass, and milk. He gives us one hundred thousand gulden worth. All our goods we get for nothing. And God sends his only begotten Son, and we crucify him."

"For nothing!" There were times when he was maddeningly dim-witted. "For nothing! Is that how you value my labor, milking, slaughtering the pigs, baking bread, brewing your beer, harvesting pears? For nothing, you say?"

325

He held up his hands in protest, mirth in his eyes. "You have given me the dearest life," he said, his face becoming sober, gazing at me in that manner of his that so dissolved my heart in affection for him. "To live with a godly, willing, obedient wife in peace and unity—union of body, but still more union of mind and manners—there is no greater wealth, dear Katie, than you, who are everything to me."

He paused, taking my hand in both of his. "Dearest Katharina von Bora, apostate nun, I give more credit to you than to Christ, who has done so much more for me. I daily must confess my devotion to you, which exceeds all bounds."

With both of my hands, I clung to his, not letting go. Biting the inside of my cheek, I felt the tears careening unheeded down my face, but I did not let go.

"When we are at last in heaven, you and I," he continued, "troubles passed, and no more pain, no more parting, neither you nor I would give one moment of heaven for the joys and delights God has freely given us in this world. Not one moment."

I nodded. He wrestled a hand free and wiped my tears. I knew it was true. I believed, yet did my heart long for him, and so grieve to lose him.

He took up his Bible. "I have long said, when this book is in the hands of all, then Luther must retire, and the Bible advance; this poor man must disappear, and God in Christ appear!"

After preaching his last sermon at his beloved Stadtkirche in Wittenberg, he set out on the journey to his birthplace, our boys attending him, at my insistence.

With heavy heart, I watched the ox cart conveying my husband from me disappear in the mist rising along the snowy banks of the river. His voice, singing with the boys, growing fainter. Then silence.

Since I was helpless—there was nothing I could do—I resolved to pray every waking hour in his absence. And so I did; as I milked the cow, as I made cheese, as I checked on the progress of my latest batch of beer—I had at last formulated beer perfectly suited to my husband's kidney and intestinal torments—as Liesel and I selected the best winter potatoes at the market, as she helped me peel them, and I prepared meals for our children and borders—always I prayed.

But I knew. In my woman's heart, I knew. When word arrived near the end of February, I was not surprised; beside myself with anguish, but not surprised.

As I had so feared, he caught a chill in the ox cart on the journey to Eisleben. But did he rest? No. After arbitrating the dispute, successfully, I was assured, he preached not once, but four times at the church in which he had been baptized sixty-two years before.

I begged Hans for the minutest details of his death, his final words.

Feeling unwell on February 16, he had quipped, "If I make it home to Wittenberg, I will lay myself in my coffin to let maggots feast on the stout Doctor." There was no doubt. They were his words exactly. I knew.

After a hearty meal, he retired to his room at the Graf von Mansfield hostelry, only a stone's throw from his birthplace. Praying at the window on the second floor, he fell asleep. When he awoke he was in considerable pain and went to his bed, knowing his end was imminent. How my heart ached. If only I had been at his side.

Hans told me of his father's final words, a recitation from the thirty-first Psalm. "Into your hands I commit my spirit; you have redeemed me, O Lord, faithful God."

"I asked him," said Hans, his arm about my shoulders as he rendered his account to me, "if he was hoping entirely in Christ." Hans squeezed my shoulders and smiled.

"And he said?" I asked.

"'*Ja*,' he said, and breathed his last."

I was numb. Walking in a dream. Was it but a black vision in the night? I awoke. To a cold empty cloister, void, hollow, unanimated by his presence.

Our cow was mooing. The needs of our animals are not suspended by my grief. There were still meals to prepare, cows to milk, pigs and chickens to feed, eggs to collect. Liesel was of inestimable help to me in those first days of my unwelcome solitude. But her greatest help was when she would throw her arms about me and weep with she who wept.

Martin Luther's body arrived in Wittenberg February 22, amidst great solemnity and reverence. The entire city mourned. Like herring in a barrel, all who were able crammed into my husband's beloved Stadtkirche where he was laid to rest.

With these final reflections, I complete my memoir. My husband gave so much of himself, worked himself to death in service not only to one town or to one country, but to the whole world. Yet was he so fond of saying, "I did nothing. The Word, God in Christ, did everything." I firmly believed him.

And now my beloved Martin Luther is gone. My sorrow, it is so deep. I cannot find words to express my heartbreak. I can neither eat nor drink, nor sleep—as it was so often with my husband.

God knows that when I think of having lost him, in all my suffering, I can neither talk nor can I find the words to write.

But I can remember. The man, my cherished husband, and his words, which, in my distress, give me hope:

Let goods and kindred go,
This mortal life also;
The body they may kill:
God's truth abideth still,
His kingdom is forever.

# AFTERWARD
## "I will cling to Christ..."

Shortly after Martin Luther's death, war threatened the city of Wittenberg, and Katharina Luther and her children were forced to flee for safety to Magdaburg. After returning to Wittenberg in 1547, renewed hostilities once again forced her to flee for her life. In her absence, the Augustinian cloister was plundered and damaged, her cattle and other stock were killed or stolen. When she returned to Wittenberg, she lived in poverty until plague fell on the city in 1552. Fleeing for her life, she was badly injured when her cart overturned near the city of Torgau. She died there December 20, 1552, her final words on her deathbed, "I will cling to Christ like a burr to cloth." She is buried at St. Mary's Church in Torgau, Germany.

# Glossary of Terms

**Danke schön**: Thank you, very much. *Danke* is thank you.

**Dirndl**: Traditional peasant dress.

**Doch**: German word meaning however or on the contrary.

**Dummkopf**: Fool or stupid.

**Frau**: In Luther's day this word denoted a lady; meine Frau would be equivalent to my lady.

**Fräulein**: Originally the German word for the unmarried daughter of a noble woman, equivalent to Miss in English; feminists have tried to eradicate the word in modern German usage.

**Gulden**: German 16th century coinage.

**Herren**: Gentlemen.

**Ich verstehen nicht**: I do not understand.

**Ja**: Common German word for yes.

**Jawohl**: More respectful or emphatic word for yes; pronounced ya-vol.

**Junge Männer**: Young men.

**Kette**: An affectionate name Luther had for his wife; *kette* means chain in German.

**Mein Vater**: My father in German.

**Meine Mutter**: My mother in German.

**Nein**: German word for no.

**Post tenebras lux**: Latin, meaning after darkness, light, which became a summary statement of the Reformation.

**Surplice**: A white tunic worn over other clerical vestments.

**Zum Wohl**: A toast to health.

# Timeline

**1456** – Johann Gutenberg prints a Latin Bible on his new moveable-type printing press.

**1483** – November 10, birth of Martin Luther.

**1492** – Columbus discovers the New World.

**1498** – Savonarola burned in Florence; Leonardo da Vinci completes *The Last Supper*.

**1499** – January 29, birth of Katherina von Bora.

**1509** – July 10, birth of John Calvin.

**1510** – Luther's pilgrimage to Rome.

**1512** – First Protestant martyr burned in Paris; Michelangelo completes Sistine Chapel ceiling.

**1517** – October 31, Luther nails his 95 Theses on the door of the Castle Church.

**1519** – Leipzig Debate with Johann Eck; Magellan circumnavigates the globe.

**1521** – April 16, Luther at Diet of Worms.

**1522** – March 1, Luther leaves Wartburg Castle.

**1524** – First hymnal; treatise on Christian schools. September, Erasmus, *On the Freedom of the Will*.

**1525** – June 13, betrothal to Katharina von Bora; Peasant Revolt; December, *The Bondage of the Will*.

**1527** – *A Mighty Fortress* (exact date uncertain).

**1528** – Lucas Cranach the Elder's portrait of Katharina von Bora; Luther mourns the death of Albrecht Dürer.

**1529** – October 1, Marburg Colloquy.

**1530** – *Augsburg Confession of Faith*.

**1536** – Calvin's *Institutes of the Christian Religion*.

**1546** – February 18, death of Luther.

**1552** – December 20, death of Katherina von Bora.

# Acknowledgements

In this work of historical fiction, I have attempted to faithfully create Martin Luther's voice from his sermons, letters, commentaries, hymns, Table Talk, and other books. Immersed in Luther's vast written work, I have carefully listened to his verbiage and the cadence of his manner of speaking, so that I could weave and adapt his speech likeness into conversations and historical situations where no exact Luther words exist. I have made it my objective in this biographical novel, not only to write an engaging work of fiction, but to be authentic and faithful to Luther's voice, his times, and his theology.

There are a host of works on Martin Luther, from which I have drawn material for this novel. But I am particularly indebted to *The Life of Luther Written By Himself*, translated by William Hazlett; *The Reformation*, by George Park Fisher; *Here I Stand*, by Roland Bainton, and *History of the Reformation*, by D'Aubigne, to name a few.

**Douglas Bond**, husband of Cheryl and father of six, is author of more than twenty-five books, a hymn writer, and an award-winning teacher. He speaks at churches, schools, and conferences, directs the Oxford Creative Writing Master Class, and leads Church history tours, including tours of Luther's Germany. Find out more at www.bondbooks.net.

# More Books by Douglas Bond

"*War in the Wasteland* is proof positive of what I have known for many years now: Douglas Bond is a great storyteller. Indeed, this novel combines all the attributes of a can't-put-it-down thriller with the intellectual tensions of a historical drama: taut plotting, strong characters, and soaring backdrop. Put this one on the top of your must-read list."

**GEORGE GRANT**, author, teacher, pastor at Parish Presbyterian Church

"*War in the Wasteland* is a gripping, informative, adrenalin-producing picture of World War I. Bond captures on every page the awful moments of fear and the reflective conversations of men who don't know if they'll survive the day."

**DOUGLAS E. LEE**, Brigadier General, USA (Ret), President, Chaplain Alliance for Religious Liberty

"In *War in the Wasteland* Bond paints a vivid picture of the battle for the soul of teen, atheist 2/Lt. C.S. Lewis."

**MIKE T. SUGIMOTO**, Professor of Asian Studies and Great Books, Pepperdine University

# Adult Novels

"Anything Douglas Bond writes is, almost now by definition, a fascinating read. But to have his skills attached to the life of John Calvin in *The Betrayal* is a double treat."
**JOEL BELZ**, founder, WORLD Magazine

"If you enjoy reading the fictional works of C. S. Lewis, you will love *The Betrayal*."
**BURK PARSONS**, editor, *Tabletalk*

"In *The Thunder*, Douglas Bond deftly escorts us into the sixteenth-century world of John Knox. Bond's careful use of language…the seamless flow, rich, vivid picture of Scotland and Reformation. The spiritual aspect of the story richer... A fine work."
**LIZ CURTIS HIGGS**, best-selling author of the Lowlands of Scotland series

"In *The Revolt*, Douglas Bond uses his unique writing style to produce a highly readable imagining of the travails of John Wycliffe, ...a vivid and exciting narrative..."
**BOB CRESON**, President/CEO, Wycliffe Bible Translators, USA

# Heroes & History

In *Hostage Lands*, Neil Perkins, a student at Haltwhistle Grammar School in England, unearths an ancient Roman manuscript. After dedicating himself to studying Latin, he uncovers a story of treachery and betrayal from the third century.

"Enjoyable reading for anyone who likes a gripping, fast-paced adventure story, *Hostage Lands* will especially delight young students of Latin and Roman history."
**STARR MEADE**, author of *Grandpa's Box*

In *Hand of Vengeance*, Half-Saxon, half-Dane, misfit Cynwulf lives apart from the world in a salvaged Viking ship, dreaming of spending his life with the fair Haeddi. When he is accused of murder, he must clear his name before he loses everything to the vengeance of the community that has already rejected him.

"In *Hand of Vengeance* Douglas Bond shines a light on the past in a way that's as entertaining as it is informative."
**JANIE B. CHEANEY**, senior writer, WORLD Magazine

# Crown & Covenant Trilogy

The Crown & Covenant trilogy follows the lives of the M'Kethe family as they endure persecution in 17th–century Scotland and later flee to colonial America. Douglas Bond weaves together fictional characters and historical figures from Scottish Covenanting history.

"Unleashes the reader's imagination—a rip-roaring good yarn."
**GEORGE GRANT**, author, teacher, pastor, Parish Presbyterian Church

"Douglas Bond has introduced a new generation to the heroics of the Scottish Covenanters, and he has done it in a delightful way."
**LIGON DUNCAN**, First Presbyterian Church, Jackson, Mississippi

# Faith & Freedom Trilogy

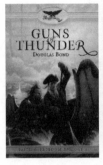 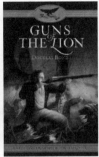 

The Faith & Freedom trilogy, sequel to the Crown & Covenant trilogy, chronicles new generations of the M'Kethe family who find freedom in 18th-century America. Adventure is afoot as Old World tyrannies clash with New World freedoms. Douglas Bond seamlessly weaves together fictional characters with historical figures from Scottish and American history.

"Action from beginning to end. I wish I'd had this kind of book to read when I was a kid."
**JOEL BELZ**, founder, WORLD Magazine

"A tale of America's revolutionary beginning, told with strength and truth. . . . Take up and read!"
**PETER A. LILLBACK**, author, *Sacred Fire*